THE DUKE'S INDECENT MATCH

INDECENT DUKES

BOOK 2

GOLDEN ANGEL

CONTENTS

Dedication   v

Prologue   1
Chapter 1   7
Chapter 2   16
Chapter 3   26
Chapter 4   33
Chapter 5   40
Chapter 6   50
Chapter 7   57
Chapter 8   65
Chapter 9   72
Chapter 10   79
Chapter 11   88
Chapter 12   96
Chapter 13   106
Chapter 14   114
Chapter 15   121
Chapter 16   128
Chapter 17   135
Chapter 18   144
Chapter 19   153
Chapter 20   160
Chapter 21   167
Chapter 22   177
Chapter 23   186
Chapter 24   191
Chapter 25   199
Chapter 26   208
Chapter 27   216
Chapter 28   225
Chapter 29   233
Chapter 30   242
Chapter 31   250
Chapter 32   258

Chapter 33   268
Chapter 34   275
Chapter 35   284
Chapter 36   293
Chapter 37   301
Chapter 38   309
Chapter 39   317
Chapter 40   325
Chapter 41   332
Chapter 42   340
Chapter 43   347
Chapter 44   358
Epilogue   365
About the Author   375
Foreword   377
45. Entry 1   379
46. Entry 2   383

Other Titles by Golden Angel   387

DEDICATION

To everyone who grew up feeling like there was nowhere they fit in.

May we all find our people.

PROLOGUE

INDIA — 12 Years Ago

<u>*Kalina*</u>

The whispers followed Kalina as she hurried down the path to her parents' bungalow, the sun beating down on the back of her neck, as if the cruelty had taken form and was burning her.

Mean whispers.

Waiting whispers.

The whisperers wanted to see her tears.

She would not give them the satisfaction. Her heavy braid bounced on her shoulder as she marched away.

"Why would she think she can play with us?" One of the children asked loudly in English, their crisp British accent distinct, making Kalina's back stiffen as the ensuing laughter echoed in her ears. It did not matter that her grandfather outranked any of their parents; word of her father's estrangement had come, even to here.

But she knew better than to turn around. Doing so would only invite more taunts.

Lifting her chin high in the air as if she did not care about their rejection, Kalina turned down the path. The safety of their new bungalow loomed ahead. She had hoped that moving to a new area would mean the possibility of making friends, but it was proving as impossible as it had in Chennai.

Though her father was English, her mother was Indian, and that was enough for the other English children to reject her. Both in Chennai and here. It did not matter how well she spoke or read or practiced her manners, she was always on the outside. Always standing out among them.

She had tried to play with the other Kshatriya children because her mother's family was Kshatriya, but they did not want anything to do with her, either. Perhaps because, although she looked like them, she was too different from them as well. She spoke mostly English, and her Urdu was accented.

Mother's family did not speak with her anymore. She had defied them for love, to marry Kalina's father. Their love shone through everything, even the disapproval of those around them. Kalina loved them just as dearly, though she wished that there were more than just them and her brother to spend time with.

Hearing the sound of children playing, Kalina turned her head to look.

Kshatriya children. She could tell by their dress and the way they were so freely moving around the bungalows. They must live nearby.

She paused, then took a step toward them.

Something about her movement must have alerted them, and the children stopped playing. Two girls and a boy, all looking to be a little younger than her, but that did not matter to Kalina. They were close enough in age. She did not mind playing with children younger than her. She could not. Her younger brother Ashwin was the only child who *would* play with her, but he was learning how to ride a horse today.

"Good afternoon," she said in Urdu, smiling brightly to try to hide her nervousness.

The children stared at her. Kalina tensed as their gazes went down her clothing. It was a proper English pinafore in her favorite color, the same rose pink as the diamonds that came from her father's mine. The other two girls were wearing brightly colored skirts and blouses trimmed with beads. Kalina had always wanted something like that, but her mother always bought English dresses for herself and Kalina.

One of the girls leaned in toward the other and whispered something, shaking her head as she did so.

Kalina felt her heart sink. If she'd been wearing clothes like theirs, perhaps... but the English children thought her too Indian, and the Indian children saw her and thought her too English.

The three turned and ran off, leaving her there alone.

Again.

Always alone.

Dropping her head, Kalina slowly turned back on her path to the bungalow.

There would be no friends here, either, it appeared.

Her mother liked to say that Kalina and Ashwin were of two worlds, but most days, Kalina felt like she belonged to neither. Not for lack of trying, but because neither would accept her.

"There is my little princess!" Kalina's father appeared in front of her, grinning with pride as he looked down at her. Her heart lifted, and she ran to him, arms up in the air to greet him. He caught her, lifting her against him. "Oof. I swear, little princess, you are getting bigger every day."

Kalina giggled.

"Of course I am, Papa; that is what is supposed to happen."

"Ah, well then. I suppose it is a good thing, though I will miss it when I can carry you like this. Were you making your way home?" He turned toward their bungalow.

"Yes."

"Where were you? You know you are not supposed to be out by yourself." The scolding was far gentler than the one she would have received from her mother. "You need to take someone with you."

"I am sorry, Papa," she said, laying her head against his shoulder, rather than admitting out loud that she had not wanted someone with her. She had not wanted anyone to see her rejected over and over again.

Or worse, accepted because there was someone watching, only to be abandoned later.

"Do not do it again, Kalina."

"I will not."

He hitched her up on his hip, pausing for a moment before speaking again.

"Did you find what you were looking for?" he asked gently.

"No." She did not know if he knew she had been looking for friends or if he just knew better than to ask exactly what she had been looking for.

Papa sighed. Not out loud. But she felt it as his chest moved against her body. She tightened her hold around his neck.

"I am sorry, Kalina," he said gently. "One day, we will move to England. Things will be easier there."

That was what Papa always said.

"Will it?" she asked. "The English children do not want to play with me. They think I am too Indian. But the Indian children think I am too English."

Still carrying her, Papa was silent for a long moment, and she knew he was thinking.

"In England, it is your rank that matters. And my father is among the highest," he said after a while. "That is your grandfather. Here... things are more difficult. Not everyone is in favor of the English presence in India. There are... things that have been done that make for ill feelings between our people. Not everyone, of course. Your mother still fell in love with and married me, after all."

"What things?" Kalina asked. She could always tell when her parents were talking around the important details, but they rarely explained what they meant.

"When you are older, we will talk about it," Papa said, the way he always did.

Now, it was Kalina's turn to sigh. She was older every day, but that did not seem to matter. No one would tell her, not even the servants. She wondered whether the other children knew. The ones who would not play with her. Maybe that was why they would not play with her.

But why would they know when she was too young to know?

But then, why would they not play with her?

It was all very confusing. And frustrating.

Rather than going into the bungalow, Papa took her around to the verandah. A cool breeze was blowing over the stone, the shade easing some of the day's growing heat. Soon, it would be time to rest. No one would be playing or doing much of anything at all.

"Do you want to hear more about England?" Papa asked eagerly.

Kalina could tell he wanted her to say yes. He loved to talk about his home. And despite the fact that she had never lived anywhere but India, and he had lived here since before she was born, he still referred to England as home.

"Yes, please, Papa," she said as he sat down in one of the chairs, still holding onto her. She snuggled against him, grateful he was there. How could she feel lonely when her Papa and Mama loved her so much? Perhaps she was feeling greedy in wanting friends, too.

Not everyone had a Papa and Mama who loved them as much as hers did, or perhaps they were just not as open with demonstrating their love. Kalina had observed many parents who were cold, impatient, or even cruel to their children. Most were not as open and loving as hers.

Maybe it was a trade?

"First of all, England is far cooler than this heat, even in the summer," he began. "There will be lords bowing over your hand and ladies flocking to admire your dresses and jewels."

Kalina giggled at the image he put in her head.

"Will everyone there be English and look like you?" she asked. Normally, she did not interrupt her father, but moving to this new home with such high hopes, only to be disappointed, had her feeling bolder than usual.

Papa hesitated.

"Perhaps among the *ton*," he said. "But when I left, there were already large communities of citizens moving from Africa and India to Britain, just as there are large communities of British moving to Africa and India. That will make you different. Special."

"I am tired of being different," she admitted.

"You speak perfect English, and your manners are impeccable. You will have all the social graces you need to be a success with the *ton*, so you will be similar to them as well."

"Because your father is a Marquess."

"Yes." He hesitated again, and for a moment she thought he might say something about the difficulties, explain further, but then his arms tightened around her. "I will make sure you have the life you deserve, my little princess."

But her father could not force anyone to be her friend. Not truly. He had tried to arrange friendships for her in the past. None of them had been real. None of those children had ever truly accepted her, though they'd been forced to spend time in her presence.

Kalina did not tell him that. It would have hurt him, and she would do anything to avoid hurting her Papa.

"Thank you, Papa," she said, because there was nothing else to say.

Leaning her head against his shoulder, she listened to him describe the joys of England... and she dreamed.

1

———

Staring up at the large manor house, Kalina took in a deep breath of the unfamiliar country air. The dark grey stone heights were impressive, foreboding even, but it was a house filled with promise. The future she'd dreamed of when she was a little girl back in India, feeling like there was nowhere she belonged.

She did not always feel like she belonged here in England, either... but thanks to a small group of young ladies who had reached out their hands in friendship, she was starting to. Lady Astrid was what her father called an *Original.* She was also a force within the *ton*, literally changing the tides of how Society viewed Kalina and her family.

Sliding her gaze over the many windows facing outward from this side of the house, Kalina paused as she saw two broad-shouldered silhouettes on the corner of the third floor. Two of the gentlemen who had been invited to this weekend? Kalina smoothed her hands over her skirts, hoping the wrinkles in her travel dress were not visible from such a distance.

There were dukes present this weekend.

Multiple of them.

If she married a duke, her father's family would be forced to accept her father back into their fold. It had to be a duke because only a duke outranked her grandfather's title of marquess. Lady Astrid had filled her house party with dukes, several marquesses, and a bevy of young ladies she favored. Kalina was grateful to be among them.

"Do you think they get their name from their house?" Ashwin asked, referencing Lady Astrid's surname of Blackstone, as he moved to stand beside her. Her younger brother was now an inch taller than her, even though they'd been the same height when they'd arrived in England. He was growing so quickly, her father had already taken him back to the tailor for another set of clothing.

"It is very dark grey stone," Kalina replied, tilting her head as she considered the possibility. "I think it more likely they used the stone because of their name rather than the other way round."

The front door opened, cutting off further conversation, and Lady Astrid came out, beaming. As always, she was dressed in impeccable fashion, wearing a rust-orange and black-striped dress that put Kalina in mind of a tiger. Her favored Cairngorm jewels adorned her throat, though the size of this necklace was smaller than the ones she wore with her ballgowns. With her dark red hair piled in a complicated coiffure, she looked exactly like what she was—a leader of the *ton*. Her mother and father were behind her, practically fading into the background when compared with Lady Astrid's presence. Kalina had met them during the Season, though they had not made much of an impression.

"Kalina! I am so glad you were able to come," Lady Astrid said, sweeping down the staircase with her hands outstretched in front of her.

The warm smile on Lady Astrid's face made Kalina's heart feel like it was blooming.

"Thank you. I am very glad to be here," she said, taking Lady Astrid's hands.

Servants were already on their way down the stairs to help with the luggage, creating a bustle in the drive as the carriages were unloaded and the Blackstones greeted Kalina's family.

Lady Blackstone looked like an older version of Lady Astrid, though her red hair was duller, her complexion paler, and her face had more lines. She smiled as warmly as her daughter, appearing sincerely welcoming of her new guests. Lord Blackstone stood more stiffly, but that was very British and not necessarily a sign of displeasure, though Kalina made a mental note of his standoffishness. She would be very careful around him, so as not to tax his sensibilities if he was uncertain about welcoming the estranged branch of the Marquess of Stilton's family into his home.

Less than ten briskly efficient minutes later, Lady Astrid had escorted their entire family into the same corner of the house Kalina had seen the gentlemen watching from, though a floor below them. Her parents were across the hall from her, her brother in the room beside hers.

"Delilah will be just down the hall from you," Lady Astrid whispered in Kalina's ear, giving her a last embrace before whisking out of the room to tend to the next guest arriving. Kalina could not help but smile as the door closed behind the forthright young lady.

Her friend.

It still felt like a dream come true.

Delilah Voight, dowager-baroness, was another new friend. A little older, more experienced in the *ton*, and somewhat scandalous, but a friend. Kalina's mother had been hesitant about her at first, but the lack of welcome after her father's family had refused to acknowledge him meant they were grateful for anyone who did not give them the cut. They could not afford to be picky in their friends.

Kalina was very glad because she enjoyed Delilah's acerbic commentary and insights into the Society she'd been thrust into.

As a child, she'd listened to her father's tales about England. As a young lady, she now knew how much he'd romanticized his home country. He had been correct about some things, though.

The *ton's* lack of acceptance was as much to do with her grandfather's rejection of them as anything else. Though there were some who muttered unflattering commentary about her mother being Indian, others were fascinated by the 'exotic' but veered away rather than displease a marquess. Kalina was grateful to those like Lady Astrid who had decided to champion their cause, though she was uncertain *why* they had done so.

She kept waiting for some terrible motivation to be revealed, but as yet, there was none she could see. Lady Astrid had no need of Kalina or her family for anything. She had her own wealth, her own status, and she was betrothed to a duke. Sometimes, Kalina wondered if she was Lady Astrid's good deed for the year.

If she was, she had no choice but to accept the charity or wallow in social exile. A state to which she did not intend to ever return.

That she sincerely liked Lady Astrid and enjoyed her company, as well as the others who had reached out a hand of friendship, made it a far easier pill to swallow.

Kalina had just finished changing from her wrinkled traveling dress to a dark pink twill day gown with the assistance of her maid, Margaret, when there was a knock at her door.

"I have it, miss," Margaret said immediately, bustling to the door. Margaret had been with Kalina since India, and she'd been happy to return to England with the family. She was a few years older than Kalina and very protective, especially when it came to men. It was a man who had convinced Margaret to travel to India with him, only to abandon her not long after they'd arrived. Before him, she'd been a seamstress, which was how Kalina's mother had found her. She still liked to sew but had decided that being Kalina's lady's maid suited her best.

Cracking the door open at first, Margaret immediately nodded and stepped back.

"Her Grace, the Duchess of Clarence," she announced grandly, beaming proudly as if Kalina had done something particularly impressive by bringing a duchess to her bedroom door.

"Kalina," Tiffany, Duchess of Clarence, said as she stepped into the room, past Margaret, who curtsied deeply as the duchess went past. Kalina bobbed a quick curtsy as well, despite Tiffany's small shake of her head and deep sigh, before she embraced the other woman.

"Tiffany," Kalina said, smiling. Behind Tiffany, Margaret was beaming like a proud mother hen again at hearing her charge use a duchess' given name. She had told Margaret that the others had accepted her to such a degree, but she supposed it was different to witness it firsthand.

She and Tiffany exchanged cheek kisses in greeting.

Truthfully, Tiffany had been her first friend before Lady Astrid. Which might be why she had an easier time thinking of a duchess by her given name than she did a marquess' daughter. That and Lady Astrid was even more formidable than most duchesses. It was incredibly difficult not to think of her as *Lady* Astrid.

Tiffany was the Duke of Bolton's sister as well as being the Duchess of Clarence, but somehow she did not have quite the same presence as Lady Astrid. She had a quiet beauty, with a heart-shaped face and high cheekbones that were the classic cream and pinks Kalina had learned the English favored. Her hair hovered between blonde and brunette, depending on the light she was standing in, and her hazel eyes were full of kindness and warmth. Today, she was wearing a cornflower-blue gown trimmed with delicate lace.

She was a gentle soul, and the friend Kalina felt the most kinship with, despite having the greatest difference in social standing.

"Astrid told me you'd arrived, and I had to come see you immediately," Tiffany said, her eyes sparkling. "Did you enjoy the trip?"

"Other than the length of time shut in the carriage, yes," Kalina said with a laugh, gesturing to Tiffany to come sit down on the window seat that looked out at the front drive. Now she could understand why the gentlemen had been watching from the floor above her. The view was quite lovely, as well as providing a glimpse of those arriving for the house party. "After the trip from India, I did not think it would be so bad, but on the ship, we could still walk about rather than being forced to sit for hours upon hours."

Margaret nodded her agreement from where she was busily

unpacking Kalina's things, not bothering to pretend she was not listening to the conversation. Kalina smiled.

"How odd to think that a journey from a country half a world away could be more comfortable than from the city to a country home," Tiffany replied, leaning forward with interest. "Were you able to walk about the entire ship?"

As Kalina described the voyage from India, she could not help but think how very strange but nice it was to sit in a window seat, speaking with a friend. England truly was everything she'd dreamed.

If she could marry a duke and give her father the position he needed to force his family to recognize him, her dreams would be complete.

There was one duke in particular... but she must be pragmatic about the situation. Just like the English. Her parents had married for love of each other, but she would marry for love of them. Both had been estranged from their families, and it pained them greatly. She could not fix her mother's relationship, but she could do this for her father.

Any duke would do.

Nathanial

Walking into the drawing room, Nathanial was struck by the lack of eyes that veered toward him. As an unmarried duke known to be in need of a good fortune, he was in need of a wife, and the entire *ton* knew it. Not every lord was willing to hold their nose and marry their daughter to a fortune hunter, duke or not, but there was a long line of those who were.

He'd ended up feeling the hunted at every ball and soiree he'd attended thus far this Season.

Not so here.

Especially because there was a large contingent of dukes present. Not just himself, the married Duke of Clarence, and the betrothed Duke of Ormonde, but three of his friends were also in need of wives

—the Duke of Montagu, the Duke of Bolton, and the Duke of St. Albans. Only Zachary, the Duke of Grafton, would be absent this weekend.

He had not been invited, likely because his former mistress had been. The Baroness Ashfield was currently across the room, standing beside the Duchess of Clarence, and appeared to be flirting with the man they were speaking to. Perhaps it was best Zachary was absent. He might have given the baroness her congé, feeling it necessary to divest himself of his mistress before searching among the debutantes for a bride, but his feelings for her had not yet waned. Watching her take up with another *amour* would be painful.

Though perhaps it would spur him on his hunt for a bride.

Something Nathanial needed to attend to as well.

Perhaps it would be easier in these surrounds, where there were fewer young ladies, and the ratio of duke to debutante less stark.

Making his bow to Lord and Lady Blackstone, who greeted him just past the door, Nathanial made his way into the room, taking the time to drink in the gathering as he moved. He had the opportunity to do so because there was no rush of debutantes his way, which was both a relief and a worry.

Would any of the debutantes here want a husband who desperately needed their dowry?

A flash of pink caught his attention from the left corner of the room, and Nathanial studiously looked away.

The right side of the room was filled mostly with the contemporaries of Lord and Lady Blackstone. Nathanial nodded a greeting to Lord and Lady Emeryn, who he'd met before. Lord Emeryn towered over his more diminutive wife, keeping close by her side as though he could not bear to be parted from her. They'd been a love match whose courtship scandalized the *ton*. Beside them was Lady Collette, who insisted on going by her first name to everyone, her substantial curves on display with a shockingly low decolletage for an afternoon gathering. The greys streaking her brown hair did not detract from her beauty nor did her age from her spirit.

She winked at Nathanial over her fan, fluttering it with invitation, and he grinned and winked back. One could never tell whether Lady Collette was serious with her flirtations or not, but not playing the game was to risk her wrath.

Several other couples milled about, not his set, and Nathanial turned away to seek his fellow dukes.

Montagu and St. Albans had perched beside the fireplace, and Nathanial made his way to them. They were warily watching the small clumps of young ladies who were in attendance, though the debutantes currently seemed happy to chatter among themselves. Off to the side, he recognized Lady Astrid's brother Rupert speaking with another young man. Nathanial had never formally met Ashwin Little, but he knew who he was.

A reminder of the woman Nathanial could absolutely not marry, despite her great fortune.

"How goes it?" he asked, coming to a halt beside Christian, Duke of Montagu, and deliberately turning himself so he could not see Ashwin Little or the corner where his sister was presently.

"They are talking among themselves rather than to us, and it's making me more nervous than if they were crowding us," St. Albans replied, rubbing at the pocket where he kept his lucky coin. Matthew was known to the *ton* as the Lord of Luck due to his unlikely number of wins at anything to do with gambling. He had a coin that he flipped to help him make his decisions, and somehow it always worked out.

Nathanial had often wished a little of Matthew's luck would rub off on him... but even if it did, he doubted he would visit the gambling tables. His father's bad luck and the family's subsequent misfortune had soured the taste of gaming for Nathanial for good.

"Do you think they are talking about us?" he asked, risking a glance over his shoulder at the gathered beauties.

"What else?" Christian snorted. "Probably deciding which of us they'll approach before dinner." Unlike Matthew, he did not seem nervous at all. Then again, there were not many with as rakish a reputation as Christian. Debutantes were not his usual fare, but he was accustomed to the attention of women. He was Society's most beautiful man, the *ton's* Adonis.

Beside him and the luckiest man in the country, Nathanial was beginning to feel more nervous about his own prospects. He needed a bride by the end of this Season, but he did not want just any bride.

With his estate buried in debts, his sisters needing to make their own debuts into Society soon, and his family's reputation in shambles, thanks to his father, he needed a bride of good fortune, good reputation, and hopefully good nature. Someone to help him find good matches for his sisters, run his estate, and improve the family's standing.

His choices on how to save his family had narrowed further and further until now, the only choice left to be made was who he would marry to safeguard their future.

Lifting his head, he looked about, and his gaze was immediately arrested by a pair of eyes so dark, they were like pools of night. The breath in his lungs felt like it rushed out all at once. His skin tingled, his body tightening, the immediate attraction stirring the way it always did when he laid eyes on Miss Kalina Little.

He wanted her. He could not deny that.

But he could not marry her.

2

———————

The Duke of Hereford was looking at her.

Again.

Kalina tore her gaze away from his, pretending that her heart was not pounding so fast, it felt like it might break her stays. Something about him always made her feel... strange. Off. Her mother had explained what happened between a man and a woman, ensuring Kalina knew enough not to be tricked into being alone with a man she did not intend to engage in such activities with.

She knew about attraction. Desire.

What she did not know was how to react to feeling such things firsthand.

Focusing on Lady Astrid, who was making introductions, helped.

"Kalina, this is Lady Nichole Dallas, Lady Karina Chipwith—"

"Please call me Kari, or else this will become too confusing," quipped the smiling young lady, brushing an auburn curl out of her chocolate brown eyes, and making the rest of the company laugh.

"—and Lady Johanna Ashmore, and her companion Miss Rose Belle."

"So lovely to meet you all," Kalina said, smiling and making sure to include Lady Johanna's companion in her greeting. Miss Belle stood half a pace back from the rest of them, her hands folded in front of her, resting on the skirts of the plain burgundy gown she was wearing. She appeared to be of age as the rest of them, young for her position, and possibly determined to prove herself worthy of it. Her skin was darker than Kalina's, her features and hair denoting her African descent, and Kalina could only imagine that she, too, felt different in this drawing room.

And they were the only two misses in the group.

Lady Johanna was Miss Belle's complete opposite in every way. Her skin was so pale, it seemed nearly translucent, her white-blonde hair was piled in curls that looked so heavy, it was a wonder her slim neck could hold her head upright, and her wide, shockingly violet eyes were otherworldly. She was the definition of delicate.

"Do you see all the dukes? Have you met them?" Lady Kari asked, fluttering her fan and peeking over at the three surrounding the fireplace. That's where the Duke of Hereford was. Kalina deliberately did not look back there.

Lady Astrid laughed.

"I did promise you all dukes. There are some other gentlemen who will be in attendance as well for you to meet. And a matchmaker will be joining us tomorrow." She smiled at all of them, but she winked at Kalina, who felt her chest tighten.

There was no shame in using a matchmaker. That's what she told herself. Lady Astrid had previously promised to contact her friend, whose grandmother was a renowned matchmaker for the *ton*. According to Lady Astrid, her friend had taken over much of her grandmother's work, though she did so in her grandmother's name to continue the mystique.

"Did someone say matchmaker?" a deep voice asked in tones of disbelief, making all of them turn.

Tiffany's brother, the darkly handsome and often serious Duke of Bolton, was standing there with his sister and her husband. The Duke of Clarence smiled widely. The two dukes were both tall, broad-shouldered, handsome, and dark of hair and eye, but their temperaments were very different.

If anything, the Duke of Bolton's demeanor seemed to have become more serious since his sister's marriage and his mother's departure to the country for her health. The Duke of Clarence, by contrast, was entirely jovial by his wife's side. Marriage suited him.

"Yes, a matchmaker. Why, did you want some assistance with finding your bride?" Lady Astrid asked archly, narrowing her eyes at him.

The Duke of Bolton snorted inelegantly, causing Lady Kari and Lady Nichole to giggle and fan themselves. He slanted a look at them, raising his eyebrows as he did so.

"Do you think I need a matchmaker, ladies?" he asked, causing both of them to fall into more fits of giggles.

Beside them, Lady Johanna stared silently, pressing her lips together. Behind her, Miss Belle glanced at the other two giggling ladies and sighed inaudibly. Kalina felt rather in kinship with Lady Johanna, who was apparently shyer and quieter than the other young ladies they'd been speaking with. Perhaps she was as delicate as she appeared.

"I doubt it, Your Grace," Lady Kari replied, batting her eyelashes coquettishly up at him.

He smiled and gave Lady Astrid a sardonic look.

"See? No matchmaker required. I am a duke after all." The declaration caused another fit of giggling from the other two ladies while Lady Astrid rolled her eyes.

"Sebastian is certain the right lady will fall into his lap, eventually," the Duke of Clarence said. "Perhaps even this weekend." He winked at the whole group of young ladies, chuckling when his wife elbowed him. Tiffany sighed at her husband's lack of tact, shooting a look at Kalina, who smiled back at her. The Duke of Clarence was too charming to be disliked.

"Well, Mei and her grandmother, Lady Hu, will be here to meet with anyone who would like to speak with them. They have connections all over the *ton* and have already successfully arranged two earls and a baron's marriage this Season." Lady Astrid looked at the Duke of Bolton rather challengingly, as if daring him to say something derogatory.

He simply smiled.

"I am sure the earls and the baron are grateful for their help." He looked around. "Now, Lady Astrid, before the matchmaker arrives, I do not believe I have met all the young ladies already here."

Before introductions could be rendered, the arrival of three more dukes set the group to titters, rapidly expanding their numbers. Lady Astrid did her duty of introducing everyone, then somehow, the group settled into two separate parts again, though the Duke of Montagu had wandered away to look out the window. That there were two lovely married ladies who were attending the house party without their husbands likely had no impact on his decision.

Kalina found herself between Lady Astrid and the Duke of Bolton. Opposite her were Lady Johanna, Miss Belle, and the Lord of Luck himself, the Duke of St. Albans. Rumor had it he would only marry a woman if a flip of his coin indicated he should. Kalina wondered if he'd flipped for her already or if her fate was yet to be decided.

He seemed an amiable enough sort. Easy to get along with. Not as high in the instep as the Duke of Bolton. But also...

Looking at him didn't make her feel the way the Duke of Hereford did.

He was part of the other group. Kalina was not going to look over at him. She was not.

Nathanial

Lady Kari and Lady Nichole were exactly the kind of young ladies he should be courting. Rich. Connected. Trained to run a household. Spotless reputations.

So, why did his eyes keep shifting to the side every time he caught a glimpse of pink?

Why did his ears strain to hear the conversation in the other group, rather than attending to the young ladies within his own? He knew the answer; he just did not want to admit it.

Her very presence in the ton *is scandalous.*

She's not an appropriate guide for my sisters. And Julianna is going to need a firm hand.

Her family not only does not have the required connections to assist our reputation, but her grandfather has also cut their branch from the family tree.

None of which was her fault, but the truth remained.

Miss Little was lacking on multiple fronts when it came to the kind of bride he required to shore up his family's reputation, which was as important to him as their fortunes. He had three sisters to marry off. Julianna should have debuted this year, by all rights, but he'd put her off so that she would not feel the same pressures that he was burdened with.

He was determined that when it came time for his sisters to marry, they would be able to do so without any consideration other than who they *wanted* to marry. Which meant *he* had to marry, with the many considerations of how to elevate their family back to the position in Society they'd held before his father's ruinous behavior.

There were times he was grateful to whoever had murdered his father, an emotion that was immediately followed by guilt for his friends who had lost their fathers at the same time. Some of them truly mourned the previous titleholder. Nathanial did not. However, he was as determined to find the perpetrator as his friends were, if only to ensure the safety of his sisters.

Several clues had recently revealed themselves... but that was not what this excursion from the capital was about. They would have to investigate further when they returned. In the meantime, appearances had to be maintained and ladies considered. It was not the past he needed to focus on, but the future.

"Have you seen the latest play at the Globe?" Lady Kari asked, fluttering her fan at him.

"Unfortunately, I have not had the time,"—he'd had the time, just not the funds—"but I heard Keane is a revelation."

"Oh, he is so talented!" Lady Kari brightened, obviously a lover of the actor, just as many within the *ton* were.

If Nathanial did get a chance to see the man on stage, it would be from the box of one of his friends. Using the Hereford's usual box when he'd not been able to pay his subscription to the theater since he'd attained his title—and it had been years since his father had done so—did not sit right in his stomach.

Using one of his friend's boxes also did not feel right.

Pride was one of the few vices he had left. When he did return to the theater, it would be in triumph and to his own box, his wife on his arm and Julianna in tow.

Listening to Lady Kari chatter on about Keane's talents, Nathanial was hard-pressed to keep his mind from wandering. Despite her other qualities, he probably should not marry a woman he could not keep his attention on. He did not want to be a cruel husband, after all.

Not like his father, who had paid their entire family no attention at all, other than to try to beget a second son upon their mother. He'd given up after three daughters, then commenced becoming King of the Wastrels.

Sebastian chimed in to Lady Kari's observations, quickly followed by Lady Nichole, who batted her eyes at him. Emboldened by his responses, Lady Kari refocused her attention on the Duke of Bolton. Nathanial barely noticed, because Miss Little was now laughing at something Matthew had said, and Nathanial's stomach suddenly felt curdled.

He looked over.

He could not help himself.

Her laughter was quiet, almost surprised, as if she had not expected to find herself doing so. Matthew appeared very pleased with himself. Miss Little's jewels gleamed at her throat, but they did not shine nearly as brightly as her smile or the spark in her dark eyes. Both of which were currently directed at Matthew.

Nathanial jerked his gaze away.

Flexing his suddenly tense hand at his side, he tried to refocus his attention on the conversation of the eligible ladies. Perhaps a change of topic was in order. Something he could participate more fully in.

Before he could think of how to turn the conversation, there was a small stir at the door—a late arrival and a very prestigious one.

"Lucifer appears," Lady Astrid muttered, barely bothering to keep her voice down as her fiancé greeted her parents. As she was standing directly behind Nathanial, he also heard her nearly inaudible sigh before she brushed past him to go greet Drake, the Duke of Ormonde and her betrothed since childhood. His mother was with him, and the Duchess greeted Lady Blackstone with the delight of long-time bosom friends who had not seen each other in far too long.

In contrast, the greeting between Drake and Lady Astrid could hardly be described as cold, but the heat was more contempt on her part and something more ineffable on his. How Drake felt about his betrothed was something none of his friends understood, nor would he speak on the matter, but there was some kind of feeling there. He claimed he would marry her at the end of the Season, after he'd had one last chance to sow his wild oats.

He did indeed seem to be intent on sowing them quite wildly.

"My goodness, the Duke of Ormonde is very handsome," Lady Kari remarked, fluttering her fan and sending a sidelong glance at Sebastian and Nathanial, as if to see how they reacted to her remarks.

"Very," Lady Nichole agreed impishly, a little smile appearing on her lips. "Though not as beautiful as the Duke of Montagu."

"No one is as beautiful as Christian," Sebastian replied, squashing any hopes the ladies had of stirring jealousy in their breasts. Both of them looked a touch disappointed that neither he nor Sebastian had taken umbrage. But if they hoped to play the friends off each other, they were going to be disappointed.

Christian was the only one of them who had made a lady swoon with nothing more than a wink, after all. And Nathanial did not care if they thought Drake handsome. He was. He was also betrothed to Lady Astrid and determined to see it through.

I wonder who Miss Little finds the most attractive of us.

No.

No, he did not.

Nathanial banished the thought from his mind. It did not matter who she found the most attractive.

"Nathanial, we need you to settle a disagreement," Gregory said, putting his hand on Nathanial's shoulder and turning him toward the woman he was so desperately trying to ignore. "Nathanial has read more books than anyone else we know. His library is stupendous."

Only because, thankfully, his father had not realized the value of the books within it, otherwise he would have attempted to sell those off as well.

"What is it you wish me to settle?" he asked, far too aware of Miss Little's gaze on him and doing his best to look at everyone equally. If he avoided her gaze, the others might notice. If he held it too long, she might misunderstand. Or someone else might. *Like myself*.

"Miss Little insists that <u>Jane Eyre</u> must have been written by a woman, even though the author's name is Currer Bell. I have not read the work myself, but Matthew read the beginning and says he saw nothing to indicate the author to be anything other than a man. What say you?"

"I think it *could* be a woman," Tiffany interjected before Nathanial could respond. The Duchess of Clarence shook her head. "But I think it could equally be a man. I do not know how I would be able to tell the difference."

"Why not use her real name, if it is?" Matthew asked, with enough arrogance that Tiffany snorted. Miss Little looked away, and Lady Johanna looked down at the floor. Her companion, Miss Belle, looked as though she wanted to snort her derision along with Tiffany.

"Only a man who has put no thought into the plight of a woman would say such a thing," Tiffany responded sassily, making both Gregory and Nathanial laugh. When he first met her, Nathanial had found her quiet and retiring. He'd even been interested in marrying her himself. Since her marriage to Gregory, a much more fiery part of her personality had revealed itself as she gained confidence in her position as his duchess. It was rather entertaining to witness.

"You can see why we need an arbitrator," Gregory said, giving his wife a sidelong look while Matthew scowled and subsided, obviously thinking about what he was missing that the women understood.

Nathanial could have told him. He had sisters, after all. If one of them was revealed to be the author of a book like <u>Jane Eyre</u>... gads, marrying her off would be impossible. The scandal of a lady of the *ton*, or even the gentry, publishing such a novel...

He shook his head.

"I think if the author is a woman, she would not wish her identity guessed," he chided.

"Oh, we are certainly not trying to guess who," Miss Little said softly, earnestly.

Having her speak directly to him made him feel as though his skin was too tight on his body, and he clenched his fist by his side, then spread his fingers wide to try to alleviate some of the discomfort.

"But just whether the author is, indeed, a woman. I think the insights into Jane's mind are far too personal to have been written by an author who is not."

"The thought had not occurred to me while reading it, but it is very possible," Nathanial conceded. "There were many instances where I found myself impressed with how her character was portrayed."

As the conversation went round, Nathanial had no trouble paying attention. Other possible women authors writing under names not their own, or as Anonymous, were brought up. It was lively, entertaining, and Nathanial found himself far too impressed with Miss Little's literary knowledge.

It would have been much better for him if she had loathed or been disinterested in books.

Instead, he found himself engaged in a deep discussion of the merits of reading the classics versus the newer publications. He was so engrossed in their conversation, he did not realize they'd moved away from the rest of the group until Lady Astrid appeared at his elbow.

"It is time for dinner," she said, smiling brightly between himself and Miss Little, a gleam in her eye that made him realize his mistake. "You can escort Miss Little in, Your Grace."

There was no gentlemanly way to refuse.

"Of course," he said tightly, turning toward the door and offering Miss Little his arm. He did his best not to react when she hesitated, then lightly rested her fingers on his coat, though it felt as if his entire body was now attuned to that one spot on his arm. "Miss Little."

"Thank you, Your Grace," she replied, ducking her head, as if she realized he was displeased. It was not her fault that they had been standing next to each other when it was time to move to the dining room. Nor was it her fault that she was not a suitable bride for him, though she would be for any of his friends who did not have the same hurdles to overcome with Society.

However, the gleam in Lady Astrid's eyes was destined to be disappointed, and he did not want to lead Miss Little on when he could not marry her.

It was going to be a tightrope walk for dinner with her at his side. Yet there was a part of him that rejoiced in the excuse to have her company for it. A part of him that he knew he needed to excise ruthlessly.

After dinner.

3

Kalina

The Duke of Hereford did not want to sit with her. Kalina did not understand why. They had been having a very nice conversation, but he'd drawn back within himself the moment Lady Astrid paired them together for dinner. He led her in, was graciously courteous, but something had changed.

She lifted her chin high.

It did not matter if he had taken up against her for some reason.

Throughout the years, Kalina had grown accustomed to rejection. She was used to brushing off the sting, so that she barely felt it at all.

Which was why it made no sense that it should hurt so much this time. But it did.

The dining room was long and narrow with an extremely long table running through the center of its length. Four multi-tiered chandeliers hung above the table, twinkling light across the expanse, while sconces along the walls helped brighten the edges of the room. Candelabras rested on the heavy wooden buffets that lined the room, adding both decoration and extra light.

Massive paintings filled the space of the walls, interspersed with smaller ones, to add interest to the visual feast. Behind the far end of the table was a large window that went nearly from floor to ceiling, hung with heavy dark green drapes. Standing in front of them, Lady Astrid looked like an exotic hothouse flower against the more muted colors on the walls and paintings. Beside her, the Duke of Ormonde escorted her to her seat beside her father at the head of the table. She did not appear overly pleased with her position, but she gracefully took her seat.

Kalina found herself between the Duke of Hereford and the Duke of Montagu, who was escorting a tongue-tied Lady Johanna. Her companion was seated across from them, between Lady Astrid's younger brother and the Duke of Clarence, and was regarding Montagu with high suspicion. Catching Kalina's gaze, Miss Belle smiled briefly before returning to her narrow-eyed study of Montagu.

"Miss Little, lovely as ever," Montagu greeted her, turning away from Lady Johanna with what seemed like relief. The poor young lady had already barely said two words together; pairing her with the stunning Montagu seemed rather unfair. Perhaps Lady Astrid was hoping to draw other gentlemen's notice to her by doing so?

"Your Grace, a pleasure to see you again," Kalina said, grateful that her mother's training had her speaking without tripping over her tongue. She knew all the proper phrases by rote, so that she did not have to think in order to speak clearly. Even she was not entirely unaffected by Montagu's beauty, though her awareness was all for the man on her opposite side. Hereford was currently greeting Delilah, who had been seated beside him.

"How was the trip from London?"

"Very uneventful." She smiled at him, too well-mannered to complain the way she had earlier with Tiffany. Though Tiffany was a duchess, she had also declared herself a friend and had shown it well enough for Kalina to unbend with her, just a touch. "Are you enjoying the house party?"

"Oh, yes. I always enjoy being in the company of so many beautiful women," he said, looking across the table at Miss Belle and winking.

Rather than swooning or fluttering, her lips pursed in disapproval. Montagu frowned, as if unsure of what to do in the face of such a response. Giving himself a little shake, he seemed to recover quickly enough despite his discomposure.

"Take Lady Johanna here," he said, turning slightly so the young woman could be included in their conversation.

Hearing her name, Lady Johanna's head jerked around, and she appeared frozen in place, wide-eyed and almost fearful. Kalina's heart went out to her. She wondered if that was what she had been like when she first arrived in England. Had Lady Astrid and Tiffany seen her the way she saw Lady Johanna? She wanted to reach out and offer the young woman a helping hand. Had it been the same for them and her?

"She has the most glorious eyes. I have rarely seen the like."

"You do have incredible eyes," Kalina agreed, leaning in slightly so she could speak to Lady Johanna without unduly raising the volume of her voice. "If you wore violet, the color of your gown would enhance them even more."

"Amethysts," Montagu declared, grinning widely. "You should be bedecked in amethysts."

"Oh..." Lady Johanna looked down at the simple gray fabric of her dress. Now that Kalina was able to examine it more closely, she could see that the fabric was a bit worn, with little holes indicating where it had either been altered or changed. If she had not been inspecting it so closely, she would not have noticed but... "What about Rose? What jewel should she wear?"

It was the most words Lady Johanna had said altogether since Kalina had met her. Both she and Montagu looked across the table at Miss Belle, who was speaking with the Duke of Clarence. As if feeling their eyes upon her, she glanced back at them, then frowned as she realized they were indeed looking at her.

"Rubies," Montague said after a moment. "Miss Belle would look resplendent in rubies, bright red as a rose."

The burgundy dress Miss Belle was wearing did become her, but Kalina had to agree. A rich, bright red would be very flattering on Miss Belle. It would also draw a good deal of attention, and so far, the companion had been doing her best to fade into the background.

"Red would be very pretty," she agreed, smiling at Miss Belle. The young lady smiled back at Kalina and shot another glare at Montagu before turning back to her conversation with the Duke of Clarence. Montagu frowned at her, his own gaze now narrowed almost in imitation of hers when she'd been studying him so closely.

"Red is Christian's favorite color." The Duke of Hereford's deep voice, suddenly joining the conversation, made Kalina jump in her seat. She felt her cheeks burn with emotion and was grateful for constant practice in composure that allowed her to appear unbothered—other than her initial start of surprise.

"Oh?" She smiled at the Duke of Montagu before turning back to the Duke of Hereford. "What is your favorite color?"

His gaze flicked down to the rose diamonds around her throat and then down to her dress of complementary pink hues with cream trim. "I am sure I can guess at yours."

Kalina laughed lightly.

"It is true, I've always loved the color pink." She smiled. "It feels such a warm, happy color. Like a hug." Realizing who she was speaking with, the heat filled Kalina's cheeks again.

Thankfully, she did not have to worry about the heat showing. Though she loved the color pink, the way the English actually turned pink when they were embarrassed was something she was grateful not to have to endure.

Quickly, she looked away from him, unsure of how he would take the comment. She had not meant to say something so personal, not after how he'd pulled away from their conversation earlier, clearly reluctant to be her dinner companion.

"It is a very flattering color on you," the Duke of Montagu interjected, breaking the tension of the moment. "As I think you know." He winked at her, and she felt Hereford bristle at her side.

She smiled back at Montagu, relieved to have him to distract her from the man at her side. Why she found the Adonis of the *ton* less attractive, yet easier on her nerves than the Duke of Hereford, she could not say, but it was true. Though she had been less nervous when they'd been speaking of books.

Before he'd pulled back.

Before she'd felt the coldness of his retreat.

"I've always been partial to pink myself," Hereford said, drawing her attention back to him. His fingers reached up to brush over the handkerchief peeking out of his coat pocket, a rather lovely shade of puce. It matched the puce and cream striped waistcoat he was wearing. "My mother grew nothing but pink roses in our garden."

"Oh, I should like to see that," Kalina said without thinking. There was something about Hereford that made her far too comfortable, blurting out her thoughts too easily, before remembering herself.

"Ah, well." It was like seeing shutters drawn across the duke's eyes. "We do not entertain much these days. Eventually, perhaps."

Blast. She had accidentally reminded him of his dire financial straits. The entire *ton* knew. Just as he had to know that she had a genuine fortune for a dowry. What hung around her neck and from her ears was the least of it. Her father had been determined to see her properly settled into English Society. That they had not been fully accepted, regardless...

She wondered what it was about herself that the Duke of Hereford objected to since she had the one thing he needed in a wife.

"We do not entertain at all," Kalina replied, smiling at him. Perhaps he kept drawing back because he did not want her to think him a fortune hunter? Even though everyone knew he required a wife with a substantial dowry. "I am grateful to be included in invitations when we are, especially to such surrounds as this. It is my first house party."

Indeed, being invited to Lady Astrid's house party had such cachet, the family had immediately received three other invitations for when they returned to London. All from hostesses who had not deigned to acknowledge her or her parents before.

"You will enjoy it," Hereford said, slanting a glance down the table to where Lady Astrid was seated. "Lady Astrid insists on being entertained at her own house parties, which means they are never dull."

"Have you attended many?"

"Not until recently, but she does have a reputation." He chuckled, still watching the lady at the end of the table as she turned her nose up at something the Duke of Ormonde said to her. "Next time, I hope to be able to bring my sister Julianna. After she debuts next Season."

"Ah, I always wanted a sister." Kalina smiled back at him as he turned his head to look at her again. "I love Ashwin, of course, but there were times when it would have been nice to have a sister."

"I have three, and I would have happily traded one for a brother."

Comparing notes on siblings, their conversation passed so easily, she barely noticed the various courses being served. From siblings, they went on to talking about their childhoods. Strangely, it sounded as though Hereford had been as lonely as she in some ways—he talked around it a bit, but it was clear he felt responsible for his sisters in the same way she felt responsible for her family.

Perhaps it came from both of them being the eldest. Though Kalina's father had never shown her anything but love, while Hereford's father... he talked around the subject, but she'd heard the gossip. The former duke had been a gambler, a wastrel, and not very pleasant as a person to boot.

That he had left his family in such dire straits demonstrated his lack of responsibility toward his family, something Kalina would never understand. Rather than following in his father's footsteps, Nathanial had clearly taken the opposite tack and was doing everything he could to be the antithesis of his father. Kalina did not need to read very far between the lines to understand that.

She thought it rather admirable.

In fact, the more she talked to him, the more she liked talking to him. The more she felt at ease with him.

To the point where she felt rather sorry when the last course was served, and only then realized that they had monopolized each other's time completely. Once they had begun conversing, she'd completely ignored the Duke of Montagu. Rather horrified at her ill manners, she quickly turned to see how he was faring...

To her surprise, he had managed to charm Lady Johanna into speaking with him very softly about the latest traveling art exhibition in London. From across the table, Miss Belle appeared torn between relief that her charge was finally having a conversation and consternation over who she was having it with.

Smiling, she turned back to the Duke of Hereford, only to realize that the meal was over. Disappointment filled her as Lady Blackstone got to her feet, nearly at the same time as Lady Astrid.

"Ladies, would you like to return with me to the parlor and leave the gentlemen to their drinks?" Lady Blackstone asked softly, smiling widely.

Internally sighing, Kalina smiled at the duke... only to find that he'd retreated behind his shell again. The openness with which he'd spoken with her had vanished, and he was once more stiffly upright in his chair, avoiding her gaze. Her heart sank.

"Thank you for a pleasant conversation over supper, Your Grace," she said, knowing it would force him to at least acknowledge her and that they had been having a lovely conversation together.

His head jerked up, something unfathomable flashing through his dark eyes.

"The pleasure was all mine, Miss Little."

Taking her leave, Kalina knew she would have to be satisfied with that.

Perhaps some time with the other ladies was what she really needed. Someone must know why the Duke of Hereford had taken against her.

4

Leaning back in his chair, Nathanial could not help but watch the ladies leave. The sway of Miss Little's pink skirts was almost seductive as she joined the throng, Tiffany coming up to link arms with her. Miss Little turned her head and said something to Tiffany that made her laugh.

"If you keep watching after her with such longing, people are going to talk," Christian said in a low voice.

"After who?" The attempt at ignorance was instinctual; it was also completely useless. Christian was hardly slow-witted, and he gave Nathanial a look of amused patience.

"You know who." Christian slanted his glance across the table to where Miss Little's younger brother and Lady Astrid's younger brother were whispering conspiratorially.

Before the last of the ladies left the room, the two striplings got up, excusing themselves from the table, and exited the room just behind the ladies, leaving the gentlemen to themselves.

"Would anyone like some brandy?" Lord Blackstone asked, gesturing to one of the footmen who came forward with a tray of glasses and a crystal decanter full of amber liquid. "I have a particularly fine barrel recently delivered from France."

All the gentlemen chose to partake, and cigars were passed around as well.

"How was your evening?" Gregory asked, turning to Nathanial with a gleam in his eye.

"He had a very enjoyable conversation with Miss Little," Christian replied before Nathanial could, making Nathanial growl. Thankfully, the others at the table were attending to conversations closer to themselves and did not appear to have heard Gregory's question or Christian's answer.

"It was a tolerable conversation." More than, but he was not going to encourage his friends in that line of thought.

"It must have been mightily tolerable as she was so engaged that she forgot I was on her other side."

"Forgot she was seated next to the *ton's* Adonis?" Gregory put his hand on his heart to further punctuate his shock. "I did not know such a thing was possible. What were you talking about that was so engaging?"

"Nothing important. It was just normal conversation." Nathanial scowled, hunching his shoulders in. He did not like all the scrutiny from his friends, and he liked even less having to face the fact that Miss Little was more than physically attractive; she was... interesting. Easy to converse with. Far easier than any other lady he'd been seated beside this Season.

"I do not understand why you are so insistent on pretending disinterest in her, when you are clearly attracted," Christian twitted.

"I have far more considerations than personal preference when it comes to a bride."

Frowning, Christian made a little hand gesture, as if telling Nathanial to lower his voice. Christian's gaze flitted past him for a moment, and Nathanial half-turned to see where the other duke was looking.

Ah. He'd forgotten that Mr. Little was seated not too far away. Though he did appear to be listening attentively to Lord Emeryn's advice about hunting hounds. Hopefully, he was not paying any attention to Nathanial's conversation with the others, but he would have to remember to keep his tone lower.

"She has a dowry," Gregory pointed out, keeping his voice lower as well. "One of the largest this Season. Other than the hostesses hoping for some of the drama surrounding the family to add excitement to their events, their wealth is a large part of what opened doors to them prior to my mother deciding to champion their cause."

The Dowager Duchess of Clarence had been the first of the *haut ton* to acknowledge the family, leading the way for her son and daughter-in-law and followed swiftly by Lady Astrid and the rest of Gregory's ducal cohort. Which was how Nathanial had been introduced to her.

Taking a deep breath to try to ease the constriction around his chest, Nathanial let it out slowly.

"Yes, she has the dowry, but not the social connections nor the experience with the *ton*. I have barely begun to right the damage my father did to our family's reputation, and I have three sisters to settle." The bands around his chest were tightening again. Now he was having no difficulty keeping his voice down, so only Christian and Gregory could hear him, and he was grateful the others were so engrossed in their own conversations.

Christian frowned.

"Julianna… she should have made her come-out this year."

Count on Christian to remember something so insignificant. Gregory frowned as well.

"That cannot be right," Gregory started to say, but his voice trailed off.

"Time does fly, does it not?" Nathanial asked wryly. He reached up to scrub his hand across his face. "Yes, under other circumstances, Julianna would have made her debut this year."

"Why did you not let her? I understand the cost, but the merchants would not have expected to be paid immediately." Gregory's frown deepened. "Or would they?"

"To me? I expect they would have made an allowance with both

Julianna and me on the marriage market, but I could not do that to her. My sisters will be able to marry whoever they want, using whatever criteria they want."

Both of his friends stared at him in silence for a long moment. Nathanial looked away, focusing on the glass of brandy in his hand, the heaviness of the cut crystal, the sharp edges pressing against his fingers as he lifted it and swirled the liquid inside.

"You mean, you will not have Julianna put in the same position as you," Gregory said softly, his voice full of sympathy and understanding.

"What if she was willing?" Christian asked, frowning. "Why does it have to be you?"

Nathanial's grip on the glass tightened, the discomfort of the crystal digging into his skin turning to slight pain as he forced himself to relax his jaw so he could answer.

"It is my responsibility. My father, as the duke, ran... everything into the ground. As the duke, it is up to me to repair it. I will not sacrifice any of my sisters upon the altar of marriage in order to fix a problem they had nothing to do with creating."

"You will only sacrifice yourself." Christian's voice was soft, almost as though he was speaking more to himself than to Nathanial. He sounded confused, like he could not understand why Nathanial would not look for a solution by *any* means necessary.

Looking up, Nathanial met Gregory's eyes. Christian had no other siblings, but Gregory had three half-sisters, who he doted on. Though they were far younger than him, arranging for their futures was something he already considered his responsibility. He nodded, his gaze full of understanding.

Gregory knew what it was to bear the burden, as well as the responsibility, of a dukedom and family. Christian had no dependents, other than two grandmothers who got on famously and were perfectly able to take care of themselves—and each other.

Perhaps one day, if he had daughters, he would understand then.

<u>*Kalina*</u>

The parlor was quieter without the gentlemen, the energy a little softer, less frenetic. The other ladies were no longer posing or artlessly flirting with their admirers but had fallen to chatting among themselves. Lady Blackstone's set made their way to the most comfortable couches by the unlit fireplace. Kalina allowed herself to be led by Tiffany toward the window seat where Lady Johanna and Miss Belle were already sitting, slightly apart from the other young ladies who occupied a nearby grouping of chairs.

Lady Johanna appeared wan, perhaps a trifle overwhelmed after being the center of the Duke of Montagu's attentions over dinner. She managed a smile, though her eyes widened at Tiffany's approach. Immediately, she jumped to her feet, Miss Belle hot on her heels, and spread her pearly grey skirts wide as she dipped into a curtsy of the appropriate degree.

"Your Grace." Both Lady Johanna and Miss Belle spoke the title almost simultaneously.

"Please, let us not stand on ceremony," Tiffany said, smiling broadly. "May Miss Little and I join you?"

"Of course," Lady Johanna said hastily, moving to the side to make room for them. "I could stand—"

"No, no, there is room for all four of us, even with our skirts," Tiffany said, laughing lightly. She waved her hand, gesturing for Lady Johanna and Miss Belle to sit. They could hardly refuse her command. Kalina sat down as well on Tiffany's other side. "Lady Astrid suggested we all get to know each other better. As both Bolton's sister and Clarence's wife, I have rather extensive knowledge of the peccadillos of their friends. Ah, and here is another who also knows the dukes quite well."

"The tragic dukes, you mean?" Delilah, the Baroness Ashfield, said as she walked up to join them. A footman obligingly appeared to pull a chair closer for her to sit in, and she thanked him before gracefully sitting down. Today, she wore pale yellow with a gold Grecian pattern edging the bottom hem of her skirts, a gold and cream *fichu* modestly covering the *decolletage* revealed by the gown's low neckline.

A single yellow gem on a gold chain hung between the delicate *fichu's* lacy drapes. With her dark hair piled high on her head to contrast with the lighter colors of her dress and showing off earbobs to match her necklace, she was quite striking in appearance.

"The tragic dukes?" Miss Belle asked, the corners of her mouth turning down and making Kalina blink in surprise. Perhaps she was a new companion to Lady Johanna? But the blonde debutante was frowning in confusion as well.

Kalina had not seen either of them before, that she could recall, but she assumed they had been attending different events than her. There were certainly enough to go around.

But how could they have been among the *ton* for any length of time without hearing about the tragic dukes?

"Those gathered here," Delilah said, gesturing broadly back toward the parlor door, and therefore back to the dining room where they'd left the gentlemen. "And the Duke of Grafton as well."

To her credit, she mentioned her former lover with nary a change of expression. Kalina's heart ached for her. She'd been Grafton's long-time lover, but now that he needed to marry, he'd separated himself from her and was looking among the debutantes for a bride. Kalina did not understand because it was obvious there were strong feelings between the two.

As much as her father had explained about English society and customs, there were some things that were so illogical, they went beyond her comprehension.

"Our fathers were killed in a hunting lodge... accident," Tiffany said, a slight pause between two of the words that made Kalina blink, then wonder if she'd heard correctly. "All at once."

"My goodness! I am so sorry ... please accept my condolences and apologies for the unthinking question." Lady Johanna gripped the pale fabric of her skirt. "I also lost my father, not so long ago. It is... very difficult."

"It is. My condolences on your loss as well." Tiffany smiled sympathetically with feeling. "I still miss him, but I do believe he would be proud of the duchess I have become."

Thinking of her own father, Kalina's heart ached. She could not imagine losing him. Either of her parents.

Pressing her lips together, Lady Johanna nodded, her gaze dropping.

"That is why they are called the tragic dukes," Delilah finished. "Though, of course, Society finds the tragedy utterly romantic as it resulted in a bevy of young, handsome dukes in need of wives all at once—and the first one was brash enough to have a love match." She shot a speaking glance at Tiffany, who blushed prettily.

"We did not mean to fall in love," Tiffany retorted. "It just... happened."

"And every debutante in Society wishes it would 'just happen' to her," Delilah teased, though there was a bit of an edge to her tone.

It was not just the debutantes who wished a duke would fall in love with and marry them, Kalina suspected.

She herself did not need love, though she did hope for companionship. Kindness. Desire. Someone who made her heart beat a little faster, yet with who she could speak easily, while the rest of the world faded away around them.

Someone like the Duke of Hereford.

Except she also wanted someone who would not pull away and close themselves off afterward. She wanted a husband who could, at least, be a true partner to her.

And he must be a duke. She was lucky enough to still have her father, and all he wanted was to be acknowledged by his family. The dukes, Tiffany, Lady Johanna... they had all lost their fathers. Life was never guaranteed.

Kalina would marry a duke and see her father have his dream of being received again by his family if it was the last thing she did.

5

———————

Though Lady Johanna remained rather quiet, Miss Belle had picked up the threads of conversation. If she was intimidated by Tiffany's station, she did a better job of hiding it than Lady Johanna's obvious anxiety. It turned out they were not from London but were the Blackstones' neighbors. Lady Johanna's late father had been a local earl, and her younger brother now held the title.

Reading between the lines and looking at Lady Johanna's attire, Kalina realized that Lady Johanna's family was in the same—or worse—financial straits as the Duke of Hereford. No wonder Lady Astrid was trying to arrange a match with a duke for the young lady. She seemed very sweet, though incredibly quiet and reserved. Being with Miss Belle helped her—the other woman was far more confident and seemed to bolster Lady Johanna's spirits.

The two were friends, she realized, rather than *tonnish* lady and hired companion. But the strictures of Society were such that Lady Johanna would not be able to attend the house party without some kind of chaperone, so that was the role Miss Belle was performing for her.

Silently, Kalina wished the young lady the best... and wondered if

Lady Johanna might accept a gift of jewelry from a near-stranger. Kalina did not have her own funds, but she had heaps of jewelry she could part with. Would Lady Johanna consider it an insult?

English pride was still something she did not have a good grasp of.

Perhaps she would wait and see if they could form a deeper friendship over the duration of the house party and decide by the end of it what to do.

A small stir of activity near the door indicated that the gentlemen had come to join them, and sure enough, a moment later, Lord Blackstone led the way in. The atmosphere in the room immediately changed, young ladies straightening their spines and the elder ladies sharpening their gazes to watch what happened next.

Kalina felt a little tingle along her own very straight spine when the Duke of Hereford strode into the room and cast his gaze about. For a moment, their eyes met before he continued looking about. When he made for a group, it was for the other group of young ladies, who had settled into the chairs. It was silly nonsense to feel as though her heart was sinking.

She turned to Tiffany, speaking *sotto voce* so as not to be overheard, though with the sudden increase in noise as the ladies greeted the gentlemen, it might not have been strictly necessary.

"Do you know if the Duke of Hereford has something against me? Or my family?"

Tiffany blinked in surprise at the question, turning to speak with Kalina in her own low tones.

"Gregory has certainly not said anything, and I cannot imagine why he would. Why? You seemed to be getting on very well."

"I thought so, too, but when Lady Astrid paired us together for dinner, he suddenly grew cold. Then he warmed again during the meal. I thought. Now..." Kalina glanced over to where he was speaking with Lady Kari, who fluttered her eyelashes and her fan at him simultaneously.

Her stomach twisted.

"Hmm." Tiffany frowned. "I do not know what he is thinking, but I can try to find out."

"No," Kalina said immediately, shaking her head. "If he has taken against me, there is nothing I can do about it... I just worried that perhaps I had done something wrong."

"Nothing I know of." Tiffany smiled warmly and reached over to put her hand atop Kalina's. "It can be difficult navigating the *ton*, but I will help as best I can. Though Astrid and Delilah have far more experience than I do." She seemed on the cusp of saying something, but then one of the ladies across the room—the older one, who insisted she be called Lady Collette—clapped her hands together, drawing everyone's attention to her.

"Dancing!" Lady Collette exclaimed, bouncing to her feet. "That is what we need! We should start our stay here with dancing!"

The rest of the company exchanged glances, but no one seemed keen to gainsay her. Lady Blackstone looked at her husband, who shrugged, then at Lady Astrid, who smiled.

"Dancing sounds lovely. Shall we decamp to the ballroom?" Turning slightly, Lady Astrid gestured toward the door. Her father, seemingly resigned to his daughter's direction, held out his arm to her mother, and the two led the way out of the room.

Right on their heels, the Duke of Ormonde gave Lady Astrid his arm, bowing slightly as he offered it. Her upper lip curled in a sneer before she could tamp down her expression, but she took his arm.

The rest of the company followed less formally. The Duke of Clarence appeared to offer his arm to both his wife and to Kalina. She smiled at him with relief, grateful to be included. Several other ladies linked arms with each other, but Kalina was not sure who she would have walked with if not Tiffany.

Delilah was already busy ushering Lady Johanna and Miss Belle along, and the other dukes she'd previously met were escorting other young ladies. Her father did glance over his shoulder as he led her mother and Lady Collette out of the room, his expression relaxing into a smile when he saw who she was walking with. When her mother glanced back as well, Kalina felt her chest fill with warmth.

Her parents had been all she had for so long. She very much appreciated that they still looked for her, even though she no longer required it.

Because I have friends.

Finally.

Such a strange concept.

Such a joy.

The Blackstone ballroom was massive, and footmen rushed around to light the huge room.

"Just this side," Lady Astrid directed, waving her hand at the half of the ballroom that contained the pianoforte. "We should not have any need of the whole space."

It left one half the ballroom obscured in shadows but, as Lady Astrid said, there was no need to fill the whole of it with light. The effort would be monumental, while their party was too small to properly make use of such a great amount of space. The footmen appeared relieved and quickly lit the side of the room she'd indicated, as well as just one of the four chandeliers.

The ballroom had a pretty pattern laid out on the floor that matched the pattern on the wallpaper, though the floor was polished wood and the wallpaper was done in cream and bronze. Tapestries depicting what looked like scenes from Greek mythology hung from the walls with sconces set between them, and lavishly ornate wallpaper decorated the space behind them.

Huge windows lined the opposite wall with heavy bronze draperies that matched the wallpaper and golden cords and tassels holding them open. It was dark, which meant they could not see outside, and Kalina wondered what the view would hold during the day. She would have to come and look tomorrow.

This was her first time out in the English countryside, and she wanted to see everything.

Lady Astrid was already settling herself behind the pianoforte, with the Duke of Ormonde hovering beside her. Giving him a narrow-eyed glance, she made a shooing motion at him. His jaw set, he ignored her clear order to move away from her and stepped even closer, reaching up to open her music.

"Oh, how sweet of you to turn the pages for Lady Astrid." The Duchess of Ormonde beamed at the two of them with the blindness of a mother who was thrilled with her child's betrothal and missed all the signs of said children's dislike of each other.

Lifting her chin, Lady Astrid's bosom rose as well as she took in a deep breath and let it out slowly.

"Very kind. Thank you so much, Your Grace."

"My pleasure, my lady."

They were the correct pleasantries, said through gritted teeth, almost as though they were verbally sparring. Everyone but the Duchess of Ormonde and Lady Blackstone seemed discomfited, but Lady Astrid broke through the moment by looking around at the rest of the company.

"Has everyone found a partner?" she asked, driving the attention from herself and the duke to everyone else.

Chairs were already being brought out for those who wished to watch rather than dance, mostly the older guests, though Lord Blackstone was already leading his lady out to the dance floor. The lady smiled at her husband with such frank delight, Kalina felt almost as though she'd trodden on an intimate moment when she looked at them, and she quickly looked away.

It was similar to how her mother looked at her father. It was also something she was unlikely to ever have; therefore, there was no point in yearning after it.

"Miss Little, may I have the honor?" The Duke of Montagu stepped up, bowing as he held out her hand, making his request.

There was no polite way to tell him no, even if she wanted to. And she didn't. Just because she wished another duke had asked first...

Kalina determinedly kept her gaze away from where Hereford was now walking toward the dance floor with Lady Nichole on his arm. She was running out of places to rest her gaze, so she focused on the Duke of Montagu.

The most handsome man in the ton.

Blond locks over a wide brow, sparkling blue eyes that promised mischief and something... more. The hard lines of his jaw were softened by the curve of his lips into a charming smile that beguiled a lady's senses and made her lose her breath, for just an instant.

Yet for all that, he did not have the same effect on her as Hereford.

"Thank you, Your Grace, I would love to." Kalina put her hand in his and smiled in appreciation that he had asked her.

All eyes turned to them as he led her out onto the dance floor, but it was different from any other time she'd been asked to dance. Then again, she'd never been asked to dance by the extremely eligible, shockingly handsome Duke of Montagu.

"They are all going to pay attention to you now," he said cheerfully as he turned toward her on the rapidly filling dance floor. The first few notes came from the piano as Lady Astrid ran her fingers over the keys.

Kalina frowned up at Montagu.

"All the other dukes?"

Leaning forward so he was almost scandalously close, he winked at her. It was like a wave rippled out from them, through the room. She did not need to look to see the reactions from everyone as the Duke of Montagu blatantly flirted with her in the middle of a ballroom. It did not matter that it was at a house party. It did not matter that he had not previously stirred her senses in the same manner as Hereford.

When the Duke of Montagu focused all of his attention—his charm—on her, it took her breath away.

"Everyone." He whispered the word, and she was so distracted by his flirtatiousness, she had almost forgotten what she had asked. The music started, Lady Astrid had chosen to begin with a reel, and Montagu grinned as he straightened and began the movements of the dance. "You'll have your pick of husbands, *ma petite rose.*"

The English habit of peppering French in among their conversation always took her a moment to process.

His little rose. Rose also meant pink. It was a masterful double entendre, and one she rather liked, considering her penchant for pink.

"But not you?" she asked boldly as she moved with him through the dance, spurred on by curiosity and his obvious desire to assist her in finding a husband. There was something very easygoing about him that made her feel like he would not judge her for being so blatant.

He laughed, and she felt the weight of the gazes watching them. The elder ladies in particular were agog with interest. She caught a glimpse of Lady Catherine Perkins, seated beside the Duchess of Ormonde, lifting her lorgnette to get a better look. It was obvious she was watching Montagu and Kalina, as were the rest of the ladies she was seated with. Even the Duchess of Ormonde had stopped beaming at her son and his betrothed and was focused on Montagu and Kalina's dance.

"You do not want to marry me." He shook his head. "And I would not dare marry a woman so close in friendship with my friend's wives. I do not want them all turning their husbands against me when I inevitably upset my wife."

"Why would you upset her?"

"I am afraid I will not make a very good husband. With so many ladies in the world, I find it hard to believe I will enjoy cleaving to a single one for the rest of my life." He chuckled, but there was something melancholy in the sound, as if his self-deprecation had something more behind it than the desire for a variety of women.

"Well, I do not think it is inevitable," she replied stubbornly. Even if he did not want to marry her, she did not like the idea of him going into marriage with the idea that he was bound to be a bad husband, as if he had no choice in the matter. "We all make our own destinies. You can choose to be a good husband if you want to."

Montagu blinked, nearly stumbling over his steps before he gracefully righted himself, and Kalina had the satisfaction of knowing she'd discombobulated him. It almost appeared as if he'd never considered the idea that he could choose to be a good husband.

He looked at her again now, and something about the way he was looking at her had changed, though she could not put her finger on exactly how it differed.

"What qualities do you think would make a good husband?" he asked. Unlike before, when he'd been breezy with his tone, like he was going through the motions of conversation rather than truly paying attention, he seemed as though he was wholly focused on her answer.

One that would force her father's family to acknowledge him.

But Montagu had not asked what she was looking for in a husband; he had asked what she thought would make a good husband.

"Someone kind. Like you." She smiled at him. "Generous and thoughtful. A man who one can converse with and relax with." Very much like she had seen with her parents growing up, they were most fully themselves when they were alone with each other and their children. "Someone who wants a partnership and is willing to work with his wife to create the future they both want."

"What about desire?" He nodded toward the Duke and Duchess of Clarence as they danced together. "Love?"

"I do not know much of desire," she admitted. Other than the way her body tingled when she was near the Duke of Hereford, but she was not going to think about him right now. "And there are many kinds of love. I do not know if one can require a specific kind for marriage. The ability to be together and enjoy each other's company would be the most important qualification, I would think."

"I see."

The Duke of Montagu was looking at her now as though he'd never seen her before, a strange light in his eyes. Kalina did not have the chance to try to find out what he was thinking, because the music ended. They separated, and he bowed as she made her curtsy.

"Christian, Miss Little, Lady Kari and I thought to trade dance partners." The Duke of St. Albans and his partner had turned toward them. Lady Kari clung to his arm, her gaze flitting back and forth between Montagu and Kalina with fascinated interest.

"Of course." The Duke of Montagu's breezy, lackadaisical manner had returned. He held out his hand. "Lady Kari." The young lady looked thrilled as she stepped forward to take it, releasing her hold on the Duke of St. Albans, who reached out his hand to Kalina, bowing as he asked her to dance. She smiled as she took it, wondering if this was what Montagu had meant by her gathering all the attention.

Though she rather thought it was Lady Kari's desire to dance with the Duke of Montagu that had prompted the trade, rather than any desire on St. Albans' part to dance with her. The handsome duke seemed genial and rather relaxed, as though he was just there to enjoy the moment. His charcoal black suit was set off by a mauve and grey waistcoat and a lacy white cravat that emphasized his strong jawline.

It really was unfair how attractive all the attending dukes were... and yet none of them stirred her attention the way the Duke of Hereford did.

"Miss Little. How are you enjoying your evening so far?" St. Albans asked, getting into position beside her as Lady Astrid began the next song.

"Very much. Are most house parties like this?" she asked, following him in the steps and mentally blessing her father for the dance instructor he'd hired the first day they'd landed in London. Her body went through the movements by rote, allowing her to move while focusing on the conversation.

St. Albans laughed.

"Not at all. Lady Collette's suggestion of dancing tonight was inspired; it's already livened things up in a manner that usually takes days to achieve. I am glad Lady Astrid accommodated her."

"I see," Kalina replied, smiling, even though she was not sure that she did. After all, she had nothing to compare it to.

As they turned and St. Albans put his arm around her, her gaze moved across the room, and she sucked in a breath as the Duke of Hereford's dark look crashed into her. He was glaring at her for some reason.

Quickly, she looked away, her heart beating rapidly in her chest as she mentally ran through her actions, wondering where she had misstepped.

6

———

Watching Miss Little dance with Christian was pure torture. It also made him a terrible dancer as he trod on Lady Nichole's toes more than once because he was too distracted by the way Christian leaned into Miss Little... the way he held her hand... the way he laughed at something she'd said. Christian never showed his true self to the ladies he flirted with, but he'd laughed for Miss Little.

Actually laughed. Not the artificial laugh he normally reserved for the ladies he interacted with, but a laugh of real, surprised humor.

And then been arrested by whatever she said next in a manner that Nathanial had never seen him engaged in before. That was when he'd trodden on Lady Nichole's toes for the third time, then forced himself to focus, though she batted her lashes and smiled at him through his apologies, regardless. After all, one did not take a duke to task, no matter how poorly he danced.

But he felt rather bad.

"Do you think he is courting her?" Lady Nichole asked, apparently reaching the end of her patience with pretending she did not see his distraction.

"Who?"

"The Duke of Montagu. Do you think he is courting Miss Little?" Impatience tinged her voice. Despite his station, the lady was becoming annoyed with him, and he could not blame her.

"No more than he is any other lady of the *ton*." Nathanial forced himself to chuckle at the jest, even though he was wondering the same thing now. In truth, he was not sure why Christian had singled out Miss Little for the first dance, nor why he'd been so blatantly flirtatious with her. The man's motives were often a puzzle to him.

"They make a very striking pair," Lady Nichole said thoughtfully. "It would certainly be a coup for her if he were to court her for a bit."

Nathanial made a noncommittal noise, gritting his teeth against expressing how he felt about that notion.

The situation did not improve when the dance ended.

Rather than being able to make his way across the room to where Miss Little and Christian were—he only wanted to dance with her to discover what she'd said that had so amused Christian, of course—he'd been almost immediately halted by the Duke and Duchess of Clarence.

"Lady Nichole, would you do me the honor of a dance?" Gregory asked, smiling at the young lady. "And Nathanial, you'll dance with Tiffany."

It was not a request.

"Of course." Nathanial bowed over Tiffany's hand. He'd actually come quite close to offering for her before she'd been discovered kissing Gregory in the library at the Duchess of Richmond's ball.

Truthfully, he still would have married her after that because he knew exactly who to blame for that particular scandal. Tiffany was far too sensible to have initiated that sequence of events. But Gregory had insisted that he be the one to marry her, and so he had.

As they'd been a love match by the time they were actually wed, it was rather lucky that Nathanial had not gone through with attempting to further his suit. It would have been dashed awkward for his wife to be in love with one of his closest friends and vice versa.

Getting into place to dance with Tiffany, Nathanial glanced over.

Miss Little was now paired with Matthew.

Matthew had said that he'd already flipped his lucky coin to decide whether or not to court Miss Little... but what if he'd changed his mind? What if he flipped it again, and it gave him a different answer?

He'd also flipped it for Nathanial and Miss Little, though he had not told Nathanial what the outcome was. He was not sure it would work for anyone other than himself. Not that it mattered. Nathanial was not going to court her, no matter what the Lord of Luck's coin flip said.

The music started, and Nathanial focused himself.

Unlike Lady Nichole, Tiffany would have no hesitation in taking him to task over bruised toes.

Unfortunately, the turns of the dance made it impossible for him not to see across the room to where Miss Little and St. Albans were now dancing. Would St. Albans tell her about the coin flip? Was the reason he was dancing with her because he'd done a new one for himself?

She turned toward him, a vision in pink, her dark beauty arresting his attention. Their gazes met for a mere moment, then she turned away again. His chest felt tight, as though he could not get enough air in his lungs.

"I see what she meant," Tiffany murmured.

Nathanial jerked his head around, managing at the last moment to keep from stepping on the duchess' toes.

"What who meant?" he asked, confused and also relieved that she had reminded him of where he was. He needed to stop watching Miss Little and think about something else. Anything else.

Unfortunately, Miss Little was exactly who Tiffany wished to talk about.

"Kalina was worried you'd taken up against her for some reason."

"I have not." Indignation was swift and strong.

Tiffany studied his face as he stared down at her. She really was very beautiful, even more so since she'd become a duchess and begun wearing dresses in the blue she favored. It was far more flattering on her than the gowns she'd debuted in.

"Then why were you glaring at her?"

"I..." Had he been glaring? He had not realized. "I was looking across the room."

"You were looking crossly across the room... at Miss Little." Tiffany gave him a hard look. "You seemed to be getting on well enough with her at supper. And before supper."

Nathanial hefted a sigh. Meddling females. He'd been relieved not to have his sisters dogging his every move. They'd been replaced with Sebastian's sister in their stead. Something that would amuse them greatly if he ever admitted it to them.

Somehow, he could not escape his sisters, no matter how he tried.

"We had two very pleasant conversations, both before and during supper," he agreed, turning in place and taking the duchess with him. Now that they were speaking intently, it was far easier to keep his focus on the dance and not step on her feet. Unfortunately, for poor Lady Nichole's toes, she had not been as engaging.

"Then what is your problem with her?" Tiffany narrowed her eyes at him. "If you are judging her for title hunting..."

"Of course not," he scoffed. "I am hardly in a position to judge that."

Though why she would care about her father's side of the family, he did not understand. It did seem rather petty. She might be able to force them to acknowledge her and her family by dint of status if she married a duke, but she could not force the Earl of Stilton to like or accept them.

But that was not his business, as he would not be her husband. That was something for whoever took that position.

And if the idea of another man, especially one of his friends, taking that position made him want to punch something... well, he would feel better once he'd chosen his own bride. It was likely his own uncertain state that made his emotions so unsettled.

Once he knew his direction, he would no longer be so distracted by Miss Little.

Far too aware of Tiffany's discerning gaze taking in every minute change in his expression, Nathanial cleared his throat.

"If you must know, I find Miss Little's company enjoyable, but as I have already determined that she is not what I am seeking for a bride, it seems prudent to keep her at a distance. I would not want to stymy her efforts to find a duke nor my own to find the wife I require." He knew he sounded priggish, haughty even, but he could not help it.

Tiffany's eyes narrowed.

"Why is she not what you are seeking for a bride?" There was a warning note in her voice that made him think there was a correct answer and a wrong answer, and a misstep would result in her extreme displeasure.

But he could not be anything but honest, even with that risk.

"I need a wife who can guide my sisters through their Seasons. One with a faultless reputation and place among Society to help diminish the damage my father did to our family." He raised his eyebrow at Tiffany. "As delightful as she is, you cannot tell me that Miss Little's place in Society is of such quality."

"Through no fault of her own."

"Through no fault of her own," he conceded. "But nonetheless."

Appearing for a moment as though she would argue, Tiffany turned her head away from him and sighed. Sapphires, surrounded by tiny diamonds, shimmered against her ears. The kind of jewels he hoped to one day be able to buy for his own wife.

But pink instead of blue.

He shook his head, shaking away the whisper that slithered through his mind. He would buy whatever jewels his wife desired. Pink was only on his mind because they were speaking of Miss Little.

Tiffany huffed.

"Well, there are other dukes," she said. "Though I thought you and Kalina made a nice pair."

Had Miss Little said something to her?

Had she asked Tiffany to intercede?

Nathanial barely managed to bite his lip against asking.

It doesn't matter.

Thankfully, the dance was ending, taking the temptation to ask her away from him.

Instead, he spent the next few dances in distracted hell as Miss Little danced with Gregory next, then Sebastian, then Drake, who had abandoned his spot at the piano when Lady Kari replaced Lady Astrid to give her a turn on the dance floor. He saw Christian turn and started heading back Miss Little's way as Drake bowed over her hand.

If he did not dance with her at all, surely that would cause more comment than dancing with her. He had certainly waited an appropriate amount of time since Christian had the thought to claim a second dance with her. No one would think twice about her dancing with Nathanial first.

He barely managed to reach her before Christian did, bowing low in front of her startled gaze.

"Miss Little, may I have this dance?"

"I... yes, of course." There was only a moment of hesitation before she accepted. "Oh..."

Her head turned to look at the piano as Lady Kari began to play the strains of a waltz. Nathanial straightened, frowning when she stepped back away from him. The idea of being denied his dance, or of her waltzing with another man, was not pleasant.

"Is something wrong?"

"I-I have not been given permission to waltz," she stammered out. "We... Almack's..." She wrung her hands helplessly in front of her, and Nathanial was hit with a sudden wave of rage.

Because of her family's position and the Earl of Stilton's refusal to acknowledge them, the high stickler patronesses at Almack's must have denied them entry. Which meant she could not receive permission to waltz from any of them, either.

Fortunately for her, the patronesses only held sway over the social scene of London, not the country, where the rules were far more lax.

Stepping forward, Nathanial took her hand and put his other on her waist, pulling her toward him and sliding his hand up her back to the proper position. Her dark eyes widened with shock, bosom heaving upwards against the low neckline of her gown as she sucked in a breath, either from surprise or the sudden nearness of his body, he was not sure.

"You are in the country at a house party," he said reassuringly. "There is no need for permission from Almack's out here. The country is where young ladies learn to waltz."

Then he stepped forward, and she automatically stepped back, instinctively following his lead, then they were whirling around the ballroom with the other couples. Unlike the previous dances, some of which had provided opportunities for easy discussion and some of which had not, the waltz was a closer dance.

More intimate.

More dangerous.

He could feel her body only inches from his, the way her skirts swished around them as his leg moved between hers every time he stepped forward. They could have spoken, yet it felt like a single word would break the spell that was growing between them.

They moved in silence, the entire world seeming to drop away until all that was left was them and the music. He had never been so aware of a woman he was dancing with in his life.

She was not trying to beguile him, yet he was beguiled.

She was not attempting to fascinate him, yet he was unable to break free of the spell that had woven around them.

When she lifted her gaze to meet his as the music ended, her eyes were fathomless dark pools that Nathanial could easily fall into. She was a siren, with no need of a song.

"Thank you, Your Grace," she whispered, stepping away.

Letting her go ached. But he had to.

He was very aware, as he stepped away and she turned to smile prettily and accept her father's offer of a dance, that the eyes of everyone in the room were on him and her. Lifting his chin, he turned away, seeking his next dance partner.

The Duchess of Clarence caught his eye and lifted one delicately arched brow at him.

This was going to be a very long house party.

$$7$$

KALINA

Rolling over in bed, Kalina yawned as she faced the large window. She'd left the curtains open a small bit so the sun could filter in through them. From what she'd gleaned, country hours began earlier than London hours, and she did not want to miss a thing.

She was at Lady Astrid's house party.

Last night, she'd danced with every duke in attendance.

She'd *waltzed.*

Staring at the crack of light between the heavy curtains, she let out a long, slow breath. Everything felt a little unreal. Like a dream. Or one of her books. But without all the dramatics.

"I am going to marry a duke," she said quietly out loud. It was the first time she had dared do so, phrased exactly that way.

She had hoped.

She had put forth her intention.

This was the first time she'd spoken it as a truth.

But after last night, she felt it in her bones. It was true. And this house party would be the means by which it would happen.

The Dukes of St. Albans, Montagu, Bolton, and Hereford were all in attendance, and all of them had seemed to take an interest in her last night. Montagu had even returned to dance with her a second time. Something that all the older ladies watching had taken note of. He would make a better husband than he thought.

Bolton had also been particularly attentive. As Tiffany's brother, Kalina felt like she was a little closer to him, knew him a little better from the things Tiffany had said about him. St. Albans, on the other hand, remained a mystery, but the Lord of Luck was hardly someone she could set her cap for, according to gossip.

If his lucky coin did not flip in her favor, it did not matter what she said or did. Kalina could not decide if he was deluded or brilliant, resting all his decisions on chance, no matter how much the outcome would affect his life. Some days, she could not imagine the loss of control; others, she thought it sounded so much easier to be guided by the whims of fate.

Regardless, focusing her attentions on the Duke of St. Albans was hardly conducive to a sure outcome.

And the Duke of Hereford?

She sighed again.

On the list. Still.

His hot and cold behavior nonetheless did not disqualify him.

Three dukes to try to impress were better than two, which narrowed her chances of securing one. She had come to the party, being unsure if there were any she might be realistically able to set her cap for, but she was feeling buoyed by the successes of last night.

Even the setback of Hereford returning to ignoring her after their waltz did not necessarily indicate failure. Perhaps he was still deciding as well and trying not to show a preference.

Though if she were to admit a preference...

A shiver went down her spine as she remembered the way his body had felt against hers. Moved against hers. His leg parting hers and stepping between them in a manner that had felt utterly indecent and given her sudden understanding of why the patronesses at Almack's felt a young lady needed their permission to dance the waltz. Understood why it was considered a touch scandalous, a little indecent.

She'd felt indecent as she whirled in his arms across the floor.

Her mother had explained to her what happens between a man and a wife. Kalina knew, theoretically, how marital relations worked. She understood the basic concept of desire.

Held in Hereford's arms was the first time she'd truly experienced such a thing for herself. Even now, her skin felt extra sensitive when she thought of it, her inner muscles clenching when she remembered his hard thigh between hers, and the way her breasts felt as though they'd swelled and ached as his chest brushed against hers.

Breath catching her in throat, Kalina squirmed, pressing her legs together as the ache between them intensified.

The sound of her door opening made her jump in place, immediately ceasing her motion, and she sat up as Margaret quietly entered. Seeing her, the other woman smiled and relaxed.

"I was not sure you would be up yet, Miss," she said, closing the door behind her. "Would you like me to open the curtains wider?"

"Yes, please, Margaret," Kalina replied, trying to relax and pretending that her heart hadn't leapt up into her throat at being interrupted. She could hardly tell Margaret what she'd interrupted.

"Such a to-do last night," Margaret said, bustling over to the curtains to pull them further open. "I expect you slept through it as usual, though."

Having already thrown back the covers, Kalina frowned, pausing where she sat on the edge of the bed.

"A to-do?"

"Yes." Margaret sent her an amused glance. Kalina's ability to sleep through even the loudest noises had always entertained her maid. She would wake up if someone touched her, but otherwise, she was a very deep sleeper. "I woke because there was so much noise in the servants' quarters. Last night, all I knew was that something was going on. This morning, I learned Lady Johanna left in the middle of the night, with her companion."

"What? Why?" Kalina sprang to her feet. Lady Johanna's room was almost directly across from hers; she'd learned last night when the dancing had ended, and everyone had made their way to their rooms. Often, she did not mind her ability to sleep through the loudest commotions; today, she inwardly cursed it.

"I do not know why." Margaret gave her a sly glance. She was clearly hoping Kalina could get more information and share it with her.

Kalina snorted, getting to her feet.

"Help me get dressed." She smiled. "The pink cambric, I think." A suitable day dress of dark pink flowers on a lighter pink background, it was one of her favorites. Flattering, without being overly showy.

It was the fastest Margaret had ever done her hair; the lady's maid practically shoved Kalina out the door in her haste to know what the gossip was. Though by the time Kalina did, she was sure Margaret would have ferreted out more information herself. Or perhaps not. It was likely her maid had already tried.

Kalina was also wildly curious and more than a little worried. A middle-of-the-night departure from a house party signified nothing good that she could think of.

Entering the dining room, she was relieved to see that she was neither the first nor the last to arrive, but solidly in the middle. The elder set was at one end of the table, while Lady Astrid, Tiffany, and the Duke of Clarence were at the other end with Lady Astrid's younger brother. Rupert looked up when Kalina came in and brightened for a moment before realizing that Ashwin was not with her; then he sighed and slouched back down again.

She hid the amused smile from her lips. It seemed her brother had found a true friend here as well.

Lady Astrid, Tiffany, and the Duke of Clarence all lifted their heads to see who the new arrival was, and Lady Astrid immediately waved her over imperiously. The gowns the two ladies were wearing immediately reassured Kalina that she had made the correct choice in her own; they were very similar in style if not in color. Tiffany's sky-blue day gown was trimmed with pale yellow ribbon, making her almost appear like sunshine on a bright morning, while Lady Astrid had chosen a flamboyant orange that, combined with her red hair, made her appear like a sunset. The colors were quite striking together.

"Good morning. I am sure you are wondering what was going on last night," Lady Astrid said as Kalina sat down.

One of the maids immediately arrived at her elbow to pour her tea while a footman fetched a plate of food for her.

"Actually, I had no idea anything had happened last night until my maid came in to tell me this morning," Kalina admitted, causing all three of her friends to blink in surprise.

"But... Lady Johanna's room is right across from yours," Tiffany said. "All the noise woke us, and we are further down the hall from you."

"I am a very deep sleeper," Kalina explained, feeling oddly apologetic. "My father always said I was the only one who could sleep through the start of the monsoons."

"Those are very big thunderstorms, are they not?" Gregory asked.

It was an inadequate description, but based on what she'd observed from London weather, it was likely the closest he would be able to imagine. Kalina nodded.

"Once I am asleep, even the trumpet of an elephant outside my room cannot wake me—my brother tried once." She shook her head. Her family adored sharing that story. Kalina enjoyed listening to it. She could not contribute anything, of course, because she had slept through the entire thing.

"Amazing," Gregory murmured. "I am incredibly envious. I do not sleep so well, even in my own bed."

"And he sleeps even more poorly when he's not in his own bed," Tiffany teased him with a little glance.

"It is true, through no fault of the bed, which is very comfortable," he assured Lady Astrid. "I just prefer to be in my own bed, in my own home."

"But now he goes wherever I want to be." Tiffany smiled brilliantly at him, and he grinned back at her with a besotted expression that made Kalina want to sigh with envy.

If any of the other dukes ever looked at her like that...

Hereford almost looked like that. Last night. While we were waltzing.

But then he'd immediately gone cold again, so it was of no significance.

Was it?

"Trust me, I have heard plenty about Gregory's desire to stay at home," Lady Astrid said dryly. "This is the first time I have encountered him at a house party, if I remember correctly."

"Very likely," he agreed, not at all put out by the observation.

"What happened with Lady Johanna?" Kalina asked, bringing the topic back around to the more pressing matter. She could not help the stir of sympathy in her breast. Not only having to leave early for some reason, but the poor lady would likely be the topic of conversation for the entire morning.

The other three glanced at each other, their expressions sobering immediately.

"A messenger came in the middle of the night to inform her that her mother was seriously unwell, and she should come home immediately." Lady Astrid sighed, smoothing her hands over the portion of the tablecloth in front of her plate. "I am currently hoping the urgency turns out to be alarmist rather than realistic, and she will be able to return."

Despite her statement, her tone of voice did not sound all that hopeful, more resigned to the fact. Kalina's heart ached for the young woman.

"She already lost her father, she said?"

Lady Astrid nodded, lowering her voice, though the group at the other end of the table appeared to be deeply invested in their own conversation.

"She did. The family... well, even before the previous earl's death, they were experiencing some difficulties. Now her brother is the earl, and he is only fourteen years old."

"Is there not a guardian to guide him?" Gregory asked, frowning.

"There is." Lady Astrid did not say anything more, but the sour twist of her lips gave forth her opinion on the person assigned to the role. She clearly did not think very highly of them.

Remembering the state of Lady Johanna's dress, Kalina could not help but feel even more sympathy for her. The family must be in dire straits indeed, and then to have her mother fall ill...

"Is there anything we can do for her?" she asked impulsively. She did not know why Lady Johanna's plight was affecting her so.

"I was hoping to this week," Lady Astrid admitted. "She was unable to make her debut in London, but she's beautiful, accomplished, and very sweet if very shy."

Almost cripplingly shy, but that was not necessarily a deterrent. Montagu had been able to coax her out of her shell a bit. Perhaps he would make a good match for her. But would he go after her?

Then again, chasing after a young lady who was returning to her extremely ill mother was hardly the act of a gentleman.

Tiffany looked at her husband.

"Perhaps we can send a package to her... something for her family if she's unable to return to the house party, regardless of..." Her voice trailed off again. Regardless of whether Lady Johanna's mother recovered.

Kalina nodded.

"I would like to contribute, if I may," she said. She would find something she could include.

Tiffany and Lady Astrid both smiled brilliantly at her. Then the door behind her opened, admitting a small parade of people into the dining room. Keeping her ears open, Kalina attended to her meal.

As she'd predicted, the conversation was initially focused on Lady Johanna and her departure, the topic rehashed every time someone new arrived. Those who did not have rooms in the same hall had missed the kerfuffle. When Kalina's family joined the throng, they were amused but unsurprised that Kalina had slept through it all.

Her father gleefully told the story about the elephant, much to the amusement of the Duke of Ormonde and Montagu, who had joined their end of the table. Hereford and St. Albans were farther away, which did not bother her in the slightest, even though Hereford appeared to be hanging on Lady Kari's every word.

As the meal concluded, conversation naturally turned to the

plans for the day. As the weather was clear, it was agreed that a ride to the nearby ruins would be ideal—for those young enough to be tempted. Kalina immediately knew her parents would join the elder Blackstones and others who opted to stay behind.

She was rather excited to see some of England's history, though Lady Astrid described it as "a bunch of stones set atop each other, which have not yet toppled over." The lady did admit that the scenery around the old church and buildings was picturesque, rather 'gothic'.

There was only one problem.

"Ah... I do not know how to ride," Kalina admitted when the conversation lulled, once she realized it would be necessary. What she did not say was that she did not know how to ride because she was afraid of horses, and the idea of getting on the back of one of the huge creatures was beyond her ken. She had not ridden elephants in India, either, though she was not as wary of them.

After seeing a horse roll over and nearly crush a young neighbor, Kalina had refused to even make the attempt.

"Oh, do not worry," Lady Astrid said, looking about her expectantly. "I am certain one of the gentlemen would be happy to take you in the curricle. Drake has experience with our set of grays."

"I was going to ride beside you. On my horse." He bared his teeth at her in semblance of a smile, which she returned with equal false sincerity.

"I would be happy to take Miss Little in the curricle," Montagu said, smiling at her.

She felt her heart lift with relief that she would not be left behind.

"Thank you," she replied fervently. "I would hate to miss the ruins."

"We certainly cannot have you left behind," he replied with feeling. There was something about the way he said it... was he flirting with her? But not the blatant flirting he had done, that he did do, with all the women who crossed his path. This seemed more intentional. More focused.

She was not sure what to think.

But Hereford was glaring at her again.

8

He should have offered to drive a curricle for Miss Little.

No, I should not have. I am trying to spend more time with the other ladies and less time with her.

Doing so would be a kind of declaration I am not going to make. At least, not with Miss Little.

Was it a declaration on Christian's part? Was he now pursuing Miss Little in earnest? Or was it one of his games?

Christian rarely took anything seriously, but something about the way he was acting around Miss Little now made Nathanial wonder...

As the horses were being saddled, he could not help but watch where Christian was helping Miss Little into the curricle. Did her hand linger just a touch too long? Was the way Christian was looking at her part of his normally flirtatious nature, or was there something more there?

Damnation, why the bloody hell had Christian offered to drive her in the first place?

"Your Grace, would you mind helping me onto my horse?" Lady Kari drew Nathanial's attention away from the curricle, where Christian was now climbing in. He said something that made Miss Little laugh as he did so.

"Yes, of course," Nathanial said brusquely, turning away from the view. It was no matter to him what Christian and Miss Little did or did not do.

Lady Kari hardly needed assistance, despite her riding skirts. Cupping his hands for her to step one delicate heel into, he lifted her anyway. She settled into the saddle easily, smiling at him with appreciation.

"Thank you so much, Your Grace."

"My pleasure, Lady Kari."

By the time the rest of the company was seated on their mounts, including Nathanial, Christian and Miss Little were well out of sight. They had to stay along the roads, while the rest of them were going to be going across the fields, so it was very likely they would arrive at the ruins after everyone else. Unless Christian drove particularly recklessly.

He had better not.

Not with Miss Little seated at his side, equally in danger of whatever maneuver Christian might make.

Sudden worry surged.

Nathanial would be worried for any young lady under such circumstances, of course. Christian was not the most reliable of the dukes present.

"I can mount a damn horse myself." Lady Astrid's sharp tones jerked Nathanial's gaze away from the road where Christian and Miss Little had disappeared. Everyone was now looking at the lady, as she did indeed get into the saddle herself, revealing that she was wearing the split riding skirts favored by the Scottish.

Standing beside the big bay she was now atop of, Drake appeared to be particularly aggrieved, scowling up at his betrothed.

Nose in the air, she ignored him, kicking her horse into a gallop and directing the steed to the opening in the gate, leaving Drake in her dust—at least momentarily. Whooping, Matthew followed immediately after her, Sebastian only just behind him, shooting a glance back at Drake that promised he would look after Lady Astrid until Drake could join them.

Nathanial waited until everyone else had passed and brought up the rear with a clearly seething Drake.

"Damnable females," Drake muttered as Nathanial brought his mount alongside his.

They were moving at a trot, not a gallop. He wondered if it was because Drake refused to give the impression that he was chasing after Lady Astrid, even though there was no one there to see him but Nathanial.

They rode in silence, slowly gaining on the group ahead of them. While they had started at a gallop, they eventually slowed to a walk, allowing Drake and Nathanial to catch up. Lady Astrid remained in front, Sebastian at her side, and they appeared to be chatting amiably enough.

Drake did not seem disposed to conversation, which suited Nathanial perfectly. Unfortunately, the ladies were not of the same mind, and it did not take long before Lady Nichole had dropped back between him and Drake. She was determined to make conversation, but Drake was not cooperative, which meant she ended up focusing her efforts on Nathanial.

"I am so glad the weather is good for an outing today," she said, smiling at him and tipping her head in a coquettish manner. "I do so love to ride."

"It is fortuitous," he agreed. "I have not been able to take a ride like this in far too long."

"It is difficult during the Season," she said sympathetically. "Hyde Park is hardly conducive to anything more strenuous than a walk."

That, and he did not have any horses to ride. They had all been sold off to pay his father's debts.

But he could hardly say so.

Instead, he acted as though that was exactly what he'd meant and nodded his head in agreement. Lady Nichole was a skilled conversationalist, easily taking him through the usual topics as they rode. She even managed to coax Drake into adding a sentence or two to the conversation, despite his obvious preoccupation with glaring at the back of Lady Astrid's head.

When they reached the ruins, Lady Nichole let out a low gasp.

"Oh, my... it's beautiful!"

Nathanial cast a look over the green rolling hills where the stones rose up from the lush grass. Ivy dotted the crumbling buildings, and the windows were long gone except for a single stained-glass rose in a pane above where the doors formerly admitted congregants. A large willow tree dramatically draped its branches beside the old church, the long fronds stirring in the wind. More trees were visible beyond the building, along with overgrown bushes and a riot of flowers that had spread out from their old beds.

The sun hung high in the sky, casting shadows across the ground that contrasted with all the brightly colored foliage. It was indeed beautiful.

Yet he could not appreciate the view when the back of his neck was prickling, wondering when Christian and Miss Little were going to make their appearance. He glanced back at the drive, which ended in a curve where it met the road. They would not be able to see the curricle until it was nearly upon the ruins.

The urge to ride to the end of it and cast a look down the road was strong, but he could not think of a reason that would pass muster. No one else was concerned about Christian and Miss Little's slower appearance. Especially because they already knew it would take the curricle longer to make its way.

Though Christian could also be dawdling. Taking longer than necessary. Deliberately giving himself more time alone with Miss Little in a manner that was socially acceptable.

His mount danced to the side, and Nathanial realized he was sitting far too stiffly in the saddle, grinding his teeth together. Giving himself a shake, he opened his mouth, and his jaw popped somewhat painfully as he forced himself to relax. Lady Nichole was giving him a sidelong glance, as though she worried he was going to lose control of his mount.

Managing a smile for her, Nathanial shook himself and

dismounted. Leading his horse over to the side where several of the others were doing the same, he found that there was a length of fence where they could secure the horses for now.

"There is a folly down that way," Lady Astrid was telling Gregory and Tiffany as Nathanial used his reins to secure his horse. It nickered, and he gave the gelding a good scratch on the side of its neck as a thank you for being patient with him. "And we can go into the church as long as we are careful. Do not lean on anything. There is also a duck pond a little further down, beyond the church."

Plenty of things to explore. Except Nathanial did not want to explore. He wanted to sit and wait for Miss Little and Christian to appear.

"I would love to see the duck pond," Tiffany said, smiling. "I have always been partial to ducks."

"Then to the duck pond we go," Gregory replied cheerfully, holding his arm out for his wife to take. Looking at them, no one would have ever guessed that mere months ago Gregory had been considered one of the foremost rakes of the *ton*. Now he was slavishly devoted to his wife and whatever made her happy. The largest proof being that he was here at the house party at all, much less willing to explore a duck pond.

"I can show you where. Nathanial, give me your arm. You can escort me. There is a matter I wished to speak with you about." Lady Astrid's imperious command was such that Nathanial almost lifted his arm without thinking.

Directing a frown at her, he waited a moment just to prove that he was not her puppet on a string before offering her his arm. It would be ungentlemanly not to after such a request.

He was also somewhat curious what she wanted to speak to him about, if she was not just using him as a shield against Drake. Not enough to fully overcome his reluctance to move away from the front of the church without having seen Christian and Miss Little, but he could hardly refuse.

As if his thoughts had conjured them, he heard the Baroness Voight call out, "Ah, look, there are Montagu and Kalina."

Turning, he saw the curricle at the very end of the drive, coming up at a decent clip. The baroness was waving at them, as if there were anywhere else they might end up. Relief flowed through him that Christian had not taken the opportunity to dawdle. Though his relief was short-lived as he watched her throw her head back with laughter at something Christian said.

His chest clenched tight.

"Nathanial." Lady Astrid's sharp tone broke through his reverie. She gave his arm a very unsubtle tug and an arched look. "You do not need to hesitate on Drake's account."

Momentarily confused, Nathanial only then realized that Drake was glaring at the two of them from a short ways away, still holding onto his horse's reins. He knew Drake knew that Nathanial was not trying to poach. If anything, he was probably annoyed Lady Astrid had claimed Nathanial's arm rather than giving Drake the opportunity to take his rightful place.

For someone who did not want to marry the lady, he could be remarkably stringent about his position at her side when they were forced to be in each other's proximity.

"Yes, well." Nathanial cleared his throat, relieved that Lady Astrid was so preoccupied with her fiancé, she had attributed Nathanial's distraction to Drake as well and not to the incoming curricle.

Now that Christian and Kalina had arrived, there was no further reason to delay.

"What can I do for you, my lady?" he asked, turning toward the direction Tiffany and Gregory had gone. The couple was only a little way ahead of them, leaning in toward each other as they walked. The faint sound of Tiffany's giggles floated on the breeze that ruffled Lady Astrid's skirts.

"The matchmaker I have coming this afternoon. I want you to meet with her. I think she will be able to help you find a bride who not only meets your requirements but also suits you personally," Lady Astrid replied, her tone softening now that she was no longer glaring at her betrothed. "You deserve more than a large dowry; you deserve someone you can rub along comfortably with or perhaps even discover finer feelings for."

Miss Little's face flashed through his mind, and he ruthlessly pushed the image out, telling himself that he was only imagining hearing her laughter. Surely, he and Lady Astrid had walked too far for that to be possible.

"You think a matchmaker will be able to help me with that?" he asked, trying to keep the skepticism in his tone to a minimum. He did not want to insult Lady Astrid, after all.

"I think *this* matchmaker will," she said, patting his arm. The confidence in her voice made him wonder if perhaps she was correct.

"Very well, if you are convinced."

He could hardly do worse than listen to what this matchmaker had to say. One thing he would have to do was make it very clear that Miss Little—no matter how well-dowered and no matter how well they got on—was not an option.

9

———————

KALINA

The Duke of Montagu was a charming companion and a dab hand with the whip. He also seemed to immediately notice that she was not entirely comfortable around the horses, though she was thankfully not sitting directly atop one. For a man who was convinced he would not make a good husband, so far, he was proving the exact opposite to her.

He kept the giant beasts to a fast but smooth walk. The road was not very bumpy, and it made for a rather nice drive. The sun was up, but not too hot, and at the pace they were moving, there was a nice breeze. Kalina tucked in her skirts about her legs to keep them from fluttering too much. She could feel the wind against her bonnet, but the bow under her chin was tied tightly enough, she had no worries about it flying off.

They exchanged several pleasantries about the weather and the Blackstones' hospitality, and when the horses did not do anything untoward, Kalina felt safer than she had initially. The curricle had her much closer to them than the carriage, but they gave no indication of misbehavior.

"So, you never learned to ride?" he asked, once she had begun to finally relax when it was clear he had full control of the horses. Not that they had been particularly frisky. She had seen worse, but she still did not fully trust them. "Was that not possible in India?"

"It was possible but..." She grimaced. "I saw a rather unsettling incident with a horse and their rider, and it put me off learning." Unsettling was the least of it, but describing what had actually happened was hardly ladylike. Besides which, she did not particularly enjoy revisiting the experience.

"Ah, I see." He pondered that for a moment. "What of learning to drive? Have you any objection to that?"

Kalina blinked. "I... have never considered the possibility."

"I could teach you," he offered, giving her a sidelong glance. "It is not very difficult."

"Oh..." Her voice trailed off as she tried to find a way to politely decline without insulting him. But should she decline? It might not be horrible to learn how to do something with horses. The English were certainly mad for them, and if she was going to be going to more house parties, she was likely to have more encounters with the beasts.

It might be nice not to have to rely on a gentleman willing to drive her.

Though she was not sure how driving herself would be viewed.

"You do not have to decide right now," he assured her cheerfully. "The offer will remain open, regardless, even after the house party is over and we return to London. I would be as happy to teach you there as I am here."

"That is very kind, thank you." Even if she never took him up on the offer, she appreciated it. Leaning back against the seat, she watched the horses moving. There was something hypnotic about their bobbing heads and the passing countryside. It was far nicer riding in the curricle than in a carriage, though she knew the carriage was better for longer distances.

She liked the open air and the feel of the breeze against her skin. The sun was warm but not beating down on her. It was a lovely experience. Especially when combined with Montagu's flirtatiously cheerful presence.

If only he made her heart flutter and her body tingle the way Hereford did...

Kalina shook off the thought.

She needed to focus on the duke in front of her, who had volunteered to drive her to the ruins, not the one who blew hot and cold over and over again.

"Do you visit the country very often?" she asked.

"Oh, no. I am much happier in the capital where there is endless entertainment," he replied cheerfully. "I grow bored rather quickly in the country. House parties like this can be quite enjoyable because there are many activities to do. I can take care of everything I need to from the city, with occasional visits to the ducal seat, but I return to London as quickly as I can. Fortunately, my steward has things well in hand."

"Did you grow up in the city?" Kalina could not help but be curious. From the way her father had described *his* father and Society, she had assumed most noblemen spent their time shuttling back and forth depending on the time of year. It was only once they'd arrived in London that she'd learned some stayed in the city year-round.

She wondered how effective they could truly be with matters of a place they rarely visited. Why they would not be more invested in the lands and people that supported them. This was her first opportunity to question a gentleman who clearly did not deeply involve himself in his estate.

"Oh, no. In the country. My father preferred it there." Something in his tone of voice changed, but she could not determine what it was. "Ah, look, see the hawk?"

Obligingly, Kalina turned her face in the direction he was pointing. Indeed, there was a bird soaring through the sky, circling without moving its wings as it glided along.

"Beautiful. Oh!" The hawk suddenly dove so fast, she nearly missed it. One moment it was there, another it was gone.

"It must have seen some prey. Ah... it did not catch its breakfast.

Poor hawk." The bird was rising back into the air, flapping its wings to regain height, before circling toward the forest in the distance.

"Well, that is certainly something I have never seen in London." She shook her head, bemused.

The duke laughed. "Very true. Though I will take the theater and Vauxhall Gardens over a hawk sighting." He chuckled. "Have you seen the recent exhibit at the museum?" Kalina shook her head, and he began to expound enthusiastically on the recent arrivals. It was clear he enjoyed beautiful things, including art.

Montagu was so engaging, it took her until they reached the ruins to realize how neatly he had turned the conversation from himself and his home. While she had learned a great deal about the museum's current and previous exhibits, as well as his opinion on the plays and operas available in London, she had not learned anything about the man himself.

She had to wonder if he had deliberately changed the topic or if he was so used to deflecting ladies' attention from anything personal, he did it automatically.

"Ah, we have arrived at the gothic ruins of London," he declared in a stentorian voice, making her throw back her head and laugh in surprise.

Kalina had always imagined that dukes would be rather stodgy, the most proper of the *ton*, but Christian was anything but.

The other group was already in front of the church, which she had expected. She would be lying if she said she was not relieved to see Lady Astrid on the Duke of Hereford's arm rather than one of the marriage-minded young ladies. It was a conundrum how she could so enjoy the Duke of Montagu's company, yet the moment the Duke of Hereford appeared in front of her, it was as though she could not breathe properly, much less pay attention to the man beside her.

As the Duke of Hereford and Lady Astrid turned away, walking away from where Kalina and the Duke of Montagu were coming down the drive, she let out a long, slow breath.

By the time the curricle came to a halt, she had her jangling nerves under control again. The Duke of Montagu got down from the curricle as the Duke of Ormonde held the horses in place.

"My lady." Montagu smiled up at her, reaching out his hand for her to take so he could help her down from the carriage.

She placed her gloved fingers in his. No tingle. No sudden fluttering in her belly. She smiled back at him, stepping down from the carriage and letting her hand drop away from his.

"Thank you for a lovely drive, Your Grace."

"Please, call me Christian."

"Then I must be Kalina to you." She tried not to show her surprise. Other than Gregory, who she knew had done so at Tiffany's behest, she had not been invited to use any of the other dukes' given names until now. Had she done something on the drive to prompt his invitation? If so, what?

Did this mean he was truly courting her?

"Kalina is a lovely name. Does it mean anything?" Rather than taking care of the horses, Christian gave the Duke of Ormonde a nod and turned away, treating the other duke like a stableboy. Though he rolled his eyes, Ormonde turned to lead the horses and curricle away until it was time to return to Blackstone Manor. Christian held out his arm for Kalina to take as she answered him.

"I do not know," she admitted. "It was my father's great-grandmother's name. He said she was his favorite relative, so he wanted to name his eldest daughter after her."

"I was named after my father's grandfather, though I think he regretted that." Christian chuckled.

She frowned at him, turning her head to look up at him as he began to lead her toward the stone ruins. Despite her interest in the sights, she was far more curious about his odd comment.

"Why would he regret naming you after his grandfather?"

"According to him, my grandfather was a paragon of virtues. Obviously, I failed to live up to his great legacy." Tilting his head toward her, Christian wiggled his eyebrows in a manner that prompted her to smile, though she did not feel that what he was saying was particularly funny. "I am quite sure my father often thought he should have named me after his least admired relative, whoever that may have been."

Kalina's chest felt oddly tight. She did not know what to say to him. Clearly, he believed that he was a great disappointment to his father, though she could not imagine how that could be the case.

"I think you are a paragon of virtues," she replied stubbornly. "Unless… are you fishing for compliments again?"

That startled a laugh out of him, drawing the attention of some of the others. Kalina kept her focus determinedly on the man at her side and not looking around to see what the other ladies might think and certainly not where the Duke of Hereford and Lady Astrid had gone. They were probably out of earshot anyway, and it did not matter what he thought.

"Trust me, my father would have disagreed with you. Vehemently." He patted her hand where it rested on her arm. "Though I appreciate your defense, I must admit, he had good reason to feel the way he did."

"As far as I can see, your only true failing is in the way you view yourself." Kalina sniffed. She had never thought to scold a duke, but the way he was so needlessly self-deprecating, so cruel to himself, was starting to get under her skin. "If you were someone else talking about you in this manner, I would have to take them to task for speaking so meanly about you—and I would tell them they must see you with clouded vision for some unknown reason because that is not the man I have come to know."

"Oh… well… you do not know me very well, you see…" But the duke looked much struck, and his smile was weaker than before. He seemed almost embarrassed. As if he did not know how to receive praise. Which she had noticed before, the last time she'd chided him for not seeing himself clearly.

"Sometimes, it takes an outsider's eye to see the clearest," she responded tartly. "And I would appreciate it if you would stop speaking so disrespectfully of my new friend, Christian." Raising her eyebrow at him, she gave him a stern look.

The way he looked back at her was almost fearful, and she could barely keep herself from giggling. He did not seem to know how to feel about her statement.

Slowly, he let out a long breath.

"Let us explore the ruins," he said finally. "Before I say anything else you need to scold me for."

"That sounds perfect."

10

NATHANIAL

"What did you and Miss Little speak of?" Nathanial asked, attempting to keep the question from sounding like a demand as he faced Christian across the billiards table. Upon returning from the ruins, the ladies retired to their rooms to rest, leaving the gentlemen to entertain themselves. Nathanial had been rather relieved, as it meant a reprieve from watching Miss Little hanging on Christian's every word.

It had been painful to witness.

The notion that it was *his* arm she should be walking on was not easy to dismiss.

His jealousy was reaching new heights with every moment spent in her presence.

Hopefully, the matchmaker would arrive soon and give him a clear path forward with an appropriate young lady to make his bride. Then he would not be so distracted by the one who would not suit his needs.

"Oh, this and that." Christian bent over the table, expertly taking aim to send the balls on its surface crashing into each other. One of them dropped into a netted pocket on the side farthest from him.

"She was very curious about the ruins. I am not sure if it was the history or the architecture that intrigued her, but she had a myriad of questions about both."

Getting into position for his next shot, he turned his head toward Nathanial, raising one eyebrow.

"Why do you ask?"

"I was wondering if you were going to offer for her." The question was blurted out before he could stop it. Because it was of no mind to him if Christian did.

Christian's fingers slipped, and his shot went wild.

Both of them stared at the balls bouncing off each other and the sides of the billiards table. Nathanial had never seen the other man miss so badly.

"Well, then." Christian straightened, clearing his throat and reaching up to tug on his cravat as though to loosen it. He ran his hand down the burgundy waistcoat he'd changed into after their return to the manor. "I am thinking about it."

Thinking about it but clearly undecided.

"Is there a reason you are holding back?" *Please let there be one. A very compelling one.*

Not that it mattered if she married someone else.

Even if it was one of his closest friends.

"Several."

Thank God.

Christian courteously waited until Nathanial had taken his next shot before answering, giving Nathanial a look as if to say, that's how it should have been done.

"I am not certain I would survive marriage to her. She is very good at scolding." He gave his shoulders a little shake, grinning, but Nathanial could see the real hesitation there. Christian's father had been incredibly strict. Privately, Nathanial did not think anyone would have ever been able to realistically live up to the former Duke of Montagu's expectations of his heir. As far as he could tell, Christian had dealt with his father's continual disappointment by meeting *that* expectation rather than attempting to rise to the occasion and disappointing him, regardless.

"Really?" Nathanial was fascinated. He could not picture Miss Little scolding someone. Much less a duke. Even when she relaxed in conversation, she was very proper.

"Yes. She did not take the way I talk about myself very kindly and told me I need to be kinder to myself." Christian chuckled, laughing it off, but Nathanial was reluctantly impressed. He knew exactly the way Christian was talking about.

None of the things he or their other friends had said to Christian had made an impression, but clearly, Miss Little had.

"Surely, that would be a reason to marry her."

"Ah, but think how disappointed she will be when she realizes I am not as she pictures. Worse, imagine how Tiffany and Astrid would react if I were to break their friend's heart." Christian's shudder was much more theatric now, and he put his hand over his heart as if he could not bear the thought of their approbation. "I would be rent asunder from my friends due to their wives' anger at me."

Though he was joking, Nathanial could not help but wonder if there was a kernel of truth in Christian's words.

"Have you given your mistress her *congé* yet?" he asked curiously.

Christian wrinkled his nose, shaking his head. He leaned on his stick as he watched Nathanial line up the next shot.

"Well... no. Though I plan to soon. I might have already if Zachary had not been such a twit about Delilah."

"You mean you have stayed longer with this mistress only to show him that he could have had Delilah and searched for a debutante bride at the same time?" Nathanial shook his head. "You overestimate Delilah's understanding. She would have barred her door to him the moment she realized he was searching elsewhere for a bride."

"She must have known that was coming."

Nathanial shrugged.

"From the way she and Zachary are about each other, I believe she may have gotten her hopes up, widow or no. If it was not for his mother pressuring him, I think she might have gotten what she wanted, too."

"Ah, yes. Well. The duchess is..." Christian's voice trailed off.

Zachary's mother was grieving the loss of her husband in a way none of their other wives had. Whether or not they had been a love match, Nathanial did not know, but it had become clear after the Duke of Grafton's death that the duchess, at least, had loved her husband. Loved him so well, she completely fell apart when she lost him. Despite it being long past the period for formal mourning, she still wore her full blacks and refused to take them off, fashion and societal expectations be damned.

Which was why it was so ironic that she was pushing Zachary to follow those same expectations in choosing his bride. A debutante, virginal and young. Not a widow, even if she was still of childbearing age.

"At any rate, I do not wish to antagonize our friends nor their wives," Christian said, returning to the topic of Miss Little. "But I must admit there is something about her. She's beautiful, of course."

"Of course."

"Very easy to talk to."

"Very," Nathanial agreed. Too easy in some regards.

"Smart. And kind."

"She is both."

"However, I would also not want to marry a woman who one of my friends has a *tendre* for." It was Christian's turn again, but he was not looking at the billiards table; he was looking at Nathanial. "I would not expect my wife's fidelity if I cannot give it to her as well, but it seems a terrible thing to have to worry she might prefer one of my friends to me."

"I..." Nathanial started to speak, then stopped. He tried to meet Christian's gaze, to reassure him that he held no such *tendre* for Miss Little... and he could not. "I cannot marry her. She is not the right bride for me. No matter my own emotions, my choice must be logical, not..." Not what his heart desired. The unspoken words hung in the air. He could not bring himself to say them out loud, could not bring himself to admit the truth.

Christian nodded slowly.

"Well, then. I am not sure I can marry her, either."

Frowning, Nathanial looked at the floor. He did not like to think that he was denying Miss Little a ducal husband, merely because they were all his friends, and yet... Still. There were others she could marry who would give her family a high station. While it was unlikely her grandfather would unbend enough to acknowledge her family unless she married a duke, surely it could not be all *that* important to gain one man's approval.

Especially since it was more likely to be a begrudging acknowledgment rather than a true welcome back into the family fold. He could even be said to be doing her a favor, so she was not wasting her life trying to follow the strictures of a stuck-up old man who cared more about whether his sons followed his commands than if they were happy. Because it was clear that Mr. Little and his wife were very happy together.

That was what he wanted for his own sisters, their happiness. He was willing to pay any price for that. That the marquess could not for his sons was a defect in him, not in Miss Little or her parents.

Christian bent back over the table.

Something caught Nathanial's eye, movement or a shadow, and he turned to look. The door was partway open, in case anyone wanted to come join them, but he did not see anyone standing there now. Perhaps someone had been walking by, or maybe he was mistaken in what he had seen. He was a mite distracted after all.

Kalina

Too wound up to actually fall asleep, Kalina lay in her bed and tried to concentrate on reading her book.

It was extremely difficult.

Her mind kept wandering.

To the Duke of Hereford.

The Duke of Montagu.

Was Christian courting her? Or was he merely being friendly? The significant looks some of the other ladies had shared with her indicated they thought he was courting her. That he had offered to take her up in the curricle both to and from the ruins would seem to indicate some kind of interest.

But how in earnest was he?

When he'd danced with her, he'd indicated he was helping her to draw others' interest. Not that he was acting for his own benefit. Perhaps today had been more of the same.

Though none of the other dukes were stepping forward in the same manner, despite Christian's actions.

Only the Duke of Hereford had looked twice at them this afternoon.

Who was the Duke of Hereford courting?

She blew out a long, slow breath.

A knock at her door made her sit up.

"Kalina, it's me." Her mother's calm voice was light, but pitched to be heard through the thick door. If Kalina had been asleep, it would never have woken her, but her mother knew she rarely napped since they'd arrived in England.

"Come in."

Pushing her book to the side, Kalina rearranged herself on her bed to be comfortable. The door opened, and her mother stepped through, smiling.

"I did not think you would be asleep," she said, closing the door behind her.

"I was trying to read, but not making much headway," Kalina admitted as her mother made her way over to sit on the bed. Like Kalina, she was wearing a fresh day dress, though hers was a pretty blue and yellow floral, while Kalina had chosen a pink sprigged muslin. "My thoughts are whirling about too much."

"How were the ruins?"

"Beautiful. Very atmospheric. Though not as old as I hoped." Kalina shrugged. "I still enjoyed seeing them."

"And the Duke of Montagu?" Her mother raised one eyebrow.

"Very charming." She smiled. "Very gentlemanly as well. I enjoyed his company."

There was a beat of silence, as though her mother was thinking, hesitating to say something, then she leaned forward to lay her hand over Kalina's.

"I know your father hopes to be reunited with his family, but I do not want you to think that the responsibility rests entirely on your shoulders," her mother said gently, giving Kalina's fingers a squeeze. "Regardless of whether you marry a duke, your father and I both love you. More than anything, we want you to be happy."

"There is no reason I cannot be happily married to a duke," Kalina replied. She appreciated her mother's reassurances, but she also knew how disappointed her father would be if he did not have the chance to reconcile with his own father and the rest of his family.

Having experienced the cut direct firsthand from her father's siblings and their children, there was a part of her that also wanted to force them to acknowledge her. To be able to force those who had seen her and turned up their noses to curtsy to her because she was no longer beneath them but in a position where they could not ignore her. Did she particularly like the part of her that felt vindicated at the thought? No. But she was too honest to deny that it would be satisfying. Gratifying even.

Her mother laughed.

"There is no reason, but marrying a duke is also not a guarantee of happiness. Unless... have you already developed an affection for the Duke of Montagu?"

No, the Duke of Hereford.

But she could not admit that when it was Montagu who she had spent time with today.

"I... like him." That was the truth. "If he were to offer for me, I would seriously consider it."

Her mother relaxed, as if she was relieved to hear that Kalina would not accept immediately, but the truth was, Kalina was not sure she and Christian would make a good match. While she did enjoy his company, his constant self-deprecation would drive her batty after a while, and he seemed torn on whether he appreciated or hated her responses to it.

Also, she was not sure she could be happy with him when she had such strong reactions to the Duke of Hereford. Yet if Montagu were the one to offer…

Yes. She would need to think very seriously on whether she would accept.

"He seems a nice enough young man. Perhaps I will try to get to know him better."

"That is what we are here for." Kalina smiled ruefully.

Noise outside her window drew both of their attention, and they got up from the bed as one to see what was happening outside. A new carriage had just pulled up in front of the house, with the Blackstone crest on its side.

"That must be the matchmaker," Kalina's mother murmured. A footman came down to open the door, holding out his hand to the woman inside.

Kalina's eyes widened. That was no Englishwoman. Unless she was mistaken, the style of the woman's outfit was Chinese, her skirt designed in the elaborate pleats of the mamian style under her robe. The fabric was a dark forest green; the embroidery decorating it made good use of what appeared to be emerald-green, gold, and cream thread. Though Kalina could not pick out the particular embroidery design from such a distance, she was certain it was gorgeous, and she would love to take a closer look.

She turned to help another, older woman out of the carriage. Clad much in the same style, though her robe and skirt were dark grey with green decoration, the older woman appeared to have some difficulty coming down from the steps. She was very petite, even more so than the first woman, who Kalina assumed was Mei, the granddaughter.

They watched as the footmen unloaded the carriage under her

direction, at which point Lady Astrid arrived on the scene to greet the women. Despite the distance and the inability to hear what was going on, it was clear that she was delighted to see both of them. Despite the difference in their stations, she greeted both with the English cheek kisses reserved for close friends.

"Well. This afternoon should be very interesting indeed." Kalina's mother put her hand on Kalina's shoulder. "Perhaps the matchmaker will have some insights. The Duchess of Clarence mentioned to me that she had heard of a matchmaker with a knack for making matches that was almost magical."

Watching Lady Astrid and the matchmaker walking up the stairs, arm in arm, before they disappeared from her view, Kalina nodded. If nothing else, she could ask the matchmaker what she thought of Kalina and the Duke of Montagu.

Perhaps, if they were able to get a private enough moment together, she could also ask the woman's opinion of the Duke of Hereford.

11

———————

KALINA

Venturing forth with her mother, Kalina quickly found that she was not the only lady who had noted the matchmaker's arrival. All the young ladies and several of the older ones had left their rooms and come to the parlor. The tea cart had been brought out and set in the center of the room, with all the necessities as well as some biscuits. Lady Blackstone was there, seated on a couch and happily chatting with Lady Emeryn and the Duchess of Clarence, leaving her daughter to escort their newest visitors around the room and introduce them.

Currently, they were speaking with Lady Kari and Lady Nichole, who were very animated, apparently thrilled to meet the matchmaker. Lady Astrid turned as Kalina and her mother walked into the room and smiled brightly at them.

Though Lady Hu appeared to be deep in conversation with Lady Nichole, Lady Astrid took Mei by her arm and turned her toward Kalina. Smiling serenely, Mei moved with Lady Astrid to greet Kalina and her mother. Up close, she was stunningly beautiful, with black hair as dark as Kalina's and rich brown eyes that were filled with warmth.

"Kalina, Mrs. Little, this is my friend Mei, the matchmaker. Mei, this is Mrs. and Miss Little."

Mei shot Lady Astrid an amused glance.

"My grandmother is the matchmaker," she said, curtsying deeper than she should have for Kalina and her mother's stations. Her English was completely unaccented, her voice soft in both tone and quality and very fluid. It almost sounded like an affect, rather than her true tone. Lady Astrid gave Mei a sharp look, but the other woman smiled serenely. "I am merely her apprentice, though I do pass on my observations and thoughts to my grandmother."

"And has your grandmother ever disagreed with any of your observations or thoughts?"

"No." Mirth danced in Mei's eyes. Her voice had changed as well, no longer quite so soft. From the back and forth, Kalina was left with the distinct impression that Mei's opinions counted very much, and Lady Astrid knew it, but that Mei preferred her grandmother to receive the credit. She thought that was probably wise, as she was unsure how the *ton* would react to matches being made by such a young lady. Especially one as beautiful as Mei.

"How do you decide on who to match?" Kalina asked, hoping to stem the back and forth between Lady Astrid and Mei and also because she was truly interested in the process.

"Well, first we must meet both parties, of course. We gather our first impressions, then we take a closer look. I do a good deal of research for my grandmother on both the subject and their families. After that..." She spread her hands wide. "Some of it is intuition. Some of it is experience. My grandmother just knows."

"And so does Mei," Lady Astrid murmured.

Mei shot her another amused look, raising her eyebrow, and Lady Astrid shrugged unrepentantly. It was clear that the two of them were very comfortable with each other, speaking to a longstanding friendship.

That made Kalina even more curious.

How did a lady of the *ton*, who had been betrothed since birth, meet a Chinese matchmaker?

"It is lovely to meet you, Mei. We appreciate you and your grand-mother making the journey," Kalina's mother said, smiling warmly. "I would certainly appreciate hearing any observations or thoughts you have on the gathered gentlemen."

As four out of six of the attending dukes were unwed and currently in need of brides, that was really who Mei and Lady Hu would be observing.

"I look forward to meeting them," Mei replied smoothly. "Right now, I would love to sit and get to know you and Kalina, if that suits you."

Kalina and her mother exchanged a glance.

"I think that suits us very well," Kalina said. Some might think that Lady Hu was the one to meet, but she trusted Lady Astrid. If she wanted Kalina to speak with Mei rather than Lady Hu, there was a reason.

Nathanial

A knock at the door of the billiards room made both Nathanial and Christian turn to see who was there. Matthew hung in the door-way, grinning widely, Sebastian just behind him with a resigned expression.

"The matchmaker is here. The ladies are gathered for tea with her in the parlor. Do you want to come meet her with us?" Matthew's interest and excitement were clear, though perhaps that was no surprise. A man who let his life be decided by a coin flip was hardly going to balk at the idea of someone directing him on a certain path.

Sebastian accompanying Matthew was more surprising. He was skeptical but still willing to see what the fuss was about.

As Nathanial had already agreed to speak with her, he was also interested in meeting her as swiftly as possible. He wanted to see if he could get a sense of her and how she made her choices, whether he might be able to trust her suggestions. While he was not so cavalier as to leave his marriage to the hands of fate, or a coin flip, an experienced matchmaker was a bird of a different color.

"I would like to," he said, setting down his billiards stick.

For a moment, Christian hesitated, then he shrugged. "I will come as well. It seems a bit of a lark, does it not?"

"No Gregory or Drake?" Nathanial asked as he stepped out into the hall with Matthew and Sebastian, Christian only a few paces behind him.

"Drake seems to have disappeared again, and Gregory is... *napping*." Matthew chuckled as he put extra emphasis on the word, making Sebastian scowl furiously. It must be very awkward to have your sister marry your closest friend. Nathanial made a mental note to keep Julianna away from his friends until she was safely affianced to someone else. He certainly did not want to think about her... *napping*... with any of his friends.

"Where *does* Drake keep getting off to?" Christian asked, and they all shrugged in response. "Do you think he's gotten a lead on... on our fathers?"

On who had killed their fathers, he meant. All of them slowed in their steps. Exchanged a glance.

"He would tell us if that was it. Wouldn't he?" Matthew frowned, not entirely sure of his declaration. Drake did tend to hold things very close to his chest. The last bit of information he'd shared was from Sinclair's heir, the new Duke of Northumberland. The man had found no threatening letters or anything that might lead to a clue among either of his predecessors' effects, though he'd promised to look. Drake had also reported that the new duke was as eager as ever to make friends with him.

However, none of them could look at Northumberland, or even hear the title, without thinking of Sinclair. It was bad enough to have lost their fathers; losing their friend so quickly in the wake of the tragedy had cemented their bonds... and the new Northumberland was left on the outside.

"Not if he were unsure of the information," Sebastian replied, his frown deepening. "He would wait 'til he was sure. We should question him when he reappears."

"He may have just gone out for a ride. The social whirl always grates on him." Though if Drake did have any new information... The confliction Nathanial was all too familiar with rose up in his chest again. His relief that his own father was gone. His grief for his friends for their loss.

Most times, he shoved the mystery to the back of his mind. He was not as eager as his friends to solve it. His focus was, by necessity, on the future and on what he needed to do right now to provide security for his sisters and his people.

He also knew his friends wanted answers. Needed them.

They wanted justice.

They deserved it, too.

Nathanial would have to fight the urge to shake the murderer's hand for what he had done for Nathanial's family—saved them from complete and utter financial ruin, most likely.

Sometimes, he wondered why his friends did not suspect him more. He'd certainly considered patricide more than once. He had not done it... but he had thought about it. The fact that so many others had died in the explosion was likely the only reason he was not viewed with more suspicion.

"We will find out soon enough," Christian said, his voice sounding slightly distant, as though he had pulled into himself.

They had gone far enough down the hall that they could hear light feminine laughter coming from the open door of the parlor.

"Unto the breach we go," Matthew muttered under his breath as they walked to the doorway. He was not wrong. The moment they appeared, every eye immediately turned to their entrance. Fans went up, fluttering, creating a wave of air puffing through the room.

Nathanial scanned the room, looking at everyone, and certainly not for anyone in particular. He spotted Miss Little immediately in one of the chairs near the unlit fireplace, with her mother beside her. They looked to have been talking to Lady Astrid and a young woman dressed in a spectacular outfit of green, cream, and gold that set off her beauty. She was now studying the four dukes with a sharp, intelligent gaze, despite her youth. *Mei* Lady Astrid had said her name was when he'd spoken with her this morning, traveling with her grandmother.

"She is no older than a debutante," Sebastian muttered, huffing and eyeing the young woman with obvious suspicion.

So as not to allow his gaze to linger, Nathanial had already moved on and spotted the older woman speaking with Lady Kari and Lady Nichole on the other side of the room. Her outfit was similar to the younger's, though in more muted colors. Not as flashy. That must be Lady Hu.

"Where are they from, do you think?" Matthew whispered.

"China, of course." There were plenty of traders, merchants, and others who had moved to London and other cities in England over the years. Nathanial recognized their particular set of features.

As he had not been able to afford much in the way of staff, speaking with merchants was a task that had fallen to him, which allowed him to meet a far greater number of people than he might have otherwise. There was an absolute madness for Chinese dishes and fabrics among the *ton*, though the spices seemed to have recently fallen out of fashion. The flavors had grown in popularity among the lower classes, so they were still available and finally at a price that Nathanial's kitchen could afford. The difficulty of travel had been much reduced over the past few decades and allowed for a much greater quantity of goods to reach England than was previously possible.

"Oh. How interesting. She's very pretty." Matthew tilted his head and reached for his pocket.

"Stop that." Sebastian grabbed his wrist, pulling it away. "You cannot marry a matchmaker even if your blasted coin says to."

Sighing, Matthew dropped his hand.

"I suppose grandmother would be upset if I do not at least marry gentry," he conceded with a hefty sigh. "I will not flip for her."

Because if he did flip and the coin said to marry the matchmaker, he would do so regardless of whether it upset his grandmother. Nathanial's lips twitched. No, he could not imagine living the way Matthew did. He had so little control already; giving up the rest of it was out of the question.

"Ah. That must be the real matchmaker," Sebastian said, tilting his head toward where Lady Hu was speaking with Lady Kari and Lady Nichole. She had barely glanced toward the dukes, while her granddaughter was still silently studying them.

"Not that you need her, eh?" Christian murmured, nudging Sebastian in the side. He grunted a noncommittal response.

Lady Astrid came to greet them, smiling widely. Nathanial steeled himself.

To his surprise, they did not meet the matchmakers immediately. They found themselves seated together with tea to coddle their innards, waiting for their turn after the ladies. Their surrounds stymied any true conversation, especially anything about their fathers or their marriage prospects. There were too many ears to overhear, and more of the older ladies arrived soon after them, drawn by their own curiosity.

The room soon relaxed into the usual banal social chatter, despite the new additions to the house party, with various conversations happening all around. Nathanial was slowly able to unwind as well, allowing him to behave more naturally when Lady Astrid brought Lady Hu and her granddaughter over to meet them.

He greeted the pair warmly, as did Matthew. Christian seemed a bit more wary, though with him that meant he reverted to his most charming social mask. Unsurprisingly, Sebastian was the holdout, staying coolly reserved with his greeting and the following conversation.

Nathanial was not sure what he had expected. Something more like an interview, perhaps. Forthright questions or at least leading questions. Instead, it was a normal conversation. More social banality.

Yet he felt as though both ladies' sharp eyes were catching everything. Every move he and the others made. Each change in facial expression. Even a moment's hesitation in speaking.

He did not dare look in Miss Little's direction, not even once.

But he felt her presence in the room, a little tingle along his skin that ensured he could not forget she was there.

12

When the gong sounded for supper, Kalina was bemused to find herself on the Duke of Bolton's arm, walking into the dining room. Several couples ahead of her, the Duke of Hereford was escorting Mei. The Duke of Montagu was leading Lady Hu on his arm just in front of Kalina and the Duke of Bolton.

Which meant she ended up sitting between the Duke of Montagu and the Duke of Bolton.

Hereford and Mei ended up across the table from her. Lady Collette was on his other side, flirtatiously fluttering her fan as she divided her attention equally between him and Lord Emeryn, her other dinner partner. Kalina did not know if she was more relieved to not have to watch him converse with another debutante or nerve-wracked over having him on the other side of the table.

She avoided his gaze, running her fingertips over the gold pattern on the plate in front of her rather than risk meeting his eyes.

"What do you think of the matchmaker?" Christian asked, leaning in and keeping his voice low. Kalina knew it was because Mei was directly across from them, but she felt Hereford's sudden interest in her and Christian. The Duke of Montagu had leaned in very close to ask her the question, and she felt heat rise in her cheeks at the implication of intimacy in how close he was to her.

Turning her head, she kept her voice just as low, all too aware of the avid watchers who noted their exchange.

"I think she is very insightful." It had not taken Kalina long to realize that both Lady Hu and Mei were deliberately keeping themselves back from the others. Rather than engaging with them, they were observing how everyone interacted with each other. They were less interested in the performance someone might put on for them and far more interested in who they truly were.

"Have you asked her to help you find a match?"

Kalina tilted her head at him.

"Do you think I should?" It was the closest she could come to outright asking if he was courting her in earnest. Ladies were certainly not encouraged to be forthright, and it would be the height of rudeness, not to mention arrogance, to presume.

He studied her face for a moment, considering.

"If you wish to." Taking a deep breath, he turned his attention to his glass as a footman passed by with a bottle of wine.

Kalina did her best not to scowl at his frustratingly inconclusive response.

The first course came around as soon as the drinks were poured, and she found that Christian had turned to Lady Nichole, who sat on his other side. Unlike when Hereford spoke with Lady Nichole or Lady Kari, Kalina did not get the same wave of biting jealousy, the same uncomfortable stirring in her stomach. She was not perturbed by Christian's attention being on someone else.

Which was a lowering thought.

Why Hereford?

Peeking beneath her lashes at him, keeping her head lowered so as not to draw attention, she watched as he smiled at something Mei said. Wondered if he was asking her for assistance in finding a bride. Wondered what qualifications he was telling the matchmaker he wanted in a wife.

And whether Kalina met them.

"So, Miss Little, did you enjoy the ruins today?" The Duke of Bolton had realized that Christian was speaking to Lady Nichole and had turned his attention to her.

She was both grateful for the distraction and reluctant to tear away from her observation of Hereford.

"They were lovely. This was my first opportunity to view anything like them here in England, and I enjoyed how picturesque the setting was."

"Are you a painter?"

"Oh... ah, no. I enjoy looking at art, but it is not one of my skills." She smiled, knowing that British young ladies were encouraged to find some kind of pastime with which to impress gentlemen— embroidery, painting, a musical instrument... All of which she had failed at dismally.

Eventually, her father had reassured her that no gentleman actually cared about such things, anyway. She did have a deep appreciation for the results, as she knew firsthand how difficult they were, and the skills of others never failed to impress her.

Bolton smiled, though it did not quite reach his eyes. She was not sure she would say he was a cold man, but he was certainly not as warm as his sister. He was far more stiffly upright than Christian, yet she did not sense any censure from him over her admission.

"I only wondered because that is often how artists describe such views. I know Lady Astrid has painted the ruins many times, in different seasons, during different times of the day."

"I did not realize." Kalina blinked, leaning forward to peer down the table at Lady Astrid, who appeared to be gripping her fork very tightly while glaring at her betrothed. The Duke of Ormonde had turned up just before the gong for supper, much to his fiancée's displeasure. "She has never mentioned it."

"I do not think she talks about it very much. I only know because Drake has one of the paintings in his library, and I asked who the artist was." Bolton did not seem to find it odd that the Duke of Ormonde, who seemed as enthused about marrying Lady Astrid as she was about marrying him, had a painting by her in his library.

Perhaps it was not odd. All the dukes seemed to accept the pair's attitudes toward each other as a matter of course, accepting all of their quirks of behavior.

Kalina found it odd, but perhaps she just did not understand the English.

It was one of those little things that reminded her, no matter how her father had tried to prepare her, that she was still on the outside.

As if thinking of him caught his attention, her father looked down the table and met her gaze. She smiled at him before turning back to the Duke of Bolton, but she could still feel his eyes on her, studying her. What he was thinking, she could not tell from his expression. She hoped he knew that she would do whatever it took to find herself a ducal husband and help him win back his family.

NATHANIAL

Bloody hell.

Christian might still very well offer for Miss Little. Despite what he'd said. His interest was clear, despite what he'd said. What had they been talking about when their heads had been bent so closely together, close enough that no one else would be able to overhear?

Then there was Sebastian on her other side. Also talking with her. Smiling at her. Ever since he'd had to banish his mother to the countryside, he'd been rather dour. Nathanial still did not know all the details, only that it had something to do with Tiffany and Gregory and their marriage, which he did not entirely understand, but it was not his business, either. Sebastian had always been a serious sort, but even more so in recent days.

If Christian did not offer for her, Sebastian might.

What was it about her that engaged the interest of so many dukes?

By the time the ladies quit for the drawing room, leaving the men to their cigars and brandy, Nathanial had already drunk twice as much wine as he usually did. Not that he turned down the brandy. The idea of Christian or Sebastian offering for Miss Little...

Bloody hell, he hoped Lady Hu was able to find him a wife soon. Surely, his preoccupation with Miss Little would disperse once he found the *right* woman to be his bride.

He quaffed his brandy.

And then again.

"Nathanial, are you all right?" Gregory frowned at him as Nathanial stood, wavering slightly on his feet.

"I... I think I need some air." Joining the others in the drawing room, watching Christian and possibly Sebastian vie for Miss Little's attention was more than he could take right now. Especially after making it very clear to Mei that Miss Little was not a prospect for his bride. Had he told her not to allow Miss Little to marry any of the others, either?

His head swam. He could not remember.

"I will go to the library. I need to sit in the quiet." Raising his hand to his head, which was throbbing, he did not need to try very hard to pretend he was too done in to listen to female nattering. Aware that his friends were staring at him, he waved his hand. "You all go on; I just need some space."

Truthfully, he should go back to his room, but in his current state, he was uncertain he would be able to make it up the stairs without help. And he was not going to admit he needed that help.

It was his own damn fault he'd gotten into this state. Once he was more clear-headed, he'd make his way up to bed and start again tomorrow. Thankfully, the others did not argue with him, and they parted at the doorway. They followed the older gentlemen toward the drawing room, while Nathanial waited until their backs were turned and stumbled down the hall to the library.

Loosening his cravat, he took a long, slow breath as he managed to get into the room without falling flat on his face. The air was a little cooler in the huge space, which made things easier. He shucked off his jacket, with some difficulty, cursing the current trend of tight-fitting fabric that made having help from his valet almost a necessity.

Only then did he fall into one of the high wing-backed chairs, slumping back against the soft velvet cushions and panting for breath from the exertion. The lamp beside him flickered, the warmth from its flame not quite reaching him. His head was truly spinning around. Closing his eyes, he groaned and let his head fall back against the back of the chair, cursing himself.

Nathanial never drank to excess. It reminded him too much of his father. But here he was, a drunken sot, and all because of Miss Little. Blasted hell. Maybe he should hope that one of his friends offered for her. That would make her off limits. Perhaps that would help end his distraction. Even though he would have to watch her wed someone else.

Reaching up, he rubbed his jaw, feeling the tightness. He was gritting his teeth together for some reason.

Would it be so bad to marry Miss Little?

She did have some powerful connections.

Perhaps she was not accepted by the entire *ton*, and she was not the Society paragon he'd hoped for, but she did have the backing of both the Duchess and Dowager Duchess of Clarence. Lady Astrid had befriended her. Delilah as well. Though a mere baroness, Delilah had moved within the circles of the *ton* her whole life, and she was friends with many of the more powerful hostesses.

But would it be enough?

That was the quandary. The unanswered question.

Would it be enough to give his sisters all they deserved? Would it be enough to help wipe away the stain his father had left on their name?

Especially with the Marquess of Stilton, her grandfather, unlikely to be pleased that his granddaughter suddenly outranked him. He might have to acknowledge her then, but it would be begrudging at best and hostile at worst. Stilton and the rest of the family might even hold a grudge against Nathanial for putting them in such a position.

Though Nathanial was a duke, with three sisters to secure futures for, he could not afford any more enemies or ill feelings than his father had already made in Society.

The door to the library opened, and he jerked upright in his chair, suddenly very aware of his lack of jacket and how his cravat had come completely undone. If the new arrival was one of the young ladies...

Relief—and some regret—poured through him when he realized it was not one of the debutantes and not Miss Little specifically. It was her father. Seeing Nathanial in the dim light next to the lamp, he raised one eyebrow, closing the door behind him.

"Sorry to disturb you, Your Grace," he said, though he continued walking into the room. He went past where Nathanial was sitting and toward the shelves. "I thought to find a book to read before bed."

Bed? Blast. What time was it? Nathanial blinked blearily as he turned his head toward the clock on the mantle. Country times meant bed much earlier than in the city, but he had not realized so much time had passed so quickly. How long had he been sitting here? *How much did I actually have to drink?*

"Has everyone gone to bed then?" he asked, doing his best not to slur his words. If they had, perhaps he could make his way to his without being seen. That would be for the best.

"Mostly. I believe there are a few of the gentlemen who decided to remove themselves to the patio for another cigar." Mr. Little smiled. "Not really my style. Ah... this might be, though."

Rather than a book, it appeared that Mr. Little had found a decanter of... something. Amber colored. Whiskey perhaps. He poured himself a glass. Nathanial closed his eyes again, trying to muster the strength to stand.

"One for you as well, Your Grace," Mr. Little said cheerfully, sounding much closer than he had before. Nathanial opened his eyes. The older man was standing over him, holding a glass out. Both hands held one.

Well. It would be churlish to refuse.

Nathanial took the proffered glass.

"Thank you." He would take a few sips. Nothing more. Bringing the glass to his lips, he took one. The alcohol burned smoothly down his throat, the earthy notes of peat and cedar sliding over his tongue, followed by a hint of something more floral. "Damn, that is good."

"Lord Blackstone's cellars are superior, I have heard," Mr. Little agreed, sitting in the chair beside Nathanial's. "I will have to ask after his supplier. I think I would like some of my own."

Nathanial wondered what it would be like to be able to just ask after a supplier and not have to wonder if he could afford whatever the cost might be.

"Ah. Well, it is very nice, I must admit," Mr. Little said, making Nathanial start. He had not realized he had spoken out loud. "I should apologize. Knowing your situation, I should not have been so thoughtless with my words."

"It is fine. Soon enough, I will know, too." Nathanial took another sip of his whiskey. A larger one. "Once I am married."

Mr. Little nodded slowly, leaning back in his chair.

"It should not be hard for a duke to find a wife with a dowry large enough to settle your debts."

"Truth. But it is more than that." Nathanial did not know why he could not hold his tongue. Perhaps it was the drink. Perhaps it was because he had been sitting alone with his thoughts, and now there was someone to talk to. Perhaps it was because the man was *her* father. He could give Mr. Little the explanation that he could not give the man's daughter. "I have to shore up... things. For my sisters."

He took another very large sip of the whiskey. More like a gulp, really. Admitting these things to his friends was difficult enough; speaking about it with a man who was nearly a stranger... Yet there was something very fatherly about Mr. Little's demeanor. As though he cared. And he had a daughter.

"You have sisters?"

"Three of them. Julianna... should debut."

"Ah. That is why we returned to England for Kalina's debut. That and I wanted my father to meet my family." There was ruefulness in Mr. Little's voice and sadness as well.

Nathanial felt for the man.

It was a terrible thing, the way the Marquess of Stilton was treating the Littles.

"My father is a hard man," Mr. Little agreed. "Very hidebound. Very proper."

"Know you wan' her to marry a duke." Damn, he was slurring again.

"I do, but more than that, I want her to be happy. Please remember that." Mr. Little cleared his throat. Nathanial opened his eyes and found Mr. Little standing over him again. He took the glass from Nathanial's hand and gripped it, pulling Nathanial to his feet. "Let me help you to your bed, Your Grace."

"Yes... bed... I should..." He could not finish the thought.

Leaning heavily on the older man, he managed to put one foot in front of the other, though it took all of his concentration. Dimly, he was aware that the house was very quiet. They went up the stairs, and it seemed to take forever.

One more staircase... but no. He must have miscounted. Maybe it had taken so long because he had not realized they were on the second staircase. That made sense. They were going down a hall.

"In here, Your Grace," Mr. Little murmured, opening a door. Nathanial could barely keep his eyes open as he stumbled in. It was so dark.

"Light?"

"No, it will hurt your eyes. Here, Your Grace, let me help you with that."

Mr. Little moved him through the room, helping him strip off his waistcoat and shirt. Thank goodness Nathanial was in his ankle-length boots, having changed out of his riding boots after returning from the ruins. It did not take much to get him out of them and down to his smalls.

"Thank you," he tried to say as Mr. Little tipped him onto the bed. He was not sure it came out right, though. Not that it mattered.

"Good night, Your Grace."

The bed was soft. Warm. Far warmer than it normally was. Nathanial felt the dark coming up to close around him.

For some reason, even though he heard the door close behind Mr. Little just before unconsciousness drew him under, he felt as though he was not alone.

13

———

Rolling over, Kalina bumped into something warm.

And hard.

Which made no sense because there was nothing warm or hard in her bed. Shifting, she tried to shove at it. It did not feel as though she was still dreaming.

She heard her bedroom door open, the way she often did when she was just beginning to rouse in the morning.

"Good morning, mi—" Margaret's voice cut off in a shocked scream.

Eyes flying open, Kalina jerked upright in the bed, her right hand flying out and encountering the warm, hard body of someone *in bed with her.* She screamed, trying to scramble back, but her legs were caught in a tangle in the sheets. It felt like her heart was going to pound right outside of her chest.

Someone is in bed with me!

Not just someone.

A man.

She felt dizzy as she finally caught a glimpse of his face, his expression turning from peaceful slumber to a frown as he began to stir as well.

Hereford.

Clapping her hand over her mouth, Kalina managed to stop screaming.

What the devil is Hereford doing in my bed?

This had to be a dream.

Though it felt very real.

Voices were already coming from down the hall, raised in alarm. Out of the corner of her eye, she could see movement as her doorway filled, people staring in.

"What the— Your Grace!" Her father's voice thundered from the doorway as he strode in, scowling furiously. "What have you done?"

"Oh my God..." someone said from the door. One of the women.

"I..." Hereford's eyes were opening.

She stared, fascinated, too horrified to move as it felt like time slowed all around her.

Hereford's gaze met hers, and he blinked. "Where... am I?"

"You are in my daughter's bed!" Her father was standing over them now, hands on his hips, black and grey dressing robe coming undone around his neck, scowling furiously. "You have ruined her!"

"Oh my God, he has to marry her!" That was Lady Kari, Kalina was sure of it, sounding caught between being scandalized and disappointed.

Kalina's stomach sank, right into a pit of shocked despair.

She was not dreaming.

She was awake.

Hereford was in her bed.

He's going to have to marry me.

The duke stared at her father for another long moment before suddenly throwing the covers back and falling off the bed. There were more scandalized squeals from the ladies in the doorway as they realized he was nearly naked. Kalina got a flash of his bare back; the sturdy muscles and broad shoulders that filled out his jackets so nicely, clearly had no need of padding. He looked like one of the carved marble statues come to life and in the flesh... not that she could truly appreciate the view in such a moment. The duke barely made it to the chamber pot before he began to heave and vomit.

Still sitting exactly where she had been since the moment she'd sat up, Kalina stared at her father. At Margaret, who was standing plastered to the wardrobe, eyes wide and her mouth hanging open in shock. At the cluster of people in her doorway, including her mother, who was staring at her father with narrowed eyes and a tight mouth.

Her heart kept beating faster and faster as the sound of Hereford emptying his stomach made her own turn over uneasily.

And her father would not meet her eyes.

"Everyone out. There is no need to linger and stare." Lady Astrid's sharp voice cut through the din.

Relief fluttered through Kalina at the sound of someone sensible coming through. Lady Astrid shooed the others away, including a disgruntled Tiffany and Gregory, before coming partway into the room herself. Her gaze traveled over everyone still inside—Kalina's parents, her maid, and the Duke of Hereford, who had finally regained control of his faculties.

He knelt on the rug, still holding onto the chamber pot, panting and looking at absolutely no one.

Lady Astrid studied him for a long moment before her hard-eyed gaze moved on to look at Kalina. The usual warmth was not in her gaze. Instead, her eyes were full of suspicion.

She knew I wanted to marry a duke. And there is something very clearly wrong with Hereford.

Freezing in place, it wasn't Kalina's stomach that sank. It was her heart.

Oh God.

She thinks I deliberately trapped him.

Not knowing what to do, what to say, Kalina found that she could not move. Could not think.

"John, help the Duke of Hereford back to his proper room," Lady Astrid commanded, moving to the side to admit one of the footmen.

A rather tall, burly footman who had no difficulty in helping the duke to his feet, his head still hanging in front of him.

It might have been from physical exertion. Or it might be something else.

Kalina did not know what to think. Her head whirled even as her body remained motionless in shock.

The footman scooped up the duke's shirt from Kalina's floor, using it to help cover the man, at least a little. His long legs were still visible up to mid-thigh as he was led from the room, his first steps stumbling before he became more sure-footed.

Pressing her lips together, Lady Astrid focused her attention on Kalina's father, who had turned to look at her. Her voice was cool. Aloof. She'd drawn back from the warmth with which she usually spoke to them.

"The library will be open for your use, Mr. Little. I will ensure the duke knows to meet you there."

There was a pause before Kalina's father answered, as he could hardly be unaware of Lady Astrid's suspicion that her home had been used to trap one of her friends into marriage. Kalina's stomach heaved. Now, she really felt like she was going to be sick, just like the duke.

"Go." Mother tilted her head at Kalina's father. If Lady Astrid's tone had been cool, Mother's was glacial. "I will stay with Kalina."

"I... yes." Kalina's father nodded. "Right then." He glanced back at Kalina, his expression unreadable. "I will take care of everything, sweetheart."

"Thank you, Father," she whispered, the first words she'd been able to summon.

Her father was going to take care of everything. Relief slowly began to unthaw her limbs as he walked out the door, followed by Lady Astrid, who closed it firmly behind her.

Immediately, her mother rushed toward the bed, reaching out her hands. Kalina lifted her own to meet them.

"What happened?" her mother asked in a low voice, squeezing

Kalina's fingers. "Tell me the truth. Did you and your father plan this?"

"What?" Kalina's voice rose in a high shriek. "Of course not!" Hurt surged through her. How could her mother think such a thing? Of course, Kalina had not...

Relief, swiftly followed by anger, crossed her mother's face, and she closed her eyes, which was when Kalina realized what her mother was thinking.

"Father did not... he would not..." She stumbled over her words, trying to think.

Of course, her father would not put a man in her bed while she was sleeping, entirely unaware. Not even to marry her off to a duke.

Would he?

"I am going to murder him," her mother muttered, the anger in her expression quickly growing. Then she took in a deep breath. "We need to get you dressed. You need to wear your best outfit. Today is going to be difficult."

Feeling utterly numb, Kalina let her mother pull her from the bed. She felt like a doll, letting her mother and Margaret make the decisions about what dress, what jewelry, and how to do her hair. It felt like they were adorning her with armor.

Which she was going to need.

Nothing had actually happened. She was still a virgin. Even she would not have been able to sleep through *that*, surely. Besides, she did not feel any different. Nothing hurt. Nothing was sore. Going by her mother's descriptions, she should have felt something if he'd... if they'd...

She was not actually ruined. But it would not matter. The duke had been in her bed, which would have been bad enough, but his clothes were also scattered across her floor. Margaret had set to collecting them while Kalina's mother brushed Kalina's hair. Society would deem her ruined.

The only way her reputation could be salvaged would be if he married her. It was also the only honorable route for him, so she had to hope he would take it.

But she did not think anyone was going to be happy about it.

———

<u>NATHANIAL</u>

Though he'd emptied his stomach, Nathanial did not feel any better. His tongue felt like he'd licked a wet dog. He was able to mostly stay on balance, though he was grateful for the footman's assistance on the stairs, which were far more treacherous than the halls.

He had not felt like this since the morning after he first looked at the estate's books and accounts after his father's death. Twice in his life now, he'd done this, but last time the worst thing he'd woken to was a headache... not a marriage.

How had he ended up in Miss Little's room?

Trying to cast his mind back, his memories of the previous evening became increasingly fuzzy through the meal. He'd drunk too much. He knew that. He'd known it at supper.

"Ah, Your Grace?" The footman murmured, drawing Nathanial's attention, and he nodded ahead.

A cluster of dukes was around his door. Gregory must have sprinted up the stairs to rouse all of them after Lady Astrid had removed him from Miss Little's room. They were all standing in the hallway in their dressing gowns, frowning in confusion.

"How the devil did you end up in Miss Little's room?" Christian asked. He was frowning more fiercely than the others, but not in the manner of a man denied something he wanted—more the way Sebastian often frowned at Gregory over Tiffany. He was giving off the distinctive aura of a protective and disapproving older brother.

Exactly what Nathanial needed this morning.

Gritting his teeth, Nathanial shook his head as he made himself straighten up and stop leaning on John footman.

"We'll talk inside," he replied grimly, gesturing to his bedroom door. The last thing he needed to do was give the staff even more fodder for gossip than they already had. Especially when he still did not have a good answer... because he did not remember.

Drake gave him a look, but obligingly opened the door, and everyone trooped in while Nathanial thanked the footman and dismissed him.

"Where is your valet?" Matthew asked, looking around as if expecting one to appear out of magic.

"What valet?" Nathanial barked, walking over to his basin. There was water in it, thankfully, though it was probably left over from yesterday. He did not care. He dunked his head into the water as he heard Drake respond to Matthew's question in acerbic tones.

"He cannot afford a valet."

Coming back up for air, his hair now soaking wet and some of his wits returning to him, Nathanial heard Matthew make a frustrated noise.

"I wish you would let us give you some funds. It can be a loan."

"I did not need a loan; I needed a bride."

Though now he was wishing he'd taken a loan from one of them. It would have needed to be an astronomical amount, and he had not wanted to be a burden on any of his friends.

But he could have taken something. Enough to get by for a bit longer, instead of insisting on taking care of everything himself. He'd still had his pride.

Pride goes before destruction and a haughty spirit before a fall.

Well, he had certainly fallen. Right into Miss Little's bed. He rubbed his head, wiping away the droplets that had begun to run down his brow.

"Well, now you have one," Gregory observed, sighing as he sat down on the edge of Nathanial's bed, folding the bottom of his navy-blue dressing gown over his lap. Sebastian sat beside him, similarly robed in dark green. Nathanial glared at Gregory, but at least the other man was not laughing.

"What happened?" Drake asked. "After you went to the library."

Nathanial rubbed his forehead.

"I overly indulged, which is why I went there instead of joining the ladies. I sat there. Thinking." About whether he could marry Miss Little, regardless of the issues with her position in Society. A moot point now. Bloody hell. "I think... I think I remember Mr. Little coming in."

The words came slowly, as did the memories. They were fuzzy. He could not remember what they had spoken of.

Aware of the other dukes exchanging glances, Nathanial took the opportunity to strip off his shirt and go to the wardrobe to pull out his own dressing gown. It was tattered and several years out of fashion, but it was also one of his favorite items of clothing because it was so comfortable. Shrugging the puce fabric over his shoulders and belting it in place, he felt marginally better now that he was no longer standing in nothing but his shirt and small clothes.

"Do you think they deliberately trapped you?" Christian asked slowly.

Nathanial let out a long sigh. "I do not know."

But he heavily suspected it. A small kernel of anger had embedded itself in his gut, and as he made the admission out loud, he felt it start to grow.

A sharp rap at the door had all of them turning. Standing the closest, Sebastian stepped forward and opened it a crack to see who it was. His shoulders relaxed as he stepped aside to admit Lady Astrid.

It only took her sharp gaze a moment to sweep the room, stopping on Drake in his rust-colored dressing gown for a brief moment before moving on to pin Nathanial with a glance.

"What the devil were you doing in Kalina's room?"

Nathanial was becoming very tired of that question.

14

"Come in and sit down. We were just discussing the matter of how Nathanial got into Miss Little's room," Drake said. Like his fiancée, his words came out as more of a demand than a request. He gestured at the empty chair by the escritoire, which no one had yet taken a seat at.

Lifting her nose in the air, Lady Astrid paused for a moment, as if to prove to Drake that she did not have to immediately jump to do as he said, before regally sweeping over to sit down. Unlike the gentlemen, she was already dressed for the day in a coral dress trimmed with copper ribbon and creamy lace. Her red hair was pulled back from her face and pinned neatly in place without any alluring tendrils or curls to soften her.

And the look that she sent at Nathanial was very hard.

"As I was just saying, I remember Mr. Little coming into the library. He gave me another drink." Nathanial ignored the groans and shaking heads that accompanied his words. Only Lady Astrid did not react, sitting as straight as a poker, ignoring Drake as he hovered at her side. "I know we talked. I do not remember about what." Leaning back against his wardrobe, Nathanial rubbed his head again.

"Did he take you to Miss Little's room?" Christian asked, though his frown was far less fierce than it had been before.

"I..."

"You need to be sure. Her room is just below yours," Lady Astrid said as Nathanial's voice trailed off. His head had already been throbbing, and trying to remember made it hurt even more. "Did he lead you there, or did you forget to go up the second staircase?"

The staircase.

Nathanial remembered the staircase.

"He helped me up the stairs. I would not have made it otherwise. I was..."

"Indisposed?"

"Four sheets to the wind?"

"Completely foxed?"

"Snockered?"

Glaring, Nathanial lifted his head to cut off his friends as they snickered in amusement. Strangely, the joking did make him feel a bit better, despite everything.

The idea of marrying Miss Little... well, part of him was not at all unhappy with the thought. The idea that she and her father had trapped him did cause him a great deal of unhappiness, which easily overshadowed the first part.

"I suppose it does not really matter, though, does it?" Sebastian asked. "Either way, he has to marry her."

"It would change how I feel about it," Nathanial muttered and saw Lady Astrid nod in agreement.

"Does he have to marry her? Christian was courting her; he could do it," Matthew pointed out. Nathanial's head snapped up, despite the pounding, and his stomach turned over again at the thought of Christian marrying Miss Little in his place. Zounds, but that would only make this whole farce even worse...

Except...

If Christian was willing, he should probably allow him.

"By that logic, so could you," Christian pointed out.

Matthew shook his head, his hand lifting to pat the pocket of his dressing robe. Even now, he must be carrying that damned lucky coin, which had told him not to pursue Miss Little.

Rolling his eyes, Christian continued, "I could, and that would save her, but not Nathanial."

Lady Astrid frowned, her expression turning speculative.

"What do you mean?" Nathanial asked.

"We could shuffle dukes around the altar to save Miss Little's reputation," Lady Astrid said, working through the problem out loud. "Though those here at the house party know it was Nathanial in her bed, if someone else were to marry her, it would be gossiped about for a few weeks until the next scandal. However, because it was Nathanial in her bed, the fact that he did not step in to do the honorable thing would reflect rather badly on him with the ladies."

Her gaze had turned to one of sympathy as she met his.

Understanding dawned.

If his goal was to marry a woman of impeccable reputation and social standing with a massive dowry, acting dishonorably with another debutante was a surefire way to scuttle his ship. No woman of impeccable reputation and social standing would marry a man who ruined another woman, then allowed one of his friends to marry her in his stead. Even his rank as a duke would not be enough to save him from Society's approbation.

Not for this Season, at least.

And if he did not marry this Season...

Bloody hell.

"If it helps, the answer to your question was yes," Matthew said, thrusting his hand into his pocket.

"What question?" Christian asked when Nathanial did not respond.

"After I flipped the coin to see if I should pursue Miss Little, I flipped it for Nathanial as well. I did not tell him what it said at the time, because I do not know if it works for someone other than me." Matthew shrugged. "But it came up heads, which means yes."

However, Nathanial had not wanted the coin the make his choice for him. He had not wanted anyone to make the choice other than himself. And while he'd been trying to talk himself into offering for Miss Little regardless of the fact that she did not meet every single parameter he'd listed for himself...

Closing his eyes, he let his head thud back against the wardrobe as his friends began to argue about whether the coin's flip had any meaning for anyone other than Matthew. Not that it mattered to him. There was only one path forward.

It felt like his chest was going to crack open, the invisible bands that had wrapped around it so tight. He was well and truly trapped. All of his choices were gone.

He had to marry Miss Little or face the fact he had failed his family, which was no real choice at all. Marrying Miss Little would save her reputation and his finances.

But she was not the lady he'd thought she was. Not at all.

Kalina

Leaving the bedroom was the hardest thing she had ever done in her life. Kalina knew she looked her best. Margaret had brushed her hair until it gleamed, braided the silky strands before winding the plaits into a complicated knot and securing it with pins decorated with tiny pink diamonds. One pink diamond hung from a delicate chain, not nearly as large as those she wore with her evening gowns, but enough to remind everyone exactly what the Duke of Hereford would be getting when he married her.

Her dress was bright rose pink, trimmed with dark green, making her look as though she was a flower come to life. The colors made her dark skin glow and her eyes shine brighter than usual.

She was as polished as the diamonds she wore.

But inside, she felt like she was dying.

Her father had gone to meet with the Duke of Hereford in the library

"Chin up," her mother murmured as they stepped into the dining room together, and there was an immediate hush from the others gathered there.

They'd heard.

They'd all heard.

Most of the ladies goggled at her, regardless of age... but Tiffany avoided her gaze by studiously staring at the plate in front of her. Delilah looked at Kalina, then looked away, applying her attention to her plate as well. Those were the two in the room she had cared about the most. Gregory was not there, and neither were any of the other dukes.

Lady Astrid had also not arrived yet.

Lifting her chin, as her mother had told her to, Kalina glided over to the buffet where breakfast had been laid out. She had never felt less like eating, yet there was no choice. Everything she understood about how English society operated, the more she behaved as if everything was normal, the more likely they were to treat her normally.

At least, Society at large would.

Her friends...

Kalina took in a deep breath to keep the ache in her chest from spreading further.

It was not as though they had been her friends for very long. She had spent far more time without any friends than she had spent with. A reversion would be back to her normal.

Maybe she was just not meant to have friends. No matter how badly she wanted them.

If it came to a choice between her father and her friends, she would choose her father, of course. He had been her support for her entire life. She'd known Tiffany, Delilah, and Lady Astrid for less than a year.

Defiantly, Kalina took her plate and walked to the opposite end of the table from where Tiffany and Delilah were seated, choosing a chair next to Mei, the matchmaker's granddaughter. Lady Hu was on Mei's other side, and Lord Emeryn and his wife were across from them.

Kalina's mother took the seat beside hers, quietly sliding into place. She was so serene, so calm. Kalina did her best to emulate her mother's tranquil demeanor.

"Good morning," Mei said, turning to look at Kalina. Her dark eyes studied Kalina's expression, which she feared might show more than she wanted it to, despite her efforts.

"Good morning," Kalina replied, and she was rather pleased at how her voice sounded. Not too high, not too strained. Almost as though this was a completely normal morning.

"I hear you no longer require my services." Mei's lips twitched, a glimmer of amusement sparking in her eyes when Kalina's mouth dropped open, and she stared at her.

Mei was teasing her.

It felt... it felt like she wanted to burst into tears at the idea that someone was not only looking at her, talking *with* her instead of about her, but was willing to tease her. She was also very aware that Mei was cataloging all of Kalina's actions. The teasing was meant in a kindly fashion, but there was also an underlying current of being examined.

Still. She was grateful.

"Well, we will see. Nothing is set in stone, as yet." She dropped her gaze to her plate. Her stomach twisted.

Picking up a piece of toast, which seemed the most harmless item, she began to butter it. It gave her something to do while she tried to convince her stomach to settle. Conversation had sprung up again along the rest of the table, but Kalina was very aware of the whispers, the sideways glances.

She did not dare look down the length of the table to see if Delilah and Tiffany were whispering to each other. She did not want to know if they were.

"From all I have observed, the Duke of Hereford is an honorable man. He will do the right thing." Mei took a sip of her tea. "I think he may even come to realize what a lucky escape he had from his chosen fate."

Kalina did not know what to say to that. It was on the tip of her tongue to comment that Mei had not had much time to observe the duke. She had only arrived yesterday. Yet, she suspected Mei saw much more, and much more clearly, than most.

As to a lucky escape and a chosen fate... Kalina could not begin to imagine what Mei was referring to. She did know that the duke and Mei had spoken at length yesterday afternoon.

Had Mei felt as though he was going down the wrong path in regard to his search for a bride?

Did referring to a lucky escape mean that she thought his marriage to Kalina was lucky?

Kalina's head hurt trying to follow the logic, yet she did not feel as though she could ask. Was not sure she wanted to.

The door to the dining room opened again, and Kalina's head jerked up. Lady Astrid swept into the room, followed by the dukes. Almost all the dukes. Hereford was absent. Likely still in the library with her father.

Taking in the room with a glance, Lady Astrid's gaze moved right over Kalina as if she did not exist. It felt like a sharp jab through her heart, and her breath clogged in her throat as her eyes began to sting. Kalina dropped her gaze back down to her plate, forcing herself to bring the toast to her mouth and take a small nibble as Lady Astrid and the cadre of dukes joined the duchess and baroness at the other end of the table.

Mei leaned in closer to Kalina, dropping her voice so only she could hear.

"Do not worry. Emotions are heightened, but eventually they will realize you had nothing to do with trapping Hereford into marriage."

Surprise nearly choked Kalina, but she managed to swallow her bread despite it. Mei's insight was even greater than she'd realized. She sounded completely sure that Kalina had had nothing to do with the events of this morning.

Afraid to hope that Mei was correct, Kalina couldn't stop the painful little spark that sprang up inside her, anyway.

15

———————

NATHANIAL

Miss Little's dowry was a literal king's ransom. He'd known it was large, but this was... huge. Gargantuan. Nearly beyond his comprehension after months of scrabbling and scrounging and trying to ensure his sisters were at least fed and clothed. It was all Nathanial could do not to stare at the marriage contract that Mr. Little had ready.

It also made him wonder how long the man had been planning this or something like it.

"Is the sum enough?" Mr. Little asked from the other side of the table they were seated at, folding one hand over the other as he rested them in front of himself. "Do you require more?"

More?

If Nathanial had been standing, he would have hit the ground. Not just because of the amount of drink he'd had the night before, either.

"This is fine." He managed to get the words out, though it felt like he'd swallowed his tongue.

It was beyond fine.

His debts would be paid. Fully. All of them.

He could fund all the backpay to his housekeeper, Miss Milford, and her brother, Daniel Milford, who had refused to leave him and his sisters. They'd scrabbled along with him, helping him find creative solutions, teaching him and the girls how to garden, how to mend their clothes, how to get by with almost nothing.

The estate could afford to invest in better seed, to create a better crop, and he would be able to make the necessary repairs to the farms and homes for his tenants so they could, in turn, produce more in coming years.

Julianna would have her debut next year. If he invested the money wisely over the next year, her dowry would be more than modest; it would be substantial. Not only would she not have to marry for money, but she would be secure for the rest of her life. So would the other two.

In one fell swoop, Mr. Little had gone beyond solving all of Nathanial's problems.

And he still resented the man for it.

For taking away that one choice.

Even more so because now he had to feel bloody grateful as well.

Nathanial blew out a long breath, trying to ease the roiling emotions that batted about his insides. He'd never felt so high and yet so low at the same time. Here he was getting everything he wanted, yet he wanted to rage at the situation.

Because it had not been his choice.

Because he was being forced into it.

"Everything looks in order," he said, once he'd finished reading through the contract. There was nothing in it that he objected to. Miss Little would keep a portion of her dowry for her to do with as she pleased, and he had no objections to that. Part of him was relieved. He wanted to think himself a gentleman, but the desire to punish her for trapping him into marriage... he would be lying if he said he did not feel it. Withholding the funds that she brought to the marriage might have a small sense of poetic justice, but just thinking about the possibility made him feel small. Unchivalrous. Not like the man he wanted to be.

He was glad the temptation had been removed entirely.

"Good." Mr. Little sounded relieved. As if he had worried that Nathanial might not do the honorable thing in light of his dishonorable actions.

Clenching his jaw, Nathanial felt the muscle tic before he managed to relax it.

"We'll have the wedding here as soon as possible. I'll send someone to London to get a special license today."

Even though he was not looking directly at Mr. Little, Nathanial sensed the other man stilling. Before, he'd been rather triumphant, though trying to hide it. Now, he was not pretending to dim his emotions. He was not happy with the idea of having the wedding here. Very well, Nathanial was not happy with being trapped into marriage.

Now they were both unhappy.

Which seemed far fairer than Mr. Little reveling in getting what he'd wanted while Nathanial simmered with resentment.

"Here?"

"Yes. I see no reason to delay. Indeed, with the possible scandal attached to the wedding, it is best to get it out of the way quickly," Nathanial replied briskly. "When the guests from the house party return to London, the deed will have already been done, and divulging that they were select guests at a duke's very private wedding will be far more titillating for them than how the wedding came about. I would like as little gossip about my family as possible, as I have a sister to debut next year, as well as two more to follow."

Lifting his gaze to meet Mr. Little's, he could see that the older man had sobered. His brow was slightly furrowed, but he did not protest. Though he had been out of Society for quite a while before returning from India, he did know how things worked.

"Besides which, for your family's purposes, additional scandal attached to your name will hardly advance your own cause." Any other day and Nathanial would not have been so gauche as to point that out. But this was today.

Mr. Little's mouth twitched, then he nodded.

"I see your point." He sighed. "I am sure Kalina will understand the necessity." Meeting Nathanial's gaze, he hesitated. "I know I am being rudely direct, Your Grace, but I do want you to know that she had nothing to do with my actions. She is as innocent as yourself in the situation I engineered."

As much as Nathanial wanted that to be true, he did not think he could trust the word of a man who'd been willing to trap him into marriage. She had certainly played her part to perfection. Screaming loudly when she awoke, drawing people to her room, then falling immediately silent once they were there. While he understood Mr. Little's desire to wipe any blame from her, that did not mean she was blameless.

In fact, if they had concocted the plan together, Nathanial would expect Mr. Little to fall upon the sword of responsibility. His admission of guilt, when he'd already shown himself to be dishonorable and when he was trying to save his daughter from reprobation, was hardly evidence in her favor.

Though... the idea that she might not have had something to do with trapping him did make him feel a tiny spark of hope.

One which he ruthlessly pushed away.

Regardless, she and her father were getting exactly what they both wanted. What he knew she'd aimed for.

So am I.

Just not in the way he'd wanted it.

Dropping his gaze from Mr. Little's, Nathanial looked back down at the marriage contract lying on the desk between them. He was an honorable man, even if he'd been dishonorably trapped. He was honest enough to be grateful for the benefits marrying Miss Little would bring him, even if he was appalled by the situation. While he'd had his reasons for wanting a different bride, good reasons that affected his social standing and his sisters' futures, that was no longer a consideration.

He was going to have to make the best of it.

Clearing his throat, Nathanial pushed the papers together, aware that he was not acknowledging Mr. Little's claim but unable to find it in himself to lie and say he held Miss Little blameless.

"We should call Miss Little here so I can formally propose," he said, trying not to sound as grim as he felt.

Making the best of the situation would include a public face of acceptance, even happiness. It was the best way forward for both of their families. What happened behind closed doors was something else altogether.

"Very well." Mr. Little got to his feet. He seemed to understand that pressing Nathanial on the matter of Miss Little's guilt was not the wisest course of action at the moment. "Ah... thank you, Your Grace."

Heat flushed through Nathanial as his anger momentarily roared inside him, his rage at the man in front of him trying to surge out. He wanted to yell. To throw something. To declare that he would never marry Miss Little and that he did not care if her reputation was ruined.

Instead, he stood stock still, breathing in deeply until he had a hold of himself again. Mr. Little had already turned away, as if he realized he had trod upon the last of Nathanial's self-control, and rang for a footman.

KALINA

Walking into the Blackstone library with her mother at her side, any hope that Mei had been able to engender for her at breakfast died a swift death when she looked upon the Duke of Hereford. Handsome as ever, despite the paleness of his face and the way his eyes appeared almost pink around the edges. He was wearing a dark grey jacket over a cerise and gold waistcoat with dark grey trousers. His light brown hair appeared rather more rumpled than usual, as if he had not taken as much time to style it.

Understandably.

When she walked in, his gaze lifted but only momentarily before he looked away, as though he could not bear to look upon her.

As painful as it had been to have her friends react to her in a similar manner this morning, this felt doubly so. If she could have stopped and bent over to hold her mostly empty stomach, to breathe through the pain, she would have. But she did not want to show him such weakness. She did not want her father to realize how badly he had hurt her.

From the hopeful way her father was looking at her right now, she could tell he thought he had done something she would be happy about.

How he could think she would want him to trap the Duke of Hereford into marriage with her, she did not know. But, unlike Hereford, his eyes were flitting back and forth between her and her mother, looking for their reactions. It reminded her very much of Ashwin when he was younger, and he had done something which he hoped would meet their parents' approval.

"Miss Little." The duke's voice drew her attention. He was looking at her again, but not meeting her eyes. In fact, his attention seemed to be riveted to her right shoulder. Perhaps because her mother stood just behind her left, and he did not want to be forced to look at her, either. "Your father and I have spoken, and he has granted his permission for me to offer for your hand. Would you do me the honor of becoming my wife?"

Despite the words, which sounded correct, his tone was monotone. Lifeless. Nothing like the man she'd gotten to know.

It was a horrible farce of a moment that should have been wonderful, and she dug her nails into the palm of her hand to keep from reacting the way she wanted to. Bursting into tears while yelling the word 'no' and running from the room would not help anything.

This was her only chance to marry a duke and give her father his family back. None of the others would have her after this, that was certain.

Whether or not her father deserved her sacrifice...

She looked at him.

His earnest expression. His hope. His uncertainty. The love that was shining in his eyes.

Her father had good intentions, of that she was sure. He would never choose to make her unhappy. So, why he had chosen *this* route, she did not know. Would not know until she questioned him.

She had never once doubted his love for her, and she would not start now. She would not reject him, the way his family had, the way her mother's family had. No matter how angry she was at him, she still loved him, and she always would.

Kalina managed to summon a smile for him. A very small one. Little more than a slight curve of her lips. She tried to put her love for him in her eyes. While she might take a while to forgive him for what he had done, she could never turn away from him. From either of her parents.

Taking a deep breath, she met the Duke of Hereford's eyes. If he'd been cold before, he looked carved from ice now, but that did not change her answer. It was the only way forward.

For her.

For her father.

Even for the duke, for she knew he needed her dowry. Desperately.

"Yes, Your Grace, I accept."

16

Everything was moving in a whirl around her, so fast that Kalina's head felt like it was spinning. The contracts had been signed. The Duke of Ormonde had been dispatched back to London to retrieve a special license from the Archbishop. Hereford had disappeared from the library without a second glance, muttering something about needing to write his family.

The idea of having to eventually face his family made Kalina's stomach turn over again.

Despite Lady Astrid's clear displeasure with the circumstances, she and her mother had jumped into action. The household was bustling with footmen and maids scurrying about, readying the manor for a ducal wedding.

Whispers followed Kalina through the house wherever she went.

No one believed that Hereford had ended up in her bed by chance.

Everyone but her mother and father seemed to believe she was at fault. Once Hereford had left the library, her mother had demanded to know what he had done, and her father had confessed what they already suspected.

He'd led a drunken Hereford to Kalina's room and left him in her bed.

He was the one who had trapped the duke into marriage with her.

Now, her mother was angrier at her father than she'd ever seen. So was Kalina, but she did not want to make matters worse between her parents, so she could not vent that anger. She was afraid if she were to show her upset, her mother would do something… drastic. Kalina did not know what. But with her whole life in turmoil, she needed her parents not to be entirely at odds with each other. She needed them to be the steady support they had always been. Which meant bottling up her own emotions rather than giving her mother more fuel for her fire.

Ashwin was hiding out with Rupert Blackstone, keeping well away from all the ruckus, and she could not blame him. His friend, at least, was standing by his side.

Though she could not blame her friends. They had known Hereford for far longer than she had known them. They knew he was an honorable man and had not actually ruined her. By now, the duke had surely told them what her father had done.

Wandering to the window of her room, Kalina stared at the long drive leading up to the manor. It felt like an entire lifetime ago that she'd ridden in the carriage along its length, to be warmly welcomed into Lady Astrid's home, full of hopes that she might impress a duke enough to gain a proposal. That life felt like it belonged to someone else.

Once again, she was an outcast.

Now, she would be leaving her parents' home for Hereford's, but he did not truly want her there.

Once again, she belonged nowhere.

Her eyes and throat burned, and she leaned forward to press her forehead against the cool glass. She felt almost feverish.

"Kalina, come help us choose your wedding gown," her mother said gently, putting her hand on Kalina's shoulder and drawing her back away from the window. Turning Kalina in place, her mother's warm, dark eyes traveled over Kalina's expression, searching for something. "You do not have to do this, you know. We can go back to India. English society is not everything."

Had she been any happier in India?

She had not felt like she belonged there, either.

If she did not belong anywhere, then what did it matter where she was unhappy?

At least here in England, she would marry a duke, then her father could be happy. In India, he had been unhappy, her mother had been unhappy, and she and Ashwin had been unhappy. Now, her grandfather would be forced to acknowledge them, giving her father what he'd hoped for. Ashwin had made at least one friend, who was standing by him. And her mother... well, at least here she was not being ignored by her family. They were too far away for them to ignore her.

"I want to stay. I want to marry the duke." She managed to push a tremulous smile onto her lips again. It did not fool her mother, who frowned at her, then sighed. Behind her, Margaret was hovering with a worried expression on her face, wringing her hands. "Do not be mad at Father, please. He was trying to help. To give me what he thought I wanted."

Mother pressed her lips together in a thin line, breathing in through her nose. Her nostrils flared, and she gave her head a little shake.

"Your father..." She took another deep breath. "Your father likely had good intentions; he often does. That does not excuse the questionability of his actions."

"I do not want you fighting while at my wedding," she pleaded. "The situation is difficult enough if you are not getting on... I need both of you."

The look in her mother's eyes softened, and she reached up to brush an errant lock of hair away from Kalina's face, tucking it behind her ear.

"You have both of us. Always. No matter how much your father makes me want to shake him sometimes. My anger at him does not affect either of our feelings toward you." She sighed. "But I will try to ease my temper. For your sake."

Relaxing, knowing that was the first step toward her mother forgiving her father, Kalina nodded.

"Would you like to choose a dress now?" her mother asked.

No, she would not *like* to, but she knew she needed to. Kalina nodded again. This was not how she'd pictured choosing her wedding gown. She'd imagined being at the modistes with her mother, picking the fabric, poring over the possible designs. Instead, they were selecting one from what she had on hand.

"I pulled out the blush because it is the closest to white, and I know that's all the rage for weddings now," Margaret said, holding up both dresses. "But I also think the pink silk would look lovely. And you have not worn it yet."

The silk was a much brighter hue, cut to perfection. It was an attention-getting dress. Kalina felt very much that she'd had enough attention. The more she could make this appear like a regular wedding to the rest of the guests, the better it would be. The blush had pink underskirts, heavily trimmed with cream lace, which lightened them. The overskirt was trimmed with lace and a pink ribbon that matched the hue of the underskirts exactly. Layers of lace bolstered the hips of the skirt where it connected to the bodice, which was also adorned with a panel of lace down the center. Tiny puff sleeves of the same fabric as the underskirt were topped with more lace that lifted into the air like little wings. The neckline was scandalously low for a day dress, but no lower than the pink silk.

It was the closest thing she had on hand to a fashionable wedding gown.

"The blush," she said, pointing to the dress in Margaret's left hand. "As you say, it is closer to white."

"Very good, miss." Turning, Margaret put the pink silk back into the wardrobe. Kalina watched it go with a kind of longing. She wondered if she would ever have the chance to wear it now or if Hereford would banish her to rusticate in the country in revenge for being trapped into marriage with her.

What her life would look like as his wife...

She could not begin to guess.

That was a problem for the future. Right now, she needed to get through the next few days, then she would contemplate what retribution she might have to live with.

Once her gown and jewelry had been chosen, Kalina shooed her mother and Margaret out of the room. She needed some space to think. Some time.

Normally, she would have thrown herself down on the bed to do so, but she found herself reluctant to approach the offending piece of furniture again. Not that it was the bed's fault there had been a man in it with her, but she was not ready to return to it.

Instead, she went back to the window and sat down on the cushioned seat. Though she stared out into the sunny day, she was not truly seeing anything. Now that she was alone, the morning replayed in her head.

Waking up.

Realizing there was a man beside her.

Screaming.

What could she have done differently?

How could she have stopped it?

Why had her father done that?

A question she had not been able to ask him as yet. One that she would need complete privacy for, just in case his answer made matters with her mother worse. But she could not fathom what he had been thinking.

A knock at her door made her jerk upright, bouncing to her feet as surprise ran through her.

"Come in."

The door opened to reveal Lady Astrid. Immediately, Kalina's mouth went dry, and her palms turned clammy as she faced the young woman who had been so kind to her... and whose hospitality Kalina's father had so abused. It did not help that Lady Astrid's expression was a smooth mask of blank neutrality, which fair screamed her displeasure.

"Is your mother not here?" Lady Astrid asked, looking around the room with a frown. "I thought you were in here together."

"No, I... I needed a moment to myself." Kalina's heart was racing in her chest, her empty stomach now filled with butterflies. "Lady Astrid... I..."

"The ballroom is being set up," Lady Astrid interrupted, as though Kalina had not started speaking. She did it so smoothly, it was entirely possible that she had not heard Kalina's stuttering words, but from the way she avoided Kalina's gaze, it was unlikely that was the case. "If you and your mother would like any input on the decorations."

The idea of trying to direct the decoration of Lady Astrid's ballroom for this farce of a wedding made Kalina feel distinctly ill.

"No, thank you." She shook her head. "I am sure you have it well in hand. Lady Astrid... I want you to know... I did not..." Because she had not expected anyone to come to her door, she was ill-prepared. She did not know what she wanted to say, much less how to say it, and yet she could not help but try.

"You did not..." Lady Astrid raised her eyebrow, meeting Kalina's gaze for the first time, and Kalina realized that the other woman was seething. "You did not intend to trap one of my friends into marriage when you accepted the invitation to my home? Or you did not mean to do it so poorly that it was obvious?"

"I... I..." Kalina silently cursed her father for putting her in this position.

"Your father did take advantage of Nathanial's inebriated state to put him in your bed, did he not?" Lady Astrid asked when Kalina could not find her tongue.

Kalina closed her eyes, gripping her skirts in her fists as the shame ran through her. Yes, her father had done exactly that.

"Then, this morning, you and your maid ensured that there were plenty of witnesses with your screams."

Oh gods... they had... though not intentionally. But if Margaret had not screamed, if she had not screamed, perhaps she could have woken Hereford. Shooed him out of her room. Hidden him in the wardrobe. *Something.* But she had reacted in exactly the wrong manner, sealing their fate.

What could she say in her defense? Was there anything at all? Her father had set the events in motion deliberately. Everything that came afterward had been put into place by his design.

She opened her eyes and met Lady Astrid's hard gaze.

"I am sorry." Her voice was a mere thread of a whisper. She was sorry. Sorry for what her father had done. Sorry for her inadvertent role in it. Sorry that the Blackstones' hospitality had been abused by her family.

Lady Astrid huffed, tilting her head back and staring up at the ceiling as if pleading for patience from a higher power. It only took her a moment to regain her control and meet Kalina's eyes again.

"What I do not understand is that we were helping you. We were all *helping you.* You did not need to do... this." She gestured angrily at the bed, directing her feelings about this morning at it in very much the same way Kalina had. "There was no good reason for it."

When Kalina stood there, mute, because she could not think of anything to say—because she did not understand why her father had acted as he had either—Lady Astrid huffed again and whirled around. The door slammed behind her, and, despite the thick carpet in the hall, Kalina could hear her stomping away because she was walking with such angry vehemence.

Slowly, Kalina sank down onto the window seat. Her head dropped, her gaze fixing on a single point on the ornate rug that filled the majority of the room. It felt like she could hardly breathe.

She pressed her hand to her chest, trying to stop the pounding of her heart, to ease the pressure on her chest. It did nothing. The emotions were welling up inside her, refusing to be pushed down, overwhelming her strength. When she closed her eyes, she felt a tear slide down her cheek to drip off the bottom of her chin.

Clenching her jaw did nothing, and a horrible sound escaped as the pain inside her expanded. Grabbing hold of one of the cushions at her side, she curled into a tiny ball and buried her face in its velvet softness to cover the sounds of her broken-hearted sobs.

17

After signing the marriage contract, Nathanial wrote a letter to his sisters, advising them of his upcoming nuptials and that he would be returning home afterward with his new bride. A week or so in the country would give him enough time to set things in place with his new funds and, hopefully, give Society enough time to find some new bit of salacious gossip for them to sink their teeth into. He and Miss Little would return quietly to London and reinsert themselves into the remainder of the Season to thwart any further gossip.

If she wanted a proper honeymoon, she would be disappointed.

Her duty was going to bring him a rich dowry, invigorate the ducal coffers, help him restore what he could of the family's reputation, and guide his sisters through their Seasons to the best of her ability. And bear him an heir.

That last would require...

Blast. His body had reacted in an altogether unwelcome manner, though eventually necessary. But he was angry. He did not want to be aroused. He did not want to be reminded of his damnable attraction to her or the way he had started to question his resistance against that attraction.

Knowing he might have eventually convinced himself to offer for her, only for them to end up together like this… somehow, it made everything worse.

He felt as though he was choking.

He needed to get out of the house.

Striding from Lord Blackstone's study, Nathanial took the back halls in hopes of avoiding the other house party guests as he made his way out to the stables. To his relief, he saw no one but servants along the way. The bustling activity was all for his upcoming wedding, which did nothing to help his mood, but it was far better than having to engage in conversation with anyone.

Reaching the stables, he signaled for a horse. With Miss Little's trepidation around the big beasts, he felt assured she would not follow him out here. Unfortunately, there were others.

He turned at the sound of footsteps behind him and groaned when he saw Christian.

The other duke was frowning at him. He came to a halt several feet away from Nathanial and put his hands on his hips.

"I do not think Miss Little was part of her father's plot," he announced.

The headache from this morning, which had finally started to subside, reemerged with a vengeance. Nathanial gritted his teeth before forcing himself to relax his jaw, as the tension only made his head throb even more.

Thankfully, one of the stableboys was already walking up with a horse for him, a frisky bay gelding who tossed his head like he was eager to run. Good. So was Nathanial.

"This is Caspian," the stableboy said, handing the reins to Nathanial.

Rather than answering Christian's inanity, Nathanial stepped into the stirrup and lifted himself onto Caspian's back. He did not groan when Christian signaled for one of the grooms to bring his own horse. He just kicked Caspian into a gallop, getting out of there as quickly as he could.

Given his head, Caspian eagerly sprang into motion, and they ran pell-mell out of the stable yard and toward the drive. The air rushed by him, stealing his breath, his focus fully on keeping his seat, and he reveled in the rush of freedom. The urge to just ride into the distance, not stopping, never to be seen again, was so strong...

But it was not realistic.

He could not abandon his sisters.

He could not abandon the Milfords.

He could not abandon his tenants.

He could abandon his future wife. Christian, it seemed likely, would step into the breach and save her reputation. Of course, the thought of Christian doing so and being the one to wed and bed Miss Little made him grind his teeth again. Well, it was only natural that he should feel possessive now.

Regardless of how it came to be, she was going to marry him and be his wife.

Jealousy was now not only understandable, it was nearly expected.

It was no wonder that his mood had darkened again by the time Christian caught up with him. He slowed Caspian to a trot, giving the horse a rest, which he needed by now. Though Nathanial had hoped Christian would not be able to find him, he must have gotten lucky in deciding which way to turn down the road.

"Why do you think Miss Little did not know?" he asked. He felt marginally calmer, a little less constricted, but he wished it had been any of his friends other than Christian following him.

On the other hand, the fact that it was only Christian might indicate that Christian was also the only one who believed in Miss Little's innocence. Or it might mean nothing at all.

"Because I do not think it is in her character to trap a man into marriage with her."

"Yes, well, as you have spent so much time with her over the past few days, I am sure you have an accurate measure of every aspect of her character." Nathanial snorted. "Before this morning, would you have said that her father had the character to trap a man into marriage with his daughter?"

"Well…" Christian's hesitation spoke volumes, though he rallied quickly enough. "I have spent more time with Miss Little than her father and gotten a better measure of her. Despite the short length of time."

"Yet somehow, I ended up in her bed last night, slept through the whole night, and she waited to commence her screaming until her maid found us." Nathanial's voice was flat. Emotionless. The anger that he'd been feeling had settled from hot to something deeper, simmering rather than raging.

"She is a very sound sleeper; she also slept through Lady Johanna's departure, and by all accounts, that was a rather noisy production which woke most of the others."

"Or was pretending she's a very sound sleeper part of their plan as well?" Nathanial snorted, shaking his head. "Because she woke up before I did this morning."

"You were snockered."

Caspian danced sideways, and Nathanial realized he was gripping the reins too tightly. He relaxed his fingers as best he could.

"Regardless. She woke and screamed, bringing everyone to her room. I'm kneeling on the floor vomiting into a chamber pot while her dad is shouting at me like he's on Drury Lane, ensuring everyone down the hall can hear him. And they can, because *now* she and her maid have gone silent for him to be heard clearly." The more he thought about it, the more certain he was.

Everything had ticked by like clockwork.

Surely, that could not be coincidence.

If he was convinced of anything, it was that Mr. Little loved his daughter. He wanted her to be happy.

Why would he participate in trapping Nathanial into marriage with her, unless he thought it would make her happy? Why they, or she, had chosen him rather than Christian, who had actually been showing interest in her, unless for some reason they thought he was the better option?

"For Mr. Little's purposes, it hardly matters *which* duke she marries. Unless, of course, it matters to her. For some reason, though

I have done my best not to encourage her, while you have done the opposite, she must have chosen me." His tone was grim, his barely suppressed anger thrumming just beneath the surface. Caspian was becoming anxious again, reading his rider's mood, but Nathanial was doing his best under the circumstances.

"And what is so wrong with that?" Christian's horse was also becoming agitated, as was he. Exasperation hung in the air around him, marring the beauty of the blue sky above him. "You'll have a wife who meets the vast majority of your requirements. You know that the rest of us will support you and your sisters when they make their come-outs. Lady Astrid and Tiffany would both be happy to guide them. I think the only reason you are upset is because you set your mind against her for some reason, even though you wanted her, and the only reason you are upset now is because you did not get to hem and haw before changing your mind and choosing her."

"Yes! Exactly!" Nathanial knew he was shouting, but at this point, he did not care. Caspian was dancing beneath him, and only the fact that he was an excellent rider allowed him to keep his seat. "I did not get to choose her. I had one choice left in my life, one place where I was only *partially* boxed in, where I had some say in how my life was going to go. You do not think it important because you *have* choices. You do not have to marry this Season if you do not want to. You do not have to do anything you do not want to do."

Christian's mouth dropped open in shock or perhaps to say something, but it did not matter. Nathanial was speaking too quickly, too loudly, to be stopped.

"If you want to rut your way through London's actresses while pretending you're searching for a bride and ending the Season without one, you can. No one will even be disappointed in you because your father is no longer around to see you doing the opposite of what he wanted. We both know you were not going to propose to Miss Little, and it is not because you were concerned over my feelings for her. It is because then you would actually be fulfilling your duties and doing what your father wanted. And you will not do that, even though the man is in the grave and will have no idea that you have finally lived up to just one of his expectations."

Panting, Nathanial had finally run out of breath. Christian stared at him, paler than he had ever seen the other man, his eyes wide and wild. He looked as if he was in pain.

Which was exactly how Nathanial felt.

Though he also knew he had gone too far.

His tongue flicked out, wetting his lips.

"Christian—"

It was too late. Christian had already whirled his horse's head around, and now he was the one galloping away from Nathanial. Running away from the truths he had not wanted to face and which Nathanial had not meant to throw at him. Closing his eyes, Nathanial took in a deep breath.

He wished Christian had not followed him out here.

But it was too late.

Too late for so many things.

Letting out the breath, Nathanial gave himself a little shake. Then he turned Caspian's head in the opposite direction from where Christian had gone.

He was alone.

Just like he wanted.

Giving the gelding his head again, Nathanial let the world rush by him in a blur of green and brown and yellow. The sun beat down on him, but with the wind in his face, he did not feel the heat.

By the time he turned around and headed back toward the manor, he was feeling marginally better. Part of him wanted to find Christian and apologize... but he was also aware of the apology owed to himself. No, he should not have said what he'd said, but he also would have never said it if Christian had not pushed him so far. If he had not felt as though Christian was taking Miss Little's side over his.

Still.

He would apologize.

Now that the bitter edge of rage had been taken off, he mostly felt tired. He did not want to be quarreling with one of his friends in addition to everything else.

"Nathanial!" Christian's voice came from behind him, and Nathanial pulled Caspian up, half turning in the saddle.

Cantering up behind him was Christian, smiling widely, as he always did.

"How was your ride?" Christian asked as he drew level, slowing his horse to a walk. He spoke again before Nathanial could answer, as if he had not just asked a question, his demeanor aggressively cheerful. "I found a lovely little field filled with bluebells. We should arrange an excursion there tomorrow if we have the time."

Ah, so it was going to be like that. Nathanial heaved an inner sigh. How very like Christian to ride off, then return, acting as though nothing had happened. It made everything much easier, yet harder, too. Part of him also wanted to ignore the necessary apology and just carry on.

"I have a feeling I will be busy," Nathanial replied dryly. "Perhaps after I leave, you can lead the charge."

"Tomorrow?" Christian raised his eyebrow in question. "That *is* quick."

Nathanial shrugged.

"No sense in waiting." And he wanted to get it over with. The more it dragged out, the harder it was going to be to keep his temper under control. He'd told Christian that his choices had been taken from him, but the truth was they'd narrowed again to a single choice —when he was to wed.

He wanted to get it done with, then he would have more choices again once he was married.

That was part of what he'd realized on his ride once he'd had some time to think. Marrying Miss Little meant he could take control over aspects of his life that he had not previously had control over. That was the upside. Almost enough to soothe his rage over how it had been done.

However, he would have to wait and see how it affected his sisters' prospects before he could fully settle with the warring emotions inside him.

Clearing his throat, he glanced over at Christian.

"I need to apologize—"

"As do I. I apologize as well. There, now you apologized, and I apologized, and we need not speak of it again." The serene expression on Christian's face, the evenness of his tone, carried a warning.

Nathanial sighed, exasperated. He had not actually apologized, but he also knew that pressing Christian further would only lead to the other man riding off again. Running was Christian's favored method of dealing with anything he found even the slightest bit uncomfortable.

He should have expected this reaction.

"Do you think there will be pudding this evening?" Christian asked, the question appearing to be the only thing on his mind as he looked up at the sky. "I could do with a good pudding."

"I am sure you could," Nathanial replied wryly.

They finished the ride up the drive. Feeling eyes on him, Nathanial looked up at the front face of the manor.

In one of the windows, a floor above his own, there was a silhouette, barely visible. He was rather forcibly reminded of how he and Matthew had watched Miss Little and her family arrive from very nearly that same position. If he'd known then what he knew now about their plans for this house party, would he have run?

He certainly would not have accepted any drinks from Mr. Little.

Was it Miss Little watching him now?

Was she feeling triumphant? Or had she begun to regret what her actions had wrought?

He supposed it did not matter. They would both be living with the consequences of those actions for the rest of their lives.

Grimly setting his jaw, Nathanial dropped his gaze and determinedly did not look up again as he and Christian rode past the house toward the stables. Tomorrow, once Drake returned with the special license, he would be married to her.

Plenty of couples married under less-than-ideal circumstances. One way or another, he would find a way to live with it.

He had no other choice.

18

———————

Rather than eating supper with everyone, Kalina requested a tray in her room. She had managed at breakfast, but she could not face the throng again. Could not face their suspicious gazes, the unspoken questions hanging in the air around them. And she did not want to see her father. Not right now. Not yet.

Especially in front of others, where she would have to pretend she was not wildly upset with him.

It was difficult enough doing so when her mother was the only important audience member.

She was midway through her meal when there was a knock at her door.

Kalina froze.

There was no help for it, though. Everyone must know she was in here. She could always pretend she had gone to bed early...

But maybe it was her father. While she had eschewed her chance to see him over dinner, in complete privacy without her mother present would not be so bad. It might also be her mother if she had finished her meal and retreated early.

Getting to her feet, Kalina brushed off her skirts to straighten them and went to answer it.

Not her mother. Not her father.

Tiffany.

Looking quite splendid in a navy-blue dress with silver trim and embroidery covering the hem of her skirt and sleeves. Tiny diamonds sparkled around larger sapphires in a ring around her neck and hanging from her ears. Her hazel eyes were wide and assessing as she watched Kalina appear.

Kalina's chest tightened at the sight of her friend on the other side of the small opening.

"Hello," she said in a low voice, unsure of how to greet the other young woman.

"Can we speak?" Tiffany blurted out the words like she was feeling just as uncertain as Kalina was, which helped a little.

Nodding, Kalina stepped back, opening the door wider to allow Tiffany entry into the room. Tiffany swept in, walking quickly, and she wondered if the duchess did not wish to be seen consorting with Kalina. It was entirely possible. Sighing inwardly and steeling herself for another scolding akin to the one Lady Astrid had delivered, Kalina closed the door behind her.

Rather than speaking immediately, Tiffany went over to Kalina's bed and turned, sitting down on the edge and staring at her. Since the duchess was sitting, Kalina decided to return to her meal. It was the first thing she'd been able to stomach eating all day, and she was ravenous.

Tiffany watched her, waiting until Kalina was seated before she spoke.

"I am sorry it took me so long to come and speak with you," Tiffany said, folding her hands in her lap as she watched Kalina.

Of course, once she'd said that, Kalina did not bring the bite of fish to her mouth, too startled that Tiffany was beginning with an apology.

"I needed to think, because I was very confused by the events of this morning."

Well, she was not the only one, so Kalina could hardly blame her for that. She put her fork down, trying to think of how to reasonably respond without betraying her father. But should she protect him? It was one thing with her mother, but if she could have a least one friend who understood that she truly had not meant to trap the Duke of Hereford into marriage with her...

Looking down at her hands, Tiffany took a deep breath.

"My problem is that I am struggling to believe that you would trap someone into marriage, even though I know you have been aiming for a duke. You have always been open about that aim. I cannot reconcile someone who is so open with someone who would hatch such a plot." Tiffany looked at Kalina again, her brow furrowed, obviously questioning.

"If your aim had always been to trap a duke, you would have been wiser to hide your desire for a duke from the beginning. Similarly, if you were going to trap a duke, Christian would have been the wiser choice, especially after the way he was dancing attendance on you the past few days. There are several dukes you could marry, including my own brother. At the moment, there has been no reason to rush to the altar... unless you are with child?"

"No!" Kalina's shocked rejection seemed to reassure Tiffany, whose shoulders relaxed slightly. Kalina's fork clanged against the dish as she set it down, shaking her head. "Absolutely not."

"Then I have to ask myself. Why last night? And why Nathanial?"

Pressing her lips together, Kalina fought against the instinct to tell Tiffany everything. But her friend was observant. And she had spent the day thinking about everything rather than jumping to conclusions.

Tiffany nodded at Kalina's silence.

"There. See? You are angry. You are very good at hiding it, but it is there. You do not have the answers to those questions, either, and if you had been part of the trap, you would."

"I *am* angry," Kalina finally admitted, sagging. "I am sad and furious."

"Why did you not say something? Why did you let Astrid think that you were a willing participant?" Tiffany asked. "She told me of your conversation. She said you apologized."

"Because it *was* my father." Kalina bent forward, giving up all pretense of formality. She buried her face in her hands, so she did not have to look at Tiffany as she spoke, the guilt and shame welling up inside her. "My father trapped Nathanial. I reacted exactly the wrong way. She was correct when she confronted me; if I had been quieter, if I had not screamed, I might have been able to waken him and sneak him out of my room with none the wiser. I might not have known, but I did participate, out of surprise and ignorance."

"Oh... my dear..." Tiffany got up from her seat on the bed and came over to embrace Kalina about the shoulders, pressing Kalina's face to her midriff. The firmness of her stays was not entirely comfortable against Kalina's cheek, but she did not want to move. At least one of her friends did not hate her. One of her friends had seen the truth, even before Kalina had tried to explain it. She would tolerate far more than a little discomfort for that.

Tiffany released her, crouching down so she could look up into Kalina's face, their hands held together in Kalina's lap. The ache in Kalina's chest was growing again. She could have sworn she had no tears left after this afternoon, but her eyes were beginning to sting.

"You are not to blame for your father's actions," she said firmly. "Unless you knew what he planned ahead of time and did not stop him, there is no fault to you."

Kalina shook her head, too afraid to try to speak because she might start sobbing over Tiffany's compassion if she opened her mouth now.

Tiffany's voice dropped to a mutter. "Trust me, if anyone has learned we are not responsible for how our parents behave, it is me."

Though she was uncertain why Tiffany would claim such deep knowledge, though she was beginning to suspect that the Dowager Duchess of Bolton's retreat to the country might not have to do with a desire for fresh air, Kalina nodded. She took a deep breath, steeling herself against the threatening tears.

"I do not want my mother to know," she admitted. "She is so

angry with my father already. If she thought I was unhappy with the outcome, she would be even more so."

"Are you unhappy with the outcome?" Tiffany asked, peering up at her. "I think that is also partly what has Astrid convinced—despite Christian's attentions, you and Nathanial seemed drawn together over and over."

Kalina's shoulders hunched.

"I... I feel a connection with him," she admitted. "If I were to choose which man to marry..." Not that she had been given a choice. "Though, perhaps Christian would be the better choice. Going by which man showed interest in me."

Tiffany studied her for a long moment.

"Perhaps. Or perhaps if he were given the opportunity for a true choice, Nathanial would have chosen you, too." Tiffany hesitated. "He has his reasons for holding back from you, but in some ways, I think the two of you are a better match than you and Christian would be."

Kalina could only hope.

Though even if her soon-to-be husband was furious with her and believed she had trapped him, she could live with it now that she had at least one friend who knew the truth.

Nathanial

It was a rather strange stag night, gathered with his friends in the billiards room of Blackstone Manor. He did not have the heart to play. Neither did he want to drink. Instead, he slowly sipped some water while watching Matthew and Christian compete.

Billiards was one of the few arenas in which Matthew's luck was not a factor, evening the playing field between him and his friends. Christian was currently winning and grinning from ear to ear over it, while Matthew was scowling and grumbling under his breath.

"This feels rather more like a funeral than is comfortable," Gregory said, going for a bit of levity as he often did. He held a crystal snifter in his hand, the amber liquid inside it practically glowing in the gas lamplight. Leaning back in the heavy armchair he occupied, he glanced over at Nathanial. "Are you sure you will not have a drink?"

"That's what got me into this mess in the first place."

"Exactly, so it can hardly make things worse now."

Despite himself, Nathanial snorted. It rather felt like gallows humor, but he could not help the spurt of amusement. Gregory was good at that.

"It could certainly be worse," Matthew pointed out, turning his attention to the conversation rather than to the table where Christian was lining up a winning shot. "She could be a poor title hunter with no dowry. And ugly. And stupid. Instead, you're going to have a beautiful, rich, clever wife."

Matthew did have a way with words.

"What are you going to do if your coin decides on an ugly, poor, stupid wife for you?" Sebastian asked with some real curiosity. "Or are you banking on the idea that it would never do such a thing?"

The Lord of Luck blinked, caught off-kilter by the question. This time, Nathanial's snort of amusement was not at all reluctant. Clearly, Matthew had never considered that his luck might go so awry.

"Do not listen to Sebastian; he described his own sister as plain and dull." Gregory shook his head. "He has no idea how to judge a woman's attributes."

That made all of them laugh as Sebastian scowled. They'd all heard Sebastian's descriptions, of course. Tiffany's style, under Lady Astrid's tutelage, had certainly improved, and she was far more fashionable now, wearing clothing that flattered her much more than her previous attire. Nathanial could only assume her mother's influence had been to her detriment. Older women could become rather set in their ways, especially with fashion.

Yet, despite her beauty, she had never stirred him the way Miss Little did.

Christian let out a shout of triumph as he won the billiards match against Matthew, thrusting one fist into the air. Sighing, Matthew turned away and put the stick back in its holder on the wall.

"Anyone for cards?" he asked hopefully.

"Only if you pay me every time you win," Gregory joked.

"There is an interesting experiment—would Matthew's luck still have him winning the game, or would he begin losing because winning would have a different outcome?" Christian mused.

Before Matthew could respond, the door to the billiards room opened, and Drake and Zachary came striding in. As usual, Zachary's monkey was riding on his shoulder, one tiny paw in Zachary's hair, his little tail curled around Zachary's neck. Rescued from an ill-tempered owner at a ball earlier in the Season, the monkey was thoroughly attached to Zachary, who had decided to name it after Sinclair, the only member of their little group to meet his untimely demise before finding a wife and heir. Well, the only member so far, but that was a black thought Nathanial pushed away from his mind. Sinclair's tragic and unexpected death had been the catalyst for all of them to put more effort into the search for a bride.

The new arrivals were immediately met with glad greetings, especially Monkey Sinclair, who accepted the attention with gravitas worthy of a duke.

"I was not sure you would come," Nathanial admitted. Since Zachary had not initially been a guest for the house party, he would not have blamed the other man for refusing the invitation now.

"And miss your wedding?" Zachary shook his head. "Besides, I needed to quit London while I had the chance. Being the only unmarried duke in the city was hardly a comfortable experience. Worse, my mother has begun campaigning for me to marry Lady Annabelle."

"Lady Annabelle Walsh?" Sebastian asked.

"Yes." Zachary cast a dark look at Drake, who was already moving to the drink cart to get himself a glass. "She has decided the only thing that will truly make her happy now is if I marry her best friend's daughter. I can only imagine where she got that idea."

"If she had asked me, I would have told her it was a poor choice," Drake replied blandly. He glanced at Zachary. "Drink?"

"Please." Zachary's tone was fervent, and he reached up to stroke a finger along Monkey Sinclair's back. The little creature chittered and leaned against Zachary's head.

Out of all of their coterie, Zachary had been the closest to Sinclair. That he was taking some comfort in his new pet was good.

"Has Lady Annabelle met Sinclair?" Sebastian asked, nodding at the monkey. Zachary made a face.

"No." His tone was clipped as he answered. So far, Monkey Sinclair had shown an aversion to women, with one singular exception—Zachary's ex-mistress, the Baroness Ashfield. Who was also a house guest, as she was one of Lady Astrid's close friends and very likely the reason Zachary had not been invited to the house party in the first place. The pair's feelings for each other made their separation extremely awkward whenever they occupied the same room.

Likely, Lady Astrid had meant to give the baroness a respite from Zachary's presence during the house party, but Fate had had other plans.

"Perhaps if you are averse to marrying her, you should hasten with the introduction," Gregory suggested, a mischievous light in his eyes.

"I think I will have to keep Monkey Sinclair away from her for as long as possible." Zachary sighed, resignation writ in every line of his body. "For the first time, my mother has been... lighter, I suppose is the best word. No longer so mired in her grief. I am reluctant to negate the change prematurely."

"You are not actually going to marry a woman just to please your mother, are you?" Sebastian sounded utterly horrified.

From the expression on Zachary's face and his lack of immediate response, he was considering doing just that.

"Let us talk about something else. Especially in a house where Delilah is also present." Zachary took a long sip of his drink. The pain in his eyes when he said his ex-mistress' name was impossible to miss. The daft fool. He had choices, and he was making all the wrong ones. "Have I missed anything other than Nathanial tripping into the parson's trap?"

They all exchanged looks.

"Just Lady Johanna's rather abrupt departure," Matthew offered up. It was the only other event of note, considering how little time they'd spent. They all fell to discussing the lady and her companion, as well as her middle-of-the-night retreat, before moving on to prodding Zachary to update them on the latest *ton* gossip.

Zachary regaled them with the story of the Countess of Spencer *accidentally* putting a fork through Lady Hatchet's hand. No one believed it was an accident, of course, as Lady Hatchet had put said hand on the Earl of Spencer only half an hour before the unfortunate incident, and onlookers had described the lady's demeanor as decidedly flirtatious. He'd shown her no interest, but it hardly mattered.

While Spencer had had a reputation for being an unmitigated rake before his marriage, his countess had an even stronger reputation for being both wild and possessive. She did not take kindly to ladies importuning her husband, despite his disinterest in the charms of any lady but his wife. His attitude had become something of a challenge for the *ton's* bored matrons, but they did so at the risk of the countess' displeasure... as Lady Hatchet had discovered.

Nathanial wondered what kind of wife Miss Little would be.

He frowned at the idea that she might become one of the bored *ton* matrons in search of an accomplished rake to warm her bed.

Equally, the idea of her being possessive of him made him feel rather pleased.

Which made him frown all the more.

This marriage was an arrangement he had been trapped into, nothing more. He should not care whether his wife was possessive of him or not. That he felt so of her would likely wear off once she'd borne him an heir. It was only natural that he would want to be the only man in her bed before she had fulfilled her duty.

That was it.

Nothing more.

19

The night before her wedding was the worst night of sleep Kalina had ever had. For the first time in her life, every time she started to drift, a noise would jerk her awake. She felt like she heard everything.

The whisper of a lady's skirts out in the hall, passing by her door.

The murmur of someone's voice coming from another room.

The hooting of the owl outside.

It did not matter that the damage had already been done, and there was no reason for anyone to appear in her room now; she could not fully relax enough to sleep. When Margaret knocked on her door and entered in the morning, she jerked awake at the sound.

"Good morning, miss," Margaret said, her voice forcefully cheerful.

"Good morning." Kalina said the words, though she did not truly believe them. Forcing herself to sit up, she blinked as Margaret opened the heavy curtains, revealing a gray and cloudy day. Perfect to go with her mood.

Margaret cleared her throat.

"I've been told to get your things ready to move this afternoon," the maid said, looking nervously at Kalina to gauge her reaction.

"Apparently, the duke has decided that you two will immediately remove to his estate following the ceremony."

"I see." Kalina rubbed her forehead. It made sense. Beginning their marriage under the scrutiny of Lady Astrid's guests hardly sounded appealing. Especially since her father numbered among them, and she presumed that feelings between her soon-to-be husband and her father would be strained, to say the least.

But she also wished she had her mother and Tiffany nearby for support.

Tiffany had promised she would speak to Lady Astrid and Delilah about Kalina's innocence in the entrapment of Hereford. She had also offered to stand for Kalina today, which Kalina would be forever grateful for. One friend standing by her side was more than she had hoped for yesterday morning.

"You will be coming with me?" Kalina asked Margaret, who nodded firmly, to her relief. She would have insisted if Hereford had tried to dismiss her lady's maid, but she was glad not to have to add to their already rocky start.

"Just try to keep me away," she said darkly, which made Kalina smile. Margaret's protectiveness over her was very appreciated at the moment. Giving herself a little shake, the maid pushed a smile onto her lips. "Now, then. You need to look your absolute best today. I'll send for a tray from the kitchen, then work on your hair."

"Thank you, Margaret." Filled with gratitude, Kalina got to her feet and pulled on her dressing gown while Margaret bustled around.

She managed to eat a little while Margaret brushed and began to curl and pin her hair. Though her stomach was decidedly uneasy, it did settle somewhat once there was something in it. By the time there was another knock at her door, her hair was perfectly coiffed, and she had on her erstwhile wedding dress. Margaret had just done up the last button.

Hurrying over to the door, Margaret stepped back.

"Lady Astrid, miss."

Sweeping into the room, Lady Astrid gave Kalina a searching

look. Immediately, Kalina bobbed into a curtsy, the way she would have before they'd become friends. The lady scowled.

"Oh, stop that. I am seriously displeased, angry even, but that does not mean you should go back to treating me as though we are not friends." The lady's tone was waspish, but Kalina was strangely glad to hear it because there was also some warmth to it. Unlike yesterday when she'd been so distantly cold. Especially because of what Lady Astrid was saying.

With how angry she had been yesterday, Kalina had assumed their friendship was over. Now, she was not so certain.

As always, Lady Astrid was intimidatingly resplendent, even more so than usual, as she was dressed for the wedding. Her gown was the deep orange of a sunset, patterned with thin stripes which were a paler shade of the same color, and trimmed with creamy lace. Rows of copper bands ringed the bottom of her skirt, adding another touch of decoration to the stunning assembly. Like Kalina, her auburn hair was pulled back, curled, and coiffed to perfection.

Crossing her arms over her chest, she glanced at Margaret, as if trying to decide whether to dismiss Kalina's ladies' maid. Rather than forcing the issue, Margaret seemed to decide that Kalina was safe with Lady Astrid and quickly sank into a curtsy before exiting the room and closing the door behind her. Leaving them alone.

Arms still crossed, Lady Astrid looked at Kalina, tilting her head as if trying to think of what she was going to say. Though Kalina could not see her feet, she got the distinct impression that Lady Astrid was tapping one of them.

"I spoke with Tiffany this morning. And Mei. Both of whom felt I misunderstood you during our last conversation." Lady Astrid scowled. "You apologized for trapping Hereford into marriage. Yet Tiffany made some very astute points about the illogic of your actions if you were, indeed, involved in his presence in your room. Did your father act without your knowledge?" It was more than a question; it was a demand for information, for the truth.

Kalina hesitated because she hated feeling as though she was betraying her father, but she nodded. He *had* done the deed. In some ways, it could be said that he had betrayed her first.

Lady Astrid sighed, dropping her arms.

"Then I must apologize for losing my temper yesterday and the way I spoke to you." She smiled ruefully. "Tiffany thinks before she acts... or reacts. I have a tendency to do the exact opposite. And once I'd had more time to think, I had to agree with all the points she made."

"There is no need to apologize," Kalina said hastily. "You were upset, rightfully so. I also reacted poorly in the moment, and I did not know what to do to make things right. I also... I know my father's actions were dishonorable, but..." She spread her hands helplessly. "He's still my father."

She wanted to protect him.

He was her father. Despite what he'd done, she loved him.

Lady Astrid huffed.

"Yes, well. Family can be complicated." She smiled wanly. "Sometimes, we do incomprehensible things for their sake." The way she said it made Kalina think that she was not actually talking about Kalina and her father, but about herself. Perhaps something to do with the fact that she was betrothed to the son of her mother's closest friend, even though she claimed not to be able to stand the man.

"Thank you for understanding," Kalina whispered, unable to speak any louder as her throat clogged up. She could hardly have enough water left in her body for a single tear, yet it felt as though she might cry again from sheer relief.

"I am sorry I did not take the time to listen to you yesterday." Lady Astrid stepped forward, holding out her hands, which Kalina gratefully took, and they exchanged cheek kisses. When they pulled apart, Lady Astrid kept hold of her hands, and Kalina blinked back the threatening tears. "I believe you can expect Delilah to speak with you at some point today as well. She wanted to come with me, but well..." Lady Astrid shrugged. "If I must apologize for something, I prefer to do so without an audience."

Kalina could not help but laugh. That sounded very like Lady Astrid.

She had not lost her friends.

Knowing that, she could face anything. Even this travesty of a wedding day.

NATHANIAL

The points of his collar were digging into his chin.

"Stop fidgeting," Matthew murmured. "You look like you are about to crawl out of your skin."

He felt as though he was going to crawl out of his skin.

Tiffany was walking down the aisle wearing a cornflower-blue gown, serenely smiling as though this was an anticipated, planned event. Despite her beauty, everyone was watching *him* far more closely than they were watching her procession. He could only hope when Miss Little appeared at the end of the aisle, he might get some respite from the scrutiny.

Though his friends all gave him supportive looks, the rest of the guests were avidly watching for his reactions. Likely tallying their thoughts for when they returned to London to spread the gossip. The best thing he could do was appear calm, collected, and unbothered by the unusual circumstances that had brought him to the altar.

"I think you need a new coin," Nathanial whispered back, even though he knew that would never happen. He was still annoyed that Matthew had flipped it for him and Miss Little, then shared the outcome in front of everyone.

Matthew snorted softly.

Tiffany took her place opposite them, back far enough that there would be space for Miss Little to stand. She caught Nathanial's gaze and gave him a smile that was both sympathetic and encouraging. He looked away. Down the aisle to where the doors were currently closed.

The music shifted. Swelled. His jaw locked as the doors swung open, revealing Miss Little and her father. She was not wearing a veil, so her expression was completely visible to everyone.

Calm. Collected. Looking at her face, no one would think that she was harboring an iota of trepidation and certainly no remorse for how she had come to be walking down the aisle. Beside her, her father's expression was also quite blank, but in his case, it was easy to see behind the mask.

Mr. Little was very happy, though he was taking pains to hide it. Unlike his daughter, he was not as good an actor.

Something else for Nathanial to keep in mind and be wary of. His bride's acting ability would have won her accolades at the Royal Theater. If he'd had any doubts about her talent after waking in her bed, seeing her performance now would have wiped them away.

The only thing that gave away any emotion other than serene contentment was the way her hand trembled when it was placed in his, and he would not have known if they had not been touching.

The dress she was wearing was the palest pink he'd seen her in thus far, lending a more bridal quality to her attire, even without the veil. Her bow-lips were slightly parted, heavy lashes concealing her lowered gaze from him as Reverend Kilpatrick began the wedding ceremony. Nathanial glanced out at the enraptured audience.

Mr. Little was still attempting to appear somber, but there was a little smile curving the edge of his lips. Beside him, Mrs. Little appeared worried, as did the younger Little. Rupert sat beside Miss Little's brother, frowning at Nathanial for some reason. Behind them were the Blackstones and Delilah, whom he assumed had chosen Miss Little's side of the guests because Drake and Zachary were seated on his. The two matchmakers were there as well.

Gathered on Nathanial's side were his friends. Gregory was watching Tiffany, unsurprisingly, while the rest of them gave Nathanial bracing nods of encouragement. Even the sight of Monkey Sinclair, wearing his own little cravat and miniature top hat while perched on Zachary's shoulder, could not coax a smile to Nathanial's lips at this moment. The rest of the guests were divided between the two sides. The number of chairs provided matched the number of guests exactly, ensuring an equal spread between the two.

Nathanial dragged his attention back to the ceremony as Reverend Kilpatrick guided Miss Little through her wedding vows. She was so focused on the words, she forgot not to look at him when she finished.

Their gazes clashed.

Her dark eyes were wide, fathomless, and his breath caught in his throat. She looked utterly innocent, completely guileless. The attraction that had always simmered between them caught and held, practically pulsing in the air around them.

"Your Grace, please repeat after me," Reverend Kilpatrick said. "I, Nathanial Archibald Montgomery Percy."

Clearing his throat, Nathanial shook off the spell that his bride's gaze had woven around him.

"I, Nathanial Archibald Montgomery Percy..."

Less than ten minutes later, the parson's trap had fully closed around him, and Nathanial was leading his new wife down the aisle, feeling as though his life had turned upside down. What it would look like from here on out, he could hardly begin to fathom.

20

Since she had never been to an English wedding, Kalina did not know how hers measured up, but she imagined there were not usually so many whispers and sidelong glances at the bride and groom. She also rather thought that the bride and groom likely spoke more than two words to each other during the meal.

Instead, Nathanial spoke mostly with Tiffany, who was on his right, and Kalina spoke mostly with the Duke of St. Albans, who was on her left. Eventually, she excused herself to go to the retiring room, which was where Delilah sought her out. Like Lady Astrid and Tiffany before her, the other lady apologized. Kalina reassured her that no such apology was needed.

"It is difficult for me," Delilah confessed quietly, brushing a lock of black hair away from her face. The lemon-colored ribbon she had woven through her curls matched the lemon dress she was wearing. The bright color was trimmed with black, which made it stand out all the more. "My first husband, the baron…"

Her voice trailed off, and Kalina's eyes widened in horrified realization.

"He… in your bed?"

"Oh no, thankfully." Delilah shook her head. "He did not ravish me, but he did not need to. All he had to do was arrange a scene at a ball, where we were caught out alone together, and he kissed me. I allowed it, thinking that he loved me. I did not know at the time that he was after my dowry." She smiled thinly. "Of course, I had to marry him, anyway, and we rubbed along well enough. Though you would think I would have learned my lesson about believing a man's protestations of love from that."

Kalina squeezed her friend's hand, not knowing what to say. At least now she understood why Delilah had drawn away so quickly.

With all of her friends, their withdrawals had actually had very little to do with their belief in her guilt and far more to do with their personal reactions to what had happened. It had hurt horribly, but now that she understood, she felt so much better.

If only she could have a similar moment with her new husband… but from Hereford's closed expression, she did not think he would welcome any such coming together. Not now. Not yet. But she could have hope that he would come around to it eventually, just as her friends had.

As she and Delilah left the retiring room, she found her father there waiting for her. Immediately, Delilah excused herself and went onward. Kalina suppressed the urge to join her. She stared at her father, trying to think of what to say. This was the first time they had been alone, without witnesses. Even before, when he'd been about to walk her down the aisle, there had been footmen present, waiting to open the doors for them.

Her father smiled hopefully at her, stirring the anger and frustration that she'd been pushing down inside her ever since she'd awoken to the Duke of Hereford in her bed. Taking a deep breath, she shoved her unruly emotions down again. They did not have time for her to vent them right now, even if she was not acutely aware of the nearby witnesses. She had kept herself under control from the moment she'd walked out of her room, applying a social mask to hide everything she was truly thinking and feeling, and she did not intend to allow it to crack now.

"Kalina... I..." Her father groped for whatever it was he wanted to say. Kalina raised her eyebrow at him. "I just want you to know that I have never wanted anything but your happiness."

Another deep breath, because if she did not breathe in, then she would end up screaming. Her lungs filled to capacity, so much that her chest ached, and she let out the air on a slow exhale.

"You thought that trapping me into marriage with the Duke of Hereford would make me happy?" Somehow, she managed to keep her tone low and even, rather than shrieking the words at him the way she wanted to.

"I thought that you might have been about to make a terrible mistake that would make you unhappy." He held out his hand. Despite everything, Kalina could not bring herself to reject him. She put her hand in his, and he gave her fingers a supportive squeeze. "The Duke of Montagu was working his way around to proposing to you. But Hereford... you two have a connection. Very akin to the one your mother and I had in our early days. But he was fighting it for nothing more than societal reasons. He would have come around eventually, I believe, but by then it might have been too late if Montagu had beaten him to the offer."

Closing her eyes, Kalina fought with her inner demons. The impulse to shriek at her father was very strong.

"Did it not occur to you that each of those was our choice to make?"

"You would not have been happy married to Montagu, not with how you felt about Hereford. Nor would *he* be happy." Metaphorically digging in his heels, her father's tone was so certain, so sure of himself, she despaired of making him understand. "Hereford will eventually realize that you had nothing to do with trapping him. Then you can both be happy together."

She hoped so. She truly did.

However, she was not nearly as certain as her father about such an outcome.

There was also no point in railing at him, no matter how much she wanted to. Kalina swallowed her temper. Her father did want her to be happy more than anything; she believed that. He had acted rashly, unwisely even, but his intentions were pure. That had to count for something.

Besides, it was too late to put the cat back in the bag, regardless. Burying her emotions, Kalina nodded.

"Let us hope," she murmured. She squeezed his hand back. "I know you meant well, Father, but you must promise to let me, and Hereford, make our own choices in the future."

"I promise." Pulling her toward him, he embraced her in a hug, which she returned. Resting her head on his shoulder, the same way she had done as a little girl when he was her hero who could do no wrong, Kalina closed her eyes. If only she had known back then how simple her life was compared to what she would face as a debutante, she might have been more grateful.

"I love you, my little Kalina."

"I love you too, Father. Thank you for trying to ensure my happiness." Maybe if she repeated it enough times, she would be able to release her upset with him.

There was a long moment, and then the sound of someone clearing their throat came from down the hall. Despite the lack of words or tone, somehow it managed to convey displeasure. Kalina's eyes flew open.

Her husband stood at the junction between the hallways, watching her and her father's embrace, a dark expression on his face.

"It is time to go," he said, without preamble. Then he turned and walked away before she or her father could respond.

Letting her go, her father patted her shoulder.

"Do not worry, all will turn out right in the end," he reassured her.

But Kalina was not a little girl anymore, and she knew better than to believe him.

<u>*Nathanial*</u>

Well, that clinched that.

His new wife had clearly snowed her friends. Lady Astrid was no longer keeping her at arm's length, nor were Tiffany or Delilah. Somehow, she had convinced them of her innocence in trapping him.

But they had not seen her father and her secretly embracing, obviously in congratulations over the success of their plan.

They had not heard her thank her father for ensuring her happiness.

Every muscle in his body felt tight and stiff with rage. It was a wonder he could see straight, as his vision felt fogged, tinged with red. Only the number of guests around them, the necessity of keeping a stiff upper lip in front of the gossipmongers, kept him from losing his temper entirely.

At least he'd had the foresight to have a horse saddled for himself, while a carriage had been prepared for his duchess and her maid. He would not be forced to ride the hours to Hereford Hall with her in close quarters. Perhaps by the time they arrived, he would be in a better frame of mind.

Even if he was not, he would no longer have to playact for an audience of the *ton*. Nor would he have to see her father, which would do a great deal for his temperament.

Striding to the front of the house where the Blackstones waited, along with Mrs. Little, who had a strained expression on her face despite the company of the Dowager Duchess of Clarence, Nathanial made his bow to the hosts. Lady Astrid stood next to her mother, sympathy on her expression, but also a kind of sternness that he was used to seeing from her. She was no longer fully on his side.

As much as he wanted to tell her about what he had just witnessed between Miss Little and her father—no, between the now Duchess of Hereford and her father—this was hardly the time and place. Especially with so many others about.

He waited, albeit impatiently, until his wife came into the foyer on her father's arm. Though her expression was utterly blank, her father seemed even happier than he had earlier in the day.

Farewells were exchanged, and Nathanial thanked the Blackstones for their hospitality and for being up to the challenge of holding an unplanned event. Lady Blackstone happily reassured him that it had been no trouble at all, especially as Astrid had taken on the bulk of the responsibility. She often did. Though today, Lady Blackstone's eyes were clear and bright, and she appeared to be feeling very well indeed.

If only Nathanial could say the same.

Escorting his wife down the stairs and to the carriage, Nathanial did not meet her gaze as he helped her up into the confines. Her maid quickly followed.

"Madam," he said stiffly, giving her a nod before stepping away.

One of the grooms was standing to the side with the horse he would be using to return home. That was one upside to his marriage. After today, he would be able to purchase his own horses and his own carriage, and provide for their upkeep. He would no longer need to rely on the generosity of others.

Trying to keep that thought firmly in his mind, rather than his bride's duplicity, he mounted the energetic bay gelding. Glancing up at the front façade of Blackstone Manor, he was unsurprised to see multiple faces lining the windows, from all the rooms on the first floor.

The Blackstones themselves, along with the Littles, had trooped out onto the front stairs to wave. His friends were grouped together at two windows. Both Gregory and Sebastian appeared sympathetic, while Christian was frowning at Nathanial as if *he* was the one who had done something wrong. Zachary and Drake both appeared more somber. Matthew was the only one who was grinning. When he caught Nathanial's gaze, he nodded his head, lifting his hand up to pat his pocket where his lucky coin was.

Daft bugger.

Nathanial shook his head, turning away and using the reins to guide his horse in front of the carriage.

The carriage that held his wife.

Who had trapped him into marriage.

Taking a deep breath of country air, Nathanial reined in his temper. They had several hours to go before they reached Hereford Hall. Hopefully, he would be able to shake off some of his temper on the journey.

But he was not too hopeful.

21

———————

KALINA

Traveling up the drive to Hereford Hall was a completely different experience from arriving at Blackstone Manor. It was more than the emptiness of the carriage, with only Margaret for company rather than her whole family; it was being uncertain of her welcome at the end of the road. Things she had not stopped to consider before entering the carriage.

Like what kind of staff would Hereford Hall have.

Whether they would welcome her.

If the duke had told them that he'd been trapped into the union rather than choosing her for himself.

Thank goodness she had Margaret, but she was also worried that she was dragging her maid into an untenable situation. Margaret would defend her if she felt it necessary, but that would likely make her unwelcome with the rest of the staff if they were loyal to the duke.

She ran through what she knew of Hereford, which was not nearly enough. Not when she was now married to him.

Due to the abrupt nature of their wedding, she'd had no chance to ask him any questions—if he'd even be charitable enough to answer them. She might have done so on the ride to Hereford Hall if he'd joined her in the carriage. On the other hand, considering how icy cold he'd been this morning, she was grateful for the respite from his chilly demeanor before they reached the hall.

"Well, now," Margaret said, peering out the window as the hall came into view. Her tone was doubtful. "That is... a very large house."

It was very large, just as Margaret said. Kalina had noticed, as they'd come up the drive, that the grounds were overgrown. The neatly manicured lawns and bushes of Blackstone Manor were long gone. The greenery here was not even as tidy as that of the inn at which they'd stopped for a stretch and a quiet bite. Her husband had ignored her presence, dining in silence, while Kalina picked at her food. Reminded that she had barely eaten today, her stomach grumbled, and she put her hand over it as if she could hush it that way.

Hereford Hall was as overgrown as the drive leading to it. Ivy crawled up the stonework and onto the roof, which appeared old and patched. While the front building appeared nearly as large as Blackstone Manor, it was not at all as welcoming. Most of the windows were shuttered, there was a large crack in one of the downstairs windows that was visible even from the carriage, and overall, the house had a depressive air about it. Though the sun was currently peeking out from the clouds, a miasma of gloom hung about the hall.

It looked as though it was well on its way to tumbling into ruins like the church at Blackstone Manor.

He really does need my money.

Which made Kalina feel just a touch better. She was contributing something substantial to their union and to the betterment of his life and his estate.

Someone must have been watching for the carriage, because the front door opened—just one of the two large doors—and a small trickle of people came out. Far smaller than she would have expected from a ducal household... on the other hand, she was already realizing exactly what dire financial straits Hereford was in.

There were three young women, one of who looked to be about

Kalina's age and two younger. The youngest was still in short skirts, her hair in neat plaits with ribbons hanging from them. She was clutching something small and furry. A dog, perhaps? From the faded fabric of her dress, Kalina guessed it was likely a hand-me-down, as was the second youngest's. From the style of the eldest's dress, she had a feeling the gown had belonged to the former duchess.

All three of them were beautiful, despite the shabbiness of their clothing. They had the same coloring as Hereford—lighter brown hair and dark eyes, though the youngest was nearer to blonde than brown. The streaks of it running throughout her hair showed in her plaits.

An older man and woman were beside them, their sturdy garb denoting their servants' status. Were they the only ones? Or had they been sent out as representatives of the rest of the household? With a new duchess arriving, the entire staff should have come out to greet her.

Unless the duke had not sent word ahead, and they were unprepared to greet the new lady of the house.

Or it was an insult.

Or they were the only staff.

Hereford had already dismounted his horse and was leading it by the reins toward the back of the carriage. No groom had come out to assist him.

Gracious.

The older couple was it.

That was the only conclusion she could come to. Even if the household was incensed by the way she'd come to marry their employer, a groom would have come to attend him and the carriages, if there had been one.

Should she get out on her own?

Her mother had taught her how to run a household, but a fully functioning, fully staffed household. All the manners that had been drilled into her kept her from doing many things for herself... but there was no one else here to do them, it appeared.

Hereford came to the carriage door and opened it.

"Madam." As before, realizing she was no longer a 'miss' sent a little tremor through her. The word as much as the coldness of his voice. Kalina gathered her courage along with her skirts so she could step out of the carriage.

Feet on the ground, she pretended not to be aware of the stares coming from their tiny audience. She shook out her skirts as Hereford assisted Margaret down from the carriage as well. The horse he'd ridden was now tied to the back of the carriage.

Almost no staff, the house in ruins, no stables or feed for the horses... Gods. Kalina could hardly credit that he'd managed to keep exactly how dire his situation was away from the gossip mongers. She certainly had had no idea. Not that it would have changed how she felt about him...

Unfortunately, there was very little she could do about how he now felt about her. Perhaps using the money she brought with her, which he obviously needed even more than she'd realized, would soften his attitude toward her. Eventually.

Coming up to her side, Hereford stiffly held out his arm.

"Let me introduce you, then we'll get the carriage unloaded. Tomorrow, the rest of our things should arrive."

Unsure of what to say, Kalina nodded her agreement as she took his arm. Noise from behind her made her glance over her shoulder. The coachman and footman who had accompanied them from Blackstone Manor had gotten to work on the cases that she had brought with her. It was only a small portion of what she'd taken to the manor. The rest of that would arrive tomorrow, but even more would make its way to the hall once her parents returned to London and sent the rest of her things onward.

As they moved to the stairs, the small group at the top came down. The older couple followed behind the three girls. The eldest led the way, her expression carefully blank. Behind her came the next eldest, who did not do nearly as good a job of hiding the suspicion she felt as she narrowed her eyes at Kalina. Only the youngest smiled, though her smile was all for Hereford.

"Nat!" she said joyfully when she reached the bottom of the steps and threw herself at him. Releasing Kalina's arm, Hereford surged into position to catch her in his arms.

"Fiona!" The resigned exasperation in his tone made it clear this was not the first time he'd had to deal with an impetuous action from her. Sighing, he held her up, gently angling himself so as not to squash the furry creature she was holding, which Kalina now realized was a hare.

Not a fluffy, sweet bunny. No, this was a wild-eyed, long-limbed, rangy brown and white hare... who, despite being along for a rather unsettling ride, lay quietly in the girl's arm.

"Fiona, you are too old to greet Nathanial that way," the eldest sister scolded, shaking her head, though there was no real censure in her tone as she reached the bottom of the stairs. Like her brother, she sounded more resigned than anything else. "Besides, you almost crushed Archibald."

"Archibald is fine," Fiona replied as Hereford hoisted her up, holding her on his hip. "He likes to jump." Her long, dangling legs made Kalina think she was nearly too big for him to do so much longer. It reminded her of how her father had done the same, holding her when others said she was too old for it, because he'd known the days when he would not be able to at all were rapidly approaching.

A little ache rose in her chest as she watched Hereford smile and shake his head.

"I am fairly certain Archibald would prefer to jump on his own, rather than with you," he said gently.

Fiona was no longer paying attention to him, though; she was staring at Kalina with interest. As if her focus directed the others, they looked at her as well.

For the first time since they'd left the altar, Kalina met her husband's gaze. With her hands folded in front of her, her heart rapidly beating in nervous anticipation in her chest, she awaited what he would say. How he would introduce her.

Taking a deep breath, he hitched Fiona on his hip.

"Ladies, I would like you to meet my new duchess. Ah, Kalina, this is Julianna, Emma, and Fiona." The brief stumble over her given name was not missed by the elder two, something flashing through both of their eyes before they dipped in curtsies to the proper level, though Fiona grinned widely at her from her spot in Hereford's arms.

"Your Grace," Julianna and Emma murmured in unison.

"Please, call me Kalina," she said immediately.

Despite the circumstances, they were family now. The idea of them using her title rather than her name made her skin crawl. They exchanged another look, then nodded at her but did not seem to know what else to say.

Hereford smoothed over the awkwardness by stepping forward, which forced Kalina to turn slightly.

"This is Miss Milford, who runs the household, and Mr. Milford, her brother, who runs... well, everything else."

"Your Grace." Miss Milford dipped into a low curtsy while Mr. Milford bowed. Both of them looked to be in their early fifties by the grey in their hair and the lines on their faces. Both of them had extremely neutral expressions, just like Lady Julianna.

"Welcome to the Hall," Mr. Milford said.

It was hard to tell if they were naturally reserved or if they were stiff because they knew of the circumstances surrounding the suddenness of her marriage to Hereford. Or perhaps they were embarrassed to be welcoming her to the hall in its current state.

"Down, poppet. I need to help Daniel and the others with our things," Hereford told his youngest sister before lowering her to the ground.

"I can help!" She frowned, looking down at the hare in her arms, then let out a sigh. "I suppose Archibald has had a good, long visit already, anyway."

Bending down, she put the hare on the ground, and it took off like a shot, heading into the tall grass on the side of the house and disappearing from sight almost immediately. Fiona waved her hand as if seeing him off.

"Goodbye! I'll see you tomorrow! Do not get eaten by foxes!"

Utterly bemused, and rather charmed, Kalina could not stop the smile curving her lips at the lighthearted farewell, all of which was said with utter innocent cheerfulness. Her smile quickly faded when faced with the harder gazes of the elder two sisters.

Feeling rather twitchy, she went to assist with the luggage, Margaret following at her heels. Hereford frowned at her, but she ignored him, taking two hatboxes in hand. If he was going to attend, so could she. Of course, she had not reckoned with the fact that she did not know where her room was. She turned and looked up at the house, pausing. Margaret stood silently beside her, holding Kalina's jewelry box.

"Follow me, Your Grace," Miss Milford said to her, holding a small trunk that held some of Kalina's gloves, reticules, and things. "I'll show you the way to your room." Something flashed in her eyes before her face blanked again, thought what emotion she was hiding, Kalina could not tell.

Nodding, Kalina followed Miss Milford into the house, aware of the bustle behind her and the way Hereford's sisters hung back. It only made sense, after all, that they should want to see their brother. Question him. She wished she could hear what he said about her, to help direct her way forward with them... but perhaps it was best she could not.

Her attention was immediately taken by the state of the house, the interior of which was just as shabby as the exterior. More so, perhaps. Though the foyer was very clean, the rug was threadbare, and there were several spindles missing on the staircase. Kalina's gaze drifted up to where there should have been a chandelier, but the large space above her was empty.

"This way, Your Grace," Miss Milford said, going up the stairs with alacrity. Was she hurrying in order to return to help with the rest of the luggage? In which case, Kalina would not dally. "We did not have time to get everything fully in order, but your room has been prepared. There are also a morning room and a small study attached to your bedroom, which are not ready for you yet."

There was a hint of trepidation in her voice—worry that Kalina would hold her responsible for not having the suite fully prepared?

She certainly did not blame Miss Milford. The lack of time and other staff to help her would have made such a task nearly impossible.

"Thank you for having the bedroom ready on such short notice," she said, infusing her voice with gratitude. Indeed, having a room she could retreat to that was her very own would be a boon. Of course, Hereford would be able to come in as well. At night. Tonight. Which was their wedding night.

A small shiver of anticipation went down her spine. Despite everything, she was very curious about what the things her mother had told her would actually feel like. Especially with him. Supposedly, such things put men in a good mood. Kalina would use any small advantage she could scrounge to improve her standing with her new husband.

"Of course, Your Grace. It's just down here."

As expected, the house was huge. The upstairs hall rug was even shabbier than the one downstairs. She had become familiar enough with English *ton* houses to realize the absence of furniture and décor in the hallway was unusual. There were squares of discoloration on the faded wallpaper where frames and tapestries had once hung.

The hallway had a very dark and gloomy air about it.

Kalina was more than a little relieved when Miss Milford finally stopped before a door and, hitching the trunk she was carrying onto one hip, opened it. Stepping back, the worthy lady bowed her head as she waited for Kalina to go through. Steeling herself, Kalina took a deep breath and entered her new domain.

The room was very pretty, though very out of fashion. The rug was not as threadbare as some of the others, and the curtains appeared to be a little ragged but perfectly serviceable. The furniture was feminine, dainty, made out of a light shade of wood that contrasted nicely with the rosier hues of the curtains and bed linens.

"It's pink," Kalina exclaimed appreciatively, wondering if Hereford had sent her color preferences ahead of him.

"It used to be red," Miss Milford admitted, sheepishly.

Kalina's heart sank a little, but no matter. She had not really expected Hereford to have made such a gesture, not considering the circumstances. Perhaps she should take the faded red to pink as a sign that the house was welcoming her, even if none of the people in it were.

"I cleaned everything thoroughly, but there was little else I could do."

The embarrassment that was clear in her voice had Kalina setting her hat boxes down and going over to the other woman, reaching out her hands. Surprise showed in Miss Milford's eyes and uncertainty, but she held out her hands to meet Kalina's. Looking her directly in her blue eyes, Kalina held the older woman's callused hands gently.

"You have worked a miracle on very little notice," Kalina said firmly. "I appreciate all of your efforts, and the room looks lovely. Thank you so much for ensuring it was ready for me."

Miss Milford's lips made a little 'o' as relief suffused her features. Then she released Kalina's hands and bobbed another curtsy. The former neutrality of her expression had shifted slightly to something warmer.

"Thank you, Your Grace. Is there anything you need? Something to drink or eat?" Miss Milford appeared rather earnest.

Kalina glanced at the window, gauging the light in the sky, which was still bright but slowly beginning to dim as the afternoon wore on. She was hungry, but did not want to ask for something when she was unsure of how bare the cupboard might be.

"What time do you normally serve dinner?" she asked.

"Six o'clock, Your Grace, about two hours from now."

She could wait two hours.

"That will be fine then, I do not need anything else at the moment. Thank you, Miss Milford."

"Happy to assist, Your Grace." Bobbing another curtsy, Miss Milford left the room.

Exchanging a glance with Margaret, Kalina let out a long sigh.

"I think his grace owes your father a greater debt than we realized," Margaret murmured, setting Kalina's jewelry box down on the vanity beside the wardrobe. "This is... well. We'll get it up to scratch soon enough."

"Soon enough," Kalina echoed, walking over to look out the window. She noted the small crack in the far most upper right pane. The flower garden below her window looked to be overgrown, a riot of greenery and colors from the jungle of plants.

One way or another, she was determined to make her new life work. There was no going back from here.

22

"What really happened?" Julianna demanded to know as soon as his wife had disappeared into the house with her maid and Miss Milford.

Nathanial shot her a look. Even though his wife was out of earshot, neither Daniel, the coachman, nor the footman the Blackstones had sent with him was. Neither was Emma nor Fiona.

Though Emma was peering at him as suspiciously as Julianna. Only Fiona was unaffected, thoroughly enjoying the activity of unloading the various boxes and trunks.

"I got married," he replied blandly.

Pursing her lips, Julianna narrowed her eyes at him in a manner that was very reminiscent of their mother. That she was wearing one of their mother's old dresses only increased the resemblance.

"Without us," she said accusingly. "And nothing but a note saying that it was happening and that you would be returning from the Blackstones to here rather than going on to London."

"There was no need to be in London once I had a bride." Though he would need to send for his things at some point. Or, more likely, Drake would send them on once he returned to the capital. He'd been kind enough to let Nathanial stay with him and not mention it to the rest of their friends.

They all knew that Nathanial was up the River Tick, but he hadn't wanted all of them to know exactly how bad it was. Matthew would have hounded him about borrowing money. Christian and Gregory likely would not have been much better. He'd avoided asking Sebastian and Zachary because their households had contained nosy females—neither of the dowager duchesses was among those he would trust with the information about how far the Herefords had fallen.

Drake had been both understanding and discreet, and he had let Nathanial keep his pride. He'd made Nathanial feel like a guest in his home rather than the charity case he truly was, and Nathanial would be forever grateful for that.

"She's very pretty," Fiona piped up from beside him, causing Nathanial to give Julianna another look. At ten years old, Fiona had not learned discretion yet, and often repeated things she heard but did not understand.

"She is."

"And rich?" Emma whispered with a glance at the men who were beginning to carry the trunks inside, trying not to sound as desperate as she felt.

One of them stood by the heads of the carriage horses, far enough away that he probably could not hear. The guilt that Nathanial felt over leaving his sisters here at the dilapidated hall rose up inside Nathanial once more. They'd been stuck here, waiting to hear what their fates would be, waiting on him, and not knowing what was going on.

"Very," he replied softly. Straightening away from the trunk he'd been about to lift, he turned and faced his sisters. Despite his feelings about how he had attained his new wife, he was glad that he could now reassure his sisters that they were safe. They would be taken care of. Their financial worries were over. Looking across their three faces —Julianna and Emma's expressions consumed with anxious worry and a touch of hope, Fiona's full of pure trust—he cleared his throat.

"My new wife had a substantial dowry—no I'm not going to tell you how much—but enough that I am going to pay off the remainder of the debts, pay the Milfords, hire new staff, and Julianna will have her debut next year."

Fiona cheered as Julianna's shoulders sagged in relief, and Emma stepped up beside her, putting her arm around Julianna and bolstering her. It was then that Nathanial realized how much pressure Julianna must have been feeling, wondering if Nathanial would be able to restore the family's fortunes or if it would be up to her. Seeing his sisters' joy was almost enough to make him think he should forgive his new wife and her father their duplicity.

Almost.

He could have gone deeper into what his plans for the money—the investments, the improvements to the estate that would yield future benefits—but he did not want to bore them. Besides, it would be more satisfying to put things into motion and see their reactions as their lives all changed. They did not need to know the details, only that he had done what he needed to in order to provide for them.

Which included marrying a woman who had trapped him.

The war between gratitude and anger had grown even stronger as he watched his sisters' reactions. The fact that he had to feel grateful at all fueled a simmering resentment.

"Does that mean I can keep my pets?" Fiona asked.

"No," chorused three voices all at once.

Fiona pouted, but everyone else was in agreement. Nathanial could only imagine how overrun the house would become if they gave Fiona permission.

"But we will start having more animals on the grounds, and I will make a special place in the stables for you to keep any of the injured ones you find," Nathanial conceded.

Fiona beamed while Julianna and Emma rolled their eyes. Neither of them was truly upset; they all agreed that Fiona was overindulged, yet none of them was willing to stop.

She was the only one who did not remember their earlier life, before their father had completely drained the estate's coffers. It also

meant she had never experienced life as anything other than a strug-
gle, her elders worrying over money, wearing her sisters' hand-me-
downs, and an increasingly dwindling staff. No wonder she had
chosen to make friends with the animals rather than the people, with
as many as had been let go or moved away after not receiving their
pay over the years.

She was also the only one who truly missed their father because
she had not realized his lies for what they were.

So, they did what they could to give her life joy. Thankfully, she
was a naturally happy child, especially with her 'pets'.

"Will there be horses?" she asked, her eyes lighting up.

"There will," he assured her solemnly. "Horses and dogs. We can
also restore the goat herd."

Fiona threw her hands in the air and spun in happy circles that
made her twin plaits fly out around her like a miniature cyclone.
"Goats!"

"Can we really?" Julianna asked, her eyes wide with shock and
burgeoning hope. Emma was surprised as well, but Julianna was
older and had a better understanding of what such things cost.

"We can." Nathanial found it easier to smile now, relaxing
slightly.

It was good to remember that there was a silver lining to this
entire situation. He'd achieved the goal of providing for his family.
He'd always known that he would need to marry in order to do so;
he'd accepted that.

It was just the manner in which it happened.

Giving himself a little shake, Nathanial pushed away the lingering
resentment. For now.

The men were returning from having delivered the trunks inside.
Between them, they'd handled all the duchess' things except one
medium-sized trunk that Nathanial could assist Daniel with.
Drawing out the pouch of coins Mr. Little had given him before they
left, to assist with any immediate expenses, Nathanial gave each of
the gentlemen a show of his gratitude.

It felt incredible to be able to do so without worrying that he was robbing his own people of what they needed.

Daniel's eyes lit up when he realized what Nathanial was doing, sheer relief and appreciation showing on his face.

"Here, let me help," Nathanial said, stepping forward as Daniel bent to lift the trunk.

"I have it, Your Grace. I'm feeling strong as an ox right now." Daniel twisted as he hefted the trunk, smiling broadly. Apparently, the appearance of money was lifting all of their spirits to an untold degree.

Fiona skipped ahead of Daniel, Emma following quickly behind her to ensure she did not get into trouble. Julianna hung back, her hazel eyes filled with suspicion.

"What *really* happened?" she asked again, giving him a look promising retribution if he was not honest with her. "You are not as happy as you should be, considering the bounty you've described. Is she a shrew? And why were we not invited to the wedding? Are you ashamed of her? Is her family in business? Not that it would matter to *me* if they were…" Her voice trailed off, as if questioning whether it mattered to him.

"Her father is the third son of the Marquess of Stilton," Nathanial said. "Though he is estranged from his family. Which is a large part of why she was looking to marry a duke. The Marquess did not approve of her father's marriage and has cut them from the will."

"She's a title hunter." Julianna looked at him curiously, raising one brow. "You are no hypocrite."

After all, he had been a fortune hunter.

Nathanial took a deep breath.

"She and her father arranged a scene at the house party by which I was forced to offer for her hand. Having done that, I decided to marry her with all due haste to hopefully stem some of the gossip and not further tarnish the family's reputation."

Julianna's eyes widened in understanding, then immediate indignation.

"Well, that is just indecent!"

Temper flared in her eyes, and Nathanial reached out to grab her hand before she could go storming into the house and up to his new wife's room to take her to task.

"It's done," he said firmly. "Her father's wealth is spectacular, and her dowry shows it. We have enough money to pay off the remaining debts, restore the estate, invest in what we need to thrive going forward, and send you off in style next year with plenty left over for Emma and Fiona to have respectable dowries."

"Really?" His sister's jaw dropped open. Her gaze slid to the house. "She's worth all that?"

"Her marriage to a duke is." He smiled thinly. "At least, to her and her father."

Staring at the house for a long moment, obviously thinking, Julianna frowned. "What about her mother?"

"From what I could tell, her mother was not part of the plot."

"Strange. I always thought it was the matchmaking mamas you would have to be wary of," she said dryly. After another short silence, she gave herself a little shake. "So, then. I suppose we will have to make the best of it. If she's awful, at least she came with the funds to balance that."

"Well... she's not entirely awful," Nathanial said, finding himself in the reluctant position of having to defend her.

"Awful enough that she had to trap a duke into marriage in order to get one."

When Nathanial did not immediately agree with her statement, Julianna turned back to him, frowning.

"What? What are you not telling me?"

"Montagu had shown interest. Though he had not come to *point non plus.* " Eventually, Julianna would hear the truth anyway, most likely. She had a knack for wringing information out of people.

"Then why did she need to trap *you*?"

"That is the question, is it not?" Nathanial murmured.

They both stared at the house. Nathanial wondered if, like him, Julianna was remembering what it had looked like before neglect had overtaken it. If she was picturing what it could look like again. Would look like again. He was not sure how much Emma remembered, and Fiona had never known anything but a home that was crumbling into obscurity... but he knew Julianna did.

"Before you left, you told me that you were going to do whatever you had to in order to marry a woman whose fortune could turn ours around," Julianna murmured. "Because you were determined that the task not fall to me."

"Yes."

"From what you have now said, she... um, your new wife, is not awful. Montagu was pursuing her. Her father is as rich as Croesus."

"Yes." He frowned, wondering where Julianna was going with this line of query.

"Was there another young lady you were enamored of whose dowry could not provide what we needed?"

"No." Nathanial immediately shook his head. Granted, the other young ladies he'd been considering for the position of his duchess would have been palatable. "I had not formed an attachment to anyone. I did not dare."

The closest he had come, in fact, was Miss Little, and her dowry had never been the issue.

"Was there an heiress with an even larger dowry that you had your eye on?"

"No."

Though he was not entirely sure of Julianna's direction, Nathanial was becoming increasingly uncomfortable at the questions being leveled at him. He shifted his weight on his feet, wondering if he dared start walking forward to end the conversation. Knowing his sister, she would follow after him, screeching her questions loudly enough for the entire household to hear if he did.

Best not to risk it.

He'd rather an audience of one for his discomfiture if he had to bear it.

Crossing her arms, Julianna turned to face him, putting her back to the house. The expression on her face was one of utter exasperation.

"Then, considering her wealth and the fact that she was 'not awful' enough to have another duke courting her, why on earth were you not trying to trap *her* into marriage?"

Nathanial opened his mouth. Closed it. Tried to marshal the arguments, the reasons why.

"Her family is scandalous. I am trying to restore our reputation along with our coffers. Because of Stilton's displeasure, half the *ton* did not welcome her family into their households. If she is going to sponsor you, Emma, and Fiona... well, I wanted a wife with an unblemished reputation and who had been brought up within the *ton* to guide you through your Seasons."

Huffing, Julianna closed her eyes. She was not as experienced in the ways of the *ton*, though their mother had taught Julianna as much as she could before she'd passed away not long after Fiona's first birthday. Nathanial knew how important their reputations were, how the *ton* worked in regard to scandal and gossip, and he'd done his best to impress that on Julianna.

Especially since she had argued to come with him this year, to try to catch a husband. But they had not been able to afford a new wardrobe, and her current state of dress would immediately catch the sharp eyes of the dowagers and matrons. Nathanial had been able to get away with wearing some of his father's old clothing simply because his father had been far more portly than himself, and tailoring the clothing to fit both him and the current fashions had not been difficult. The same had not been possible for Julianna.

Now, he was even more glad that Julianna had not debuted this year. Her belief that he should have trapped Miss Little into marriage rather than the other way round gave him some insight as to how she might have handled her own Season. Both of them were determined to save their family, but Julianna was more focused on the financial aspect than the social. Only because she did not understand the social ramifications.

Taking a deep breath, Julianna huffed again.

"I can see you are upset that she trapped you, despite the fact that her fortune is literally going to restore our home and provide for our futures and even though you did not have another woman in mind for your bride." Julianna arched one delicate brow at him.

"Of course, I am. Do you not want to choose your own husband?" he asked irritably. Julianna desired control as much as he did.

"Of course, I do," she replied, echoing his first statement. "That is the only reason I let you delay my Season, to give you the chance to make that possible for me."

As if she could have forced the issue. But Nathanial did not say that. He'd rather let her think she'd been able to make the decision on her own, rather than being backed into the corner the way he had been.

"Well. I suppose we shall see how she settles in." Julianna made a face. "I do not know whether to be furious at her for trapping you or grateful."

"That makes two of us."

Nathanial hefted a sigh. It was time to go inside and face his new life.

With his new wife.

23

———————

Not long after the trunks of her clothing and things had been delivered to her room, there was a knock at the door. Before Kalina or Margaret could answer, the door burst open and Hereford's youngest sister came barreling into the room, bright-eyed and eager, followed by the middle sister, who appeared scandalized and apologetic.

"Fiona! I am so sorry, Your Grace, we've been trying to teach her manners, but..." Emma's soft-spoken apology was accompanied by her throwing her hands up in the air in obvious frustration at the inability to control her younger sister.

"Please, call me Kalina," Kalina said immediately. She almost added on that they were sisters now, but bit her tongue against it, not sure how Hereford's sisters would feel about her once they knew how she had attained the position. Smiling kindly at Fiona, who beamed back at her, she leaned forward to put her hands on her knees, bringing her closer to Fiona's height. "Knocking was appreciated, but it is best to wait until you receive an invitation to enter someone's room. What if I had been changing my clothing? Or taking a bath? You would have interrupted my privacy."

"Oh." Fiona thought about that for a moment. "I have seen my sisters changing."

"Have you seen Miss Milford or Mr. Milford changing?"

"No, they would be upset if I… oh." Fiona made a face as she realized.

Kalina could not help but smile.

"It sounds as though your sisters would appreciate it if you waited for an invitation to enter as well."

"We would," Emma confirmed with a sigh. She walked forward, putting her hand on Fiona's head and brushing back some of the flyaway hair, tiny tendrils that had worked their way out of Fiona's plaits. "But it is very hard to tell this imp no in a manner that sticks."

Fiona frowned.

"I will start waiting," she said, almost defiantly. Then she looked at Kalina again. "You are very pretty. Are you from Africa?"

"No, India." Kalina smiled, straightening up again now that she had made her point about privacy. "Though my father is from England."

"Oh. I wondered. Nathanial said he had to marry a lady."

"Fiona!" Emma's scandalized whisper was back, along with a long-aggrieved expression.

Kalina laughed, waving reassuringly at Emma. She did not mind Fiona's bluntness, and she could only imagine how few people the girl had met at her age, living in this house. House parties were certainly not a thing that had happened here for many years, if there had even been any during Fiona's lifetime.

"My grandfather is the Marquess of Stilton." Estranged and did not acknowledge her or anyone else in his family, but blood was blood. It was the reason they had received any invitations at all initially. Mostly due to the *ton's* avid interest in anything of a scandalous nature.

"And your mother is from India?"

"Yes, as am I."

"What is India like? Are there animals there?"

Smothering a laugh, Kalina gestured to the small chaise on the other side of her bed. The girl's enthusiasm was infectious, as was the warmth of her welcome, which was far more than Kalina had hoped for. She realized Fiona was too young to understand all the implications behind her and Hereford's sudden marriage and arrival at the hall, and she was grateful for it.

"Would you like to sit down, and I will tell you all about it?"

Fiona immediately ran to the chaise, Emma following more hesitantly. She clearly felt the need to keep an eye on Fiona but also was unsure of Kalina.

She understood there was something more than a quick marriage.

Kalina only hoped she could at least make a good impression before Emma learned the truth, perhaps keep Nathanial's sisters from thinking too badly of her. At the very least, she did not want Fiona to take up against her.

She had a feeling the youngest of the Percys could be devilish if she chose to be.

As Margaret unpacked Kalina's things, she sat on the bed and told Emma and Fiona all about India and the animals there. Fiona was especially fascinated by Kalina's description of elephants.

Because her back was to the door, it was only a prickling of her senses that made Kalina aware there was an addition to their audience.

She turned to look over her shoulder. Hereford and Julianna were standing there, listening intently as well. Her husband's gaze met hers for just a moment before he looked away. Julianna was studying her closely, as though she was trying to figure Kalina out.

"Julianna! Did you know that elephants are so big you can ride them?" Fiona asked as she jumped up and ran over to her sister. Grabbing Julianna's hand, she tried to pull her into Kalina's room.

"I did not know that. I have never seen an elephant before." Julianna resisted Fiona's attempts to drag her forward. Lifting her gaze to Kalina, she smiled, but it did not reach her eyes. "I apologize; you must be tired. We'll leave you to rest."

Fiona made a disappointed noise, but at her sister's urging, she quit the room after waving over her shoulder at Kalina. Emma glided noiselessly after her, though she smiled and nodded at Kalina before she left, and her smile seemed genuine. After his sisters were gone, Hereford stood in the doorway, looking about the room, not meeting her eyes.

She wondered when the last time he had been in this room.

Possibly when his mother had been alive. He was looking at it as though he did not recognize it. Or perhaps he was just that determined to avoid looking at her. Nervously waiting for him to say something, she was aware of Margaret on the side of the room, appearing to make herself as small as possible but also watching Hereford closely. If he did anything to discomfit Kalina, her maid would defend her.

Kalina would have to have a word with Margaret.

She was uncertain whether she could stop Hereford from firing the maid if he decided to. Though her understanding was that, as lady of the household, she was nominally in charge of the staff, especially her own lady's maid, he was still the duke. The head of household.

That rankled because it did not seem fair that her husband controlled the money she had brought to the marriage. She kept her portion, and that was it. But there was nothing she could do about that.

She could, hopefully, keep Margaret from speaking out of turn and being fired.

"Supper is at six o'clock," he said after a long moment, still not meeting her gaze. "Unless you would prefer a tray in your room?"

Though the notion tempted, Kalina would not be such a coward. It was better to start as she meant to go on, and she was determined to make a good try at this marriage. This life.

Besides, she'd enjoyed Fiona's company, and Emma's, though the latter had been much quieter. Eating together would also give her a notion of how to gauge the Percy sisters' reactions to any revelations their brother made to them this afternoon. Kalina lifted her chin.

"I will eat dinner with the family."

He nodded, started to turn.

Stopped.

"It will not be... there has not been time to send Miss Milford to the village for any additional food. The meal will be..." His voice trailed off again.

"I am sure whatever is served will be filling, and that is all I need," Kalina said firmly. If she was able to eat very much at all.

Hereford nodded again and turned, pulling the door shut behind him. Both Kalina and Margaret let out their breath at the same time.

"He's a bit of a cold fish," Margaret muttered, turning back to her task.

But he had not been.

Not until he'd been trapped in a future with her.

Tears pricked her eyes again, and Kalina took a deep breath, pushing them away. Sometimes, it felt like all she did was push down her emotions. Her wants. Her desires.

Shaking her head, she got up from the bed and went to assist Margaret in sorting through the jewelry she'd brought. It did no good to dwell on such things.

None of it could be changed, anyway.

Though... as she was putting her favorite rose diamond necklace to the side, it occurred to Kalina that her life was more her own now than it had ever been before. She'd done what she had sworn to do. She had married a duke. Her father was now so well-connected, his father would not be able to completely ignore him anymore.

That had been her goal for long enough that she felt the lack of it like a void. What did she want for herself now?

What kind of future could she make here at Hereford Hall?

Staring down at the glittering gems in her hand, she realized she had no idea what she wanted now that there were no expectations laid at her feet. She could finally choose for herself, and she did not know what she desired because she had never thought about what she might want for herself.

How very, very strange.

24

———————

NATHANIAL

Supper passed without incident.

What Julianna revealed to Emma, Nathanial did not know. Both of them were cautiously curious about his wife, but neither relaxed during the conversation. His wife was rather guarded as well, compared to how she had been at Blackstone Manor.

Normally, Fiona would inject a much-needed bit of levity to any occasion, but today she was pouting because she had been forbidden from bringing her recent acquisition to the table—a baby fox she'd found crying of hunger whose mother had never returned to it. Both Emma and Julianna had given him guilty expressions when he'd been introduced to Telemachus, but he had only sighed. Attempting to keep Fiona from rescuing animals did nothing to stop her; she just attempted to hide the creatures about the house.

With as many unused rooms as there were, it was better to know what she was up to.

Though Miss Milford and Daniel often ate with the family, they'd insisted on a more formal dining situation now that he was married. He suspected they also wanted to interrogate his wife's lady's maid about the new mistress of the house. Still, as staff was going to be added to the household very quickly, he supposed it was best to start getting used to it now. Besides, after all they had done for him and his sisters, Nathanial was not inclined to deny them whatever they asked for.

His wife kept the conversation going by asking about his sisters' interests, the house, and the surrounding areas. Only Julianna was able to answer much about that last. Nathanial could have as well if he'd been able to bring himself to do more than grunt.

At one point, Julianna shot him a look of pure exasperation at his unusual reticence, but Nathanial could not bring himself to be engaging. His brain was too busy thinking of all he needed to do on the morrow to start setting the estate to rights, while his emotions were torn between gratitude and resentment. None of which was conducive to conversation.

He was also very aware of the rapid approach of night.

His wedding night.

He was going to need to consummate the marriage.

The need for a rich wife had come from his father's ill-handling of the estate and the family finances. The need for a wife, however...

When his father had first died, along with all the other dukes in the hunting lodge fire, Nathanial had been shocked. Then he'd been relieved. His grief had been more for Fiona's loss than his own. He'd been very aware of how his father was draining the family and what he would eventually inherit. Getting it sooner actually meant they were in better shape than they could have been.

His father had sold off everything that was not entailed, and he'd emptied the house as well. Julianna had managed to save some of their mother's jewelry from him, only to be forced to sell it after their father's death to pay off the worst of the debts and keep them all from starving. Nathanial's meager savings he'd been able to keep from the allowance his father had given him had barely made a dent.

Nathanial was determined that his sisters would never have to endure such a thing again. He did not trust anyone else to take care of them the way he did. His current heir was a distant cousin who lived in America and had never visited the estate, nor did he have any real connection to Nathanial or his sisters.

If something were to happen to Nathanial…

The hunting lodge accident had been the first tragedy; what followed had been even worse.

They'd barely left mourning for their fathers when Sinclair, Duke of Northumberland, had followed his father to the grave. His cousin had inherited. Granted, despite Nathanial's personal dislike of the fellow, William Seymour was at least the kind of gentleman who would take care of the dukedom's people. He had installed Sinclair's mother in the Dowager House along with his own mother, and from all appearances was doing the best he could under the circumstances.

Whether that would hold true for Nathanial's heir, he did not know.

He would not risk it.

Therefore, he needed to beget his own heir as quickly as possible, but the idea of engaging in intimacies with a woman who had tricked him in the most foul manner…

The worst part was that, physically at least, he did want her. He could not stop watching her out of the corner of his eye. The way her lips parted when she lifted her spoon to take a bite. The way her breasts moved against the low decolletage of her gown—which was not even truly that low, *and* it was modestly covered with a *fichu*, appropriately for a family dinner. Part of him itched to touch her silken skin and hair.

Another part of him wanted to turn her over his knee and spank her until he'd vented his anger about her treachery.

"Perhaps tomorrow we could visit the local shops?" His wife suggested, turning her head to look at him with her big dark eyes. They were full of uncertainty, which was at least something. She did not seem to know quite how to behave toward him. She should have thought of that before she trapped him into marriage.

Still, she was offering to take his sisters shopping, which they desperately needed, but he did not have the time to do.

"Yes, that should be fine." He would have a word with Daniel before he went to bed this evening. Their neighbor, the Earl of Harrington, always let them borrow a carriage when they needed it. Nathanial suspected he'd also been giving Daniel money on the sly to keep the family afloat, but he did not ask because he already felt he owed the earl and his wife for the generous offerings of their resources and the fact that they'd never gossiped about the Percys' dire straits.

"Yay!" Fiona sat up straight, throwing her hands up in the air. "A new dress!" Something she had never had before. Though Julianna and Emma's reactions were not quite as exuberant, they both sat up straighter, bright-eyed with eagerness. It had been a long time since any of them had worn anything but hand-me-downs—and Fiona had never had a dress of her own.

Seeing their happiness, watching his wife's smile spread wider as she took in his sisters' reactions as well, he could almost feel contentment.

Almost.

If only she had waited. If only she had not trapped him.

No matter what she did now, it did not make up for it; that underlying thread of the original deceit remained.

He could not forget it, no matter how much he wanted to.

He also had to wonder if what he was seeing now was more acting. More duplicity. The way she'd drawn him in at the house party. Not just him either. Christian. Astrid. Tiffany and Gregory. Delilah. They'd all befriended her. Enjoyed her company. Hell, Astrid and Tiffany had already forgiven her.

What her goal might be, he could not fathom, unless she was trying to ingratiate herself so that he would forget the antecedents of their marriage. Would that he could.

It was not until Julianna glanced at him with concern that he realized his smile had faded and he was gritting his teeth. Immediately, he traded out his expression for a more neutral one. Still, the joy he'd gotten from his sisters' reactions had already faded when reminded of the truth.

Thankfully, the meal was coming to an end.

Normally, the lady of the house would invite the other ladies to withdraw with her, leaving the gentlemen to their libations. His wife paused, looking around the table, obviously uncertain of what to do. After all, this was a family dinner, not a formal one, and she did not know how the Hall normally operated.

They had not been so formal in years, not since long before Nathanial's father had died.

Julianna saved her.

"Time to get ready for bed, Fiona," Julianna said, smiling.

Normally, Fiona was not averse to going to bed, but the excitement of a new family member had obviously gotten to her, and she pouted, slumping down in her chair.

"I want to stay up late." Obviously hoping that her new sister-in-law would be a softer touch than the rest of her siblings, Fiona turned to her with wide, appealing eyes. "Can I stay up late? Since it's a special occasion?"

Nathanial could have interceded, but he was curious as to how his wife would handle the situation.

She only hesitated a moment before smiling kindly.

"Tomorrow is going to be a *very* busy day. I think getting as much rest as you can is a good idea. Besides, the faster you fall asleep, the faster morning will come, and the sooner we'll be on our way to the shops."

Rather than sulking at being denied, Fiona sat up straight with excitement.

"The faster I shall have my new dress!" She jumped up out of her seat and ran to the door before impatiently turning. "Julianna, come *on.*" Then she disappeared down the hall, her footsteps quickly fading at the pace she was moving.

Laughing, Julianna got to her feet.

"She does not need me to help her get ready, but she likes the company," Julianna explained. "I will probably follow her straight to bed. As you said, tomorrow will be a busy day."

The smile that wreathed her face at the thought did make Nathanial's chest loosen a touch. As did Emma's smile as she got to her feet.

"I should like to make an early night of it as well," she said. Truthfully, she was probably going back to her room to read before she went to bed. Any of the manuscripts or books that had been worth anything had been sold, of course, but that had still left a substantial portion of the library intact. Emma often had her nose in a book.

Nathanial valiantly suppressed the urge to tell her to stay, to keep him from being alone with his wife. It was not his sisters' responsibility to manage his marriage for him.

"Good night," he said, at the same time as his wife. He just managed to keep from glancing at her as his sisters left the room.

Sitting perfectly still, back straight, she looked at the dishes left on the table. Before she could say anything, Miss Milford came bustling in, probably alerted to the end of the meal by Fiona's abrupt and rather noisy departure. She smiled and bobbed a curtsy.

"Are you finished, Your Graces?"

"Yes, thank you, Miss Milford," Nathanial said, getting to his feet. To his left, his wife slowly rose to hers as well. Her plate was cleared, though she had not put much on it to begin with. Whether the meal had not been to her liking or if she'd just not felt like eating, he was not sure.

It would not matter to me except I need her to be healthy to bear my heir.

That was obviously why he cared. If she was experiencing some kind of emotional distress over realizing what marriage to him meant, which affected her appetite, surely that was the least of what she deserved.

Stepping away from the table, he offered her his arm, though he found he could not look her in the eye, pinning his gaze on her shoulder instead.

"Madam."

"Thank you." The soft rejoinder was almost too quiet to hear.

He was very aware of how alone they were as he escorted her out of the dining room. The soft clinking of china and silver behind him, attesting to Miss Milford's immediate attendance to her duties, followed them through the door, then was cut off after the door closed, leaving them in awkward silence in the hall. Though Nathanial wracked his brain, he could not think of what he might say to her.

So, they walked on, beside each other but not truly together. The gulf between them aggravated him as much as he felt he required it. He was far too aware of the swishing of her skirts next to his leg, the warmth of her fingers on his arm, even through his jacket and shirt sleeves. Nathanial clenched his jaw and loosened it again as he led her back to their rooms.

His was directly beside hers.

The first time he'd entered the marchioness' rooms since his mother's death had been at the beginning of this Season, when he'd wanted to ensure it was ready for a bride. He'd been back several times since, though the rooms remained empty.

But now she was there.

His wife.

On their wedding night.

Even as his arousal stirred, part of him rebelled against the idea. Railed against being put in a position where he had to bed a woman he'd specifically *not* chosen as his wife, no matter that he'd desired her.

Each step toward her door felt heavier. The air around them felt like it was stifling him. The silence was far too loud in his ears. His sisters had rooms farther down the hall in the wing, yet he could not hear them.

By the time they reached his wife's door, he could barely draw breath.

Her hand trembled against his arm as he opened the door for her. It swung open to the brightly lit room. Obviously, her maid had been in to light the way in anticipation of her arrival.

From his position at the door, Nathanial could see the large canopy bed, draped with the faded red fabric that had adorned it since his mother's day. The distance between the door and the bed yawned wide, and he leaned back away from it, metaphorically digging his heels in.

His wife looked up at him, her lips slightly parted, long lashes sweeping against her cheek.

"Are... are you coming in?" She sounded hesitant. Unsure.

But not unwelcoming.

Nathanial felt his mouth go dry.

The conflicting urges within him—to haul her into the room or to run down the hall to his own refuge—battled inside him. It felt as though he was being torn apart by the indecision.

Her head tilted back, like she was hoping for a kiss.

"I have a headache," Nathanial blurted out.

Turning, he fled the field, already cursing himself under his breath, but he did not look back to see how she received his excuse. He strode—quickly, but he was not running—as fast as he could to his own room and did not take a full breath until he was inside with the thick wooden door between him and his wife.

Closing his eyes, he leaned back against the hard surface, letting his head thud onto it. There was another door, of course, the one between their rooms, but he was not going anywhere near that.

Not right now.

Not until he could wrestle his unruly emotions into some semblance of concord.

25

———————

KALINA

It was her wedding night, and she was still a virgin. A virgin who could not fall asleep.

Kalina turned over, trying to get more comfortable in the bed. The mattress was comfortable enough, despite its age. The sheets were soft, worn from use. But _she_ could not get comfortable.

For a moment, she'd thought Nathanial would kiss her, and all would be well... but he'd practically run from her. Shut himself away inside his own room. So close but so far away.

She'd thought about knocking on the door between their rooms, but decided against it. It had already been embarrassing enough ringing for Margaret to help her get ready for bed. Though her maid had been cheerful getting her ready for bed, as if she expected that Hereford would be in after she left.

But he had not come. Eventually, Kalina had blown out her candles and lay down.

The last thing she wanted to do was force him to spend time with her when it was clear he did not. Hopefully, tomorrow...

Part of her desire was pure curiosity, but another part was that he made her feel things. She wanted to explore that. And if he had come into the room with her, she might have felt like they'd traveled along the road toward forgiveness. Her mother had said that being in the bedroom together was the most intimate thing a couple could do.

She'd hoped...

But no.

Perhaps there was no way to make up for the way her father had tricked him.

Turning onto her side, Kalina buried her face in the pillow, letting the soft cushion soak up her tears.

Closing her eyes, she took long, deep breaths. In. And out. Felt her heart slow to a calmer pace. The tension in her body began to leak out of her. Relaxing her. She focused her mind on her new sisters. Julianna and Emma were both more reserved with her, but Fiona had been nothing but warm and welcoming. A soothing balm to her battered emotions.

She could make a place for herself here.

Tomorrow, she would be happy to take them shopping. Visit the village. And explore her new home. Surely, Fiona, at least, would be willing to show her around the many rooms. Miss Milford would likely help, too. Margaret had said the older woman was very welcoming and happy that the new duchess had brought her own lady's maid.

Peace slowly settled over her, and she was just beginning to drift off when she heard a noise. At first, she dismissed it. Houses creaked, after all. Or perhaps she'd already fallen asleep and was dreaming. She was right on the cusp.

But then she heard the sound of fabric shushing against itself, coming closer to her.

Her heart began to race again, and she turned over.

A large, solid shape was approaching her bed, the outline of shoulders and head shadowed but visible as her eyes peered through the darkness.

"Your Grace?" she whispered, because she did not feel comfortable calling him by his first name. Not after everything.

And he had never given her permission to.

"Hush," he murmured, though the one word was enough that she recognized his voice. His shoulders moved, and some of the silhouette slid away, revealing a leaner shadow.

He must have been wearing a dressing gown, she realized, as he began to crawl onto the bed. She felt the dip in the bed, felt trepidation and hope rise inside her. As much as she wanted to say something, she could not think of what... and besides, he'd told her to hush.

There was something freeing about the silence. If she could not say anything, then she could not say anything wrong. If they did not speak, then they could not accuse or insult, either.

Hereford tugged the sheets down away from her. Uncertain of what to do, Kalina found herself utterly breathless.

Though he'd technically been in her bed before, she had not been aware of it for the majority of the time. Having him come into it now... Her heart was racing inside her chest, and her skin felt exquisitely sensitive as the heat of his body came alongside hers.

Not on top of her exactly, but hovering over her. One knee moved between her legs, and she felt her nightrail shift as her knees parted, lifting to admit him.

His head lowered, and for a moment she thought he might kiss her, but instead his lips landed on her throat rather than her mouth. The sensation of him touching her sensitive skin there made her gasp. Especially when her hands lifted to touch him and found nothing but bare skin.

The only fabric between them was her nightgown.

Heat suffused her, sudden arousal pooling in her core as a hot need filled her. What she needed she had only the barest idea of, though she understood what was supposed to happen. He would need to put his male part inside her, and then move until he reached completion, spending his seed in her body to plant and grow a child.

Her mother had said it could be very pleasurable, though she had not explained exactly how.

Nor had she warned Kalina about the way her skin would feel tighter, her nipples budding and becoming more sensitive as the soft fabric of her night rail moved against them, or how her insides would clench and send little ripples of pleasure through her. Her mother could not have possibly described what it felt like to have a man's lips traveling over her throat, his hands pulling her night rail up and sliding his palms up her sides, igniting her senses.

"Oh!" She could not suppress the soft gasps, the little moans, as Hereford touched her in a manner that was utterly indecent and wildly exciting. Her body moved, hips lifting up, reaching for... something.

Hands cupped her breasts, and she gasped again, shuddering as the sensations went through her. Her nipples ached, and she whimpered into the darkness, clutching at Hereford's bare shoulders, shifting underneath him. There was a needy pulse between her legs, a growing ache that begged for more, even though she did not know what she wanted more of.

"Please," she begged.

"Hush."

The word was quiet but firm.

One of his hands lifted, covering her mouth as his head lowered to her breasts.

Kalina cried out against his fingers as his mouth closed around her nipple, the wet heat sending a shot of pure pleasure from the little bud straight to her womanhood. He sucked, hard, and the throbbing ache inside her responded, but her moans were muffled against his hand. His other hand kneaded the opposite breast, fingers plucking that nipple, teasing and tugging, while his tongue laved over its twin.

She writhed, fingers digging into his shoulders as he used his mouth and hand to stoke the fires of her desire. In this arena, she was a complete novice, and he was the master of her senses.

Lifting his head, he released her breast, grasping her wrists instead and pushing them up above her head. He did not speak, just wrapped her fingers around the spindles of the headboard, holding them in place. When he let go of her hands, she kept them there.

The feeling of vulnerability as she lay stretched out beneath him, her night rail pushed up above her breasts, one nipple wet and throbbing, the other tight and aching, only increased her ardor. Yet, following his unspoken command, letting him take the lead and submitting to his direction, aroused her even more. As much as she wanted to touch him, just as the silence was freeing, so was the inability to move.

She could not say anything wrong, nor could she do anything wrong. Everything was up to what he wanted.

Bending over her again, he took her other nipple in his mouth, and Kalina moaned. She did not speak or beg again, but whimpered and gasped and cried out as much as she needed under the sensual assault. Curving his fingers over her other breast, his free hand slid down along her side, over her hip, then between her legs where he was kneeling.

The feel of his fingers touching between her legs, sliding through the wet petals of her womanhood, nearly made her levitate. The wooden spindles she was holding creaked as she tightened her grip, her hips lifting.

She was slick, hot, and could feel his fingers exploring her. Stroking her. Caressing her.

One of them found her opening and pushed inside her, and the strange sensation of something invading her body made her cry out in surprised pleasure. No wonder her mother had said this was the most intimate thing a man and wife could experience together.

Kalina felt utterly undone as his finger moved, going deeper, retreating for a moment, then questing forward again. The heel of his hand pressed against the curls over her mound, rubbing gently, and sending an utter shock of pleasure through her. Her toes curled as her head thrashed back and forth.

The urge to beg was growing, but she knew he did not want her to speak.

Part of her almost did, just to feel his hand over her mouth again.

But she wanted to show him that she could follow his direction. That she could give him whatever he needed, whatever he desired. She could make up for how he'd ended up married to her.

At least, she could try.

Another long finger slid inside her, and she moaned, shuddering as she gripped the spindles harder, pulling on them as the sensations made her entire body want to curl from head to toe. It was such a strange sensation, yet entirely pleasurable, even as she felt the stretch and the invasion. She'd felt similar stirrings before, but they had never come to this point, never grown in this manner.

The pressure on her mound increased, his fingers stroking inside her as he suckled her nipple. The intense pleasure grew, coiling inside her tighter and tighter until she could not bear it anymore.

Ecstasy burst within her, the sudden release of tension starting in her core and flaring through her body in a starburst of rapture. It pulsed and throbbed against his hand and fingers. Her cry of pleasure cut through the dark, wordless and passionate.

His mouth moved away from her nipple, but she barely noticed as his hand kept moving, kept pressing, pushing her on wave after wave of sensational bliss as his tongue began to trace patterns on her stomach. Kalina could barely think straight anymore, gasping and shuddering for breath as the intensity of the sensations consumed her body.

The soft wetness of his tongue moved lower and lower. It was not until she felt his hot breath against her mound and swollen lips that she had the first suspicion of his intention.

But no... he couldn't...

Except, it seemed, he could.

His shoulders pressed her thighs wider as his tongue laved over the sensitive flesh between her legs. Kalina shrieked in surprise, trying to close her legs around him, though she did keep her hands firmly gripping the headboard. Sliding his fingers from her body, he wrapped his arms around her legs, his hands pressing against the soft skin of her inner thighs as he pried them apart.

If she had not already been lying down, she might have fainted as he kissed her nether lips, parting them with his tongue and licking up the wetness between. It felt utterly scandalous, even compared to how he'd been touching her before. The sensations were more than she could stand, yet she had no choice.

Air wafted over her sensitive nipples, still moist from his attentions, while her body began to clench and tighten again. She thrashed her head back and forth on the pillow, gasping as the tension built even faster this time, the ministrations of his feasting tongue and lips sending her pleasure higher and higher.

The crest was heaven and hell, as she was so much more sensitive than before, the assault of sensations so much more intense. Rather than bursting inside her and spreading, they rushed through her, pummeling her like a monsoon storm. Tears had gathered in her eyes, sliding from the corners and down into her hair and her pillow, but they were not tears of pain or distress.

They were tears of overwhelm.

Of soul-wracking pleasure.

Of being physically shattered, yet made whole at the same time.

When her husband finally lifted his head, Kalina was practically delirious. Her head spun. Her body throbbed. She felt utterly boneless.

"Let go of the bed." His voice was deep. Rumbly. Husky.

Kalina released her grip, and her fingers ached from having held it so tightly for so long.

Gripping her hips, he turned her over.

She gasped at the sensation of her nipples brushing against the sheets as he pulled her hips back toward him, forcing her to bend at the knees and lifting her bottom into the air. Everything felt so sensitive, she could hardly bear it, yet she knew she must because he had yet to actually engage in what her mother had described as the marital act.

Something thick and hard prodded at her womanhood, much thicker than his fingers, then began to push in. His fingers wrapped around her hips, holding her in place as he began to stretch her open, and she cried out at the shocking sensation of being duly invaded. As strange as his fingers had felt inside her, this was even more so.

It did hurt, a little, the way her mother had warned her it might, but she was so slick, so relaxed from the bouts of ecstasy, it was far easier than it might have been if he'd attempted this when he'd first entered her bed. With her cheek pressed against the pillow, Kalina moaned, shuddering as he retreated, then thrust in deeper. Far deeper than his fingers had gone.

The intimacy of having him inside her so fully, stretching her so wonderfully, was even more so than even his mouth. She could feel him sliding deep into her body, connecting the two of them in a dance as old as time. His guttural groan as he pulled out, then thrust forward for a third time, sliding all the way inside her until his groin bumped up against her bottom, sent a shiver down her spine.

"Bloody hell, your pussy is perfect for my cock," he muttered.

The strange words revolved around her head. A cat? And a rooster? Odd choices, yet somehow, here in the dark, they fit together as perfectly as he did with her.

Kalina did not know if she was supposed to answer since he had told her to hush, but a moment later, he was pulling away again, then thrusting in, and it did not matter because she had no voice, anyway. He moved inside her, retreating and advancing, his fingers gripping her tight as he thrust into her from behind. The sensation of his slick glide, some part of him slapping against the swollen nub of her clitoris as he did so, sent her on paroxysms of pleasure again.

There was no climb—she had already reached the precipice multiple times. This was almost as though she was caught up in the wind and taken up to the clouds, twisting in its grip and unable to escape the waves of pleasure that were so intense, they were almost painful. Every thrust had his cock touching some part of her that sparked and flared with renewed rapture, and she sobbed in agonizing ecstasy as the sensual assault went on and on and on.

His pace picked up, taking her harder, faster, and she cried out, the sound muffled by the pillow as she turned her face into it. The wetness of where her tears had soaked into the fabric moved over her skin as the overwhelming sensations wracked her already rattled senses.

Hereford let out a wordless cry, burying himself inside her. She could feel him, hard and hot and thick and pulsing. Her body gripped him, squeezing the thick length of his cock, as warmth filled her.

His seed.

Slowly, the grip on her hips relaxed. One arm slid under her, holding her against him as he rolled them onto their sides, his hardness still buried inside her. Kalina felt the warmth of his body against her back, his hard muscles holding her tightly.

His nose was buried in her hair, and he inhaled deeply, his grip on her waist slowly loosening.

Everything felt right with the world.

With him wrapped around her, her body both exhausted and sated, she closed her eyes and immediately fell asleep.

26

Deliciously sore, cheeks hot with heat because she was not sure how she was going to look her husband in the eye this morning, Kalina braved the dining room to break her fast. Even before she entered, she could hear the chatter of higher voices alongside Hereford's deeper one, so she knew the rest of the family was there.

She had slept for longer than she usually did.

Margaret had had to rouse her rather forcefully to keep her from oversleeping.

Perhaps that was no surprise, considering the lateness at which she had actually fallen asleep—and the exertion of her activities immediately before. Those activities were the reason for her hot cheeks.

She was uncertain how she was to act toward Hereford now that they'd engaged in such intimacies. Now that he'd put his mouth on every part of her, now that he'd been *inside* her. Yet there was no other option but to carry on.

For the first time, she somewhat understood the British attitude of keeping a stiff upper lip. It did help get one through embarrassing moments.

Steeling herself, she took a deep breath and opened the door to the dining room. Four pairs of eyes met hers, two of them turning in their seats to do so. The heat in her cheeks flared even higher.

"Good morning," she said, doing her best to keep her voice even.

"Good morning," three voices chorused back immediately.

Her husband's response was a touch slower. More mumbled.

She was acutely aware of Hereford's eyes on her as she moved over to the buffet, though when she glanced over at the table, he had already turned his gaze down to his plate.

Her stomach flipped over in disappointment.

Any hope that last night had changed anything between them was gone. Though he'd given her such pleasure, touched her so intimately, fallen asleep wrapped around her...

Even the fact that he'd quit her bed at some point had not necessarily indicated anything. She did not know when he'd left. For all she knew, he'd retreated just before Margaret had come into the room.

Or right after she'd fallen asleep.

Dropping her attention back to the selection of food in front of her, she picked up a plate. Despite the way her stomach was now churning, she was still ravenous. And it was going to be a long day. She needed to eat something.

"I want a rainbow of dresses!" Fiona was saying as Kalina brought her plate to the table. A glass of water had already been set out for her, along with a teacup. The pot of tea sat in the middle of the table.

As she sat down, Julianna picked up the pot and poured Kalina a cup of tea. She could not help but feel grateful. If the sisters were not overly demonstrative in welcoming her, they were at least not cold.

Not like their brother.

The way that he looked at Fiona, the way he smiled, nearly took her breath away with a desire to have him look at her like that again. With warmth. With appreciation. With interest.

"Start with three dresses first," he told his youngest sister. "I have things I need to attend to today, but soon you will be able to get more."

"One for each of us?" Fiona asked, glancing at her other two sisters, obviously wanting to be sure she understood what her brother meant. All of them were wearing hand-me-downs again. The dresses were out of fashion, the colors slightly faded, though they'd been well taken care of. They did fit very well, which indicated some sewing ability by at least one person in the household.

"Three for each of you."

"Each?" Julianna whispered, her eyes wide. Her gaze darted to Kalina, then away again.

It was obvious where the largess was coming from.

"Huzzah!" Fiona threw her hands up in the air, apparently forgetting that she was holding her fork in one of them. Some of the eggs that had been on the tines went flying to the floor behind her. She half-turned to look as she realized her mistake. "Oops."

Kalina startled as something red and furry darted out from underneath the table, heading directly for the fallen eggs. Her mouth dropped open when it came to a halt. Reddish fur, bushy tail... was that a fox?

"Fiona." Hereford's voice was both amused and full of resignation. "You know Telemachus is not allowed in the dining room. How did you even get him in here?"

"I did not!" Fiona said, jumping up and hurrying over to the fox. She picked him up, and he did not protest. The fallen eggs were already gone, and he was licking his chops with satisfaction. "He must have snuck in. He's very wily, you know."

"Mmm." The sound Hereford made was noncommittal.

"What are you going to do about Telemachus once we get dogs?" Julianna asked.

"Oh, they will be the best of friends," Fiona said cheerfully, carrying Telemachus out of the room.

The three older siblings looked at each other.

Emma sighed.

"You know, the way she is, she might even be right. Telemachus has never bothered Archibald or the hens or any of the other animals she's brought in."

"I'm not worried about Telemachus bothering the dogs; I'm worried about the other way around," Julianna said quietly, glancing at the open doorway.

"The dogs will be out in the kennel, and Telemachus rarely leaves the house other than to go in the garden." Hereford shrugged. "Their paths should not cross."

"Until Fiona crosses them," Emma muttered quietly beside Kalina, quietly enough that neither of her siblings appeared to have heard.

Kalina made a mental note to find a way to keep an eye on Fiona. She was not old enough for a lady's maid, but she could certainly use some kind of governess... one who was very good with animals.

Fiona came skipping back into the room, effectively ending that conversation and returning it to the more important one of shopping. At first, silently eating, Kalina listened to the sisters discussing what kind of dresses they might get, only to find herself drawn into the discussion as they began to ask her about the current fashions in London.

At the head of the table, Hereford stayed silent, listening attentively. Did he think she would steer his sisters wrong? She hoped he did not think that lowly of her character.

Though if he did, she could hardly blame him.

The others were finished with their meals before her, having started so much earlier. The three sisters dispersed to go ready themselves for the trip, chattering happily. Kalina looked at her husband, who was also finished but far too polite to leave her at the table alone. At least he felt she was due that much courtesy.

Looking at him, she could not help but feel the heat rising in her cheeks again. Now that they were here, she was glad that he had come to her in the darkness. It had given the experience a dreamlike quality. One that helped separate it from the cold man she now faced. If she'd actually seen him as he'd touched her...

But she had not.

"They will likely need more than gowns," she said quietly, because she did not know what else to say to him. She was not going to bring up the previous night, after all. Everything in their past only touched on the sore topic of how she'd become his wife. His sisters were safe.

"What?" He blinked, looking at her for the first time and meeting her gaze.

Kalina's heart leapt up into her throat as his hazel eyes locked with hers, but she managed to keep speaking.

"They will likely need more than gowns. They'll need small clothes. Possibly nightgowns." She hesitated, but pushed on because she had a feeling that he had not thought beyond the immediately obvious since that was all he'd stated. His sisters might be loath to press for more, but that was what they needed. "Hats and bonnets. Gloves. Fiona's shoes appear to pinch her feet."

Hereford sat for a moment, his expression blanking. Not as if he was angry, but as though he was running through a tally in his head of what it would cost. She had a feeling that was second nature to him.

Having seen the state of Hereford Hall, she was no longer as sure that her dowry would cover all necessary debts and repairs, yet his sisters needed to be properly outfitted. She was also not sure of his relationship with the local shops. The ones in London would continue to cater to the *ton* on credit, but eventually, even they would close their doors for nonpayment.

"I do not have enough ready cash, but as long as they do not opt for anything extravagant, the local shops should be willing to extend the credit. They know we would not ask for it if we did not think we could fulfill it."

Kalina nodded, relieved that he had not taken umbrage at her comment and that she would not have to announce that it would be two gowns each in order to afford the rest of the necessities.

Now that her plate was cleared, her husband moved his chair back.

"If you will excuse me, I need to spend the day going over the accounts."

"Of course," she said, getting to her feet so he could as well.

"Madam." He nodded his head in acknowledgment, turning and striding from the room. Kalina felt her heart sink as she watched him go.

She understood why, but she'd hoped...

It appeared that last night had not earned her any softening of his attitude toward her.

* * *

NATHANIAL

The clatter of a carriage arriving outside drew Nathanial from his desk to the window to watch his sisters and wife exit the house along with her lady's maid. Even from a distance, the difference in their dress was obvious. His wife looked every inch a duchess, in a dark rose gown that was the height of London fashion and adorned with intricate lace in unusual patterns and a matching hat perched smartly on top of her head. His sisters... the material that made up Julianna's dress was far finer than that of Emma's or Fiona's, but it was so far out of fashion, it was clearly too old to be hers. His wife's lady's maid was better dressed.

They will have new dresses by the end of the day.

He blew out a long, slow breath.

At some point, he would also need to make his way to his tailor.

He was grateful that his wife had pointed out there were more than gowns to consider. Nathanial was not certain what state the girls' small clothes were in, and he would not have thought to ask. Julianna and Emma would certainly need new underthings to go with their dresses, as fashion demanded.

Watching his wife and sisters get into the Earl of Harrington's carriage, he imagined a day—not too far from now—when they would get into a carriage bearing the Hereford coat of arms and not the Harrington's. A carriage very much like the one he'd traveled in with his parents when he was younger. Back when he'd thought his father could do no wrong.

Some days, he was uncertain whether his anger at his father was more for shattering that illusion or for the mess he'd left them in.

As the carriage rumbled back down the drive, Nathanial turned away from the window. He had a lot of work to do, and for once, it was not pinching pennies or scrounging or tearing his hair out over lack.

Instead, he would finally have funds… and he wanted to ensure that he did far better to provide for his family than his father had. He'd already prioritized the debts they still owed—he'd done that ages ago—but the amount his wife's dowry provided went well beyond that.

He had investments he wanted to make.

He had a list of things he wanted to do for the Hall.

He had a list of staff he *needed* to hire and an even longer list he *wanted* to hire.

Neither of which had gotten as much attention from him as the debts.

Nathanial needed to figure out what he could do to improve their lives, the estate, and balance that with an eye toward the future.

He had barely gotten into it before there was a knock on the door.

"Come in." Lifting his head, he tried not to show his impatience. It was rare he got to enjoy tending to finances or be excited about it. The interruption was not entirely welcome, but with his family out of the house, it could only be one of the Milfords.

Miss Milford opened the door and stepped in. Her expression was particularly blank.

"Your Grace," she said, bobbing a curtsy. "I came to confirm to you that her grace's sheet was marked, as expected."

"Thank you, Miss Milford," he said, and she bobbed another curtsy, taking herself out the door and shutting it firmly behind her.

Despite his eagerness to get back to the accounts, Nathanial leaned back in his chair, turning the news over in his mind. He'd felt certain, last night, that his wife had been a virgin, but he'd still asked for confirmation. Thinking about his wife brought him a certain amount of tension, and he'd thought that might be the worry…

Now that he had the confirmation, he knew that the question of his wife's virginity had not been his concern. There was no loosening of tension, no release of frustration. It *had* occurred to him that one reason for trapping a duke might have been because she was already with child... but he had not truly believed it.

Not thought it fitting her character.

But considering her first deception, he'd wanted to be sure.

If only his new certainty made him feel any better.

Last night had been another kind of revelation. Her passion, her obedience...

But he'd also discovered what a light sleeper she was.

When he'd entered her room, she'd been still, her breathing even. Yet she'd woken as he'd approached the bed, before he'd even come alongside it, giving herself away. Perhaps she no longer felt the need for deception, but it had confirmed the initial one.

No wonder he'd felt the urge to spank her at that moment. He'd barely been able to tolerate hearing her voice. And yet that urge had eventually been subsumed by the desire to kiss her. She'd been everything he could have wanted in a wife on their wedding night.

If only it had come about in a different manner.

Well. At least he did not have to worry about a cuckoo in his nest. Which should have made him feel far better than it did.

But he was still left with the question—why him?

27

———————

The carriage was well sprung and extremely comfortable. She had not recognized the coat of arms on the door, but a little questioning of Hereford's sisters made for easy conversation on the way into the village. The Earl of Harrington was one of their neighbors who frequently allowed them to borrow a horse or the carriage when they needed. From the careful way Julianna phrased her explanation, it was clear they tried not to tax his generosity. He was not often in the country, though his wife had spent most of her time there with her daughter until the daughter married Lord Hyde.

Learning about the neighbors took up most of the drive to the village, which had not been on the road Kalina had ridden in on, so she stared out the window in curiosity. She was not entirely sure how to judge by English standards, but it seemed a rather large village, bustling with activity and people.

The carriage came to a halt in front of a shop with a large glass window, dresses and fabric displayed in it. A moment later, the footman who had accompanied the coachman was opening the door to the carriage. Fiona squealed with excitement, bouncing in her seat, and her joy was infectious as the others disembarked from the carriage. She put a smile on all of their faces, as well as several passersby.

There were also several who looked askance at Julianna and Emma's dresses, and even more who looked at Kalina with curiosity.

"Do you come to the village often?" she asked Julianna quietly as they entered the shop.

"No." Julianna looked away, not meeting Kalina's gaze, as if she was ashamed of the answer.

"Can I have a dress out of this?" Fiona asked. She was already more than halfway through the shop and holding up a prettily patterned multi-hued fabric.

Kalina was about to answer when a sharp voice snapped out, cutting her off before she could begin.

"Do not touch that." A woman appeared from the back of the shop, coming forward. She was older, handsome in features, with pale skin that set off her dark hair and eyes. The frown on her face made her less attractive than she might have been otherwise.

Her gaze glanced dismissively over Margaret—who had taken up station by the door—Kalina, and Emma, but widened when they reached Julianna.

"My lady." She immediately dipped into a curtsy and held it, head bowed so they could not see her expression.

"Mrs. Galbraith." Julianna smiled tightly, sending a reassuring look to Fiona, who had frozen, still holding the edge of the fabric she'd been so entranced by. "You have not met my sisters, Lady Emma and Lady Fiona."

"My apologies, my lady, I did not realize she was with you." The apology sounded sincere enough as Mrs. Galbraith rose, but she also glanced at Fiona again, as if she expected the girl to start running amok. Then her gaze moved to Kalina. Traveled over her clothing, taking in the fabric, the fine work, and the jewels winking at Kalina's throat and dangling from her ears.

Kalina had dressed to impress, knowing how important it was to make the right impression as Hereford's duchess. She also wanted to avert any issues when it came to receiving credit from the shopkeepers. While she did not make an ostentatious show of wealth, any seamstress or modiste who saw her attire would immediately clock her as having money to spend.

"And this is my brother's new wife, the Duchess of Hereford." It rolled off Julianna's tongue easily enough, but hearing herself referred to as such gave Kalina a start that she had to hide.

Mrs. Galbraith outright stared at Kalina in shock before Julianna made a small noise, and the woman dipped into another curtsy.

"Your Grace. I... had not heard that the duke had married." The woman stumbled slightly over her words.

Kalina almost felt bad for her, except that there was something about the woman that made it difficult for her to find sympathy for her. Perhaps it was because she had snapped at Fiona when she had not been doing anything wrong. Fiona had recovered her movement, but now she was standing stock still with her hands behind her back, her joy dampened.

"It was quite recent," Julianna said, causing Emma to press her lips together. Yesterday was quite recent indeed. Kalina was happy to let Julianna navigate the waters with the locals, as she would know them better even if she did not often come into town.

The modiste was looking at Kalina again, her gaze traveling almost impudently over Kalina's face, a slight frown curving her lips.

"Is something wrong?" Kalina asked, raising one eyebrow.

"No, no, of course not, Your Grace. I just... I suppose I was not expecting him to marry a... a foreigner." Mrs. Galbraith sniffed, smoothing her skirt down with her hands even though it did not need it. "Nothing personal, of course, Your Grace, it just seems strange that our nobles would want to marry outside of our own."

Nothing personal. Of course. It never was. Not to Mrs. Galbraith because she was not on the receiving end of the thinly veiled insult. She would not like any foreigner marrying her duke. But it still felt intensely personal to Kalina.

She could at least take heart from the fact that Julianna and Emma were both now staring at Mrs. Galbraith, open-mouthed with shock and disapproval at her temerity to speak so dismissively of

Kalina's heritage. Margaret was bristling, obviously ready to jump to Kalina's defense. Their reaction, and thinking of how Lady Astrid would reply to the woman, gave Kalina the courage to respond as she wanted to, rather than swallowing the insult.

"Perhaps if England wants fewer foreigners, she should stop claiming other countries as her own," Kalina replied with a thin smile. "That is how my mother became part of the British Empire." Mrs. Galbraith blinked owlishly, rather taken aback. But Kalina did not give her a chance to respond. She turned to Julianna. "Is there another dress shop here?"

"Yes." Julianna shot a look at Mrs. Galbraith before turning away to meet Kalina's gaze. "It is just down the road."

"Good. We will be going there now." Kalina raised her chin up, about to pivot on her heel, when Mrs. Galbraith came stumbling forward.

"Wait! Your Grace, I think you misunderstood me." Mrs. Galbraith held her hands out beseechingly. "I did not mean to insult you. I was speaking generally, not to you personally."

"Yet I am one of the people you are speaking generally about." Kalina looked down her nose at the woman, who was only trying to correct herself now that she realized she was going to lose custom over it. "Did you really expect me to stay here and pay you for the privilege of being made to feel unwelcome?"

From the suddenly pinched expression on Mrs. Galbraith's face, she had. Kalina nodded when the other woman did not respond immediately.

"Come, Fiona." Kalina held out her hand, and the young girl immediately ran to take it.

Mrs. Galbraith bristled, and by the time they had reached the door, the woman had found her voice again.

"This is why no one likes you foreigners," she shrieked. "You have no sense of how things are supposed to be done!"

Holding her head high, Kalina swept back out onto the street, pulling Fiona with her. Her heart was pounding in her chest, and her jaw was locked tight against the angry tears that wanted to fall, but she kept a serene expression on her face. There was no way she was going to give that woman the satisfaction of knowing that she'd hurt Kalina in any way.

She also could not turn around and point out that Mrs. Galbraith was only reaping the rewards of her own actions. Not without behaving exactly the way the dressmaker expected her to, and Kalina would rather eat her hat than give her any satisfaction.

"Why was she so mean?" Fiona asked once they were out on the street, the door cutting off Mrs. Galbraith's outrage. At least she had the sense not to follow them out.

Holding tightly to Kalina's hand, Fiona looked up at her with confusion. Kalina took a deep breath, wrestling with her unruly emotions. Thankfully, Margaret came to her rescue. She had a rather unique perspective, coming from the outside but having observed what Kalina and her family had been through.

"Some people don't like anyone who is different from them. Whether they come from a different place, look differently because of their skin or hair, or believe something different." Margaret sniffed derisively. "They reject what they do not know. Some of them are afraid."

"Afraid of what?"

"Mostly afraid they'll be treated the same way they treat others who are different, as far as I can tell." Margaret made a face. "I saw that a lot in India. There are those who lash out, trying to protect themselves, even though they are not under attack. In fact, in India, it was we British who were doing the attacking. We were the foreigners in their country, and we've been making it part of the British Empire. Something Mrs. Galbraith obviously did not think about. In India, it was her grace's father who was the unwelcome foreigner."

"Oh." Fiona's eyes widened, and she looked up at Kalina. "I do not want you to feel unwelcome."

"You have made me feel very welcome," Kalina said, smiling down at her and giving the girl's hand a reassuring squeeze. She came to a halt, stepping to the side to get out of the way of any passersby, and turned back to the older two sisters. "Ah... I do not know where I am going."

"This way." Julianna stepped forward, and Margaret fell back to walk alongside Emma. The footman, who had been waiting outside the shop, trailed them. If he thought anything about their abrupt departure from the shop, or if he'd overheard any of the conversation between Fiona and Margaret, he did not show it in his very blank expression. "I cannot apologize enough, Kalina. I had no idea... if I had realized..."

"Do not worry. I do not hold you accountable for her actions," Kalina said smoothly, smiling at Julianna. She could tell her sister-in-law had been sincerely distressed by Mrs. Galbraith's words at the moment, as she was apologizing now. "You would have had no reason to know she felt such a way."

Because, of course, the woman would hardly have behaved in such a manner to Julianna herself.

Despite Julianna's claim that the sisters did not visit the village often, numerous passersby saw her and dropped a quick curtsy, along with a speculative look at Kalina. The people out and about were mostly born and bred English, but she slowly relaxed as she realized she was hardly the only person with darker skin in the village. Several of the shopkeepers appeared to also be some of the 'foreigners' Mrs. Galbraith was so unhappy about.

Kalina glanced at Julianna, but she seemed to find it unremarkable that so many knew her on sight. Perhaps she used to visit the village more.

"Here we are," Julianna said, gesturing to the door of another shop. She looked at it dubiously. "I must admit, I have not been here before. Mrs. Galbraith's mother was my mother's seamstress."

"I am sure we can find something," Kalina reassured her. If she had to, she would send Julianna and Emma to Mrs. Galbraith's on their own, though she hoped it did not come to that.

She was reassured on multiple levels the moment they stepped into the shop. It was clean and orderly, with high-quality fabric displayed in a multitude of colors. A mother and her daughter with dark brown skin were on the far side of the shop, heads bent over a bolt that they were discussing.

"Hello, hello!" A friendly round woman with grey hair, apple cheeks, and bright eyes came over to greet them immediately. "Welcome. Oh my, Lady Julianna!" She immediately dipped into a curtsy.

"I am sorry, I do not know your name," Julianna said, though she seemed unsurprised at being recognized despite that.

"Of course not, my lady. I am Mrs. Collins. My parents moved away when I was younger, but I still remember what your mother looked like, and you are the spitting image." Mrs. Collins tilted her head, smiling fondly at what was clearly a good memory. She had also cleared up the mystery of how so many in the village recognized Julianna, especially if Julianna was wearing one of her mother's dresses, as Kalina suspected. It would enhance the resemblance.

"Thank you." Julianna smiled at Mrs. Collins. "This is my new sister-in-law, the Duchess of Hereford."

"Oh! Your Grace!" Mrs. Collins immediately sank into a deep curtsy. "I wish you very happy indeed. My apologies, I had not heard that his grace had married."

"It is rather recent." The side of Kalina's mouth twitched as she echoed Julianna's previous answer. Emma lifted her hand to her mouth, covering her smile. "The duke and I appreciate your well wishes."

"Of course! What can I do for you today, Your Grace? My ladies?" Mrs. Collins beamed at the giggling Fiona as she straightened. Everything about her demeanor was the complete opposite of Mrs. Galbraith's, and Kalina relaxed further.

"Do you have any ready-made dresses?" Kalina asked. One ready-made dress for each of the sisters, then they could order two more, but she very much wanted them to be able to each walk out with a new gown.

"Oh, yes, right back here." Mrs. Collins waved her hand, turning her head as the woman on the other side of the shop called out to her. "Go ahead and take a look, and I will join you in a moment."

The fact that Mrs. Collins went to attend to her other customer, who surely could not have been anywhere near in rank to Kalina, made her feel even better about the woman. Smiling, she went with Hereford's sisters to look at the ready-made dresses.

Several hours later, they exited the store, all wearing new small clothes, gloves, and dresses. Mrs. Collins had packed up the old ones and promised to deliver them to the Hall along with the finished dresses that had been ordered. Beaming widely, she thanked them for coming and, again, gave Kalina her best wishes on her new marriage.

Stepping out into the street, Kalina smiled wide as she watched Fiona spin in a happy circle, quietly chanting "new dress" over and over again. Though more reserved, both Julianna and Emma were beaming as well, continuously glancing at their reflections in the shop glass as they went from Mrs. Collins' shop to the milliners', then on to the cobblers. All of them had their measurements taken, except Fiona, as she was still growing, and she received a new pair of shoes with some space to grow into.

Whispers about the duke's marriage had spread quickly, and several of the town worthies came to introduce themselves, including the mayor's wife, who apologized for her husband's absence. Kalina was not certain if someone had said something about her exit from Mrs. Galbraith's shop, but there were no more incidents. She was warmly welcomed by everyone who approached her.

They had luncheon at the local inn, which served a variety of meat pies and a delicious potato and leek soup with a thick, crusty bread. The innkeeper, Mr. Ward, had quickly shown them to a private room where they could eat without interruption, for which Kalina was grateful. Though she'd expected some stir about her arrival, she had not realized how deep the curiosity would run. Not just about her either, but about Hereford's sisters.

She was beginning to realize how much they'd kept to themselves over the years, likely both because they had not been able to afford to do otherwise and also to keep up appearances. Of course, it would have been impossible to completely hide that the dukedom was struggling, but she wondered if anyone had realized how badly or if the family had only convinced themselves they were fooling their neighbors.

As they finished their meal, Fiona leaned back in her chair and looked around.

"Now what?" she asked, a little trepidatiously but also a bit hopefully.

They could return to the Hall, but Hereford had said they had the carriage for the entire day, that the earl did not need it. And Kalina had some of her own money in her reticule. Certainly more than enough to get a treat for all of them. She was not ready for the day to be over yet. She was enjoying herself, the sisters were warming up to her, and she had no desire to return to Hereford's coldness sooner than she had to.

"Is there somewhere nearby that sells sweets?" she asked Julianna, whose eyes lit up.

"There is indeed."

As far as her first day as the Duchess of Hereford went, Kalina felt it was a resounding success.

The only thing she was uncertain of was whether her husband would agree.

28

———————

For the first time since inheriting his title, Nathanial was able to feel truly satisfied with his work. It turned out everything in life was easier when the money to cover basic necessities and beyond was available.

Again, that feeling of resentful gratitude welled up inside him.

If he could only work his emotions past the resentment... but every time he thought about it, his mind lingered on exactly *why* he was resentful. About how his choices had been taken from him, when he'd had so very few in the first place. About how much he'd liked her.

Enjoyed her company.

Only to discover she wasn't who, or what, he'd thought she was.

Maybe he would be less resentful if she had not pretended to be an honorable young lady. If she had not made him like her.

A knock on the door to his study made him jump. Though he knew the Milfords were about, he had not expected to be interrupted.

"Come in."

Daniel opened the door, stepping inside with a frown on his face.

"Mr. Galbraith, from the village, requests an audience, Your Grace."

No wonder Daniel was frowning. Nathanial's lips turned down in the same manner. There was an unspoken agreement in the area that everyone adhered to, which was not to call on Hereford Hall unless it was a dire emergency. Not that Nathanial would have been able to help with many emergencies before, other than personally lending his own muscle to a cause.

Which he had done a time or two.

But from the look of disapproval on Daniel's face, whatever brought Mr. Galbraith here today, it was not an emergency.

The man owned one of the village's dressmaker shops, which his wife ran.

Ah. He must be here to ascertain that Nathanial was now up to snuff before having his wife start on the dresses for the girls. No wonder Daniel was disapproving. He would be insulted at the implication, no matter that there was reason for it.

Nathanial was a little as well, but he hid it. He could not blame a man for wanting to ensure he would be paid what he was owed. There were plenty among the *ton* who took advantage of their position to keep from paying their bills for far longer than was conscionable, Nathanial's own father included. He was determined to take a different route, now that he could.

"Show him in." He knew he sounded weary when he said the words, but it was more resignation that Mr. Galbraith would see more of the Hall than most had since Nathanial's father's demise. Still, he could not go out to the foyer to greet the man. Thankfully, it was a short walk from the front door to the study, so he would not see everything about how depilated the Hall had become.

At least Nathanial's study was in good condition, thanks to the fact that his father had rarely used it, even before Nathanial's mother's death. Though if he had actually done some work in it, perhaps the family and the Hall would not have gotten into such a state.

No use in thinking of what ifs, though.

Nathanial stood as Daniel showed Mr. Galbraith into the room, wearing a finely tailored suit and holding a brown cap in his hand. The man was much as Nathanial remembered him, although a little older now. He'd not lost any hair, but there was grey showing at his temples and a few more lines on his face than before. He'd served as Nathanial's tailor when Nathanial was younger, while his wife ran the dressmakers that Nathanial's mother had shopped at.

Theirs had been one of the first debts that Nathanial had paid off when he inherited, before he'd realized exactly how many his father had owed.

"Your Grace." Mr. Galbraith bowed low before approaching Nathanial's desk and standing in front of it. Daniel remained in the doorway listening, and Nathanial did not bother to dismiss him. Hopefully, this would be quick, then Daniel could show Mr. Galbraith back out. "It is good to see you home again."

"Thank you, sir. Please, sit. What can I do for you today? I assume my sisters and wife visited Mrs. Galbraith." That was a good lead-in for Mr. Galbraith to express any concerns about payment. Nathanial would rather get straight to the point than dance around the subject, especially since he would actually be able to pay the man.

"Ah, yes, and I believe there was a misunderstanding between my wife and the new duchess." Mr. Galbraith did not sit; rather, he wrung the hat he was holding in front of him, appearing rather agitated. Nathanial blinked as he realized that whatever had brought Mr. Galbraith to his door, it was not concerns over being paid.

"A misunderstanding?"

"Yes, I believe your wife misconstrued something Mrs. Galbraith said. It can be hard, you know, Your Grace, with someone unaccustomed to our ways." Mr. Galbraith turned the brim of his hat between his fingers, spinning it like a wheel as he smiled earnestly, but his eyes were full of worry.

"What was it exactly that Mrs. Galbraith said?" Nathanial folded his hands in front of him, giving Mr. Galbraith a hard look. He would be questioning Julianna as soon as they got home, although she was just as likely to come running right to him if there had been any serious contretemps.

"Well, see, I don' rightly know exactly what was said, Your Grace. I twasn't in the shop when the ladies visited, but Mrs. Galbraith was in a right state after they left. She said the new duchess, ah, well, that the new duchess took insult to something she said and wouldna give her the chance to explain." The way he stumbled over his words and his demeanor pricked at Nathanial.

"What do you expect me to do about it?" he asked after a long moment, when it appeared that was all Mr. Galbraith had to say.

"Well, I was hoping you could talk to your duchess and sisters, see, Your Grace. Explain that my wife did not mean anything. We would hate to lose your custom, Your Grace, especially after all the work my wife did for the late duchess." Mr. Galbraith had stopped spinning his cap, and now he clutched at it, digging his fingers in. "My wife, you know, she was just surprised. No one knew you'd married and, well, I think she expected an English lady, you know?"

Despite all the stumbles and roundabouts, Nathanial got the general idea of what Mr. Galbraith was saying.

He frowned at the man.

"I was not aware that I had an obligation to choose a bride based on your wife's expectations, Sir." He knew his tone was icy, and it was not entirely Mr. Galbraith's fault, but Nathanial was so damn tired of everyone's expectations. Especially because he now had a feeling that Mrs. Galbraith had very likely insulted his wife when they went to shop there, likely not realizing she was the new duchess.

"Of course not, of course not, Your Grace," Mr. Galbraith said in a rush. "It just took her by surprise, you know, that you had not, and well, it's been hard with all the foreigners taking up space in the village."

Nathanial raised his eyebrow.

"You mean the foreigners who started businesses that have helped the village to grow? The ones who assisted with the harvest for trade, who we would not have been able to get all the harvest done without them?" Nathanial had been very happy to welcome new additions to the village, and they'd proven themselves time and time again to be nothing but beneficial. "I do not recall you helping with the harvest, sir."

"Ah, well, yes, bad back, you know..." Mr. Galbraith coughed. "I am not saying all of them, but there have been troublemakers, too, Your Grace. Like, when the Martins' cows got into the hay field because the Dormer boys wanted to see what would happen, or so they say."

"If I remember correctly, your boys let the Martins' bull in with the Wainwrights' cows when they were about the same age."

"Oh, well." Mr. Galbraith seemed at a loss for words at having his own sons compared to the Dormers. Yet of the two incidents, the consequences of letting the bull in among the dairy cows had been far more destructive. Either he'd forgotten or he had not conflated the two.

"Mr. Galbraith, where my wife and sisters choose to buy their dresses is their prerogative. If you think there was a misunderstanding between your wife and mine, that is something that is best handled between them. I cannot, and I will not, try to force my wife to use a particular dressmaker, no matter that she used to make dresses for my mother." Nathanial spoke crisply, laying out the matter as he saw it and giving Mr. Galbraith no room to interrupt or try to explain further.

"I am sure I can count on you to make my wife feel welcome in her new home. When the opportunity arises and Mrs. Galbraith can apologize for the misunderstanding."

"Ah... yes." From the way Mr. Galbraith's expression had fallen, that was not quite the response he'd been hoping for. He knew that he'd been dismissed, though, and bowed. "Thank you, Your Grace."

"Daniel will see you out." He glanced back at where Daniel was in the doorway and gave him a little nod. Daniel would know that meant Nathanial wanted him to return to the study afterward.

It did not take Daniel long to return. Nathanial was leaning back in his chair, thinking, when the other man came in. He gestured at the leather wingbacks in front of his desk, offering one to Daniel, who took the one on the left.

"So. What do you think?"

Daniel snorted, shaking his head. Unlike Mr. Galbraith, he didn't pepper his speech with Nathanial's title, as he'd long had permission to speak freely with Nathanial.

"I think Mrs. Galbraith probably let her views on foreigners drop in front of your duchess, likely insulted her to boot, and then had another two thoughts about it when she finally realized all the lost commissions the duchess represented. If there's one thing the Galbraiths care more about than the 'foreign invasion,' it's their till."

"The foreign invasion?" That was a new one to Nathanial.

"There are just a few who call it that. Most of us are grateful for the new blood. There's been no more trouble than what our boys usually cause, but of course those like the Galbraiths grumbled three times as much about it while pretending their own are angels." Daniel snorted again, making his opinion on that matter clear.

"Anything I should be worried about? Especially when it comes to ensuring my wife faces no more attitudes like the Galbraiths?"

"Nah, Your Grace, no need to worry. Like I said, most of us know what's what. It's done us far more good than bad, and the bad has not been truly bad. Just youthful mischief. Honestly, we'd all rather keep them than the Galbraiths. Like you said, he didn't lift a finger to help with the harvest." Daniel chuckled.

"Is there another dressmaker available?" Nathanial thought he remembered there being one, but he was not entirely sure.

Thankfully, Daniel nodded.

"Mrs. Collins will have them handled. And the Galbraiths cannot even complain overly much. Mrs. Collins used to be Abigail Pritchard." Daniel grinned.

Nathanial vaguely remembered the Pritchards and their daughter from his childhood, when he'd visited the village far more often. It was good that she'd come back. And, as an Englishwoman and a former local, she probably got under the Galbraiths' skin more than if she'd been from outside of the country, giving them less of an excuse to complain about a competing shop.

"That's good. Thank you, Daniel. Now. Let's talk about hiring."

Which would certainly include quite a few people in the village, likely many whom Mr. Galbraith would find objectionable. Which was just fine with Nathanial. Without them, and without the dukedom's backing, the village could just as easily have died out.

Now that he had the money to give more support to the village, that included those who had saved it. No, they had not lived here for generations, but they would for generations to come if he had anything to say about it.

Just like his family.

By the time he and Daniel were done talking through the possible local hires and had made a list of positions they would still need to fill, he heard the sound of the ladies returning. It was hard to miss since Fiona came into the house shrieking his name —only the joy in her voice kept him from jumping up and panicking.

Exchanging an amused glance with Daniel, he got to his feet and went to greet his sisters.

He had not realized how much he would enjoy seeing them properly outfitted. His wife hung back, allowing his sisters to have their moment under his gaze. Fiona was dancing around with pure happiness, Julianna was beaming, and even Emma was standing a little straighter and preening.

Though the gowns were not perfectly fitted to them, they were more than acceptable for general day dresses around the Hall. They looked more like sisters of a duke now.

"Beautiful," he said as Fiona twirled for him, smiling widely at her.

"Thank you! I am glad we got them from Mrs. Collins. Mrs. Galbraith was mean." Fiona twirled again as Nathanial blinked. "I'm going to go show Telemachus!"

Before he could respond, she'd run off again. He looked over at the others. Emma was saying something to his wife, so he did not think they'd heard what Fiona had said, but Julianna obviously had. She made a face.

"I'm glad you all had such a good outing," he said, tilting his head in the direction of his study. "Julianna, can I speak with you for a minute?"

Neither his wife nor Emma seemed to see anything amiss with his request as they glanced up to smile at Julianna. He led his sister down the hall, very curious as to what she would have to say.

By the time she'd finished her recounting of the day, Nathanial was fuming and wishing he'd gotten the full story before Mr. Galbraith had had the temerity to appear at his door. If he'd known...

Well. It seemed his wife had handled the situation on her own, and he had been smart enough to see through Mr. Galbraith's hedging. If the Galbraiths wanted the support of the Hereford Duke and Duchess, they were going to need to apologize *abjectly*.

And Nathanial would do what he could to help the attitudes of anyone else in the village who needed a correction.

No one was going to be allowed to disrespect his wife.

29

———————

KALINA

The second night of her marriage was very much like the first.

Tossing. Turning.

Wondering if her husband would come.

Wondering if she'd detected a slight softening in his attitude toward her after today's shopping trip with his sisters. Certainly, Julianna and Emma were warmer with her now than they had been before today. But she was not sure if her perception that Hereford might be following suit was nothing more than hopeful imaginings.

As she began to finally drift off, the door between their rooms opened. She rolled over onto her back, breathless.

Eager.

Hereford came to the bed, dropping his dressing gown, much as he had the night before, and climbed beneath the covers with her. Unlike last night, her body already felt roused, ready for him. She knew what was possible now. The hardness of his body sliding against hers made her shiver.

Before she could open her mouth to say anything, he lowered his lips to her throat and kissed her, his hand sliding over the curve of her hip and then skimming up her body to cup her breast. Kalina moaned, sliding her own hands over his arms. As freeing as being unable to touch him had felt the night before, she now reveled in touching him.

Exploring him.

His mouth moved lower, to her breasts, to suckle her nipples. Kalina shuddered, wrapping her legs around his body as he sucked hard, dragging his teeth over the tender buds. Every part of her body came alive at his touch, pleasure heating her from the inside out. She grasped his head, her fingers sliding through his hair, and she heard his groan. Felt him rock against her.

A moment later, he was pushing her hands back up above her head again.

"Let me touch you," she pleaded.

"Hush."

Wrapping her fingers around the spindles again, he put his hand over her mouth as he went back down to her breasts. Rather than obey this time, Kalina opened her lips—only to find the tips of his fingers thrust between them. Emboldened, frustrated, she sucked on them hard, dragging her teeth across them as he began to ply his attentions to her breasts again.

Though she did not release the spindles, she was not entirely passive anymore, either. His fingers twisted in her mouth, turning the pads side-down, and she ran her tongue over them. With his head at her breasts, she felt his cock rubbing against the seam of her pussy, sliding back and forth in the growing wetness between her lips.

Nipping at his fingers did nothing to spur him onward. He continued to tease her, growing her passion as she writhed beneath him.

When he finally pulled his fingers from her mouth and settled down between her legs, she was aching with need. She gasped as his tongue parted her nether lips, seeking the little button of pleasure at their apex. Moaning, she moved her hips upward, trying to get more of the pressure her body was demanding.

Then she gasped as she felt something at the entrance of her anus, slick and hard, pushing on the tiny opening. One of his fingers, lubricated from being in her mouth.

Did he know?

Of course he does.

But that was where he wanted to touch her.

His finger pushing into her bottom, his tongue sliding against her wet folds... it did not hurt exactly, but it was not comfortable, either. Surely, that was not decent...

Yet she could not find it in herself to deny him.

If this was what he wanted, she wanted to give it to him. Even as she gasped and clenched, her body automatically trying to push his finger back out, pleasure swirled within her. His mouth moved over her, and he sucked the nub of her clitoris into his mouth as his finger burrowed deeper inside her, making her writhe and dig her heels into his back as he tormented her with sensual pleasure while also pushing her senses to a new height as he began to pump his finger back and forth where it should not be.

His arm moved over her. With his shoulders under her thighs, propping her legs up atop him, his mouth on her pussy, he now wrapped his free arm over the top of her hips, holding her in place so he could do what he willed with her. All the while, Kalina could merely grip the spindles of the bed and gasp and writhe and moan.

She wanted to touch him so badly.

But she wanted to please him more.

By the time he flipped her onto her stomach, she was breathless from pleasure, whimpering from how sensitive every part of her felt. The sudden thought that he might mean to put his cock in her bottom slid through her, but then he was thrusting into the wet heat of her pussy and obliterating that fear from her mind. Kalina pressed her forehead against the bed, moaning as he rode her, hard and fast, sending her senses spiraling out of control yet again.

Sliding his fingers down beneath her, he began to rub the little nub that he'd previously suckled, stroking the over sensitized piece of flesh.

"Please..." she begged, squirming against his thrusts and fingers, caught between them. "I cannot..."

She could not possibly handle another peak of pleasure. Just floating on the haze as he moved inside her was barely tenable.

"Again." His fingers moved more forcefully. "One more time."

The cry that burst from her was barely human as he rubbed rough circles over her slippery flesh, his cock thrusting deep inside her. It was as though her body could not deny his command, no matter how far beyond the bounds he pushed her.

Once again, once he had spent himself inside her and utterly exhausted her, he rolled them onto their sides, his cock still embedded within her. Her head pillowed on his arm, back curled against his front, she felt his hand slide up her body to cup her breast. Holding her tight, his breath slowed along with hers as she slipped into sleep.

In the morning, he was gone again.

That was her life now.

During the night, a passionate husband who drenched her with pleasure. During the day, he was far removed from her. Not exactly icy, but not warm either. The distance hurt her nearly as much, though she clung to hope that perhaps he was a little less distant every day that passed.

Thankfully, there was plenty to fill her time with and distract her.

The first few days, she spent exploring the house and getting to know Nathanial's sisters, assessing what they would require. Fiona needed a governess, certainly, though she could read and do simple arithmetic. Her preference was to be outdoors or with her animals, and Kalina was able to witness firsthand exactly how skilled she was with an injured or frightened creature.

To her amusement, she learned that Archibald, the wild hare, was a daily visitor to the Hall, as if he wanted to check in on the young girl who had once rescued him. She was the only one whose touch he tolerated. Kalina could not help but wonder what Monkey Sinclair would make of Fiona, as he was reluctant to interact with any woman other than Delilah.

Emma's reserve lessened with every day that passed as she became more comfortable with Kalina. She was not at all unwelcoming, or even all that quiet; she was just incredibly shy. As she became more accustomed to Kalina's presence and more comfortable with her, she very quickly became much more talkative. She tended to follow Julianna's lead in everything, but she was very clever, and her interest lay in the gardens.

She took Kalina through them, pointing out the various plants and weeds, describing the work she'd done to try to keep them at least somewhat in line. Eventually, she'd had to retreat to a small space just behind the house, but that small plot of the garden was gorgeously maintained. Much to Kalina's amusement, quiet Emma was happiest when digging in dirt and chattering about plants.

Both Julianna and Emma would need a dance instructor, as neither of them had been taught any of the dances they would need to know. They'd been tucked away in the country for far too long. Both of them also needed to choose a musical instrument and possibly a singing instructor if either of them had a pleasing enough voice.

None of which would help them to run a household, but such skills were expected in order to land a husband.

Hopefully, one who would behave in a less confusing manner than her own.

After the first few days, the house began to be a bustle of interviews. Hereford was hiring local men to refurbish the rooms in the house. Kalina, with Miss Milford and Julianna trailing behind her, went through the rooms she would be expected to play hostess in, detailing her instructions. Julianna seemed to find it very educational.

The dresses from Mrs. Collins arrived, much to the delight of all the sisters. They fit perfectly and were finer than the ready-made gowns. Though Emma still wore Julianna's old dresses when she went out to tend the garden. Kalina made a mental note to have an apron made for her.

As she began interviews with the household, with Miss Milford at her elbow, she had Julianna sit in as well. She had never been trained to run a large household or how to hire new staff, though she had seen plenty let go.

She was clearly eager to learn, though, like her brother, she kept herself slightly removed from Kalina. The two were obviously close, and Kalina had the feeling that Julianna had been Hereford's confidant here in the house for a long time. She likely knew far more about how Kalina and Hereford's marriage had come to be than either Emma or Fiona—not that Fiona would have necessarily understood.

Emma had warmed up to Kalina very quickly, though. Julianna seemed to be withholding judgment, though she was friendly enough during their interactions.

After a week of marriage, Kalina had just become used to the whirlwind in the house when her husband made an announcement over breakfast.

"We are going to need to spend today packing, and tomorrow we are removing to London."

Everyone lifted their heads to stare at him, including Kalina. He had certainly not said anything to her about it. But then... why would he feel he needed to? It was not as though she needed to be consulted.

"All of us?" Julianna asked.

Kalina took heart from the fact that Julianna was clearly surprised as well. Apparently, Hereford had not told anyone of his plans.

"All of us. There are workmen coming in for the roof and some of the walls and floors where they need to be repaired. The Milfords will be staying to oversee the work, but it's going to be noisy and disruptive and... well, I thought you might all like a trip to London," he admitted, sheepishly.

The way he looked at Julianna now was almost boyish, hopeful for praise and uncertain he was going to receive it. The look made Kalina's heart ache for him, as she wondered how long it had been since he'd been able to do something like this for his sisters.

"Yes!" Julianna was nearly bursting with excitement. Emma had gone quiet again, but she smiled readily as Hereford's shoulders relaxed.

Only Fiona was frowning.

"But what about my animals?"

"Telemachus can come with us," Hereford said gently. "Miss Milford has already promised to finish taking care of Robin until he can fly again." Robin being the bird with an injured wing whom she'd recently rescued. "Archibald will have to stay here. Daniel is going to look out for him daily and ensure that everyone knows he's to be left alone."

Eyes filling up with tears, Fiona nodded.

"There will be more animals in London," Kalina told her gently. "We can visit Hyde Park, where there are ducks on the Serpentine. Perhaps we can go to Newmarket for the races one day as well. And there's the London Zoo, and I believe they have an elephant."

That was what finally brightened Fiona up.

"An elephant?" She looked at Hereford, as if asking him for confirmation Kalina was not bamming her.

He nodded.

"And a lion, zebras, bears, and kangaroos."

Fiona's eyes went wide, no longer so tearful. She looked torn.

"Daniel and Jane will take care of Archibald and Robin?"

"Yes. If you have any special instructions for them, you can give them today. We'll leave just after breakfast tomorrow."

"Where are we staying?" Kalina asked, curious. As usual, her husband looked at her shoulder rather than her face as he answered her.

"Manchester Square. I managed to find a house for rent. Apparently, the Earl of Fife and his family had to leave London rather precipitously." His mouth twitched, and Kalina gathered there was more to the story, which was likely untoward for young ears.

"What does precipitously mean?" Fiona asked, distracted from the deep thinking about instructions for animal care that she'd been doing.

"Very quickly," Kalina and Hereford said at the same time.

Surprised, he met her gaze, and the shock of it made her heart suddenly start beating triple time, feeling as if it might jump right out of her chest. For a long moment, their gazes held, like a hypnotic spell. She could not look away, yet she felt wildly uncomfortable looking directly at him.

No wonder he did not usually meet her eyes.

"Are these dresses good enough for London?" Emma asked suddenly, looking down at herself doubtfully. She was wearing one of the ones that had been made expressly for her.

"They are," Kalina reassured her quickly. "Neither you nor Julianna will be able to attend any balls, though there are some teas I might be able to take you to, and your dresses will be perfectly acceptable for those. The readymades you can wear at home."

"There will be modistes in London, as well, and you can all visit Bruton and Bond Streets," Hereford said. "By the time we return to Hereford Hall, you'll all be properly outfitted for the coming year."

"*More* dresses?" Fiona asked incredulously, making Kalina cover her mouth with her hand to smother a laugh. As excited as Fiona had been about having a new dress, it seemed that she was perfectly happy with the three that she now had.

"More dresses," Hereford replied with utter seriousness, though there was mirth dancing in his eyes.

Once again, Kalina felt her heart ache.

She liked her husband.

In fact, she could easily see herself falling in love with her husband.

But she doubted he could ever love her.

At least when they got to London, she would have her friends. Clarence House was not far from Manchester Square, which meant Tiffany would be close. Delilah was practically next door in Portman Square, and Lady Astrid's London home in Grosvenor Square was easily within walking distance. As was Hyde Park.

Her own family was a little farther afield, but at the moment, a little distance between her and her father was likely for the best.

As she watched her husband smiling and joking with his sisters, unsure if he would ever warm to her again in such a manner, it was all she could do not to hold a simmering resentment against her father. With every day that passed, she was realizing what she had gotten herself into for the rest of her life...

She knew her father had been doing his best to give her what he thought would make her happy, but it was feeling more and more like he'd trapped her in a cage where she could envision the life she could have had with Hereford if he'd chosen to marry her but never actually get to live it.

30

Nathanial

They entered London quietly, with little fanfare. The house he'd rented was a row home. His wife would be able to have teas and at-homes but not throw a ball. A dinner party would be the largest gathering possible.

Hereford House had been rented out before the Season started. That money had been what was feeding the girls and the Milfords for the whole Season, as well as giving Nathanial the blunt he'd needed to remain in London searching for a bride. Though he could have exerted his ducal authority and returned to the house, he was not looking to make any more enemies among the *ton*. It would also have required hiring a great deal of staff, not to mention the interest it would have garnered from the rest of Society.

Nathanial's goal for the rest of this Season, until Julianna's debut, was to be as uninteresting as possible.

Not only did the Baron of Fife's departure from London mean that his house had opened up, but it had also provided a gossip cover for Nathanial's return. Who cared about a duke who was now off the market when there was a new scandal to exclaim over?

The Baron and his Baroness had been caught *delecto in flagrante* with the Earl of Denby's eldest, unwed, daughter in the conservatory at her engagement ball. The daughter had been sent to the countryside, the Baron and Baroness had immediately departed for Scotland, and the lady's fiancé had remained in the capital, putting on a show of indifference.

It was the perfect time to return. Tongues would wag far harder for a broken engagement and a scandalous encounter than something as *passe* as a nobleman being trapped into marriage. Even a duke.

As expected, their arrival did not go entirely unnoticed, but there was no surge of nosy guests appearing at their doorstep. Thankfully, Drake had sent over several of his staff to assist until Nathanial could hire his own. Drake swore Nathanial was helping him out, as it would give the under butler and the woman training to replace his housekeeper some practice doing things on their own before eventually moving upward in his own household. There were also several footmen and maids, all of whom had been forewarned about Telemachus and had very little reaction to a fox running underfoot.

The first day, Nathanial had acquired a collar and leash so Fiona could take Telemachus to the park at the center of the square, with the promise that she understood that was the only place he could go outside while they were in London. The last thing Nathanial wanted was to have some young bucks deciding on an impromptu fox chase in the middle of the city. Fiona would be devastated, and who knew what kind of damage could be caused.

Hopefully, the pink bow she'd tied to his collar would make it clear to all that he was a pet.

By the end of the second day, several invitations had come to the door for upcoming events. The *ton* was acknowledging their return to the capital. Though part of him wanted to hide away, he knew it was best to meet them head-on. He and his wife needed to present a united, utterly boring front.

With any luck, by the time Julianna debuted next year, the fact that their marriage had been under rather scandalous circumstances would be barely a memory in the *ton's* mind. It was all about appearances. If they saw a boring married couple who were completely amicable and altogether unremarkable, they would accept that and move on.

Which meant he needed to speak to his wife.

She was in the drawing room, helping Fiona sound out some of the more difficult words in a book about animals they had found at the bookstore the day before. As things went with his sisters, he had to admit he could not have hoped for better when it came to how she cared for them.

While he'd had some concerns over whether she'd be an appropriate guide for them through the *ton*, she'd thrown herself into the role with enthusiasm. A dancing instructor had already been hired for both Julianna and Emma, and a pianist by the name of Arabella Goddard had been hired to brush up their rusty piano skills. Julianna remembered a bit more than Emma, but neither had had a piano to practice on for a very long time. Fiona had never had lessons, and she was starting now, under his wife's tutelage.

No, he had no complaints about his wife's conduct in regard to his sisters.

Whether her family's issues would affect his... Well, they would need to venture into Society to determine where they landed in the *ton's* eyes.

The opportunity arose on the third day when Gregory and Tiffany came to call.

"I am sorry we could not get here sooner, but you did not give us much notice of your arrival," Tiffany scolded him, kissing his cheek. "Where is Kalina?"

"I sent one of the maids to fetch her. I believe she's currently helping Fiona, my youngest sister, with her fingers on the piano."

Tiffany lit up with interest, and Nathanial belatedly remembered that she was a music lover and an incredibly accomplished pianist herself. Unfortunately for her, and fortunately for him, his wife was already arriving at the front hall.

"Tiffany!"

"Kalina!"

The two embraced, and the simmering resentment that had been somewhat soothed at Hereford Hall began to bubble up in Nathanial's chest again as he witnessed how easy it was for Tiffany to accept Kalina as her equal. Though Tiffany and Gregory's marriage had also started with a scandal, it had hardly been Tiffany's fault. If anything, it was Gregory who had trapped her into marriage, though that had not been his intention at the time.

"Well." Gregory clapped Nathanial on his shoulder, breaking the dark mood that was starting to settle on him. "Married life looks good on you." He was looking around at the house, not at Nathanial, thankfully, as Nathanial did not know how to react to such a statement.

"It is good to see you," Nathanial said, rather than replying to Gregory's statement directly. He was still eyeing Tiffany and his wife, and doing his best to hide his disgruntlement. "Since you're here, you can help us."

"What do you need help with?" Tiffany asked, smiling as she stepped away from his wife.

"Well, you can start with what the current gossip is about us, and we'll go from there." Nathanial managed to smile.

***

K̲a̲l̲i̲n̲a̲

It was so good to see Tiffany and have her friend's belief in her reaffirmed. Sometimes, with Hereford, her guilt crept up and swamped her. Living with someone she had wronged, even if she had not meant to, was not easy. Tiffany's easy renewed acceptance of her helped.

Marriage suited her friend. Tiffany was beaming and beautiful in a sky-blue day gown decorated with a darker blue calico pattern, which matched Gregory's dark blue waistcoat. The two of them together made a striking pair.

Hereford and Kalina informed their current butler, Stalling, that they were not at-home to any visitors other than family and fellow dukes—Kalina quickly tacked on Delilah's name to the list as well—before escorting Tiffany and Gregory into the drawing room. Kalina rang for tea, musing on how natural it felt even after so many days of living at Hereford Hall, where she and the girls would get their own.

Gregory and Tiffany took the couch, naturally, while Kalina and Hereford sat in the chairs across from them. The delicately carved furniture looked almost comical when being used by the men, though Gregory seemed more comfortable than Hereford did. It did not escape Kalina's notice that they fell into the seating arrangements naturally, without any discussion.

In fact, if it had been reversed, she rather thought she and Hereford would both have been stiffly uncomfortable beside each other on the couch, whereas Gregory and Tiffany would have been loath to be parted by the chairs. It emphasized the difference in their marriages.

Quickly, Tiffany and Gregory brought them up to date on the town gossip, which was how she finally heard the details of the Fife scandal that had sent him and his family flying back to Scotland. No wonder the house had been suddenly available. She could also appreciate that in the wake of such titillating gossip, her and Hereford's return to London would be of less interest to the *ton* than usual.

That did not mean that they'd fully escape the *ton's* scrutiny.

The conversation halted briefly when the tea arrived and resumed immediately after the maid closed the door behind her.

"At least a third of the *ton* thinks Kalina trapped you into marriage for your title, another third thinks you trapped her into marriage for her dowry, and the last third thinks you're a love match," Gregory said baldly, rather than dancing around the issue while Kalina poured tea for each of them.

Kalina blinked in surprise at the last, which distracted her from her guilt at knowing that some of Society laid her father's misdeeds at Hereford's feet.

"A love match?" Hereford asked in astonishment. Kalina glanced at him, but he was staring at Gregory in frank disbelief. "Why on earth would they think that?"

"Ah, well, our fault, a bit, I think." Gregory smiled sheepishly. "It worked for us after all. And a story about how you went to the house party to see if you would suit and then after Christian began to show interest, it pressured you to move..."

"Of course, there are those at the house party who know the truth, but it has confused the issues at least," Tiffany put in. "It does not hurt that they also saw the two of you getting along quite well. Just last night, I heard Lady Collette telling her friends that she would have put money on your match at the beginning of the house party if she'd had anyone to bet with."

Hereford muttered something under his breath Kalina could not quite make out, but it was probably for the best. She was not sure what to make of any of it. While she'd become used to the *ton's* interest in her and her family, she was hardly an expert on how to move forward.

"What have my parents said?" she asked, curious. At some point, she was going to have to face her father again, and though she'd forgiven him at her wedding, after living the reality of his decision for days now, she was not sure she could be so sanguine when she saw him now.

She was aware of Hereford shooting a quick glance at her, but now it was her turn to avoid his gaze. Lifting her teacup to her lips, she took a small sip. The flavors were weak compared to what she'd grown up with, but she'd become accustomed to them here in England. Such as it was.

"They've been quietly keeping to my mother's side," Gregory said. "No one will dare say anything with her beside them, and she's recruited the Dowager Countess of Spencer and Lady Blackstone to her cause. Not that Lady Blackstone needed much encouragement, as it was her house party. And she brought the Duchess of Ormonde along with her, of course. Even the most outrageous of the harpies watch their step with that kind of support rallied around your parents."

Kalina noted that he did not mention Lady Astrid. While she might have forgiven Kalina and believed in her innocence, forgiving

Kalina's father would probably take more time if such a thing ever occurred at all.

At least her father had not been allowed to do more damage. Now that she thought of it, perhaps that was another reason the ladies had gathered round her parents. Not just to keep the harpies away, but to ensure her father did not make any further missteps.

That was a relief.

"So. What's the best way forward from here?" Hereford mused, though it sounded more as though he was speaking his thoughts out loud than asking for opinions.

Gregory answered him, anyway.

"To keep the gossipmongers off your back? Present a united front. Give them, if not a love match, at least contentment. The lack of response will make them lose interest far more quickly than anything else, especially when they already have a far juicier morsel to chew on."

There was a little twinge of guilt at taking advantage of another's misfortune, and Kalina felt very sorry for the earl's daughter, but she knew she was not at fault. They were merely taking advantage of the timing of an event that none of them had any hand in.

"The *ton* is not interested in content or happy marriage," Tiffany agreed. "Right now, speculation is far more engaged in which duke will be the next to marry. With Nathanial no longer available to the marriage mart, my brother, Christian, and Matthew are fair under siege."

"What about Zachary?" Nathanial asked, frowning at her.

"Rumor has it he'll be engaged to Lady Annabelle soon, a rumor which is heavily supported by his mother and hers. Which, of course, has only invigorated the interest in the other three." Tiffany's blank expression did not give away any of her own feelings on the matter, though she must have some.

With such rumors swirling about, and by his own mother no less, Delilah must be heartbroken. Kalina's own heart went out to her. Even though he was not yet engaged to the young lady, from the way Tiffany spoke, it sounded almost inevitable.

"Right then." Nathanial leaned back in his chair, then immediately sat upright again as the wood creaked. "That goes along with my own thoughts. If we're amicable with each other and unremarkable in most ways, interest will not linger on us."

Amicable.

The word should not make her heart ache so, but it did. Looking across her teacup at Gregory and Tiffany, caught in the trap her father had set, Kalina finally had to face the truth.

She had not wanted a duke, other than to please her father.

Nor had she wanted an amicable marriage.

She'd wanted a love match.

31

———————

NATHANIAL

The note came as he was getting ready for Lady Darning's musicale, the afternoon after Gregory and Tiffany's visit. Nathanial had been readying himself with the help of his new valet, Bennet, when Stalling came to his room with the note. Thankfully, Nathanial had dismissed both of them before opening it, because he was not certain he would have been able to hide his reaction.

It is time to pay what your father owed.

He sucked in a breath as he stared at the letter, which was far too reminiscent of the stack of threatening notes he'd found in his father's things. The notes that had, at one time, made him think that his father might have been responsible for the death of all his friends' fathers, in a roundabout way. He'd worried that his father's actions had gotten them all accidentally killed.

But when he'd revealed the existence of the notes, he'd discovered that his father had not been the only one receiving threats. Gregory's father had a stack as well, and they'd recently uncovered the fact that his father's old steward had been the one sending them. The man had fled before he'd been discovered, and they had investigators looking for him, but so far, he had not been found.

It had reassured Nathanial that it was likely not his father who had been inadvertently responsible. They were still unsure how Gregory's steward was involved, and none of them thought he was the mastermind—indeed, his last note had indicated a larger plot—but at least Nathanial had been able to wipe that guilt from his mind.

Taking a deep breath, he put that aside and started mentally tallying the list of debts his father had owed, not just to businesses but to the various members of the *ton*. All the debts he had inherited along with his title, damn his father.

Ton. Most likely ton.

The paper was heavy in his hand, thick and high quality. He snatched up the envelope again. There had been a wax seal on it, which he had barely paid attention to, though he should have. His mind had been too focused on the plan for this afternoon and evening, the first engagements with the *ton* since his marriage.

The wax was dark red, which indicated nothing, and Nathanial did not immediately recognize the coat of arms displayed on it. He'd never been one for memorizing such things. The ones he knew mostly belonged to those that he'd seen frequently on either correspondence or his friends' carriages or both.

This was neither of these.

Was this a new debt or an old one?

"It's possible I've already paid," he murmured. The last of the banknotes had gone out from his desk just before they'd left for London. Perhaps this had been sent before the bank note had been received.

He would have to ask around to all those he'd paid. Ensure that they'd been paid properly. Impatience swept over him at the knowledge. He wanted to be *done* with his father's legacy.

Folding the note, he tucked it back into the envelope and put it on his nightstand. He would deal with it later. First, he needed to get through the musicale, then the Styx's ball. Those were the two events that Tiffany and Gregory had helped him and his wife choose from the small stack that had arrived as their first excursions.

Lady Darning's musicale would be a well-attended event,

featuring an opera singer and Tiffany herself, which was a large part of the reason for attending. All of his fellow dukes would be there, as would Lady Astrid and his wife's friends. From there, the ladies would move on to a private tea at Tiffany's, which he thankfully would not be expected to attend. But he would escort his wife to the Styx's ball tonight.

Tomorrow, they would do another set of rounds, a rather exclusive luncheon hosted by the Duchess of Windham, then a masquerade in the evening at Camden House. The new Marchioness was hosting her first large event and, according to Tiffany and Gregory, it could not be missed without causing comment among their set now that they were back in London.

At every event, their role would be the same—to play the proper, boring, unconventional married couple.

He was not going to pretend to a love match, the way Gregory and Tiffany had to weather the scandal of being caught in the library. He did not have it in him. Not when his emotions were so conflicted already.

Torn between forgiving her and holding on to his righteous anger.

Eventually, he would forgive her... he knew it. His sisters were too happy. The family's financial troubles were over, thanks to her. She was doing a remarkable job as his duchess, regardless of how she'd attained the position. And the way she responded to him at night...

He would forgive her.

It was creeping up on him, but he was not able to completely let go of his anger, his resentment. Not yet. He could imagine a day when he could, though, and that was good enough for him to feel more settled.

If the *ton* accepted their ruse and there was no more scandal or drama or anything that would harm his family's reputation, it would be much easier to forgive her. With his friends rallying around them, that would help. Especially with Tiffany and Astrid at his wife's side.

The bustle of servants as Nathanial made his way to the foyer impinged on his senses, interspersed with Fiona's laughter. She was in the music room with Julianna and Emma, apparently enjoying herself. When he reached the front hall, his wife was already there waiting for him.

As always, her beauty hit him straight in the chest. Her lustrous dark hair was piled in gleaming coils on the back of her head, a dusky pink hat with three creamy feathers perched smartly on top. As always, the pink set off the color of her skin, adding a rosiness to her cheeks. Her dark eyes gleamed brightly as they lifted to meet his. The gown she'd chosen was perfect for an afternoon musicale, with a high neckline and a bodice that nipped in at the waist to emphasize her figure. The color was a matching pink to her hat, with a cream underskirt and cream ruffles lining the edges of her sleeve, drawing attention to her delicate hands. Small pink diamonds, large enough to be seen but not so large as to be gaudy, shone at her ears and throat, reflecting the light in her eyes.

The uncertainty in her expression as she met his gaze was quickly covered by calm serenity, and she folded her hands in front of her. The pink kid gloves covering her fingers were a shade darker than the rest of her ensemble, drawing attention to her graceful movements.

"Madam." Nathanial held out his arm. "Shall we?"

Neither of them smiled as she put her fingers on his arm, yet he felt her touch like a brand.

Their first public outing as man and wife.

Once again, he felt that little hint of resentment. Taking his wife out for their first excursion should have felt nothing but triumphant... instead, he was going to have to go before the *ton* and pretend their marriage had not started with entrapment. Pretend that he was entirely content in his situation, when the truth was he was not.

Taking a deep breath, Nathanial shook the thoughts off as he led his wife out of their rented house and to the carriage.

Kalina

The silent carriage ride with her husband was unnerving but thankfully short. She did not know what to say to him, and he did not seem to be interested in speaking with her. Staring out of the window as the streets rolled by, he appeared to be deep in thought.

Kalina stared down at her gloves and the lace ruffles on her sleeves, examining them even though she did not need to.

She wished she could think of something to say.

Something engaging.

Something that would make him smile.

And forgive her.

And fall in love with me.

She might as well wish for the moon on a string.

He jerked to attention when they reached Lady Darning's home. Kalina was not surprised when Lady Darning's eyes widened and brightened when they arrived. The lady and lord stood just inside the door, greeting their guests before they were escorted to the music room.

Kalina had been introduced to Lady Darning before, but had not met her husband until now. The lady was several inches shorter than Kalina, generously curvy, with brown hair that was expertly coiffed. Beside her husband, she appeared even shorter than normal. He was a good inch taller than Hereford with broad shoulders that filled out his jacket, movements that hinted at extensive musculature, and a completely bald head.

Unlike some of the _ton_, he did not bother trying to hide his lack of hair, but stood proudly without anything covering his pate.

Just as she had with Lady Darning, Kalina liked him on sight.

One of the reasons she'd pushed to accept the invitation to Lady Darning's musicale rather than Lady Sterling's luncheon was that she'd remembered how Lady Darning had been kind to her and her mother when they'd met. Lady Sterling had not been unkind, but neither had she been welcoming.

If Kalina was going to raise a lady's cachet with her and Hereford's first public appearance, she'd rather it be Lady Darning.

"Your Grace." Lady Darning curtsied low as Lord Darning bowed to the appropriate degree. "We are so honored by your attendance." Lady Darning rose, her eyes gleaming with interest. "I seem to have attracted quite a few dukes to my musicale today. I must admit, I did not expect such an august turnout, even with the Duchess of Clarence's agreement to play. Especially so soon after your wedding."

She was prying for information, though doing it very politely, and Kalina did not blame her at all. It was going to be a hot topic for a while yet, no matter the groundwork their friends had laid for them.

"We are always happy to support our own," Hereford said, smiling. "Besides, I never miss a chance to listen to Tiffany's talent."

"This will be my first time hearing her. Ilene insisted I could not miss it," Lord Darning said with a fond glance at his wife. Whether he was a music lover himself, it was clear he was happy to indulge his wife in her request—or command, as it were.

"You will not regret it."

Hereford's words proved true. Seated between her husband and Lady Astrid in the audience, Kalina found herself entranced by both the opera singer and Tiffany's piano playing. She was aware of the whispers that had flitted through the other guests when they realized she and Hereford were present, but once the music started, they hardly impinged on her conscience.

She was too enthralled by the performance.

Which was a relief.

Another benefit of this outing being a musicale was that the expectation was that they would *not* talk very much.

Once the music ended, there was conversation, of course, but it revolved around the performance they had just watched. A few ladies tried to delicately pry for more information about Kalina and Hereford's marriage, as Lady Darning had, but none of them pressed very hard. Most were too excited to talk about what a talent Lady Tiffany had.

The matchmaking mamas were clearly relieved that she was safely married off already, rather than enchanting the eligible gentlemen of the *ton* with her music. Kalina noted that Gregory was sticking quite close to his wife's side as she accepted the compliments of several of the gentlemen who had attended the performance.

The ladies opted to walk around the corner to Clarence House, as it was such a lovely day and not a very far walk. The gentlemen followed a little farther behind, escorting them from afar. Once they reached the house, the gentlemen announced that they would be going onward to their club and leaving the ladies to their tea.

Gregory and Tiffany said their farewell to each other, an affectionate exchange that bordered on scandalous, given they were on the street. Hereford bowed to Kalina and went to join St. Albans, while Ormonde appeared to be trying to do the pretty with Lady Astrid, while she was impatiently attempting to shoo him off. From the glint in his eyes, Kalina thought Lady Astrid might have a better chance at moving him along if she was not quite so determined to order him about.

Delilah stared at the front of the house while Grafton stared just as avidly at her, as though he was willing her to look at him. Monkey Sinclair had been left at home, so as not to disrupt the musicale, and it felt almost odd to see him without the little creature on his shoulder. His attention to Delilah was less odd, but Kalina also found herself rather exasperated with the man.

If he was not going to propose to her, indeed, if he was preparing to propose to another, he needed to leave her alone.

As all of this was happening, a carriage rolled up, and Kalina was startled to see Mei, the matchmaker's granddaughter, descend without her grandmother. Tiffany came forward to greet her, while her brother looked askance at the young woman's presence and muttered something about none of them needing a matchmaker. Which prompted Lady Astrid to give him a sharp look and inform him that Mei was there for tea with the ladies, and that the world did not revolve around him.

Quickly subsiding into scowling consternation, the Duke of Bolton led the group away down the street while the ladies flowed into the house. Kalina could not help but glance at them as they went. Her husband, surrounded by his fellow dukes. She wondered if he would discuss their marriage with his friends. What he would say.

Taking a deep breath, she followed her friends into Clarence House.

Perhaps they would have some advice on how she could convince her husband to forgive her. It could not hurt to ask.

32

Nathanial

"Well then, how is marriage?" Christian asked as they strode out of earshot of the ladies.

It was all Nathanial could do not to look over his shoulder to check if his wife was still outside.

He scowled at Christian. There had been something about the way he'd asked that made it seem as though he was inquiring less on Nathanial's behalf and more on his wife's.

"Very good," he said shortly. "My wife is more than satisfied; you do not need to worry about that."

"I am not going to seduce *your* wife," Christian replied, somewhat exasperated. "I am a better friend than that. No matter how attractive she is."

Nathanial humphed.

"Even if his actress did give him his congé," Gregory joked.

Christian sighed, casting him a look.

"Renee and I agreed—"

"She decided she was tired of him spending half his time at balls," Gregory informed Nathanial, cutting Christian off.

"That our enjoyment of each other had run its course." Now it was Christian's turn to glare, reaching up to fiddle with the rose-red pocket square at his breast. "I cannot blame her, as I have not been able to give her the attention she deserves."

"It does not hurt that she'd already found a new benefactor, a wealthy American who is courting her with diamonds rather than rubies," Drake put in from the side, his lips twitching with amusement.

"I cannot help what a woman has preferences for." Christian shrugged. "Besides, she was becoming rather tedious with her demands." Very possibly because she had already decided to end things with Christian and had deliberately done so to make the transition easier, but Nathanial did not point that out. Christian would have already thought of it. Likely, he did not mind.

Though he enjoyed his mistresses and preferred long-term affairs over short ones, he never seemed to become truly attached to any of them.

"What else have I missed? Anything important?" Nathanial asked, causing those around him to exchange looks.

"We'll tell you at the club," Drake murmured, which made Nathanial's senses prickle. Whatever they'd learned, it must be of significance for them not to want to speak of it in the street.

Which meant it had to do with their fathers.

His gut tightened.

"That matchmaker Lady Astrid brought to the house party made another match," Matthew offered up after a moment. "Lady Nichole and the Viscount of Burberry are now engaged."

"Well. I will have to wish the couple happy," Nathanial said after a moment, realizing that his wishes for the newly engaged couple were sincere. Even though Lady Nichole had been one of the ladies he'd been interested in at the house party, he was not unhappy to hear of her wedding someone else. He hoped she and the viscount were very happy together.

"She's working on a match for Lady Kari, too."

"Not with any of you?" Nathanial raised his eyebrow.

"Apparently not." Matthew appeared more amused than anything else. Sebastian was snorting and shaking his head again, likely at the idea that one of them might need a matchmaker at all.

So far, he had been proven right, but Nathanial doubted Sebastian would want to travel the same road as him and Gregory. He was far too proper to be sanguine about scandal precipitating his marriage. Him and Zachary.

Nathanial glanced over his shoulder.

"No engagement on your front?"

"Not yet." Zachary grimaced. "But my mother has recruited my uncle, and now both of them are encouraging the match. Likely, I'll be married to Lady Annabelle by the end of the Season. Or at least engaged." He said it with all the cheer of a man walking to the gallows.

Nathanial shook his head. It was one thing to marry a lady when forced to by honor or even finances, but he could not imagine having a true choice and ceding it to someone else. No matter how Zachary's mother was grieving, making such an important decision for her son seemed like a step too far to help her recover.

But it was not his place to say.

If Zachary was willing to let his mother choose his bride... well, he was the one who was going to have to live with that. For the rest of his life.

Nathanial wanted to ask after Delilah, but doing so would only pain Zachary more. He'd ask Gregory or Matthew for the gossip later when Zachary was out of earshot.

They rambled on to the club, securing a private room upon their arrival. Thankfully, it was a quiet day at White's with very few gentlemen about. They were quickly ushered into the room, and drinks were served, along with some food to nibble on.

"So," Nathanial said once the server had exited, closing the door behind him. He settled back into his chair, crystal glass in hand. "What have I missed?"

"It's what *we've* missed," Drake replied rather grimly. "Namely, our chance at catching Montblanc in England. We're fairly certain he made it onto a ship to America."

"Well... damn." Nathanial leaned back and took a long sip of his drink as Drake repeated the report he'd gotten from the investigator who had picked up Montblanc's trail.

"We've given the man money to follow Montblanc to America," Sebastian put in. "But whether he'll be able to find him over there..." His voice trailed off, and he shrugged.

"Which leaves us empty-handed for clues again, other than we know *someone* planned the whole thing." Matthew made a face. "But we do not know who they were aiming at, much less who was the mastermind."

"Other than Montblanc was very much aiming at my father," Gregory murmured. Montblanc's niece had been a victim of the old Duke of Clarence's depredations, and Gregory had the half-sister to prove it. According to Gregory, she had begged for clemency for her uncle, but Gregory could hardly promise her anything when they did not know the extent of Montblanc's involvement, only that he had fled.

"But was he the person behind it, or did they just use Montblanc's anger to their own ends?" Drake shook his head. "I would not assume anything. Especially as both you and your mother agree that Montblanc had no reason to take up against any of our fathers, and he was not the type to sacrifice the innocent for his revenge."

"No, if anything, he was defending the innocent." Gregory grimaced. He had no illusions about the kind of man his father had been. Even worse than Nathanial's father, who had been neglectful and selfish but had not been physically violent and never abused the maids.

"Which leaves us back where we began." Nathanial sighed.

"Actually, I want to have another look at the notes your father received," Sebastian said. He was the one who had first noticed that several of the notes Gregory's father had gotten were done by the same hand, though efforts had been taken to disguise the fact. "We never looked very closely at the notes that were not by Montblanc.

Now that we suspect he may have been used by the mastermind behind it all, it's possible others may have been recruited to the same cause."

Nathanial blinked and took in what Sebastian was saying. A conspiracy was what he was describing. One that had ended with eight dead dukes.

"Bloody hell." He took another large quaff of his drink, appreciating the burn as it slid down his throat.

And here he'd thought his marriage was the largest of his problems.

Kalina

"I told you they would realize," Mei said, smiling warmly when she greeted Kalina, who had to laugh in response. She was wearing another outfit of dark green and ivory and gold, though slightly less elaborate in decoration than the one she'd donned for the house party.

Surrounded by her friends, all of who believed her innocence, had lightened her heart considerably.

"You did. If only you could induce my husband to do the same." Kalina sighed as she sank onto the chair at the table. They were in Lady Astrid's salon, a bright room decorated in the shades of a countryside sunset with creamy oranges dominating the color scheme. It could have been overwhelming, but she'd offset all the brighter hues with rust, copper, and cream, as well as delicately carved dark wooden furniture.

With the curtains open and sunlight streaming in, it was a relentlessly cheerful room, which felt exactly like what she needed right now.

"You have not told him?" Lady Astrid frowned as she began to pour the tea for all of them.

It was not a surprising response. Lady Astrid was a direct kind of person. Kalina admired the trait, but found herself unable to emulate it.

"There has not really been an opportunity to bring it up in conversation," she replied truthfully. "His sisters are normally around when we are together."

"Surely at night..." Tiffany let her voice trail off.

"We do not talk. In fact, we have not exchanged a single word at... at night." Kalina felt her cheeks heating in embarrassment as her friends all looked at her. Tiffany was married, of course, and Delilah was a widow, but this was not proper conversation for Mei or Lady Astrid.

"Do not concern yourself about my delicate ears; I have heard far worse." Mei smiled cheekily, lifting her teacup and gently blowing on the hot surface. "Seen worse, too. The seamstress beside my grandmother's shop has a daughter who is having a rather torrid affair with an earl's younger son, and they are not very particular about where they copulate. It's been very educational."

"Good lord, Mei," Delilah said, laughing despite herself.

Mei shrugged, unrepentant. "My grandmother already had a collection of books that she gave me to ensure I understood matters of the body. Attraction, chemistry, the physical aspects that draw people together, these are things that are necessary for a matchmaker to understand in order to make successful matches."

"Do not hesitate to speak frankly in front of me, either," Lady Astrid said. "I may be a virgin, but I doubt there is anything you could say that would surprise me."

Both Tiffany and Delilah looked at her consideringly. Lady Astrid raised her eyebrow as if daring them to try her. After a moment, Tiffany shrugged and turned her attention back to Kalina.

"What do you do at night? Does he come to your bed, or do you go to his?" Tiffany asked.

It truly did feel as if the room had gotten hotter, but Kalina wanted her friends' advice. As long as she was not going to scandalize Mei or Lady Astrid, both of who seemed unperturbed, she might as well tell them all.

"He comes to mine. After dinner, we go to our separate rooms, and he does not come in until much later, usually when I am almost asleep. The first time, I did not even realize it was him at first. Now, I am used to it."

"He comes creeping in the darkness?" Lady Astrid frowned. "That seems... odd."

"Every night?" Delilah asked.

"Every night. And we do not speak. By the time we are done with the, ah, act, I am completely worn out." Kalina's cheeks were hot again. "I fall asleep, and when I wake, he is gone. Though any time I have tried to speak, even if it is not to have a conversation, he hushes me. Sometimes he even puts his hand over my mouth."

Tiffany blinked, her eyes unfocusing as if she was imagining what that might be like, while Lady Astrid frowned. Delilah raised her eyebrows, but seemed more thoughtful than censorious.

"What would you say if not conversation?" Mei asked.

Kalina supposed the seamstress's daughter and the earl's son must do their best to be quiet, as their affair was illicit.

"Please, more, right there, stop you toad, that's the wrong spot..." Lady Astrid murmured under her breath, but as Kalina had paused before answering, they all heard her perfectly clearly. The tension that had grown around the table broke as they all burst into laughter.

"You speak to Drake that way?" Tiffany asked, holding her hand over her stomach as she laughed.

Lady Astrid gave her an arch look. "Who said anything about Drake?"

Everyone's mouth dropped open, the laughter abruptly cut off because, of course, they had all assumed she was conducting any such activities with her fiancé.

"Astrid!" Tiffany's voice was a squeal.

"Oh, shush, I already told you I am a virgin. But if he is running around having his bit of fun, I see no reason I cannot explore a bit as well, as long as I remain *virgo intacta*. That's all that supposedly matters."

"But if you're discovered..."

"Then he will likely break off the engagement. Oh, no." Despite the sarcastic way she said the last two words, some of her uncertainty leaked through.

Kalina could not help but think that if Lady Astrid was dancing with danger in such a way, it was at least in part to have some revenge on her fiancé for his own behavior. Which might matter to her if her pride was pricked, but it felt like more than that.

"We are going to discuss you and Drake eventually, but I believe Kalina has the more pressing need at the moment," Delilah interjected, shaking her head. Her husky voice was full of amusement. "Kalina, you may have to go to him, and I do not mean in his bedroom. Somewhere that is more neutral territory, but where he still feels in control. His study, perhaps."

"I do not know how to start. I walk in and say, 'I am sorry my father trapped you into marriage with me, but I promise I had nothing to do with it'?" She sighed. "Why should he believe me? That's if he lets me finish my sentence."

"You need to catch him off guard with something surprising," Mei suggested. "Something to take him aback, so he cannot muster an immediate response."

"You could always ask him to spank you." Tiffany blushed as every eye landed on her.

"*Spank her*?" Lady Astrid sounded more than a touch incredulous, despite her earlier claim that they would not be able to surprise her.

"Yes. As Mei said, it would catch him off guard, especially if he is feeling a desire to punish her in some way. And it would give her the opportunity to tell him the truth."

"But it will hurt." Lady Astrid was making all of Kalina's points for her, so she kept her mouth shut.

To her fascination, a hot red blush spread over Tiffany's cheeks.

"Well, it depends on how he does it. It can hurt, but..." Tiffany shrugged. "And I do not believe Nathanial would be the type to want to harm her, even if he does feel as if some punishment might be justified."

"She has a point," Delilah murmured, drawing everyone's attention to her.

Mei's eyes had gone very wide. Apparently, Lady Astrid was not the only one who was surprised, though Mei sat quietly listening in much the same way Kalina was.

"It can be not altogether unpleasant. In fact, it can be very pleasurable, eventually, and especially as she is the one asking for it... Sometimes, such things can make men more amenable to conversation afterward."

"You and Zachary..." Lady Astrid looked utterly aghast.

"Yes. In the past. Though I very much feel as though he is the one in need of a spanking now." Delilah sniffed haughtily, but real hurt lurked in her dark eyes.

Still, Kalina laughed along with the others. The idea of Delilah spanking the upright Duke of Grafton was certainly an amusing mental image.

"How can a spanking be pleasurable?" Lady Astrid demanded to know.

"It is like a balance against the pleasure. It stings, but with the pain there comes a rush of..." Tiffany waved her hands in front of her, as if at a loss for words.

"I think I understand," Kalina said softly, thinking of how she felt when Hereford's teeth dragged over her nipples or when his finger had slid into her bottom. Pain but also pleasure, twined together. Discomfort that she bore for him, which added to her overall ecstasy.

"Well, I am sure I do not," Lady Astrid huffed, but it was clear her curiosity had been piqued. She looked at Delilah. "But what about you? You've taken up with Conyngham; do you engage in such activities with him?"

"Oh, no." Delilah laughed. "Conyngham is just a bit of fun. He's easy to be around and quite skilled when it comes to pleasure, but we are not like that."

But she had been 'like that' with Grafton. Kalina could only imagine it would be a while before Delilah opened her heart to another man.

The conversation wound onward, Lady Astrid skillfully deflecting any questions about her own experiences and who they may have been with, while Tiffany and Delilah compared notes about what kind of spankings they enjoyed. Mei and Kalina listened with wide eyes and open ears, and the thought turned round and round in Kalina's head.

What if she asked her husband to spank her?

33

NATHANIAL

His wife was distracted. Nathanial studied her out of the corner of his eye as they approached Lord and Lady Styx in the receiving line. The hosts were currently greeting the Earl and Countess of Spencer, but their eyes were already on Nathanial and his wife, alight with eager anticipation. No one could blame them, as there were several events this evening, but Hereford and his wife had chosen theirs.

Like with the Darnings, it would add to Lady Styx's cachet.

Since she greeted them with true warmth, just as Lady Darning had, Nathanial did not mind at all. This particular ball had been his wife's choice, and so far, she was proving adept at knowing where she would be the most welcome.

"Your Grace." Lady Styx curtsied. "It is a singular pleasure to welcome you to our house." Rather tall with bright red hair, her freckles should have been unfashionable, but she'd always defied Society and embraced them rather than trying to downplay them. Her husband was her equal in height, with olive skin. Like her, he eschewed Societal fashion and had chosen to grow his hair long—all of it. His beard touched the top of his cravat, and his mustache covered most of his face. Though he had drawn his hair back in a queue to keep it out of his face, his disdain for current fashions made him a match for his wife.

Their dramatically styled clothing suited them perfectly.

"Thank you for having us here this evening." His wife smiled genuinely, holding out her hand and exchanging cheek kisses with Lady Styx, who beamed widely at the affection. There were plenty of others in the receiving line who would note her closeness with a duchess—one who had not always been welcomed by others before attaining her title. Lady Styx was being rewarded for her offering friendliness before it had benefited her personally.

"Congratulations on your marriage," Lord Styx said, with utter sincerity, looking at Nathanial. "I believe you have a rare find indeed."

Considering Lord Styx had a reputation for liking very few people other than his own wife, Nathanial found himself rather bemused by the compliment. His wife had garnered more allies than he'd realized among the *ton* during her time in it, regardless of her father's family's lack of approbation. Personally, Nathanial valued Lord Styx's opinion far above the Earl of Stilton's.

But his impression remained, as the Styx's moved on to the next guest in the receiving line... his wife was distracted by something. Lost in her own thoughts. But by what?

He had not seen her after the tea this afternoon. Had one of her friends said something to her? Or had something else happened that was causing her distraction?

Why was she not focused on him the way she had been before?

The realization that he'd rather liked her being solely focused on him previously was unexpected. Harrowing, even. Nathanial was not sure he wanted to care where her attention was.

But the unavoidable truth was that he did.

"Are you looking for someone in particular?" he asked as they entered the ballroom, wondering if perhaps she was supposed to be meeting her friends.

His wife looked at him as if surprised. As though she'd forgotten he was there, despite the fact he was escorting her into the ball on his arm. If Nathanial's feathers had been ruffled before, now they were positively disturbed.

"Oh... no. Is there someone I should be looking for?" Her gaze cast out, which was when he realized that previously her attention had been thoroughly inward. The contrast made that clear.

If she'd truly noticed anyone else in the ballroom before his query, he would be surprised. Unfortunately, he did not feel as though he could ask what she was thinking. That was hardly the kind of safe conversation they engaged in—if they spoke at all when it was just the two of them.

Nathanial tried to remember if he'd ever spoken with his wife, alone, since their marriage.

He did not think he had.

Besides, this was hardly the surrounds for such a conversation. They were supposed to be *comfortably* married. Amicable. Not hanging on to each other, the way Gregory and Tiffany did, which was tolerated by their peers only because they were understood to be a love match. If he started behaving oddly, attentively, that would only draw more eyes to them and engender more questions about their match, which was the opposite of his aim.

But he did not like it.

The uncomfortable thought occurred to him that in order to be more settled in his marriage, he might actually have to talk to his wife.

Kalina

The Styx's ball was lovely, other than a few extremely awkward moments when Monkey Sinclair deserted the Duke of Grafton for Delilah... while the Duke of Grafton was escorting Lady Annabelle, and Delilah was waltzing with Conyngham. The earl had grinned as the monkey chittered at him as though scolding him, obviously not put off at all, but Delilah's face had gone still as a stone at the sight of Lady Annabelle on Grafton's arm.

Kalina did not tell Delilah that she later overheard Lady Walsh crowing over the triumph of her daughter catching a duke. The whole situation was painful enough, and Delilah already knew what was in the wind.

She was rather distracted by her own husband, who seemed to be blowing back and forth with his own wind. Though he did not cling to her side the way Gregory did with Tiffany, neither was he as absent as she had expected. He did step away to join his own conversations, but eventually made his way back to her. And after her dance with Lord Jarrett, she found her scowling husband had returned to her circle and immediately claimed her on his arm again.

Which was all very confusing because that was not what had been discussed when they'd made their plan with Tiffany and Gregory.

On the other hand, no one seemed to find it remarkable. Lord Jarrett simply nodded and smiled, taking himself off with a smug expression on his face, as if he knew something no one else did. Exactly what he felt he knew, Kalina was not entirely sure, but that was the impression she received from him.

By the time they made their excuses and said goodbye to their friends and hosts, Kalina was thoroughly confused.

They reached the carriage, and Hereford sat upright across from her. It was dark within the confines of the carriage, but she got the feeling he was looking at her. Studying her as best he could despite the dimness of the light. The close scrutiny made her feel a little breathless.

They were so rarely alone.

And when they were, it was even darker in her room. She could not see him there, nor could he see her.

But right now, only the upper part of his face was cast in shadow. She could see his jawline. His lips. Part of his cheek. The way his shoulders shifted against the seat behind him. His hands, where they rested on his thighs, one long finger tapping against his leg. A finger that had been inside her.

Something that was much easier to forget when they were surrounded by his sisters or the servants or the *ton*.

Here, alone, in the intimate darkness of the carriage, she was very aware of his fingers. His hands. Her body reacted because she knew exactly how she could make him feel.

The silence hung heavy in the air, making her want to squirm in her seat. She pressed her thighs together at the unexpected arousal that just being alone with her husband caused.

"Did you enjoy the ball?" she asked, finally, because she could not bear the growing tension.

The tapping finger on his thigh stilled, and he cleared his throat.

"I did. Lady Styx is an excellent hostess. Did *you* enjoy the ball?"

"I did. Thank you."

The conversation was stilted, awkward, but it soothed her a little. At least it was not complete silence.

"I believe Zachary is going to need to cease bringing Monkey Sinclair to events."

Kalina laughed softly at her husband's observation, relaxing even further. The monkey was certainly a safe enough topic of conversation.

"He does seem intent on causing problems."

"You notice he kept the monkey on the opposite shoulder as the lady on his arm." Hereford chuckled. "She looked rather nervous."

"I would be too, considering Sinclair's reputation with the ladies." She did not mention the exception that Monkey Sinclair made for Delilah. They both knew, but it did no one any good to comment on it.

"Not just the ladies; did you see the way it reacted to Zachary's uncle?"

"What? No, I must have missed that."

Hereford laughed outright.

"I think it must know Zachary's uncle is assisting his mother with the push to marry Lady Annabelle because the way that monkey hissed at him..." He laughed again, shaking his head. Seeing the edges of his lips curled up in a smile—a smile directed at *her*, no less —made Kalina's heart pound in her chest.

But they reached the house too soon. The smile faded. The conversation ended. Hereford helped her down from the carriage, but even with her hand in his, she could feel his withdrawal again.

Once more, she was escorted to her room and left there.

Once again, he came to her, just before she drifted off to sleep, and climbed into her bed in the darkness.

As always, he hushed her.

When she tried to speak, anyway, he turned above her and lowered his cock into her mouth while his tongue was still deep in her pussy. Kalina was horrified and fascinated by his manner of gagging her. The tip prodded at her lips, and he uttered one harsh word.

"Open."

Immediately, she did, and his cock pushed into her mouth.

He tasted salty. Meaty. The thick length of him slid over her tongue and came up against her throat, making her gag. She shuddered at the sensation as he withdrew, then slid back in, using her mouth the way he did her pussy. It was hard to breathe, making her feel rather dizzy from the lack of air as he moved above her, his fingers prying her legs farther apart as if the act of using her mouth spurred his desire to use his own to greater efforts.

Despite how wildly perverse the act was, how utterly indecent, there was a part of her that reveled in it. That heard his moans, felt his shudders, and wished she could see his face as his cock moved in her mouth. Wondered what he would look like as he used her in such a manner.

That wished they were not completely in the dark.

Eventually, when she could do nothing but cry out in pleasure, he pulled his cock free from her lips. Wringing wave after wave of pleasure from her body with his own mouth, he kept her writhing and moaning until she was too tired to even go up on her knees for him. Instead, she ended up on her side, her husband straddling one of her legs, the other lifted over his shoulder, as he pumped into her hard and fast.

The position allowed his hand to move over her breasts, tweaking and tugging on her nipples, then drift down to her swollen, overstimulated pearl of pleasure. She was nearly insensible from the overwhelming assault on her senses by the time he went rigid, holding himself inside her as he reached his own pinnacle.

Letting her leg drop down, he kept his cock within her body, snuggling up behind her the way he always did... after.

She was too exhausted to try to form a sentence, but her thoughts still whirled even as sleep crept up to pull her under.

While a love match might be out of her reach, she wanted to be able to have conversations with her husband. She wanted this intimacy in more places than the full darkness of her bedroom in the middle of the night.

She wanted him to forgive her.

Tomorrow, one way or another, she was going to ask her husband to spank her.

34

———

It had to be done before the Windham luncheon.

That was the only time Kalina could be assured of having enough time and there being no interruptions. Fiona's new governess, Miss Temple, was doing lessons with her, Julianna and Emma were with their dance instructor, and Hereford was alone in the study. There was no guarantee that another such opportunity would arise between the luncheon and the Camden Masquerade this evening.

Which meant it had to be now.

Heart beating a rapid tattoo in her chest, Kalina knocked on the study door. Waiting until she heard the slightly muffled invitation to 'come in' to open it, all the while wondering if she was going to lose her courage and run.

Having to face her husband and make such a scandalous request was not something she would have ever imagined herself doing. None of this felt like her, like the person she'd always been. But, on the other hand, she did not know that she had ever wanted something for herself so badly as she wanted her husband's forgiveness.

Opening the door and facing him, seeing him in the light of day, watching the startled expression fall over his face before he blinked and returned it to a neutral one, she felt far more vulnerable than she did when she was naked in the dark with him. Perhaps it would have been easier to say the words then, to make her request at night, if only he would let her speak.

But he would not.

Which meant she had to do it now.

He got to his feet as Kalina closed the door behind her.

"Yes, ah... what can I do for you?" There was something odd about the way he stumbled over his words, like the sentence came out unfinished even though it was complete.

Kalina went to stand in front of his desk, hands folded over each other in front of her so that they would not show how she was trembling. She was wearing her favorite, most comfortable morning gown, the light pink and white striped muslin that made her feel airy and bright. Even that did not help with the urge to turn and run or to stammer out something else and flee.

She had to get the words out, right now, or she would never be able to say them.

"I want you to spank me." They came out in a rush, tumbling over each other, barely intelligible even to her own ears. Hereford stared at her. She stared back at him.

She was going to have to say it again.

She could not possibly say it again.

Kalina was about to retreat when her husband shook himself out of his stunned silence.

"Did you just say you want me to *spank* you?" He sounded both shocked and confused.

"Tiffany suggested it." Well. She had not meant to say that, but they were the first words that came to mind. Blame her friend for the audacious request. "As... as a penance?" Fumbling for what she meant, she came out with the wrong word. Or perhaps it was correct. She might not have known about her father's plans, but she still felt guilt.

If he spanked her, he might feel better about it all... and so might she.

"As a penance," he repeated slowly, like he was turning the words over in his head as he said them. "Yes. I can see that. That..." He paused and took a deep breath. "I accept your offer."

For a moment, it was as though she could not understand what he'd said. The words took several heartbeats to process. Only when he pushed his chair back from the desk and sat down in it, while she was still standing, and put his hand on his thigh, did she fully comprehend his response.

He accepted my offer.

He wants to spank me.

As penance.

Kalina knew what a spanking was, but other than a one-time swat from her mother as a child when she'd stolen a *gulab jamun* from the kitchen, she'd never received one. The sweet dough ball had been more than worth the slight sting and her mother's half-exasperated, half-amused scold.

Feeling as though some strange entity had taken over her body, Kalina found herself walking around the desk and facing her husband. Hereford tilted his head back and patted his thigh. The dark brown trousers he was wearing went well with the dusky rose waistcoat over his crisp white shirt. The lighter brown jacket he had on at breakfast had already been removed and was draped over the back of his chair. He looked impeccably handsome. The light in his eyes as he looked up at her gave her hope that perhaps Tiffany had been correct about this tactic.

"I... just, over your lap?" Her hands fluttered uncertainly at her sides as she looked at him.

He nodded his head, patting his thigh at the same time. The stern expression on his face made her feel even more jumpy, despite the desire that she could see in his gaze.

Taking a deep breath, Kalina awkwardly put herself over his lap. At least, she felt awkward. If he thought her so, he did not comment on it. Instead, he moved his hand out of her way, and she heard him let out a long breath as she settled her stomach against his thighs, her side against his stomach. Putting her hands out in front of her, against the softness of the rug beneath his desk, she wriggled to try to feel less vulnerable... but it was no use.

Especially when he tugged her skirts up to reveal her drawers. Despite the brightness of the room, she could not see him in her current position, but she was suddenly, acutely, horribly aware of how he would be able to see every bit of her. There was no darkness to hide behind in here.

The feeling of him parting her drawers at the split, revealing her buttocks to his gaze, and the hand that came down to rest over the curve of one cheek, made her shudder. Though she tried to turn her head and crane her neck, hoping to get a glimpse of her husband's expression, she was unable to see it well enough.

All of his focus was on her exposed bottom.

Heat filled her cheeks and pooled between her thighs, which confused her. She had not expected to feel the same desire as she did at night, when he came to her bed, yet her body was responding in the same manner as it did then.

He lifted his hand.

Brought it down on her bottom.

She cried out, as much in surprise as at the impact.

It did hurt. Stung even.

Yet the immediate sensation that followed was a kind of rush of excitement. More emotional than physical, despite the fact that it started there.

His hand came down again.

And again.

Kalina squirmed as the heat in her bottom began to grow, the sting increasing every time his palm slapped against her flesh. It did hurt, yet the arousal between her thighs grew with every swat. Tiffany had not mentioned this aspect of being spanked.

Had she not experienced it?

This was supposed to be a penance.

Was Kalina supposed to be enjoying it?

Perhaps she was not, yet she could not change her body's reactions. Her heart was beating faster and faster as she panted for breath. Squirming on her husband's lap, she could feel the slickness between her legs, rubbing together, pressing together, adding growing pleasure to the stinging heat blooming across her cheeks.

His hand came down again, right in the center, and Kalina moaned, even as tears sprang to her eyes from the intoxicating mix of pleasure and pain.

<u>NATHANIAL</u>

Hearing his wife's moan, Nathanial froze.

Uncertain of how she would respond to being spanked, he'd been holding back, peppering her bottom with firm, crisp swats because he did not know how much she would be able to take. Hearing her moan...

He looked down at her bottom, then dipped his fingers between her thighs.

She was wet.

Silent thunder roared in his ears, a white rushing noise that drowned out the rest of the world as it turned over, then righted itself again, but with an entirely new perspective from what he'd had before. As though, suddenly, he could see everything in a new light.

Perhaps his wife had trapped him into marriage, but that did not mean she was the wrong wife for him. She had just gone about it in the wrong way.

Though he'd been willing to accept her offer of being spanked as a penance, he'd also been thrown off by the suggestion. Spanking his wife was not something he'd looked for because there was no way to know what a debutante would find acceptable. He had not even dared to hope that he would find a wife who would accept, much less enjoy, such a thing.

Now, here she was, over his lap, aroused and moaning from the punishment he was applying to her upturned bottom. His cock, already half-hard from having her over his lap and finally being able to see the parts of her that had always been hidden by darkness, was instantly, painfully erect.

Nathanial gritted his teeth against the shocking surge of lust that ran through him. Never in his life had his desires been so tested.

But she'd wanted to pay a penance.

His hand came down harder, stinging his palm.

And his wife moaned again, shuddering against him, the stiffness of her stays under her dress rubbing against the bulge at the front of his trousers and exacerbating his own problem. He spanked her again. And again. Her skin darkened and heated under the steady swats, and with every increase in intensity, it did nothing but increase her moans and cries.

"Oh, please..." Her soft gasp was not a plea to stop.

No, it was the same plea she made in the darkness of night, when he was in her bed, pleasuring her with his mouth.

It had the same effect now as it did then.

Nathanial hauled her up off his lap, sitting her on the desk before him, and she emitted a little squeal as her bottom met the hard wood. She looked up at him, dark eyes shiny with sparkling tears, a single track running down her cheek, her swollen lips parted. They'd always met in the dark. He'd never had anything but his imagination to tell him how she looked.

Now, he knew he'd never be able to get the sight of passion and need on his wife's face out of his mind.

His lips crashed down on hers, his body sliding between her thighs. Her skirt was already up around her hips. One arm around her body to hold her against him, his other hand fumbled between them, undoing the front of his trousers—or at least, attempting to when most of his focus was on her lips.

How she tasted.

How she molded to him.

How her tongue met his in a dance of pure need.

He did not just kiss her—he claimed her. And when he finally managed to free his cock and pull her to the edge of the desk so he could plunge inside her, he reveled in the sensation of both his cock and his tongue ravishing her senses. Kissing her breathless as he began to move, hard and fast, his hands holding her at the edge of the desk, her hands wrapped around his neck as she kissed him back with all the passion a man could hope for.

He wanted to devour her.

Leaning forward, he felt one of her hands slip away, going behind her to help keep her in position as he thrust, sliding his cock deep inside her before retreating.

Her lips slipped away from his as their movements became more frenetic, more impassioned.

"Oh... oh God..." Her soft, high voice caressed his ears. But that was not what he wanted her to say.

"My name. Say my name."

Her pussy clenched around him, drenching him with her arousal, and he thrust hard into the soft, wet haven.

"Hereford!"

Nathanial growled against her throat, nipping at the soft skin there.

"My name, Kalina."

The way her muscles tightened around him was a spasm, a convulsion of ecstasy.

"Nathanial! Oh God... Nathanial!" She cried out his name, louder each time, as he moved harder and faster, his name on her lips sending him into an animalistic frenzy of need. He could not get deep enough inside her, could not be close enough to her to satisfy himself.

Falling back into his chair, he took her with him, her legs straddling him, and she moved against his body, rubbing herself against him as her own ecstasy spiraled. For the first time, he was able to watch as she threw her head back in pure feminine bliss, crying out his name as she peaked, clenching around his cock as his own need came to its inevitable climax.

Sliding one hand up to the back of her neck, he pulled her forward, claiming her mouth again as his hips lifted slightly, devouring her cries of passion as his cock spurted inside her. The clenching of her muscles milked his length, pulled spurt after spurt of seed from him, leaving him utterly wrung out and panting, her lips soft and hovering just above his.

He'd kissed his wife.

And now that he'd started, he did not ever want to stop.

Kalina lifted her head. Stared at him, as if she did not know what to do now.

Neither did he.

He was still inside her. It felt as though the wall between them had come tumbling down. But what did they do without it?

How did they act?

What did he say?

A knock at the door made both of them jump, especially as the door rattled a moment later.

"Nathanial? Why is your door locked? Is Kalina in there? Is she well? I thought I heard something." Fiona's questions came rapidly and had a similar effect on both him and his wife. She jumped to her feet, hands immediately going to her hair as her skirts fell into place —rumpled and wrinkled, but thankfully, Fiona would hardly know what it meant.

The loss of her warmth against him, around him, was deeply felt, despite how he jumped to his feet as well, righting his own clothing and securing his trousers back in place.

"Give us a moment, Fiona." His wife's voice was higher than usual, the look in her eyes wild and horrified. Yet when she looked at him, met his gaze, the horror faded and was replaced by something softer.

Something hopeful.

"Go," he said softly with a nod. Stepping forward, he brushed a lock of her hair back into place. Thanks to the positions they'd been in, other than her skirt, she was remarkably tidy. "She'll want your attention before I take you away for the day."

Kalina nodded.

They were standing very close together. His hand was still on her hair.

Nathanial lowered his lips to hers.

This kiss was different. Passion had been sated. Desire banked.

That was not what this kiss was about.

It was softer. Sweeter. Her lips clung to his, her hands coming to rest gently on his chest.

"Kalina! I want to show you what I did with Miss Temple this morning!" The door rattled again. From a distance, they heard the muffled sound of Miss Temple calling Fiona's name, and the governess was clearly coming closer. "Nathanial, stop hogging Kalina!"

His wife's laughter pulled her away from him.

"I think I need to go and have a word with Fiona about listening to her governess," she whispered.

Nathanial let his hands fall reluctantly away from her hips, where they'd come to settle. Although he could intervene as well, he did not want to step on his wife's toes, and overseeing Fiona's governess ran under her purview.

The spanking had achieved exactly what he'd needed, he realized as he watched his wife go. It had broken through the barrier he'd erected, and for the first time since marrying her, he no longer felt the lingering resentment overshadowing every interaction.

He was free of it.

He watched Kalina open the door to his study, laughing as his youngest sister threw herself into her arms, immediately babbling about her morning, with an exasperated Miss Temple standing beside her. Warmth filled him at the sight, and he realized far more than his physical needs felt satisfied. The freedom from that resentment, from the barricade he'd put between them, meant that for the first time since their wedding, he felt as though he saw everything clearly.

He was hit with the sudden realization that he'd accidentally gone and fallen in love with his wife.

Bloody hell.

35

———

The luncheon at Windham House was exceptional. It was also far more exclusive than she'd realized it would be. Dukes, duchesses, and the Windhams' close circle. Thankfully, that meant several of her own friends were there as well, or the experience would have been far more terrifying.

Though all of those present very quickly reverted to a first-name basis, Kalina could not help but feel like an imposter among the *haut ton*. She had not been born to the title, nor had her husband chosen her to receive it. Her father had tricked him into giving it to her.

The lingering pain in her bottom was a stark reminder of that fact. Though she also smiled every time she was reminded. That interlude with her husband had been... entirely different. The carriage ride to Windham house had been far more comfortable. They had not spoken of her spanking or the immediate aftermath, but had companionably discussed Fiona and Miss Temple before reaching the house.

It had been rather lovely.

Of course, once they'd arrived, they'd been unable to have any further private discussion, but she had hopes for the future. Tiffany seemed to notice the difference between them, her eyes widening with question for Kalina before Kalina nodded back. She could not keep the smile from her face as she did so.

Despite any lingering discomfort, which was as much a reminder of pleasure as anything else, Kalina would have done such a spanking three times over for the change it had effected between her and Nathanial.

After the luncheon, the gentlemen and ladies separated. The ladies went to the garden rather than the drawing room, as it was a lovely day outside, and Lydia, the Duchess of Windham, apparently wanted to show it off. It was a truly lovely garden. To Kalina's surprise, she found herself walking arm in arm with their hostess.

Nerves fluttered through her when the stately blonde tugged her off to the side, away from Tiffany and Lady Astrid, who were bent over an exotic-looking orange bloom. Kalina could see why it had drawn Lady Astrid's attention. She rather wished she was over there with them. Their elegant hostess was more than a little intimidating.

"I am so glad you and Nathanial came today. I was hoping to speak with you privately," the duchess said, once they were out of earshot of the others. Immediately, Kalina steeled herself for some kind of rebuke. She could only imagine what an established duchess might have to say to a new one who had attained her position by trickery and deceit. "There are rumors that Nathanial was trapped into marriage with you."

Kalina did not respond. She did not know what she could say. It was true. There was very little defense she could make, and trying to explain what had really happened felt like a betrayal of her father. Besides, saying anything at all would go against the plan Nathanial had outlined for dealing with the *ton*.

Just because Lydia was a duchess, as far as Kalina knew, that did not change the way he would want her to behave. No one else had made such a blunt statement, which bordered on rudeness and so had always been easy to sidestep.

While she knew her silence damned her, there did not seem to be anything else she could say instead.

To her surprise, Lydia patted her arm where they were entwined, in a kind of consoling gesture.

"Ah. I'd wondered if it was true. If you ever need to speak to anyone who will understand, please feel free to come to me." Her smile brightened when Kalina's head snapped around to stare at her. "You did not know?" She leaned in, whispering. "Rumor has it, the Duchess of Windham trapped her duke into marriage as well. And at a house party no less."

Kalina's mouth dropped open in shock.

"You?"

"Me," Lydia confirmed with a nod, then her attention was drawn to another woman coming down the pathway toward them with a mulish expression on her face.

Dressed in a pretty dark pink gown that dipped daringly low in front, almost scandalously low for a daytime dress, the pretty brunette was obviously on a mission. The Countess of Spencer had quite the reputation as an *Original*—though cut from a very different cloth than Lady Astrid—and despite her lesser rank, she was even more intimidating than some of the duchesses.

"Yes, Cynthia, can I help you?"

"Are we done with the gardens now? I want to play cards." Cynthia glanced at Kalina. "Do you know how to play cards?"

"It depends on which game." Kalina loved playing cards, but there were very few people who would ever play with her. Ashwin had quit in disgust years ago, which quite limited the options of games she could play with her parents.

"Have you ever played American poker?" Cynthia cocked her head.

"Yes... but I do not think my husband would approve of my gambling." Now that matters seemed to have improved between them, she did not want to risk any act that might upset the boat again.

"Oh, we do not play for money," Cynthia said, turning and gesturing for Lydia and Kalina to precede her. "We play for secrets and favors." She winked, though she was obviously feeling impatient.

Lydia just laughed and smoothly moved forward, pulling Kalina with her.

It did not take long to install themselves in the card room. Kalina found herself at a table with Cynthia and Arabella, the Duchess of Windham's sister-in-law, and Tiffany. Cynthia and Arabella were clearly very close and both eager to play cards. At the other table, Lady Astrid had joined Lydia and Lydia's other sister-in-law, Christina, as well as Lady Marley, whose first name was Daphne. Kalina had not had the opportunity to speak with either of them for more than a greeting, but it was clear the two were as close as Cynthia and Arabella were.

After winning several rounds of poker, Kalina made sure to lose one. Cynthia was beginning to look a bit pouty, as was Arabella, and even Tiffany was eyeing her a bit askance.

"How are you doing that?" Tiffany murmured when Kalina won the round after that—she truly had intended to lose, but Arabella had done a better job of bluffing than usual, and she had not realized the other woman had nothing in her hand.

"I've always been good at card games," Kalina admitted, though she did not explain that such a statement was vastly understating her skill. Games of pure luck were not her forte, but if there were skill and an element of chance... somehow she'd always been able to keep track of the cards. Which had been played, which had yet to be played. She had not realized that it was not a universal skill at first, though she'd quickly learned.

Her father had always warned her not to boast about it.

"I would very much like to see you play cards with Matthew sometime," Tiffany muttered, frowning down at her own hand.

It did not take long before Cynthia decided they should move on to whist—and she insisted on pairing with Kalina. Arabella, on the other hand, seemed to take the tack of wanting to beat Kalina after being so badly trounced at poker. Bemused, Kalina almost felt bad when she and Cynthia handily won.

By that time, masculine voices were coming closer, the gentlemen returning to join the ladies. Kalina could not help but tense when the men began to filter into the room and saw the ladies playing cards. She immediately sought out her own husband from the small crowd. Though he frowned when he saw the cards, his gaze lifted to hers and relaxed, as if he understood that she had not gambled away anything they needed.

She could only imagine how he felt about such things, considering his father's reputation.

Knowing what she now did about the Duke and Duchess of Windham, she watched closely as the duke moved to stand beside his wife, his hand on the back of her chair. Though he was imposing in stature, the moment his gaze met hers, it softened. There was real warmth between them. Affection.

Maybe even love?

But Lydia had said she'd trapped him into marriage with her.

She'd offered to speak with Kalina, but she'd already given Kalina something far more important than advice or even a listening ear.

She'd given Kalina hope.

Nathanial

Unlike the luncheon earlier in the day, the Camden ballroom was packed, which came as no surprise. As a major event of the Season, everyone who could attend *did* attend. The crush of people being masked also meant there was a sense of gaiety and freedom that came with identities being marginally hidden. Of course, most everyone was recognizable despite the masks, but they pretended not to be.

His wife clung to his arm, which he was not unhappy about.

As he did not want the *ton* speculating over his emotions, especially when he had barely recognized them himself, the masquerade meant he did not have to pretend indifference or contentment. No one would comment that he and Kalina spent their entire evening together if they so chose.

The only one who might have questions about it was Kalina herself.

Nathanial did not know if he was ready to answer those questions. Neither did he want to quit his wife's side. Especially when he saw more than one rake eyeing her low-cut decolletage. Masquerades, though they allowed for couples to cleave to each other without comment, also tended toward all sorts of licentious behavior.

Normally, as Kalina had not yet borne him an heir, she would be considered off limits for a flirtation or affair by the vast majority of the *ton*... but not all of them. And if Nathanial wanted to keep his and Kalina's names out of the gossips' mouths, punching a man for flirting with his wife at the Camden Masquerade was hardly the way to do it.

As if the thought had summoned the most flirtatious man in the room, Christian shouldered his way through two other gentlemen to reach Kalina's other side. He was wearing a golden mask set with rubies, emphasizing his golden blond hair. The ruby red of his waistcoat was also patterned with thin gold thread and golden buttons decorated with lions' heads gleaming from them. The folds of his snowy white cravat were in the Napoleon style, adding an air of deliberate casualness to his sartorial splendor.

Straightening his shoulders, Nathanial ran his free hand over his own waistcoat, which was a dusky rose pink he'd had made to match his wife's favorite ballroom dresses. It was a hue he rather favored as well.

"Duchess." Christian smiled down at Kalina. "You looked ravishing." He lifted her gloved fingers to his lips, and Nathanial had to suppress a growl.

Christian would cease flirting when he ceased breathing, and not a moment before, Nathanial was sure of it. He knew his friend meant nothing by it, but he could not help but remember the moments at the Blackstones' house party when he'd been worried Christian might have an interest in Kalina. Even if his friend had declared he did not think he would offer for her.

The fact he'd even considered it for a moment was farther along the path to marriage than Christian had ever ventured before.

Not only that, but Nathanial had no true idea about how his wife felt about the Adonis of the *ton*... other than she'd chosen to trap him into marriage rather than Christian. Perhaps he had nothing to worry about on that score.

"Thank you, Your Grace," Kalina said, smiling, then she slipped her hand away from Christian and put it atop the one that was already curved around Nathanial's arm. It was all he could do not to visibly preen. He settled for a smug smirk in Christian's direction, satisfaction settling in as his friend smiled at him and turned to scan the rest of the ballroom.

What he could see of it, at least. Christian was only an inch taller than Nathanial, and Nathanial could not see very much other than glittering masks and jewels, bobbing feathers from the ladies' hair, and the occasional glimpse of another tall gentleman's face. He doubted Christian's view was much improved.

Still.

"If you see Durham, I need to speak with him," he said to Christian.

Elijah Stuart, Earl of Durham and heir of the Marquess of Camden, was the last person on the long list of nobles Nathanial had repaid but had not been able to confirm the payment. Though the coat of arms on the envelope he'd received had not been Camden's, Nathanial had no idea what Durham's sigil would look like or if it could be for a different honorary title.

What he did know was that the bank had contacted him earlier to inform him that everyone, other than Durham, had received their payment. If Nathanial could not find the man tonight to give the earl the money his father had owed, then he would seek him out tomorrow. But since he was here...

He very badly wanted the last of his father's business done with.

Christian nodded, while Kalina looked up at him curiously. Nathanial smiled at her, finding the expression oddly natural. He'd been holding back so many smiles before or was unable to give in to them while he simmered with resentment, and now was able to let his face do as it wanted. Still, he did not want to worry her over things like debtors, not when there was no reason to do so.

Nor was he eager to remind her of his previous need for her dowry.

Not when things had changed so drastically between them, and he was still trying to find his way through his feelings.

"I think I see Durham," Christian said suddenly. "This way."

With Kalina on his arm, Nathanial followed Christian through the crowd to the side of the room. Durham was standing there with a blonde woman Nathanial was fairly certain was his wife. Another couple was beside them speaking with Lady Astrid.

Nathanial greeted them and introduced Kalina, receiving introductions back and confirming that the blonde was the Countess of Durham. She smiled sunnily at them both. The dark-haired woman standing beside her was Durham's cousin, Mrs. Browne, and the man was her husband, Captain Browne. With Kalina quickly pulled into conversation with the ladies, Nathanial quietly asked Durham for a quick word.

Which left him utterly puzzled at the end of it. Durham had not received payment because he'd refused it—he scowled at the idea of holding Nathanial accountable for his father's debts. He refused to reconsider his position, no matter that Nathanial protested that he had the money now. They ended up making a gentleman's agreement that Nathanial would owe Durham a favor for the future, which left him both grateful and satisfied... and perturbed.

Then, who was the note from? All the letters he'd found, all of his father's vowels that he'd uncovered, had been signed.

Clearly, the sender of the recent note had expected him to know who had sent it. They must have assumed he would recognize the seal. He would have to share it with his friends. Surely one of them would know whose it was if there was an expectation that he would recognize it on sight.

Turning away from Durham, he found himself immediately distracted from the mystery by the sight of the Marquess of Camden's youngest son clearly flirting with Nathanial's wife.

The surge of possessiveness that thundered through him had him moving before he could think.

36

———————

As always, Lady Astrid had the most unusual friends. Lady Durham and Mrs. Browne were both stunningly beautiful, the former as light in hair and eyes as the latter was dark. Lady Durham's mask was gold, while Mrs. Browne's was midnight black. Both of them eyed her with speculation as she was introduced.

"We can speak freely in front of Kalina," Lady Astrid assured the other two women, with a quick glance at the gentlemen to assure herself that they were preoccupied. Durham and Nathanial had their heads together, and Captain Browne had been drawn into conversation with one of the gentlemen beside him. "She is in this, too."

"In what?" Kalina asked, trying not to feel suddenly adrift. She did not want to be cast out of whatever she was, but she also had no idea what Lady Astrid was speaking of.

"Astrid thinks someone murdered the tragic dukes' fathers," Lady Durham said, keeping her voice low. "The investigations Evie and her husband did into the matter came back inconclusive, and Evie is not yet convinced that Astrid has it aright."

"I am slowly becoming more so," Mrs. Browne interjected, frowning. "It is difficult because, as usual, the men are trying to keep the ladies out of things. Not my husband, of course, but I assume yours has told you nothing about the possibility that the hunting lodge accident in which his father was killed may have been no accident?"

Kalina's head was reeling, and it was all she could do not to allow her shock to show on her face. Once again, long years of keeping a neutral expression regardless of the provocation came to her rescue.

It took her a moment to find her voice.

"He has not."

All three women snorted.

"I told you, they are trying to keep us out of it," Astrid said, rolling her eyes. "All except Gregory, which is the only reason I know about Montblanc, thanks to Tiffany. At least one of the men is being sensible."

"Well, they are married," Lady Durham pointed out. "Perhaps Drake will be more reasonable after your wedding." Even as she said the words, it was clear she did not believe them, and Astrid snorted in response.

"Obviously, it did not change Nathanial since he has failed to inform Kalina. Men." Astrid's dismissive tone made her opinion very clear.

"He has not told his sisters," Kalina said, feeling she could be certain of that. "They would have told me. I think. I am not sure he would have—our marriage did not come about in the usual manner."

"I have already informed them," Astrid reassured her with a wave of her hand, though she frowned at Kalina. "Does he still believe you had a part in trapping him?"

"I am... not sure." She had not said so outright. Neither had he. Since the change in his demeanor toward her, she'd been almost afraid to bring it up again. If she insisted on her innocence, he might become angry if he thought she continued to lie.

With things going well now, there seemed no reason to bring it up again.

Astrid shook her head.

"The two of you need to communicate."

"That's a bit calling the kettle black, is it not?" Mrs. Browne asked, arching a dark eyebrow at Astrid, who glared at her.

"Drake and I are hardly going to get along better by communicating *more*. What is he going to talk to me about? How many women he's seduced this week?" Lady Astrid shook her head, reaching up to brush a fiery curl away from her face. "No matter. What's important is the dukes." She turned her attention back to Kalina. "We still do not know why they were murdered—"

"*If* they were murdered," Mrs. Browne murmured.

"Which means we cannot be certain the current generation is not also in danger and possibly ourselves as well since we're intended to carry the next generation," Lady Astrid finished, with another sharp glance at Mrs. Browne.

Kalina's hands immediately went to her stomach as she took a sharp intake of breath.

Mrs. Browne sighed.

"It is better to be safe than to be sorry in this instance. And, to be truthful, I am mostly put out that Anthony and I missed something in our investigation." She glanced at her husband, who was still turned away in conversation. "One thing I do believe we can be certain of is that it was not a foreign plot, unlike the attempt on the Duke of York's life not so long ago. In fact..." Her voice trailed off as she gestured to someone.

They must have been close by in order to be able to see her in the crush. Proving Kalina's thought true, a moment later, a young, handsome man appeared at her elbow, grinning broadly. He was well turned out, every inch of him impeccably pressed, yet somehow he gave off an air of casualness that made one feel immediately comfortable with him. The mask of bright green over the upper half of his face obscured his forehead, but showed off his eyes to perfection, as they were the exact same shade as the gaudy accessory.

"This is my cousin, Adam Stuart. Adam, you remember Lady Astrid, and this is the Duchess of Hereford."

"Ladies." Still grinning, the man gave an elegant bow, despite the lack of space to truly do so.

It turned out that the young Mr. Stuart had recently been over-seas, and he quickly confirmed for his cousin that there was nothing on the continent to suggest that anyone there had anything to do with the tragedy. He also mentioned that there was no sign the Russians had their fingers in English pies again.

Kalina could only infer that meant the previous attempt on the Duke of York's life had been by them. Her jaw felt locked into place to keep it from dropping as revelation after revelation was dropped in front of her. When Lady Astrid had assured them they could speak freely in front of her, they had certainly taken her at her word. Kalina had had no idea there had ever been an attempt on the Duke of York's life, much less the rest of it.

She was uncertain why Mrs. Browne and her husband had been investigating anything, much less why she took her cousin's word about an entire continent, but Lady Astrid seemed to take their statements as fact. Kalina decided she could do no less. At least for now. She may have questions later, but this was clearly not the time.

Turning to her, the young Mr. Stuart gave her his best smile. He was charming enough that Kalina found the corners of her lips lifting automatically in response. She would not have been able to help herself, even if she had wanted to hold back a smile—which she had no reason to currently—but she recognized his charisma.

"You were born in India, correct, Your Grace?"

"I was. My family came here recently, not long before the start of the Season."

Immediately, his eyes lit up with interest.

"I have always wanted to visit India. Is it true there are entire seasons with nothing but rain?"

"That does not sound so different from London some weeks," Lady Durham quipped with a smile.

Kalina laughed, but Mr. Stuart shook his head with all intent seri-ousness.

"No, Josie, it's completely different."

"I know, Adam, I am only jesting." She did not seem to take affront, patting her brother-in-law on the arm with a fond look for him before turning to Kalina. "Adam is an intrepid explorer these days. Given the chance, he will certainly talk your ear off about both India and the trip from there to here."

The roguish smile was back, and he bestowed it intently upon Kalina. "I certainly will."

Indeed, he was able to pepper her with several questions before her husband suddenly appeared at her side, scowling for some reason. Immediately, Kalina was concerned. Had his talk with the earl not gone well? Yet the earl had rejoined them as well. He was not smiling, but the fond way he was looking at his wife before he whispered something in her ear did not indicate any unhappiness on his end.

Taking her hand in his, Nathanial wound her fingers around his arm, glaring at Durham's younger brother as he did so.

"Stuart."

Mr. Stuart's dark eyes danced with amusement.

"Hereford. I understand congratulations are in order." He winked at Kalina, unfazed by Nathanial's deepening scowl.

Kalina was not certain she understood what was happening.

Her husband seemed... jealous?

But in order to be jealous, he would have to care about her.

Wouldn't he?

"Thank you, Stuart. Now, if you'll excuse us," he put a little emphasis on the 'us' just as the first notes from a violin trembled through the air, "I believe this is my dance with *my wife.*"

No, she was not imagining it. Not jealous though. Possessiveness. And maybe a touch of jealousy.

Because she'd been talking to another man?

Kalina did not have time to think, did not have time to question it before she found herself being pulled through the crowd by her husband. The dance floor was also crowded, elbow to elbow, but somehow he stepped into the swirling mass, making a space for them without stepping on anyone's toes and pulling her along with him. Breathless, Kalina found herself rotating in his arms.

Which was when she realized what they were dancing.

"The waltz! I'm not..." She was not supposed to waltz in London... when she was a debutante. But she was married now. And waltzing with her husband. Kalina relaxed. No one had told her explicitly, but it made sense that she would not need permission from the Almack's hostesses to waltz now.

She was not doing anything wrong that could hurt the family's standing.

———

<u>*Nathanial*</u>

Looking down at his wife, Nathanial wished her pink mask did not obscure so much of her face. It was difficult to decipher the expressions flashing across her face when he could not see half of it.

She was not... what?

And then she'd halted. Relaxed. Stopped trying to pull away from him.

Was she thinking about Adam Stuart?

Or was she thinking that she was not supposed to dance with Nathanial since they were pretending to have a warm relationship?

Did he dare ask?

Did he want to know the answer?

Twirling her across the dance floor, he relaxed now that she had, too. He did not want to ruin the dance. Instead, he let go of his questions and let the music flow over them, through them, carrying them in an intimate bubble across the crowded floor. It did not matter how many people there were around them, it was though everyone else did not exist.

It was just him and his wife and the music.

When it ended, he could feel his heart pounding as he stared down at her. The urge to lower his mouth to hers was strong... but even with the masks, that would cause a serious amount of gossip. It was *not done*. Especially between a wife and a husband.

If he threw such niceties out the window, he might as well declare his feelings right here in the middle of the Camden ballroom. And he was not ready to do that. Not when he felt so unsure how she felt about him. Considering that she'd trapped him into marriage, making such a declaration would put him in a very vulnerable position. Again.

Too vulnerable.

Clearing his throat, he stepped away, taking her hand in his.

"Thank you for the dance, my dear." It felt formal. Too formal. It broke the spell the music had woven around them. Her smile changed, just a touch. Most people might not even notice, but he did.

"Thank you, Your Grace."

He frowned down at her. He had not meant to make things *that* formal. She was his wife. She should use his name.

"Nathanial," he corrected her in a low tone. Thankfully, no one around them was paying attention to their conversation, so they could not hear him insisting his wife call him by his given name.

Dark eyes blinked at him through the mask.

"Nathanial," she repeated on a husky whisper that made him want to drag her from the ballroom and do utterly indecent things to her.

He had half a mind to do just that, but when he turned, he found his intentions thwarted. His blood ran hot and then cold as he stared at the man in front of him, the man he had not seen since the house party, since the wedding. Since Mr. Little had trapped Nathanial into marriage. Mrs. Little was on his arm, though her gaze was completely focused on Kalina.

The rage and resentment he'd managed to beat down in regard to his wife rose up inside him again, and he stiffened, going straight as a poker. Beside him, he could feel his wife's reaction.

"Mama. Papa." Kalina stepped forward to greet first her mother, then her father. Nathanial nodded at both of them, feeling as though his muscles might creak from the effort.

"We heard you were here and wanted to come say hello," Mrs. Little said, her gaze now going back and forth between Nathanial and Kalina. He had no problem with her, other than the man she'd married. Unlike her husband, her shock and horror had been entirely authentic—and Nathanial had seen the anger she'd directed at the man in the wake of that awful morning.

She'd had no such thing for her daughter, but Nathanial could hardly blame her for that. Indeed, he realized now, after having had more time to get to know his wife, it was very likely Mr. Little had a heavy influence over his daughter. Kalina wanted to make the people around her happy, always. In many ways, one could call her easily led.

Which was why Nathanial had been able to forgive her so easily, he now realized. Not only because he'd seen her true remorse, but because the more he'd come to know her, the more he'd been able to see how she might have been led down a path she would not have normally gone in order to please her father. Kalina was no manipulative mastermind, but she was someone who would do anything for a person she was loyal to.

For someone she loved.

I want her to be that way with me.

The revelations punched him in the gut, and he was not sure he would have had them without being faced with the actual mastermind of the plot behind his wedding. The resentment over not being able to be truly angry, considering that he'd gotten everything he could have wanted in a bride, bubbled up inside him again, making him clench his jaw.

His wife and her mother exchanged their news while he and her father eyed each other warily.

Not the most enjoyable first encounter post-wedding but not altogether bad.

And when he and his wife returned home, he took out some of his frustration by having her grip the spindles of her headboard until he'd wrung three orgasms from her with his mouth and his fingers before plunging between her thighs and driving her to a fourth climax with one finger deeply embedded in the ass he fully intended on claiming soon.

37

—————

Waking up alone in her bed, deliciously sore all over, Kalina reached out to touch the indent her husband's head had made in the pillow beside hers. She wished she knew how long he stayed.

She wished he would stay until the morning.

Things had been going rather well last night until they'd run into her parents. The joy that she'd felt upon seeing them again, even her father, had not been matched by her husband. Especially not when it came to her father. Which she could not blame him for.

Part of her was happy she'd been able to see her parents, and it had made her realize how much she missed them and her brother... but part of her wished that Nathanial had not seen them. Though at least he was not angry with *her* afterward. At least, he had not seemed to be. If anything, he'd been more passionate than ever before.

After Margaret helped her get dressed, Kalina made her way down to the dining room, joining the rest of the family in the meal. Nathanial smiled when she came in. All three of her sisters-in-law brightened.

It was a lovely meal as she received a recounting of everything the girls had done the day before. All of them were making progress on their lessons, especially Fiona, who seemed to have finally settled in with the idea of learning. She was enjoying working on her reading now that Miss Temple had found a book on animal husbandry for her to practice with.

Nathanial promised Julianna a trip to Newmarket for the next day to pick out a horse, which Emma and Fiona could come along as well. Kalina made herself smile at Nathanial's offhand comment that she could choose a horse as well.

Absolutely not.

But perhaps she could choose two... and a gig... She did not want to ride a horse, but learning to drive two of them might be easier for her. If nothing else, she could hang back with Emma, who also did not seem particularly enthused by the idea of having her own horse.

Fiona, of course, was already demanding one for herself. Nathanial's lips twitched, but all he told her was, *we'll see.*

After breakfast, the family scattered to their separate diversions. Nathanial brushed his lips over Kalina's before going to his study to work. The girls had their lessons. For once, she did not have any events to attend during the day... she could have opened the door to visitors and announced herself at-home...

Instead, she decided to visit her family.

It felt almost odd to return to the house she'd lived in at the beginning of the Season. The house had not changed, but she had. The home no longer felt like *her* home. Perhaps because she had not been there long enough for it to feel so, but that did not explain everything. She had been at Hereford Hall for even less time, but that was where she thought of when she thought 'home' now.

"Your Grace." Darcy, her parents' butler, bowed low when he opened the door. Kalina wanted to tell him not to, but she also knew there was no point. He was very proper, and the way his eyes shone with pride as he straightened told her that he was happy to be able to address her as such. "Welcome back and best wishes on your recent nuptials."

"Thank you, Darcy." She smiled at him. "Are my parents home?"

"Your mother is in the kitchen, speaking with Chef Julliard."

"Thank you." Kalina did not require an escort in her parents' home, and Darcy just bowed, letting her go on without him. As she was walking down the hall to the back of the house, sudden pounding footsteps alerted her to her brother's presence even before he called her name.

"Kalina!"

Turning, she beamed widely as her brother appeared and practically threw himself at her for a hug. When Darcy had said only her mother was home, she'd assumed Ashwin would be with her father, and she was thrilled to see her little brother. She hugged him back tightly.

"Ashwin."

"How are you?" He pulled back and looked at her closely, looking her over with intent scrutiny in his dark eyes. It was a look that was very reminiscent of their mother.

"I am good."

"You are? The duke is treating you well?" The question was asked with all the somber seriousness and protectiveness of a man, not a youth. When had her little brother become so grown up?

"He is, I promise. I am very happy with both my marriage and my husband." She did not even have to lie; she was very happy. She would be even happier if her husband's feelings for her grew, if he fell in love with her. But even without that, she was happy right now. "I am looking forward to introducing you to his sisters."

Ashwin snorted and rolled his eyes.

"More sisters. Just what I always wanted." Despite the sarcasm threaded through his voice, she could hear the fondness in his tone. Laughing, she reached up to tousle his hair.

And she did have to reach *up*.

It was rather disconcerting to be gone for such a short time, then have a revelation about how big her little brother had become. Somehow, with all the excitement of the Season and her focus on her father's mission, she had not noticed until now.

"I am going to see Mother. Do you want to come?"

She was only a little disappointed, considering what she wanted to talk to her mother about, when her brother shook his head and stepped away.

"I am in the middle of my studies for the day. Father wants me to go to Oxford next year, and I need to make sure I can pass the exam. I just heard you come in and wanted to make sure I did not miss you." He gave her a doleful look. "This is the first time you've come by."

"Well, you can always come visit me. And meet your sisters. I think you're going to adore Fiona and her fox."

Ashwin's eyes rounded.

"Her fox?"

Kalina could not help but laugh.

"We will have you all over for supper soon," she promised. "A family event." As soon as she was certain that her husband's temper would manage an entire evening with her father. Perhaps she was being overly optimistic in saying soon, but that was what she hoped for.

At the very least, she would find a time when she could introduce Ashwin to her new family. She did not think Nathanial would blame her brother for anything that had happened.

"I look forward to it." He wrinkled his nose, but she could see the curiosity gleaming in his eyes. He might be torn about the idea of meeting more people, wondering whether or not they would accept him, but the mention of a fox definitely interested him.

Giving her brother one last hug, feeling buoyed by the encounter, Kalina continued on to the kitchens. A familiar but surprising scent filled her nose as she got closer, and her eyes widened. She had not smelled that since India—and even then, they had never had that scent in their own home. It had always been in others.

Quickening her pace, she came to the kitchen and found her mother there with Chef Julliard and one of the kitchen maids, directing them on adding the next ingredients to the curry. The spicy scent brought sudden tears to Kalina's eyes and an unexpected wave of nostalgia for India.

All of them turned and looked up as Kalina came in, and the chef and maid immediately dropped into a bow and a curtsy.

A wide smile brightened Mama's face, and she opened her arms, coming around the counter with them spread wide.

"Kalina!"

"Mama."

They hugged, and Kalina clung for a long moment, breathing in the scent of her mother's rose perfume combined with the simmering curry. Over her mother's shoulder, she could see the chef and maid smile and exchange glances before turning back to their task.

"What are you doing here?" Her mother pulled away enough to look her in the face. "Were we expecting you?"

"No. I just... I wanted to see you."

"Of course. You're always welcome here. Come, come, let's go sit down. Chef and Mandy have this well in hand." Her mother gently shooed her out of the kitchen and along the hall toward the back parlor.

"You have them making curry."

Her mother hesitated a moment before answering. "I do."

"Why? We never ate curry in India." They entered the back parlor, and Kalina went to her favorite chair, sitting down and frowning at her mother. It was not that she disapproved; she just did not understand.

"Because I knew we were always coming here," her mother said, sitting down in the chair she always took, opposite Kalina. "I wanted to ensure that you and Ashwin had a palate for English food." She sighed, looking down at her hands. "And I suppose I was doing my best to reject my family the way they had rejected me after I married your father."

"Why?" Kalina asked. She'd always been curious, and for the first time, it seemed that perhaps her mother was willing to open up and talk about it. When Kalina had been younger, the topic had not been explicitly forbidden, but she'd never felt that she could ask. "Father has been doing his best to work his way back into his family's good graces... why not you?"

"Oh, I tried. At first." Mama sighed, a heavy, heartfelt sigh. "They were so angry at me for not following through with the marriage they'd arranged for me. My parents could not handle what they called *my* rejection of them. They did not see it as me claiming my own life; they did not care that I had fallen in love. I had rejected the match they'd made for me, so they rejected me. Very much the same way your father's family rejected him, but they were far away, and my family was close. I tried, over and over again, but after you were born and my mother would not even look at you, I decided I was done."

She lifted her gaze now to look at Kalina, sadness and warmth in her eyes.

"I could handle their rejection of me and work to try to change it. I would not let them reject and hurt my children. I stopped reaching out. I decided if they were to reach out to me, I would not reject them... but they did not."

Kalina's heart went out to her mother. She had not known all of these details. Her mother had never talked about it before, and she'd assumed it was too painful. Now she could see the anger that simmered there as well before her mother banked it again.

"But why did we never eat curry at home?" Kalina had had it, usually when they'd been invited over to someone's house for supper. The instances had been rare, but she'd loved both the taste and the smell. It was never served in their house.

"I suppose that when they rejected me, I decided to give them good reason to." Her mother smiled wanly. "It was my way of actually rejecting them, not just choosing to marry a man I wanted. I always thought they would come around, but when they did not, I decided to throw myself into being as English as I could because I knew eventually we would come home."

"But Papa is still looking for acceptance from his family because he never had to face it in person?"

"He is also far more of an optimist than I am. A bit of a dreamer, really." Mama smiled fondly. "And, unlike me, he did not have a match arranged. His father was incensed that he'd married without consulting him first, but his sin against them was far less than what my family perceived as my sin against them. Even after I accepted my family would never forgive me, he still had hope for his."

Kalina studied her mother's face, which showed sadness but also serenity.

"So, now you are eating curry?"

"I miss it. I have also come to realize that I do not have to reject everything in order to separate myself from my family." She smiled, but it was full of concern as she looked at Kalina. "When I married your father, I took control of my own destiny in some ways, but my family still influenced my decisions. I have to wonder now if that was a mistake."

"Because of me?"

"Because of the way you felt pressured to marry for your father's sake," her mother gently corrected her. She huffed. "I am still angry with him about that. We chose to marry each other—me against my family's wishes and him without consulting his. You were choosing to aim for a duke, and I did not want to interfere with your choice, but then your father did. He took from you what we had, what we sacrificed for." Mama shook her head. "I could kick him."

"But you will forgive him, eventually?" She wanted that for her parents. Although she knew it was her father's actions, and not hers, that had them at odds, she could not help but feel somewhat responsible. "He was trying to get me a love match. In his own deluded, not-very-well-thought-out way."

"Ready, fire, aim, that's your father." Mama smiled ruefully and closed her eyes. "I know who I married. But he also needs to understand that his actions have consequences, and not just for you. The choice should have been yours to make."

"I know," Kalina said softly. "But I think it will come out well enough in the end. Nathanial is no longer angry at me, though he still is at Papa. I cannot blame him."

"Neither can I."

"I do think Papa is right, and he was the better choice for me." Because she was falling in love with him. She did not know if she would have with Christian. Though she'd enjoyed his company, they'd been missing something ineffable, something she and Nathanial surely *did* have. "Even if he went about everything in the wrong way."

Mama wrinkled her nose.

"I wish that your happiness did not depend on him being correct. I cannot wish that he be wrong because I do want you to be happy… but I also want him to be wrong."

Laughing, Kalina reached out her hand and took her mother's.

"He can be both right and wrong at the same time." She squeezed her mother's fingers.

It was a very pleasant rest of the visit, catching up on what her family had been up to since that tumultuous house party, telling her mother about Hereford Hall and Nathanial's sisters. Unlike Ashwin, her mother was very much looking forward to meeting them.

She would have to speak with Nathanial and see how tetchy the subject of her father remained and whether a supper might be possible soon. If not, perhaps she could take his sisters somewhere her mother and brother could meet them, without him or her father present. Just to keep from chafing his sensibilities.

Feeling much better now that she'd been able to talk to her mother—though she did *not* tell her mother about the spanking that had changed her and Nathanial's relationship—she did thank her for making sure Kalina was informed before her wedding night.

Disembarking from the carriage, she swept up into the house, humming cheerfully under her breath. She was on her way to the back garden when she turned the corner and saw Julianna sitting beside the closed door to Nathanial's study. Her sister-in-law's eyes widened, a pleading expression settling over her face. She pressed her finger to her lips, clearly begging Kalina for silence.

More than a little intrigued, Kalina came closer, and Julianna's eyes widened even further as Kalina stood over her and pressed her ear to the door. Whatever Julianna was so interested in, Kalina wanted to know, too.

38

———————

NATHANIAL

Deep in the steady flow of work, the unexpected knock at Nathanial's door made him jump.

"Yes?" he asked, looking up, ink pen still poised over the letter he'd been writing to Daniel. Stalling opened the door and stepped in.

"The Marquess of Carmathen requests an audience, Your Grace." Stalling's demeanor was slightly disapproving. Carmathen had a bit of a reputation, even among the *ton*. He rarely graced ballrooms with his presence, though his title would make him welcome despite his reputation (if he was not run off by the irate husbands who detested his lack of interest in discretion when bedding their wives), and rumor had it that he might actually *own* a gaming hell.

No one had proven it, but just the rumor was enough to cause most of the *ton* to look at him askance. Bad enough to be involved in business in any way, although the strictures around that were loosening in certain circumstances, but a gaming hell was no respectable business.

What could he want with Nathanial?

Gaming hell.

More likely, he'd had business with Nathanial's father.

"Show him in, please, Stalling."

"Yes, Your Grace."

Stalling had gone from slight disapproval to pure disapproval, but he was too good a butler not to do his duty. Nathanial could not help but miss Daniel's lack of standing on ceremony as he finished his missive to the man. When they returned to Hereford Hall, he would likely leave Stalling here to help set up Hereford House once the renters had departed.

A stiffly upright butler was expected in London. Out in the country, he'd prefer someone more relaxed.

Just as Nathanial finished signing his letter, Stalling returned with the Marquess in tow.

"The Marquess of Carmathen," Stalling announced, stepping aside for the other man to enter.

Perhaps a few years younger than Nathanial, the Marquess was several inches taller than Stalling and with broader shoulders as well. Not just physically imposing; the way his sharp gaze moved around the room, taking in every detail, his mental acuity was obvious. They had never met before, but Nathanial's immediate impression was that the Marquess was both clever and dangerous.

He was dressed impeccably, despite his dissolute reputation. The edges of his shirt collar were sharp against his square jaw, he was clean-shaven, and his dark hair was expertly styled. Dressed in all black, other than his white shirt and neatly tied cravat, he appeared almost like a painting of what a proper gentleman should look like. Even Stalling would not be able to complain about his appearance.

Yet there was no doubt that, even in a room with a duke, the Marquess was confident of his own standing and power.

"Carmathen."

"Hereford." The Marquess bowed, not quite as deeply as he should for a duke, yet close enough that no complaint could be made without appearing petulant. Nathanial's lips twitched in amusement.

"Come, have a seat." He gestured to the wingback leather chairs across from his desk. Carmathen prowled forward, his focus now on studying Nathanial as he chose the seat on the left and lowered himself into it.

Nathanial met his gaze steadily. Carmathen's lips curved.

"You are not much like your father," Carmathen observed.

A small huff of air escaped from Nathanial's lungs as the marquess confirmed why he was there.

"I am not," Nathanial agreed. As far as he was concerned, the Marquess had just paid him a compliment. Indeed, when Carmathen's smile widened, it was clear he had meant it as one.

"I will be frank with you, Hereford, your father lost quite a bit gambling with me. I do not necessarily believe a son should have to pay his father's debts when his father left him nothing... however, it seems you've landed on your feet."

"Ah." The mystery of the letter recently delivered to Nathanial suddenly became clear. He turned slightly and pulled open the uppermost right drawer on his desk, taking out the letter on top and the envelope with the seal he had not recognized. "I take it this was from you."

"It is." Carmathen frowned. "Did you not know?"

Nathanial slid the letter and envelope across the desk to the other man. Curiosity writ over his features, Carmathen leaned forward and picked it up. Giving the letter a brief glance, as it required nothing more in order to read it, he snorted.

"I must apologize. My steward is in charge of collecting my debts, and he has a flair for the dramatic. Although I do see he added my seal. Nothing more is usually needed, as those receiving the letter would know it immediately."

"I did not recognize it," Nathanial admitted. "I planned to start asking my friends if any of them did."

"Just as well I showed up then." Carmathen tossed the letter and envelope back onto the desk and leaned back. "Unless you wanted everyone to know we're doing business."

"To be honest, I would hope that the business can be concluded quickly." He wanted everything from his father's business done and over with. "What did my father owe you?"

The smile that flashed across Carmathen's face was not at all reassuring.

"Your sister's hand in marriage."

It was like a blow to the chest.

"*What?!*" Shock. Outrage. Horror. He knew all of it flashed over his face before he could cover it.

Carmathen did not seem insulted at Nathanial's reaction to such a union; if anything, he was amused.

"As he did not have the means to pay for the vowels he owed me, he offered your eldest sister. Julianna, I believe her name is?" Carmathen tilted his head. "My understanding is that she's not out in Society yet, but she is old enough to be. Dowry free, of course."

"You want my sister as your wife?" Nathanial sputtered. That was the only way he could describe the way the words came out of his mouth. He felt like strangling his father. But someone had already blown the bastard up.

Once more, Nathanial could only wish that someone had done it sooner.

"Well, I do need a wife and an heir, eventually. There was a certain appeal to avoiding the marriage mart altogether. And your father described her as beautiful and biddable."

"Well, he was half right," Nathanial drawled. Biddable? Julianna? His father must have been desperate.

"Given the family's financial circumstances have changed, and you began paying off the debts, and since you did not answer my steward's note, I wondered if you even knew of the vowels your father left with me. Not just me, by the by. Our last game was with Cornwall and Trent, though neither of them was promised a sister. Just me." That flashing grin again. Carmathen was amused. Nathanial had never been less so. "I decided to come in person to discuss the options."

"Options?"

"In case you wanted to pay off the amount your father owed me, rather than providing me with a bride."

Nathanial nearly collapsed with relief that Carmathen was going to be reasonable. Of course, that was the first thing he would have offered, but he had no idea how intent Carmathen was on having Julianna as his bride. He could not imagine the two had ever met. Julianna had certainly never mentioned an engagement.

Likely, her father had not told her either.

"Yes. That would be preferable to everyone involved, I believe." He eyed Carmathen. "Especially if you are looking for a biddable bride."

"Ah, so she is beautiful." Carmathen chuckled, leaning back in the chair. "I did wonder which half your father was right about."

"Beautiful and strong-willed. I don't believe the word 'biddable' has ever been used to describe her in her entire life," Nathanial said dryly. In fact, just hearing the adjective would have Julianna spitting fire.

"Well, then. I'll be happy to take the money and consider it a lucky escape."

Carmathen also knew the amount due to Trent and Cornwall. The latter's name kept sticking in Nathanial's head. Something about it was ringing a bell, but he could not fathom why.

As usual, the amounts were astronomical. Not the kind of money he carried around with him. Especially with what his father owed Carmathen. If Nathanial had not immediately sunk money into the estate and investments... but once he'd had a return, he would be able to pay off the vowels he had to hand over to Carmathen. The man offered to take Julianna off his hands again, biddable or not, but Nathanial refused.

Not if there was another option.

That had been the whole point of his own marriage—to allow his sisters their choice. Not for Julianna to be bartered off due to his father's gambling.

"I suppose I shall be patient a little longer." Carmathen patted his pocket where he'd put Nathanial's note. "I certainly will not need a bride before next Season at the earliest."

Nathanial glowered. Carmathen was enjoying himself far too

much at Nathanial's expense. It might even serve him right to saddle him with Julianna. She'd make his life a misery.

But he could not do that to his sister, even if Carmathen deserved it.

"You'll have your money," he growled. "As will Trent and Cornwall."

"Cornwall may forgive the debt," Carmathen commented. "He was the one who invited your father to the hunting lodge. He got sick before the trip. Devil's own luck, that one. You could always try to appeal to his guilt."

That was it. That was where Nathanial had heard the man's name before. He just had not realized that his father had owed Cornwall money.

The man had not been on the trip, so it was likely no one had spoken to him about the explosion and fire. A trickle of awareness spread down Nathanial's spine. Someone needed to question Trent.

As his mind whirled, Carmathen's gaze unfocused, and he turned his head slightly. Before Nathanial could ask what he was about, the man sprang to his feet and was across the room in the blink of an eye, opening the door that he'd come through previously.

Nathanial's wife and sister tumbled at his feet, Kalina tripping over Julianna, in a whirl of fabric and skirts. He shot to his feet, fingertips on the surface of his desk, staring with his mouth open. Had they been listening at the door?

KALINA

Listening through Nathanial's study door had been frustrating, but too tempting to resist. Julianna had the better perch, with her ear to the keyhole rather than trying to listen through the thick wood. Kalina could only catch so much.

Enough to hear that Nathanial's father had owed the man inside money. And others. The man would have never been able to pay such sums back. Had he planned on leaving all his financial troubles to

Nathanial? She had not had the opportunity to meet the old duke, and now she was glad of it.

She could not fathom a parent being so uncaring of his children and their futures, so selfish as to leave them with problems he created and never even tried to solve. He got what he wanted when he was alive and left the mess for Nathanial to clean up once he was gone.

The anger she felt at a dead man she'd never met was shocking.

There was suddenly quiet in the room, and Kalina frowned, pressing her ear more firmly to the door. Had they lowered their voices for some reason?

With so much of her weight pressed against the hard wood, her knees against Julianna's shoulders where the other woman knelt, there was nothing to keep her upright when the door suddenly gave way. She shrieked as she tumbled forward, over Julianna, falling in a heap of skirts at the entrance to the room. Julianna was knocked over by her own fall, leaving them both floundering at the feet of a very tall, very handsome man.

"Well, hello there." He purred the words as he stared down at her and Julianna, his gaze flicking back and forth between them.

"Good morning." Kalina did not know what else to say. He held out his hand, and she took it, allowing him to help her to her feet, which was when she realized how much taller he was than her. Or maybe he was just very good at looming. Though he dropped his hand fairly quickly, she'd been able to feel the strength in his fingers.

Though he held his hand out to Julianna, she eschewed taking it, getting to her feet on her own with a haughty sniff.

"I am not marrying you."

Kalina groaned inwardly as a flash of something flared in the man's dark eyes. She could have told Julianna that some men took such blunt statements as challenges—and those were not men to trifle with.

Thankfully, Nathanial had gathered his wits and was coming around his desk to take control of the situation.

"Kalina, Julianna, this is the Marquess of Carmathen. Carmathen, this is my wife, the Duchess of Hereford, and my sister, Lady Julianna."

"Your Grace." Carmathen bowed to her. Then he turned to Julianna, a dangerous smile flashing across his lips. "Lady Julianna." The way he said her name was like a caress, and Julianna sucked in a breath as her eyes went wide.

Nathanial appeared as though he wanted to punch the marquess, but of course, he could not.

The man had not actually *done* anything.

"I think I need to speak with my wife and sister privately," Nathanial said, giving Carmathen a dark look.

"Of course." The marquess smiled at Julianna and winked at her. "It was a pleasure to finally meet you, little fox." She bristled, and Nathanial's face went red while Kalina watched, fascinated. The marquess turned to her and gave her another bow. "Your Grace."

And with that, he was gone, whisking his way out the door and closing it behind him.

Nathanial scowled.

"You are both in so much trouble."

39

Whatever punishment her husband wanted to subject her to, it was not forthcoming. Instead, he and Julianna railed at each other for several long minutes, and Kalina moved out of the line of fire as they shouted at each other. Apparently, Julianna had known that her father had arranged a match for her with Carmathen... and neglected to tell her brother in hopes the issue never surfaced.

Nathanial was resigned at discovering that Kalina knew everything about his father's death, thanks to her friends, which left most of his focus on Julianna. He was furious with her for allowing him to be caught off guard by the debt to Carmathen and not trusting him to protect her from an unwanted wedding.

They were finally interrupted by Fiona, holding Telemachus, wanting to know what all the shouting was about. Julianna went off in a huff with her younger sister and the little fox, declaring that they were going to the park.

Rather than address the fact that Kalina had been listening at his study door along with his sister, Nathanial immediately sent notes to the other dukes, asking them to come. When she found out that he felt the Marquess of Carmathen had given him a potential clue into the death of his father, Kalina immediately insisted that one be sent to Lady Astrid as well.

While they were waiting for the others to arrive, Nathanial went over the full discussion he'd had with Carmathen.

He'd just finished when Stalling came to announce the Duke and Duchess of Clarence's arrival, at which point they relocated to the drawing room. Kalina greeted Tiffany and Gregory, then rang for tea while they all settled themselves. It did not take long for the room to fill up. Everyone had come immediately—thankfully, it was early enough in the afternoon that they had all been home when Nathanial's summons arrived.

Zachary was the last to arrive, Monkey Sinclair clinging to his shoulder, the monkey's tail twined around his neck. As usual, the monkey was wearing a ribbon that matched Zachary's waistcoat; today's was a pale yellow that looked a touch wrinkled.

"My apologies," he said, frowning. His face appeared paler than normal. "I would have been here sooner, but my horse threw me the moment I got in the saddle. Somehow, a burr got stuck under the blanket. Thankfully, I landed on a pile of hay in the stable yard; it could have been much worse."

"My goodness!" Tiffany fussed over him until he waved her off, seeming shaken. He was not entirely displeased about being fussed over, just a bit embarrassed. Kalina poured him a cup of tea to bolster him.

Once they were done assuring themselves that Zachary was unharmed, all the attention in the room turned to Nathanial. The dukes were arrayed around the room, allowing the ladies to sit. Only Gregory had a space on the couch, beside his wife, of course, but Nathanial hovered beside where Kalina was sitting, one hand behind her on the back of the chair. Drake was several feet away from Lady Astrid's chair. The rust-orange pocket square in his jacket matched the color of her morning gown almost exactly, Kalina noted with some amusement.

Very much the way her gown matched Nathanial's pocket square today.

"So, what is this new clue you have for us?" Sebastian asked, getting right to the heart of the matter. Pacing back and forth behind the couches, he seemed more agitated than some of the other dukes. Tiffany twisted in her seat and held her hand out to him.

With a deep sigh, he walked over and put his hand in hers, using his other to smooth down his emerald-green waistcoat. A useless gesture as, unlike Zachary, his was completely unwrinkled.

"The Marquess of Carmathen visited me this morning," Nathanial said, ignoring the quick indrawn breaths of several of the other dukes. Lady Astrid sat up a little straighter. "Unbeknownst to me, and I do not know where my father's record of the vowels went, my father owed the marquess and two others gambling debts. Trent and Cornwall. Cornwall is the one who invited my father to the hunting lodge, but he did not attend himself... according to Carmathen, he fell sick before the trip."

Everyone in the room was silent, working through it in their heads.

"If he did not attend, then he has never been questioned," Lady Astrid said in a low voice.

Nathanial nodded.

"What would be the point if he was not there? But I did not know. As far as I know, no one looking into the matter would know that my father owed him money. Money that he could not possibly ever repay."

It was motive. Slim, but it was there. Kalina felt sick at the thought. On the other hand, from everything she'd learned about Nathanial's father, it might have been for the best for his children. However, she knew Tiffany and Sebastian truly grieved their father's death, as did Zachary. His mother was distraught over it. Kalina was not certain of the others, but surely almost all the dukes had someone who mourned them.

"Do we know if he actually fell sick?" Drake asked. "Or was that just an excuse?"

"I had that thought as well." Nathanial made a face.

"Are you going to question him when you pay him?" Christian

asked from where he was leaning on the mantle. His arms were crossed over his chest, his expression inscrutable. Whatever he was feeling, it was not apparent on his face.

"I can try, but I do not think I am the best person to." Nathanial looked around. "I was thinking one of you might approach him. Even if he did not have anything to do with my father's death, even if he knows nothing, he may be loath to speak with me about it. And if he does know something, he might be more forthcoming with someone whose father he did not send to their death."

"I can speak with him," Matthew offered. "We run in the same circles sometimes. He's a heavy gambler. I believe he's at a house party at the moment, but there's a tournament this Saturday at the Tramp's Den that I do not believe he'd miss."

"At where?" Tiffany asked, frowning as she turned her head to look at Matthew. Gregory shot the other man a dark look.

"Nowhere you need to concern yourself with," Gregory assured his wife, patting the hand he held. On her other side, Sebastian's expression made it clear he was in full agreement with his brother-in-law.

"It is no place for ladies," Drake said firmly.

Only because Kalina was sitting beside her did she see the way Lady Astrid's fingers twitched in her lap.

Though the conversation wound around, after a bit, the gentlemen decided to decamp to Nathanial's study and excused themselves from the ladies. Kalina did not mind because she wanted to speak with Tiffany and Lady Astrid privately. Though she was also curious about what the gentlemen wanted to speak of without them, and she was sure the other two were as well, both of them were just as eager to have their own discussion.

As soon as the door was closed behind the gentlemen, Tiffany leaned in toward Lady Astrid.

"What is the Tramp's Den?" she demanded to know.

"A gambling hell, down in the Warrens," Lady Astrid answered calmly, taking a sip of her tea as if it was normal for a young debutante to know about a gambling hell in the most dissolute part of

London. No proper young lady should *ever* be in that part of the city, much less know what businesses were located there. Kalina stared at Lady Astrid.

She was becoming accustomed to Lady Astrid knowing all sorts of things she should not, but this was a step further than she would have guessed. Determined not to show her shock on her face, because she was not going to judge Lady Astrid's myriad of connections, she was at least comforted that Tiffany was as surprised as she was.

"I am not going to ask how you know that," Tiffany said, shaking her head and sitting back. "Well, what do you think?"

"I think I am going to speak to Mei and see what she can find out about Carmathen, Trent, and Cornwall," Lady Astrid replied immediately.

"All three of them?"

"Of course." Lady Astrid lifted her teacup to her lips and took a sip. "The gentlemen might be focused on Cornwall, but Carmathen knew enough to drop the hint, and who knows what Trent might know. At the very least, I want information on them, as I know very little about all three of them. Mei is uniquely placed to gather the basics without kicking up a fuss."

Which was very true. Kalina hardly had the contacts to ask. Lady Astrid and Tiffany might, but of course, then questions would be asked about why they wanted to know. As Mei was assisting her matchmaker grandmother, her queries would be assumed to be part of their trade.

"We should also see what Delilah knows of them," Tiffany offered. "She hears things we do not."

Lady Astrid nodded her agreement before looking at Kalina.

"How likely is it that Carmathen will push this marriage to Julianna?"

"Nathanial thinks he is content to be paid back." Kalina stopped. Hesitated. Lady Astrid raised one eyebrow in query. "But there was just something about the way Carmathen looked at Julianna."

"Ah." Lady Astrid tapped the side of her teacup thoughtfully, her lips slightly pursed as she tilted her head. Kalina could almost see the thoughts running through her mind, even if it was impossible to know what they were. She was plotting *something.*

"Why?"

"I was wondering if he might be a suitable match for Lady Johanna."

Both Tiffany and Kalina blinked in surprise. That was such a turn from anything Kalina might have guessed.

"Is she that desperate?" Tiffany asked. "His reputation is..."

"Yes and yes. Her mother has been getting sicker. There is only so much I can do for the family, so much help they'll accept. My parents are no help, unfortunately. Lady Johanna is a distant cousin on my father's side, but it is very distant, and they have accepted Lady Johanna's reassurances that all is well enough."

"You have not?"

"I think the family is in far more dire circumstances than Lady Johanna let on. You know how it is with the *ton.* Admitting their misfortunes could scupper things for her younger brother, the earl. Just look at the hoops Nathanial jumped through, and that's with a much loftier title." Lady Astrid gave Kalina a significant look.

She nodded in understanding and looked at Tiffany.

"Hereford Hall was in shambles when we arrived. His sisters were all in hand-me-downs. Fiona received her first new dress, made for her, after our arrival. It was so much worse than he let on."

"And he's a *duke.*" Lady Astrid shook her head. "Imagine how much worse it would be for a earl's sister. Carmathen might have a reputation as a scoundrel of the first degree, but from what I know, he's an honorable scoundrel, and he takes care of his people. If he married Lady Johanna, he'd not only ensure her family was well off, but he'd also teach her brother the ropes of being a earl. He would do it all quietly, without bringing attention to the family's situation."

"Is she truly that bad off?" Lady Tiffany asked tentatively. "She had a companion with her, after all."

Lady Astrid made a face and lowered her voice.

"Miss Belle is actually a cousin. An illegitimate one. She was acting as Lady Johanna's companion because there was no other option. And, being illegitimate, she hardly expects to be presented to Society." Lady Astrid's eyes flashed with disapproval and something else. A look that she had often gotten in her eye when looking at Kalina before the house party.

Kalina would be willing to wager all the money Nathanial had left from her dowry that Lady Astrid had plans for Miss Belle's future, as well as Lady Johanna's.

"I will see what Mei can find out about Carmathen and his interest in marrying." Lady Astrid nodded. "In the meantime, how are things with Nathanial? The two of you seem to have worked out your... differences."

"Tiffany gave me some very good advice." Kalina smiled at the other duchess. "Things have been much better since then."

"You mean you let him spank you?" Lady Astrid made a face as she set her teacup down, causing Tiffany to stifle a laugh.

"I requested that he do so." She shared a look with Tiffany, whose mirth was dancing in her eyes. It was not often that they got to see Lady Astrid discomfited. "And Tiffany was correct... it was both pleasurable and painful. It also seems to have brought us closer than before."

"I did notice that you are calling him 'Nathanial' now and not 'Hereford'," Tiffany commented.

"I..." Kalina's voice trailed off. When had that happened? She was not certain. Recently, as Tiffany had said, but she could not remember exactly when the shift was made.

She did, though. She thought of him as Nathanial. Called him Nathanial. And... he'd started calling her by her name, too.

It was a small thing, yet large enough for Tiffany to comment on it.

"Oh look, you've flummoxed her."

Lady Astrid laughed delightedly. "Well, I am happy to hear that things are moving apace. Although I am not certain that I can condone this idea of being spanked, of all things."

"You cannot know until you've tried it," Tiffany pointed out.

Lady Astrid pressed her lips together. Obviously, she did not like not knowing. Especially when two of her friends did. Make that three, since Delilah had revealed she and Zachary had also engaged in such activities during her time as his mistress. She eyed Tiffany.

"You have become very uppity since your marriage," she observed.

Tiffany caught Kalina's eye and winked before turning back to Lady Astrid and giving her a pointed look.

"I had the best to learn from."

"Mmm." Lady Astrid lifted her teacup to her lips again, but it did not entirely cover her smile.

40

———————

N*ATHANIAL*

"Why did you want us to talk alone?" Christian asked, once they were ensconced in Nathanial's study, with his pocket square stuffed in the keyhole—just in case. The little bit of pink fabric looked out of place against the hard wooden door, but hopefully, it would assist with any would-be eavesdroppers. Kalina had admitted it had been difficult to hear everything through the door—Julianna had had a far easier time of it.

"Well, we can hardly speak of things like the Tramp's Den with the ladies present," Drake said, making a face at him as he turned one of Nathanial's wingback chairs to face the others and sat down in it. He looked at Matthew, who was doing the same with the other chair. The rest of them stood about, leaning or resting against various pieces of furniture. Nathanial leaned against the doorjamb, keeping one ear open for the ladies. "Do you want backup this weekend?"

"It could not hurt to have some others there." Matthew looked around at all of them with a frown. "Not Nathanial, of course. Even if it were not your father he had invited to the hunting lodge, your presence at a gambling hell would draw far too much attention."

"The same with Sebastian and Gregory, especially since Gregory has barely left his wife's side since their marriage," Drake pointed out. "I can come. No one will look askance at my presence there."

"I cannot. I have to escort Lady Annabelle around this weekend," Zachary said, looking miserable about the prospect. He reached up to stroke Monkey Sinclair's back, and the little creature chittered in response, putting his tiny paw on Zachary's ear as if trying to console him.

"Are you really going to marry her just to make your mother happy?" Christian asked him dubiously. The idea of doing something to make a parent happy was the antithesis of how Christian had lived his life.

"It's more complicated than that," Zachary replied, looking away.

"Well, I can go as well," Christian said, shaking his head as he turned his attention back to the rest of them. "I've been to the Tramp's Den before."

"I think no more than three of us should attend." Sebastian glanced around to see if anyone disagreed with him. "Any more and someone might start to wonder what so many of us are doing there. I agree that the three of you will cause the least comment."

"It will be a welcome break from the marriage mart." Christian grinned at Sebastian. "Are you ready to be the only eligible duke available to the mamas?"

The jab struck Sebastian, who clearly had not thought through that fact. Gregory and Nathanial were married, Zachary would be with the debutante the *ton* now expected him to propose to, so without Matthew and Christian attending the balls…

"Bloody hell," Sebastian muttered, reaching up to scrub his hand over his face. "Well, nothing for it. It makes sense, and this needs to be the priority."

"Do not worry," Gregory said, clapping his hand on Sebastian's shoulder. His wide, amused grin declared that he was thoroughly enjoying Sebastian's discomfort. "We will not let you be too overrun. You can hide behind Tiffany's skirts if need be."

Chuckling, Nathanial leaned his head back against the wall. It truly was nice being on the other side of marriage and not having to worry about such things now. He had his wife.

The conversation quickly veered around to other matters. Gregory wanted to know if Monkey Sinclair was warming up to Lady Annabelle—he was not, despite her best efforts. Zachary griped over the fact that the little creature's sole exception to misogyny was Delilah. Some men might have taken such an occurrence as a sign, but Zachary did not.

Christian, Matthew, and Drake had their heads bent together, discussing how they might best be able to question Cornwall without rousing his suspicions. Sebastian appeared to be lost in thought, probably trying to decide how he was going to ward off the matchmaking mamas with so many of his fellow dukes absent from the weekend's activities.

Finding a bride had not been the cakewalk he'd expected at the beginning of the Season.

It had not for any of them. Both Gregory's and Nathanial's marriages had been predicated by scandalous circumstances that required them to act honorably. He could not see Sebastian landing himself in such a situation.

One never knew, he supposed.

Eventually, everyone left to prepare themselves for their evening's events. He and Kalina attended Lady Greywood's ball before returning home, where he had a good excuse to spank her for listening to his meeting with Carmathen. Once her bottom was good and hot, he turned her on her back and used his mouth on her, his fingers sliding between her heated cheeks to stretch the tiny hole there.

His cock pulsed as she writhed for him, crying out with pleasure from his tongue in her pussy and his fingers in her arse. Only once she was limp and satiated from pleasure did he mount her, wallowing between her thighs, listening to her whimper, feeling her shudders as he stimulated her oversensitive flesh.

Nathanial loved wringing every last drop of pleasure from her body, his own ecstasy exploding through him as he emptied himself into her.

Panting, he nestled his face into her neck, enjoying the closeness, the way her hands trailed up and down his back. Felt her yawn. Lifting his head, he brushed his lips over hers in a kiss.

"Don't go," she whispered when he pulled away.

"I am not."

He took a few minutes to clean himself up with the water from her basin before returning to her with a wet cloth to clean the evidence of their lovemaking from between her legs. She shuddered as he ran the cool, damp cloth over her puffy, sensitive lips, her back arching in a manner that made his cock twitch.

By the time he climbed into bed beside her, pulling her back into his arms, she was already asleep. Worn out from his attentions. Grinning, Nathanial closed his eyes and followed her down.

It was the first time he spent the full night in his wife's bed.

Waking up beside her was a revelation. She was nestled sweetly in his arms, her breathing even and deep. Long black lashes brushed the top of her high cheekbones. The silky tresses of her hair were strewn across the pillow, midnight black against white in a stunning contrast.

She was soft and warm, and he did not want to let her go.

Why had he not stayed in her bed before?

You know why.

But that time had passed. He knew his feelings, even if he had not spoken them aloud. Admitting them to her felt far too vulnerable, especially considering how their marriage had come about. He had no idea how she felt about him.

He considered attempting to sneak away from her side now, before she woke, before she realized he'd spent the night at her side. Did doing so reveal too much of his emotions?

It might, but he still resisted the idea. Nathanial wanted to be here. Besides, it was his right as her husband to stay in her bed if he so wished.

Another benefit to being in her bed in the morning was that he could now wake her up in a far more enjoyable manner than he usually awoke.

Bending his head down, he brushed his lips against her neck.

"Kalina," he murmured, whispering her name so his breath wafted across her skin.

She did not stir, and he moved his lips over her collarbone.

"Kalina." A little louder this time as his mouth began to make a trail down to her breast. He kissed the top slope.

Nothing. No reaction from his wife. Nathanial frowned, a suspicion beginning to take root in his mind.

Moving his mouth over her breast, he watched her face as he took one pert nipple between his lips and sucked. Hard.

She let out a little moan with her breath, her expression changing only very slightly. Nathanial released her nipple and sat up. Watched her. Her face smoothed out immediately, and she turned her head to the side, her deep, even breathing resuming. He stared down at her.

She was still asleep.

A heavy sleeper.

But she had never been when he'd come to her bed. She'd always woken up immediately. Everyone had said... but he'd seen the proof otherwise. Until now.

Unless she was faking *this*?

"Kalina." He said her name loudly. Forthrightly. A demand. It was like a sharp clap in the air. There should be *some* reaction if she was awake, even if it was a minute change to her expression or breathing.

Nothing.

Nothing changed.

His wife was nearly impossible to awaken.

Events reordered themselves in his mind. The resentment he'd felt was now replaced by guilt and... and a new kind of anger. Why had she not told him? Why had she not said anything after that first day?

Why had she let him spank her when she'd done nothing wrong?

And now he wanted to spank her again for insisting he spank her in the first place, which made no sense, yet it did.

"Kalina," he growled, giving her a shake. She sighed, turning her head back and forth, then letting it flop back down again. Still not awake. She was every bit as difficult to wake up as had been reported.

The times he'd come into her bedroom... maybe she was less difficult when she first went to sleep?

Or maybe she had not been asleep at all.

Well.

He would see if she could sleep through *this.*

<u>*Kalina*</u>

Pleasure slid through her dream, making her senses tingle. It was a dream, she knew that, a memory of how Nathanial enjoyed burying his face between her legs. A dream... yet the pleasure felt so real.

She moaned.

But not just in the dream.

Kalina heard her moan, from a distance, as though her real self was miles away.

Why was she moaning?

The pleasure surged, a direct hit to the little nubbin between her thighs, and she gasped as the sensations drew her up out of the dream. Floundering, confused, her hands moved toward her pussy, only to meet the top of her husband's head.

Nathanial *was* between her thighs, again, his mouth suckling at her tender bits, waking her with pleasure.

"Oh!" She shuddered as she finally came fully awake, surprised and pleased to find her husband still in her bed and shocked at his actions.

Rather than taking her to completion, Nathanial lifted his head, his hazel eyes glittering at her as he stared down at her.

"Kalina." His voice was even. Neutral. And it sent a shiver up her spine. "You are very difficult to wake up."

"I... you knew that."

He raised an eyebrow at her.

"Did I? You have woken quite easily every time I have come to your bed in the evenings."

"I have not been asleep," she explained. Her body was aching, her needy pussy pulsing. As if he could read her mind, his fingers slipped between her thighs, sliding between the slick folds, stroking her and making it hard for her to think as she answered him. "There have been a few times I was close to, but once I realized you would be coming regularly, I could not fall asleep until after you had."

His finger slipped inside her, making her moan as her hips lifted, her body clenching around him.

"So, the night at the house party. You truly did not awaken when your father put me in your bed."

Kalina shook her head back and forth, reaching up to grasp the pillow beneath it, gasping as he crooked his finger inside her, stroking an exquisitely sensitive spot.

"Kalina."

"What?" He was teasing her. Tormenting her. Her body was buzzing from the sensual assault, and he wanted to ask her questions? How was she supposed to focus on what he was saying under these circumstances?

"The night at the house party. When your father put me in your bed. You truly did not wake until the morning."

"I did not." She shook her head again, mewling as the base of his hand pressed against her clitoris, hard enough that her hips lifted into the air... then the pressure was gone. His fingers were gone.

The world turned upside down and righted itself as he flipped her onto her stomach. Kalina barely had time to take in a surprised breath before his hand came crashing down onto her bottom, still sensitive from the spanking he'd given her last night. She shrieked in response as the hot sting jolted through her.

41

KALINA

Gasping, Kalina tried to shake the sleep from her head as Nathanial's hand came down again on her upturned bottom. If the sensations weren't so sharp, she would have thought she was still dreaming.

"What?" She'd meant to ask why, but she was still grappling with the suddenness of the spanking and the way her body was pulsing with need from the way she'd been woken. It was certainly not the worst way to wake up, but she would have preferred seeing it through to its inevitable conclusion, not having her pleasure interrupted by a spanking.

"Why did you let me believe that you were part of it?" Nathanial's voice was full of aggrieved frustration as well as self-recrimination. "You asked me to spank you, for God's sake! You let me believe you were trying to atone for something you had actually done!"

"I—" She shook her head, trying to make sense of it all, then shrieked as his hand came down again. "I just wanted you to forgive me!"

"Forgive you for what? You had done nothing wrong!" His hand came down again with a sharp smack, then rested on her upturned bottom. The extra warmth emanating from her skin made his palm feel hot against it.

"Then why are you spanking me?" She looked over her shoulder at him, utterly confused, especially when he glared at her.

"Because you had me spank you for something you did not do."

Clearly, it made sense to him.

Kalina was uncertain if she was just too tired or if the concept was just too convoluted.

"I am sorry?" It came out as more of a question than a statement. Kalina tried to roll onto her back, but his fingers dug into her bottom, keeping her in place, like he was uncertain whether or not he was finished with it and therefore refused to let it out of his reach.

"What are you sorry for?"

"Um... asking you to spank me?"

She really was not entirely sure. Nathanial scowled at her. Even if she was just repeating what he'd said, maybe it was her uncertain tone that he was unhappy with now.

But she really did not understand.

"I would never have spanked you if I'd realized you truly had nothing to do with trapping me," he growled. "It would not be... it is not..." He floundered for the words, but Kalina was starting to understand.

It was not fair.

Nor was it honorable of him to punish her for something she had not actually done. And Nathanial had already proven how important it was to him to do the honorable thing.

Kalina thought she understood now.

"He is my father. I still bear some of the guilt. I could have reacted better when I woke. If I had not screamed..."

His hand rubbed her bottom, fingers brushing over the sensitive crinkled rosebud between them, and a shiver went up her spine in reaction.

"Your maid was screaming, too."

"Well, yes, but I added to the problem."

Nathanial snorted and lifted his hand to get her another hard swat.

"Ow! What was that for?"

"For being a martyr. You are hardly in control of your father's actions or your maid's reaction."

"I thought you were upset with me for asking to be spanked," she groused.

"For asking to be spanked when you did not deserve it. Personally, I think that taking on the burden of others' actions as your own deserves a bit of punishment." He rubbed her bottom where he'd just swatted it, sending pleasure pulsing through her. "Though I admire your loyalty, that goes a touch far. The only actions you are responsible for are your own."

His fingers brushed over the entrance to her bottom again, pressing against it when she did not answer.

"Do you not agree, Kalina?"

"You have taken on the debts your father owed as if they were your own." She huffed. While she might be guilty, so was he.

Nathanial's fingers stilled.

"That is not quite the same, and you know it. Besides, it is not done out of loyalty but necessity. Especially if I am going to establish my sisters with any kind of good standing."

That was true enough. The family would have been ostracized if Nathanial had not made good on his father's debts, especially considering the number of high-ranking nobles his father had owed large sums of money to. Which was not fair, but it was how Society worked.

Whereas the only person ostracizing Kalina had been her husband.

"I wanted you to talk to me," she muttered. "And I felt guilty because... he's my father."

"I admire your loyalty to him, but I'd prefer your loyalty be to me," Nathanial said quietly.

"It is!"

"Is it? I had to discover that you had misled me on your own. I cannot help but wonder if that was at least partly to ease things for your father."

Well, he was not entirely wrong there. Kalina was not sure what she should do about it. She stayed silent because she now felt guilty. She had not deceived Nathanial when it came to tricking him into her room—that had been her father. But she had deceived him when she'd allowed him to think that she'd been a part of the plot.

Which meant she could not entirely blame him for being upset with her.

If she thought he'd wronged her, and he had not, she would also be very upset to discover that he had accepted responsibility for the deed and let her think that he was guilty when, in fact, he was innocent. So, by trying to make things right between them, she had actually wronged him.

And it was far too early in the morning to be trying to pick through such a Gordian Knot.

"I think I need to demonstrate how thoroughly you are *mine* now," Nathanial said. "Stay right here. Do not move."

He got up from the bed, leaving her bent over on her knees, warmed bottom in the air, and facing her pillow. Long strands of her hair hung down on one side of her head.

What was he doing?

She wanted to know.

But he'd told her not to move.

So, she did not move.

Her ears strained to hear him instead, and she did not have long to wait before he came back into her room. The bed moved and dipped as he climbed back on, this time positioning himself directly behind her rather than at her side.

What did he mean that he was going to demonstrate that she was his?

Something prodded at the entrance to her bottom, slick and hard. His fingers. She'd become accustomed to penetrating that tiny hole at this point, though usually with his mouth on her pussy when he did so. Without that distraction, the sensation of his fingers pushing into the narrow passageway was far more intense.

"Oh!" She rocked forward, but his other hand grasped her hip, holding her in place.

"You've been very naughty, Kalina," he said firmly as his fingers twisted inside her, going deeper, spreading the slick lubrication he'd coated them with along her tight channel.

She gasped as he moved his fingers with purpose, stretching her open.

It hurt, and it didn't.

It was incredibly uncomfortable but somehow pleasurable at the same time.

And she would happily take the discomfort to please him.

For some reason, being told she was naughty while he inflicted a perversely naughty act on her bottom made her arousal climb and her pussy pulse.

"I understand you will always be loyal to your parents and your brother, but your loyalty belongs first and foremost to me." The fingers retreated. He shifted behind her, and something much thicker pressed against the loosened entrance. Pressed and moved, making her gasp and shudder as it began to stretch her far wider than his fingers had.

His cock, she thought faintly. *He is putting his cock there.* "You will not tell me a falsehood again, not even to protect your father."

He thrust forward, his cock sliding along the lubricated path his fingers had created, and Kalina cried out at the sharp sensation of being so thoroughly invaded. So entirely filled. It felt like all the breath was being forced out of her body as he stretched her virgin bottom open with his cock. The snug fit made her muscles spasm and cramp, like they were trying to push him back out of her, but he just moaned in response, tightening his grip on her hips.

The pain was bearable, especially tinged with pleasure as it was. Certainly, it did not hurt any more than the spankings he'd given her, yet it felt so much more intimate. She felt vulnerable in a way she'd never experienced before. It was the penance she had not known how to give.

She would take it. Every thrust. Every cramp. Every ache. She would take and celebrate each of them as he plundered her depths, if that was what he wanted. If it was what pleased him.

"Say it, Kalina," he ordered, withdrawing slightly, then thrusting back in again, even deeper this time.

"I will not tell you a falsehood again!" She shuddered, crying out as he withdrew and thrust, this time filling her completely. The sensation was shockingly intense, her toes and fingers curling as her body was assaulted by the agonizing ecstasy of such an indecent act.

"Not even to protect your father."

"Not even to protect my father," she repeated dutifully, moaning and clenching as he withdrew again.

The sensation of his cock receding was even more intense than its invasion, rasping rawly along her senses, leaving her gasping for breath before he thrust in again and forced the breath from her lungs as he filled her. Her pussy spasmed emptily, greedily, wanting his cock for itself, yet there was another part of her that gloried in the shocking intimacy of having him in such a forbidden, wicked manner.

It felt like a reckoning.

A claiming.

"You are mine," Nathanial growled, moving harder, faster, taking her more forcefully.

Kalina cried out as the pain and pleasure collided inside her, spiraling through her and winding her tighter and tighter. One of his hands moved down her hip, between her legs, to stroke the swollen bud that was throbbing between them, and she felt like she might collapse.

"My Kalina. My wife."

His fingers pressed on her clitoris, rubbing, circling.

She was going to climax while he was in her bottom.

The wave of pleasure rose within her, his thrusts between her heated cheeks sending aching pulses through her body. She writhed, caught between his hand and his hard thrusts, dropping her head down so that her cheek rested against the silky fabric of the sheets beneath her as she cried out. The overwhelming rush of sensations was almost too much to bear.

The girth of his cock seemed to thicken inside her, the already rigid length stiffening further as he slammed into her from behind. His fingers moved relentlessly, forcing her to the peak of erotic rapture and over the edge... and she fell, crying out his name as she went over the cliff.

———

NATHANIAL

The tight grip of his wife's virgin ass as she came for him was too much for him to resist. Her muscles clamped around him, spasming, and he groaned as he thrust into her bottom completely, using his hand on her pussy to hold her tightly against him as he groaned and flooded her bowels with his seed.

Kalina whimpered, rubbing her bottom against him, still clenching and milking his cock of every last drop.

Letting out a long sigh of air, Nathanial wrapped his arm under his wife's hips and turned them both so they were lying in bed again. Him behind her, his cock still embedded in her sweet arse, her body cradled against his. Pressing a kiss to the back of her neck, he fondled her breast, feeling both of their racing hearts begin to slow, their panting breaths return to normal.

"Are you still upset with me?" she whispered once she'd caught her breath.

"Not at all." Nathanial toyed with one pert nipple between his fingers, giving it a little tug. Her bottom clenched around his cock, which was still half-hard, and the small squeeze made it jerk inside her. He kissed the back of her neck again. "You took your punishment like a good girl. All is well between us again."

He took a deep breath.

"I need to apologize to you as well. I did not know but... I did not ask either. And I am honest enough to admit that if I had asked, and you had told me you had no hand in trapping me, I would not have believed you. Everything I saw..."

She sighed, wriggling slightly against him, her bottom rubbing his hips. The movement might have dislodged his cock, but he had not shrunk enough, and he was not sure he was going to at this point. Even though he had just climaxed, he could feel his arousal beginning to stir again.

"I could have tried to tell you," she said softly.

"I am not sure it would have mattered, though I wish I had been given the opportunity to believe you. But I do not like that you asked to be punished for something you did not do." He tightened his hold on her. "*Never* do that again."

"I will not. I do not like it when people are upset with me." Her hand stroked over his arm at her soft admission. "But I especially do not want you to be upset with me."

"Trust me, upset is the last thing I feel right now," he murmured, cupping her breast as he rocked his hips forward. His cock was quickly growing in size. He felt, as much as heard, her whimper as it began to stretch her wide again.

This time, they remained on their sides as he took her slowly, tenderly moving within her already well-used bottom, his cock sliding back and forth on the cum he'd already filled her with. He stroked her pussy, drawing little circles around her clit, until they tumbled over the finish line of ecstasy again.

Afterward, he rang for a bath.

All in all, it was one of the most enjoyable mornings he'd ever had, even if it had not gone quite as anticipated. He wished it could last forever, but of course, it could not. Eventually, they had to leave.

Face the real world.

He wanted to make his wife as happy as she made him... but in order to do that, he had to face—and forgive—the man who had wronged him so egregiously.

42

Arriving at the house the Littles had rented for the Season, Nathanial took a deep breath, tapping his cane against the stone walk beneath his feet. It was difficult not to feel a certain way about visiting his in-laws, especially without his wife as a buffer.

But it was necessary.

Just as he wanted Kalina to put him first, that meant putting her first as well.

And that meant finding a way to rub along with his father-in-law.

Taking another deep breath, he lifted his chin and went to knock on the front door. It took less than two minutes for him to be escorted inside to where Mr. Little was in the library. The older man stood as Nathanial was shown in.

Though Kalina resembled her mother far more than her father, there were some similarities between them, mostly in their movements. The way Mr. Little stood calmly waiting, the slight hint of worry in his brow. If Nathanial had not gotten to know his wife so well, he was not sure he would have caught the concern in Mr. Little's expression.

"Your Grace. This is an unexpected honor." Mr. Little gestured to the leather chair across from the one he'd been sitting in. "Would you like to sit down?"

"Yes, thank you."

Mr. Little nodded at the butler, dismissing him. To the right of Mr. Little's chair was a tray with a decanter and several snifters on it.

"Brandy?"

"Please." It sure as hell could not hurt, and it might even help.

After pouring Nathanial a generous amount and handing it over, Mr. Little added a bit to his own snifter, which had not yet been finished. It was another sign of the other man's nerves, which strangely helped Nathanial to feel more relaxed. Since the first day, he'd felt as though Mr. Little had no regrets and was completely self-assured in the correctness of his actions. To see him less than fully confident was strangely reassuring.

Nathanial took a sip of his brandy before speaking, as he was uncertain of where to begin. He'd had the entire walk over to think about it, and had not been able to come up with exactly what he might say.

Especially since part of him had expected Mr. Little to be blustery and defensive from the start, not nervously welcoming.

They sat in silence for a long moment.

"Well. I thought perhaps it was time for us to speak," Nathanial said finally. "Man to man, as it were."

Mr. Little nodded slowly.

"I suppose you want an explanation."

"I would appreciate one." He did not think the man would be able to explain things in such a manner that Nathanial would agree with the actions he'd taken, but he did want to know what had driven the man to act.

"I knew Kalina was aiming for a duke. Lady Astrid and Tiffany were clear about that and their support of her. We all understood your desire for your daughter to outrank your father and why. But considering Montagu's interest in her at the house party... why me? Why resort to such a possibly ruinous tactic? What if I had not done the honorable thing? You risked everything you were working toward, everything Kalina had done for your goal. Why?"

The question came out more forcefully than he'd intended, and he found that he was angry not just on his behalf, but his wife's.

She deserved more from her father.

Mr. Little studied Nathanial for another long moment, as though he was formulating his words, and Nathanial clenched his jaw against saying more. If he did not give the man the opportunity to speak, he would never get his answers. But it took some effort because he wanted to shout at the man.

Taking in a deep breath, Mr. Little put his snifter down on the little table beside him, the amber liquid swirling from the movement.

"I realized I wanted my daughter happy more than I wanted my father to acknowledge me." His eyes were calm. Steady.

It was so far from anything Nathanial might have expected the other man to say, he did not know how to assimilate the information.

"You two were making a hash of things," Mr. Little continued, his voice low, thoughtful. Almost as though he was remembering all of it. "Montagu was circling, and you were making excuses about why you could not marry Kalina. I heard you, you know, one night when you were speaking. But everyone could see the spark between you. It reminded me very much of me and my wife when we met." His lips curved in a nostalgic smile. "Unlike you, we did not fight our own emotions; we only had to fight her family and eventually, mine."

"I..." Nathanial started to speak, then stopped because he did not actually know what he wanted to say.

In many ways, Mr. Little was correct.

He took another swallow of brandy while the older man kept talking.

"Everyone could see that you and Kalina were drawn to each other. Marriage to Montagu would not have made her happy, not when you exist. Then the matchmaker came, and I knew I could not leave anything to chance. You both would have been miserable, married to others. I realized I wanted her happiness, above all else. Even if she never spoke to me again. Even if I ruined my chances of my father acknowledging me. It was a risk I had to take because I wanted to give her a chance at happiness. If you had not married her, we would have left England for her sake again. Gone to the Continent to travel. Or perhaps to America."

Mr. Little was no longer looking at Nathanial; he was talking almost to himself, remembering the contingency plans he'd made if Nathanial had not done the honorable thing.

"What if I had not forgiven her? What if I had turned out to be an utter cad who mistreated her horribly because you trapped me into marriage with her?"

"I had plenty of opportunity to observe you at the house party, Your Grace. Often, when you had no idea I was doing so. That was not in your nature. You are an honorable man, and I knew that no matter my actions, you would not harm Kalina."

Harm? No.

Spank? Yes. And Nathanial still felt like a cad for having done so the first time. Though he did realize that was his wife's fault, not her father's. Though part of him wanted to blame the man because he'd rather be mad at his father-in-law than at his wife.

But if Kalina should not take responsibility for her father's actions, neither should he place blame on her father for hers.

In some ways, he even understood the man.

The temptation to do something similar to Zachary and Delilah was strong. Watching Zachary ruin his life by marrying the wrong person, for nothing but sheer stubbornness and a sense of duty to his mother, was wildly frustrating. If he could think of a way to force those two to the altar... would he do it?

Maybe.

But that was different. Because he knew them, knew how they were together, and knew without a doubt that they were in love with each other, even if neither would admit to it.

He and Kalina...

They'd had a spark. He'd been resisting. Mr. Little was not wrong about that.

"It still should have been my choice." That was the sticking point. The one he could not get away from.

"It should have." Mr. Little's easy agreement took the wind right out of Nathanial's sales. "My wife has pointed out to me that, regardless of my opinions about the choice you were making, it was yours to make. Just as we made our choice when we married each other. For that, I do apologize. As my wife says, sometimes I act without thinking. This was something I should not have done. I do not expect forgiveness to come immediately, or easily, or even at all, though I do hope we can rub along civilly, for Kalina's sake."

"I as well. That is why I came today."

Something flashed across Mr. Little's face. Relief? Satisfaction? Perhaps a little of both. Nathanial could not deny that he would have been miserable seeing Kalina marry someone else, especially one of his friends.

Knowing that her father had not been thinking of himself when he'd tipped Nathanial into Kalina's bed, that he'd been thinking of them... well, it did not make everything better, but it helped. He was glad to know the man had a contingency plan if Nathanial had not done the honorable thing.

"I do not know if I can forgive you yet," Nathanial admitted. "But I think we can at least get along for now. For Kalina's sake."

Now the expression on Mr. Little's face was definitely one of relief.

"I am glad to hear that, Your Grace. I've missed my daughter. Though it does me good to see her happy... far happier than she was when we first arrived."

"I am curious... what would you have done if I was not a duke?" This seemed the most opportune moment to ask such impertinent questions since Mr. Little was speaking so frankly. Whether or not they'd ever talk like this again... he wanted to strike while the other man was more vulnerable, more willing to share his inner thoughts.

"I should never have put the burden of reconciling me with my family on her. Though, to be fair to myself, she also took far more of the burden onto herself than I ever meant her to. It was something I had thought of, but it was never the requirement she took it as." Mr.

Little shook his head. "I wanted it, but she made it into her mission. That is something you have to be very careful about, Your Grace. If you tell Kalina that you desire something, she will ignore all her own needs to make it happen."

Nathanial had noticed that about her.

He supposed that was why, when her father noticed that *she* wanted something—that something being Nathanial—he'd acted so precipitously.

When he looked at it that way—being wanted so badly by Kalina that her father had trapped Nathanial into marriage with her—it was almost a compliment. One that completely ignored Nathanial and Kalina's choices and any sense of agency in their own lives.

But a compliment.

He needed to grasp whatever reasons he could for forgiving his father-in-law. That was the whole point of coming here today.

Taking a long sip of his brandy, Nathanial leaned back in his chair.

"How is Kalina settling in with your sisters?" Mr. Little asked.

"Very well. They love her and she dotes on them." Any worries he'd had about Kalina's ability to guide them through the *ton* had dissipated. Anything his wife did not know, her friends would be able to assist her with. She might not have the same social standing as a lady whose parent was not estranged from their titled father, but she had social allies. Strong ones. "My youngest sister in particular, Fiona, adores her."

Slowly, Nathanial settled as he and Mr. Little conversed, starting with Nathanial's sisters, which led to Mr. Little sharing some memories of Kalina when she was a child, which led to them talking about India. They skirted any sensitive subjects, such as Mr. Little's family, Nathanial's father, and anything financial, but it ended up being a rather enjoyable and revealing conversation.

They would certainly be able to be in each other's company in the future after this. By the time Nathanial left the Littles' house, he was fairly certain he would eventually even be able to forgive his father-in-law.

Eventually.

Acknowledging that they would see each other at the Tremaine ball later that evening before Nathanial left, he headed home feeling rather chuffed. He would be able to surprise his wife tonight by being able to speak with her parents without antagonism. Something that should make her happy.

Which, along with making his sisters happy, was all he wanted now.

43

Clinging to her husband's arm, Gregory and Tiffany trailing behind her, Kalina greeted Lord and Lady Tremaine. Their daughter, Louisa, stood beside them. A stunning beauty, she appeared to be pouting as she looked between Gregory and Nathanial and sighed before dipping into a curtsy of the appropriate degree. It was not the first time a debutante had looked at her husband in such a way.

The Season had begun with six eligible dukes—technically seven, but Northumberland was still in mourning and had not joined the social scene yet. Now, two of them had married, one was practically engaged with the announcement expected any day, and half of the opportunities for this Season's debutantes to marry a duke were gone.

Lady Louisa must have had hopes.

Kalina could not help but feel for her. She heard Tiffany graciously greeting the young woman as Nathanial led Kalina away and into the ballroom.

It was a crush, of course.

They were announced and began their descent down the staircase when her husband stiffened. Kalina glanced at him, but his gaze was off to the right of the ballroom. She started to look, but could not tell what had caught his attention when he kept moving again. It did not escape her notice that he escorted her to the left when they reached the bottom of the stairs.

Whatever he had seen, he did not want to bring her near it, which only piqued her curiosity even more.

She craned her neck, trying to find what he'd been looking at without being obvious that she was looking. It only took her a moment to give up. There were far too many people, and she had no idea what he'd had such a reaction to. She felt fairly certain the cause had not been her parents, as he'd informed her earlier in the evening that he'd visited her father, and they'd had a good discussion.

Which she had been delighted and relieved to hear. Also touched that he'd gone and done such a thing for her.

It had led to a rather wicked encounter in his study where she'd used her mouth on *him* for the first time. That had mussed her hair to the point where they'd arrived at the ball later than intended, as she and Margaret put it to rights.

She knew she looked rather splendid now, her hair piled up in a complicated knot on her head, shimmering with pink diamonds that matched the ornate necklace around her throat and jewels dangling from her ears. Twin bracelets decorated each wrist, adding to the sparkle. Her dress was several shades darker than her diamonds, which accentuated their color, and was trimmed with an even darker pink ribbon that matched Nathanial's waistcoat and pocket square.

No one would ever guess that a few hours ago she'd been on her knees in front of her husband, doing such wildly perverse things.

It did make one wonder about the things other couples got up to behind closed doors...

Did others in the *ton* do such scandalous things?

She could not imagine.

Yet, she would not have imagined herself engaging in such acts, either.

The proof that her husband had not been guiding her away from her parents appeared in front of her face a few moments later when she saw the circle of people Nathanial had aimed them toward. A completely genuine smile bloomed on her lips.

Her parents were there, with Ashwin, who was standing beside Rupert Blackstone. The two young men had pulled themselves slightly apart from the others. Lady Astrid stood beside Kalina's mother, with Mei and her grandmother on her other side. Seeing them approach, Delilah stepped back to give Nathanial and Kalina space to join them between herself and Lady Hu.

The matchmaker brightened when she saw them coming, her dark eyes dancing. She leaned lightly on an ornate cane, the brown and gold going very nicely with her outfit. Beside her, Mei wore green and gold, possibly the same outfit she had worn at the house party, or at least one very similar to it. She smiled widely at Kalina and Nathanial as well.

"I am very happy to see you together," Lady Hu said after greetings had been exchanged, nodding firmly. She gave Nathanial a look. "Mei informed me of your wishes, but I think that you ended up with the right match."

Kalina pursed her lips together at the reminder that Nathanial had not initially wanted to marry her. But there was no denying facts. And he had certainly come around since then.

It did not hurt to have a matchmaker confirm that they were good together. Her father beamed at Lady Hu's comment, but was wise enough to look away, his gaze directed at the dance floor as if he was smiling at what he saw there rather than the matchmaker's assessment.

"Thank you, Lady Hu." Nathanial's tone was caught somewhere between amusement and resignation. "That does seem to be the general consensus."

"Well, some things are obvious. Others will require a more delicate touch." Lady Hu lifted her gaze to the stairs where the Duke of Grafton had just been announced, along with his mother, the Duchess of Grafton, his uncle, the Marquess of Selter, Lady Annabelle Walsh, and her parents.

Delilah had stiffened, her chin lifting slightly, though she kept her back firmly to the staircase, not bothering to look at her former lover as he escorted the woman Society expected him to marry. Zachary's gaze flitted around the room, coming to rest on the back of Delilah's head.

If the young lady on his arm noticed, she did not show it. Wearing a pale white dress with very pale blue trim, she clung to his arm. On his opposite shoulder, Monkey Sinclair sat, the saffron colored ribbon around his neck matching Zachary's waistcoat exactly. Kalina could not help but wonder how many ribbons Zachary had bought for his pet. The effect was entirely adorable, even though her stomach tightened at the sight of them, knowing how his presence would affect Delilah, though she pretended otherwise.

She could not help but think that Zachary did not look happy, either. However, his mother looked elated, beaming at the couple in front of her as she was escorted down the stairs by Zachary's uncle, the Marquess of Selter. The Walshes followed behind them, positively preening.

With such a united familial display, there was no doubt that an offer of marriage was in the wind. Kalina's heart ached for Delilah. Even a little for Zachary, though part of it was his own fault for letting his mother dictate his future. He looked like he was marching toward his doom, not a marriage he desired. On the other hand, even she had heard about his mother's deep grief after the death of his father, although there was no sign of it on her face.

Kalina knew something about life-altering decisions to make a parent happy.

But knowing what she knew now of love... she was so grateful to have it. She could not imagine losing it. And Zachary knew exactly what he was losing by letting Delilah go and marrying Lady Annabelle instead.

So, she did feel a bit sorry for him.

Just a bit.

"Well," Lady Astrid said brightly, also ignoring the group headed down the stairs. "Has anyone seen the new exhibit at the museum? I heard it's quite stunning."

Determined to follow her lead, everyone rallied, as if Delilah's heartbreak was not walking past. The conversation about the new exhibit lasted until the quivering sound of a bow being run over violin strings alerted everyone to the musicians readying themselves.

Nathanial immediately turned to Kalina.

"My lady. May I have this dance?"

"You may," she replied, laughing at the twinkle in his eye. She was very aware of her parents watching them and the way her father was beaming. It seemed as though her mother was softening toward him, now that she could see how happy Kalina was.

Which made her glad. She did not want her parents at odds with each other. Especially because of her.

Smiling up at her husband, she followed his lead toward the dance floor—and nearly stumbled when he came to a sudden halt. He'd gone stiff again, just like he had on the stairs, and now that she could see his expression, there was a cold hauteur that she had only seen in the first days of the marriage.

But it was not directed at her; it was directed at two men in front of them. One was older, wrinkled, with grey hair, and leaning heavily on a cane. The other... the other looked an awful lot like her father. Several years older than her father, but close enough in appearance that it was obvious they were related. Looking back at the older one, she realized he was very much what her father might look like in another twenty or so years.

She had never actually seen them up close like this before. Though she knew they'd been at several previous events she and her family had also attended, they'd stayed well away. Mostly, she'd seen their backs when her father had watched them with longing but did not attempt to approach.

Kalina's stomach flipped over.

"Your Graces." The Marquess of Stilton's wrinkles looked to be from frowning a great deal, and his eyes might be the same color as her father's, but they held none of the warmth her father's did. Neither did her uncle's. Both of them were stiff as pokers as they bowed. "I thought it time to... congratulate you on your marriage."

If anything, Nathanial somehow stiffened even further. Kalina had no idea what to say, so she bit her tongue.

She'd never really thought about what would happen when she was faced with her grandfather. She certainly would not have expected a ballroom confrontation with every eye turning in their direction. If she'd pictured anything at all, it would have been a more intimate gathering. One with apologies and acceptance. Not slyness and a contemptuous undertone.

The man in front of her was a snake.

She glanced at her uncle, who did not meet her gaze. His focus was entirely on Nathanial. As was her grandfather's.

Until they suddenly flicked to the side, and she was aware of her father standing there. Without her mother. Not because he did not want to include her, she realized immediately, but because her father was always going to protect her mother. He would never put her in front of these two men without being assured of her welcome.

Which was why he was now at Kalina's side, providing a second shield. Bolstering her.

"Father. George." Her father's gaze flicked between his parent and his brother. He bowed. Very slightly. The expression on both of their faces had turned to pure contempt, and she could not imagine how hard it was for him to see them look at him so. She wished she could reach out and hold his hand, but that would only weaken their position in front of the *ton.*

Society respected strength. Stiff upper lips.

"Finally got your wish, eh, John?" The marquess looked down his nose at her father. "Bought yourself a place in Society that I cannot ignore."

Rather than answering him, her father looked at her and Nathanial.

"Go on," he said softly. "You were on your way to the dance floor." They did not need to be here for the marquess to sharpen his claws on. The unspoken words hung in the air.

Her father was willing to face this alone, but Kalina did not want him to have to.

Thankfully, her husband was doing an excellent imitation of a brick. He did not move an inch, nor did he look away from the marquess and his heir.

Until suddenly he did. Incredibly rudely. Kalina found herself spun around as her husband gave the marquess and his son the cut direct, turning without acknowledging them, without taking their leave. Gasps echoed through the ballroom. Even the musicians had not begun playing yet. Every single guest was too caught up in the drama playing out before them.

Kalina's heart was beating so fast in her chest, she thought it might jump right out of it. She was used to being at the center of attention, but not like this.

"Hereford!" That was not her grandfather; it must be her uncle, and he sounded utterly shocked. He could not have expected to be given the cut by a duke because Kalina had certainly not expected it. "You cannot be taking their side."

This time, Nathanial whirled around without bringing her with him, but Kalina turned just as quickly. Both the Marquess and her uncle looked horrified, but her father... her father was watching Nathanial with a strange combination of relief and pride. Gratitude. She'd thought he would be horrified that Hereford had just given his family the cut. This was not the reaction she'd expected.

"You mean my wife's side?" Nathanial's voice was low, lethal with warning that her uncle did not heed.

"We all know you were trapped into... this." Her uncle waved his hand at her, still not looking at her, as if she was not truly a person to him.

Even though she had no feeling for him, being treated as if she had no feelings, no worth, still stabbed her through the heart. Especially because he was right.

"A house party, from which you return with an unexpected wife? A wife who we all know was angling for a duke? The whole of Society knows you would not have *chosen* such an... an indecent match."

Her husband moved so quickly, Kalina did not have time to stop him before he plowed his fist into her uncle's face. Gasps and screams rent the air as her uncle stumbled back, holding his nose, blood already seeping through his fingers and staining the pristine white of his gloves. Hands over her mouth in utter shock, Kalina could only stare.

"Speak of my wife again like that and we'll have a meeting at dawn," Nathanial growled, fists clenched at his sides. She could not see his face because he had placed himself in front of her, a knight defending her honor. "We are a love match."

The Marquess did not go to help his son. He stood there, eyes glittering with malevolence as new gasps and titters swept the ballroom. Kalina stood stock still; that had not sounded as though Nathanial was trying to cover up the truth, the scandal.

It sounded as though he meant it.

There was a flurry of movement, and Kalina found herself standing between her mother and Delilah. Lady Astrid and Tiffany were there as well, placing themselves slightly in front of her. The Dowager Duchess of Clarence stood beside Kalina's mother, keeping slightly to the side as she tried to see the Marquess' reaction—as short as she was, she likely could not see much because Kalina's father was now standing beside Nathanial as well, with Ashwin and Ruper just behind him.

But it was the line of dukes who caused the marquess to take a step back.

They stood shoulder to shoulder, a menacing line of power, confidence, and muscle—with a single tiny monkey who chittered threateningly before falling silent again. All seven of the tragic dukes had joined together to defend their own.

Which was when Kalina realized that there was no need for the family her father had sought to provide by reconciling with his father... This was their family. The people who stood beside them, no matter what.

She finally had a place where she belonged.

"You go too far, all of you," the marquess started to say. What more he might have said, they would never know because he suddenly shrieked and stumbled forward, arching his back. The line of dukes tensed, like they were not sure whether to defend themselves or try to catch him, but he managed to keep from actually falling over at the last moment.

Whirling around, he glared at the Countess of Spencer, who stood there with an empty glass and an expression of wide-eyed innocence on her beautiful face.

"Oh my," she said, putting one hand up to her cheek and then bobbing into a curtsy that was just short of the exact degree due to a marquess. "My apologies, my lord. I tripped."

The Marquess glared at her, trying to reach behind himself to feel the wet spot on his back. It was not very visible due to the black of his coat, but it must have been very uncomfortable because he was squirming in place.

Before he could turn his ire on her, the Earl of Spencer, a darkly handsome man with an extremely impressive glower, stepped up to his wife's side. Though their rank was lower than a marquess', their reputation for wild and unpredictable behavior, as well as their connections, made them a force within the *ton*. The fact that the countess was willing to spill her drink on a marquess was proof of that.

And they had their own large circle of influence as well.

The Duke and Duchess of Manchester moved to their side, and Lydia caught Kalina's eye across the way, giving her a supportive smile. The duke's sister and her husband, the heir to Viscount Hood, moved out of the crowd as well. Lady Arabella, whose outrageous antics within Society rivaled the Countess of Spencer's, immediately stepped to her side. The Marquess of Dunbury and his wife, Lord Hyde and his wife, the tall and tawny Marquess of Hartford and his wife...

Kalina's grandfather and uncle were caught between the two groups, the rest of the ton looking on with bated breath.

"What an unfortunate accident. You are going to want to have that tended to immediately," Lady Arabella said to the marquess, smiling in a way that was more like baring her teeth. "It is too bad you will have to miss the rest of the ball."

"Yes, well." The marquess' gaze darted back and forth, but no one stepped forward to help him.

No one stepped forward to support him.

He lifted his chin and gestured to his son, who was still holding his nose, though he was no longer glaring at anyone. He seemed to have shrunk in on himself.

"Come, George, I need to go home." He said it as if it was his idea, but everyone in the ballroom knew that he had been routed.

It was dead silent as he and his son began their long march up the stairs with everyone watching. Lord and Lady Tremaine met them to exchange a farewell as good hosts. Lady Tremaine looked caught between horror and delight—such public contretemps was not her style, but her ball was going to be the talk of the Season after this.

A consummate hostess, the moment the marquess and his son disappeared from her ball, she had the musicians start again. And Kalina finally felt like she could fully breathe again.

She thanked her friends for their support and hugged her mother. Nathanial was doing the same. He and her father exchanged gruff nods.

When her father embraced her, Kalina felt her chest pang.

"I am sorry," she whispered, knowing that was not the outcome he'd hoped for.

"I am not," he whispered back, surprising her. "You are far more important to me than either of them."

Very nearly brought to tears, Kalina pulled back and pushed a smile onto her lips. It would not do for Society to see her crying, not after such a resounding social triumph.

The Countess of Spencer came by to offer her very insincere apologies for interrupting their 'conversation.' Kalina rather liked the unusual woman, and it was clear that she and Lady Astrid were quite friendly with each other.

Then her husband returned to her side and offered his arm once again.

"My dear. May I have this dance?"

She looked up at him, wonderingly. She wanted to ask him if

what he'd said about being a love match was true, but this was not the time nor the place. It would have to wait.

Putting her hand in his, she smiled up at him and let him lead her to the dance floor.

She whirled round the ballroom in his arms, happier than she'd ever been in her life, knowing that her friends and family were watching, some of them joining her and Nathanial on the dance floor. The people who truly mattered.

Her people.

Though she knew any chance for reconciliation with her father's family was gone, somehow it did not matter. She felt free.

Happy.

Fate had ignored what she'd thought she'd wanted and given her what she needed instead.

44

Thankfully, after Stilton and his son left the Tremaine ball, the rest of the evening passed without incident. Not only that, but the tone of Society had changed. The gathered forces against Stilton and his ilk had been powerful, confident, and varied.

Suddenly, everyone wanted to speak to him and his wife.

Everyone was welcoming.

The *ton* knew which way the wind blew.

Without realizing it, without intending to, he'd restored his family's social standing by standing up for his wife. Considering the vagaries of the *ton*, it could have easily gone the other way. Nathanial was not blind to the fact that the number of dukes and powerful figures within Society that had taken his side, while Stilton had had no one, had greatly contributed to that outcome.

Still.

He felt much easier now, knowing that there was no reason his sisters should not be successes when they debuted.

While he would never trust the majority of Society to stay firm if the wind blew against him and Kalina, tonight, he got to see who would stand beside them and the effect it would have. They would be able to weather every storm.

His sisters' futures were assured, in every way they could be.

And he was in love with his wife.

He had not intended to make such a public declaration, but it had not harmed their standing. When gentlemen spoke with Kalina, they eyed him warily, as if he might punch their noses, too. A side effect he was not at all upset about.

His wife would never be one of the bored matrons of the *ton*, taking lovers while her husband dallied with his mistress. Not if Nathanial had anything to say about it.

Once their social duties were done, he was ready to leave.

"Shall we?" he murmured in Kalina's ear.

"Yes, please." She smiled at him, appearing relieved rather than resigned to leaving the ball early.

Nathanial could only imagine how stressful the events of the evening had been on her.

They made the rounds of their friends, Kalina's family, and the others who had stepped up to support them before taking their leave of the Tremaines. Lady Tremaine did not appear sorry to see them go. Nathanial suppressed a smile. They had not quite reached the levels of scandal the Baron and Baroness of Fife had, but he was certain that tomorrow, Lady Tremaine's ball would be the most talked-about piece of gossip.

This time, he did not mind being the center of a scandal.

Getting into the carriage with his wife, Nathanial sat down beside her rather than across from her. With a soft sigh, she leaned her head against his shoulder as the carriage began to move, rocking them slightly. He reached out and put his hand on her lap, sliding his fingers over and between hers to hold her hand.

"Thank you," she whispered.

"For what?" Turning his face to the side, he brushed a soft kiss over the top of her head. Her fingers were curled around his, and he swept his thumb against her soft skin.

There was a pause.

"Everything." She laughed, a soft little laugh that made him smile. "But especially for how you handled my grandfather. And my uncle. They were..."

"Awful." He supplied the word when her voice trailed off.

Taking a deep breath, she nodded. He felt the movement against his shoulder.

"They were awful. Which feels terrible to say of family, but it is the truth."

"My father was also awful, so I understand."

She giggled, but it only lasted for a moment before she quieted.

"I am glad my father did not reconcile with them."

"I as well." He was very glad that her father had put her first again, even when faced with the outcome that he'd returned to England for. It was not worth it for the man to grovel at the marquess' feet, but some would have, anyway. They would have kissed the ring, toed the line, and put up with their wife and children being treated terribly, all for the sake of 'family'. Nathanial sighed. "I suppose this means we'll have to spend every holiday with him."

He said the words teasingly, and—as intended—they made his wife laugh again, lightening her mood.

The carriage rolled to a halt in front of their house.

Getting out, Nathanial turned to help his wife. A sudden thought gripped him as she stepped onto the first stair down from the carriage, and rather than helping her all the way to the ground, he reached out and lifted her into his arms. Kalina gave a little shriek of surprise as she found herself being carried rather than stepping down. Her arms clung around his neck, helping to secure her against him.

"What are you doing?"

"We did not have a proper homecoming as newlyweds," he replied, giving the coachman a nod as he turned away and began to walk up to the front door of the house with her in his arms. "So, we are doing it now. I am carrying you over the threshold."

"Oh." Her voice was soft. Wondering.

Nathanial grinned. He felt... giddy. That was the word for it.

The expression on Stalling's face when the butler opened the door for them was even more entertaining. The very proper man seemed confused and a touch worried.

"Is the duchess hurt?" he asked anxiously, watching Nathanial coming through the doorway.

"No, Stalling, she is unharmed. We are in for the night now." Nathanial strode past him, making for the stairs.

"He looks utterly flummoxed," Kalina whispered, laughing softly.

Nathanial did not particularly care about what Stalling thought right now. He whisked Kalina down the hall to his bedroom. Their bedroom. Because they no longer spent their nights apart. Which also likely scandalized Stalling, not that he would ever be so gauche as to express an opinion on the matter.

Right now, all Nathanial wanted was to get his wife alone.

Kicking the bedroom door shut behind him was extremely satisfying. Letting her legs drop, he held her close against him, so he could bend down and claim her lips in a searing kiss. With her arms still wound about his neck, she met his passion with her own, their tongues stroking together as his hands began to travel over her body.

Clothing dropped to the floor, piece by piece, some with a bit more difficulty than others. Nathanial moved his hands and mouth over her silken skin as more and more of her body was revealed to him until he could finally tip her back onto the bed and kneel on the floor beside it. Grasping her by the hips, he pulled her body toward him so her legs were draped over his shoulders, giving his mouth and tongue full access to the sweetness of her pussy.

"Nathanial!" She shuddered, her fingers sliding into his hair as his tongue slid through the center of her folds, tasting the honeyed sweetness of her arousal. Sliding his hands up her body and over her breasts, Nathanial pressed on with his task, licking and sucking as he massaged the soft mounds filling his palms. His fingers closed around the taut buds of her nipples, pinching them, while he feasted between her thighs.

With half her body draped over him, there was nothing she could do but writhe as he played with her to his heart's content, teasing her, tormenting her with growing pleasure but denying her the climax her body ached for.

He was denying himself as well.

His cock ached, bobbing in front of him, eager to bury itself inside her.

"Please, Nathanial..." Her fingers flexed in his hair, tugging hard enough that it sent a shudder down his spine. Her words were gasped out between panting breaths, her back arching as she thrust her breasts up against his palms. "Please... I need you."

One last, long lick up her center, where he lingered on the little bud of pleasure at the top, then Nathanial gave her what she needed.

Rising to his feet, her ankles pressed against his shoulders, he lined his cock up with her body. The wet heat slid over his tip, and he groaned, her cry ringing in his ears, as he thrust in hard. Burying himself inside her, he leaned forward, and her legs slid against his body until he could turn his head and kiss one of the slender ankles his hand was now wrapped around.

Kalina could not quite reach him in this position, other than to brush her fingertips over his chest, and her arms fell down to either side of her head, framing her beautiful face and the river of her long black hair. She was a goddess. His goddess.

"I love you," he told her.

Her eyes widened in shock as he retreated, his cock sliding inside her, then thrusting home again.

"I love you."

Kalina

Tears sparked in Kalina's eyes as her husband buried himself inside her with the words she most longed to hear. The warmth building in her core, the heated passion, surged within her as his body rocked against hers, his hands sliding down her legs and back to her breasts.

"I love you," she whispered back. His hands closed over her

breasts as she shuddered as her back arched, his hips moving as he thrust into her again. Her returned confession seemed to have set off a spark within him, and he began to move faster, harder.

Kalina cried out as the pent-up passion he'd tormented her with bubbled over, her climax exploding through her as he filled her over and over again. The pleasure spiraled wildly out of control as he kept going, driving her higher and higher, the waves of ecstasy wrecking her senses.

She tipped over the edge while he kept going, sending her into a state of agonized rapture as the sensual assault hovered between pleasure and pain from the sheer intensity. Reaching for his hands, she grabbed his wrists as tears sparked in her eyes, her legs wrapped around his waist, trying to hold him in place, trying to cease the relentless pounding.

Instead, he switched their holds, taking both of her wrists in one hand and pinning them above her head, so she was utterly helpless beneath him. His other hand slid between their bodies, finding the little nubbin of her clit, swollen and overstimulated, and began to rub and pinch the tiny bud.

Kalina screamed as the intense sensations shot through her, her pussy clamping down around him. She fought against his wrists, her thighs squeezing his body, trying to push him away as the sensations swamped her, becoming almost too much for her to bear.

More tears slid down the sides of her face, soaking into her hair as the onslaught overwhelmed her.

The pain-pleasure combination pulsed through her until Nathanial slammed home and groaned as he began to throb within her, emptying himself into her shuddering body. Kalina gulped, panting for breath, her muscles finally going lax as his hand moved away from her tortured nub.

Her husband half-collapsed over her, his forearms pressed against the bed on either side of her arms as he feathered kisses over her jaw.

"I love you," she whispered in his ear. She wanted him to know that she did not only feel such things in the heat of passion.

Felt him shiver against her.

"I love you." He pressed a kiss to her jaw before lifting his head to look down at her, his fingers smoothing the flyaway hair back from her face. "I know our marriage did not begin the way either of us wanted, and as much as it bothers me that your father was right about us... I do love you."

Kalina laughed. There was a part of her that was annoyed that her father was correct as well.

Good intentions. Questionable methods.

But it had gotten the job done.

"I feel the same. And I do love you, with all my heart."

Taking her lips in another kiss, Nathanial wrapped his arms around her, lifting her up with him as he straightened, so he could roll them both into the bed.

Kalina happily fell asleep in his bed, in his arms.

The next morning, they sat at the breakfast table with his sisters, who were all happily chattering. The contentment, the joy, that settled over her was bone deep.

"I say," Fiona said, picking up her slice of toast to butter. "Did anyone else hear a scream last night? I woke up in the middle of the night, and I swear I heard someone screaming."

Both Emma and Julianna shook their heads no.

"You must have only dreamed that you woke up and heard it," Julianna said.

Nathanial and Kalina locked eyes over the table. She brought her teacup up to her lips to help hide her expression, while he winked at her.

Hush.

He mouthed the word before sinking down behind his newspaper.

Heroically suppressing her giggles, Kalina asked the girls what they wanted to do for the day, skillfully changing the subject. This was her life now. And it was better than she could have ever dreamed.

EPILOGUE

The hazard tournament had been fruitful for Matthew's pockets but not for the information they'd been hoping to uncover. The Earl of Cornwall had never appeared. Since speaking to him and finding out why he had not attended the trip to the hunting lodge, especially after inviting Nathanial's to the lodge, had been the point of attending, that was disappointing. When Christian had finally been able to obliquely question the man's friends, they all swore they were surprised by his absence; as far as they knew, he'd planned to attend.

He, Drake, and Christian had seen through the rest of the night, as leaving at that point would have been suspicious. Matthew was too close to winning to leave without comment.

When the Tramp and his lady indulged in their usual voyeuristic show after the end of the tournament, he quickly took his winnings and got out the door while everyone was distracted, Christian and Drake on his heels.

"I do not suppose you could *try* to lose every once in a while," Christian grumbled. "Sometimes it is unlucky to be winning, especially when it draws the ire of every man in the establishment."

Matthew shrugged.

"That's not how it seems to work." In truth, he had no idea why his luck always worked out like that. Sometimes, he considered it fate's apology for saddling him with his father.

"Well, I'm off to home. It's late." Drake made a show of yawning widely.

"I as well." Christian shook his head. "My carriage is down this way. Do either of you need a ride home?"

Taking ducal carriages into the Warren was not wise—one was likely to return to find the coachman gone or dead and any ornamentation on the thing stripped.

But Drake shook his head.

"I have one at the end of that street." He gestured vaguely in the opposite direction that Christian had indicated. "I will likely see you tomorrow or the day after."

"Good night," Matthew said, frowning, because something about Drake's demeanor was bothering him.

"Good night," Christian echoed, and looked at Matthew as Drake ambled off down the street, hand stuck in his pockets. It was so very casual. Too casual. "What about you?"

"Ah..." Matthew reached into his pocket and pulled out his lucky coin, causing Christian to groan.

"You cannot even take a ride home without using your coin?"

"I am not sure I am ready to go home."

"You cannot be serious. You cannot stay here; you will be coshed and robbed."

"That does not sound like the kind of luck I have." Matthew grinned at his friend. Being hit over the head and his pockets emptied was not something he'd ever worried about, no matter the sum of money he carried or where he was. He'd never had it turn out badly before; why would things change now? Sadly, the same could not be said for things like his carriage, which is why he'd taken a hackney into the Warrens.

He flipped his coin into the air.

Should I follow Drake?

The question did not need to be asked aloud, thankfully, since he did not know what Christian would think. He was not entirely sure he understood the impulse to follow his friend and see what he was about. The man had just turned down another street.

The coin landed in his hand, and he swung it over to lay it flat on the back of his opposite wrist.

Heads.

He was to follow Drake.

Shrugging his shoulders, he grinned at Christian.

"It seems my night is not over yet."

Rolling his eyes, Christian shook his head.

"If it was anyone but you…"

"But it is me. I will be fine." He was a touch concerned about Drake, though. "You are more than welcome to accompany me if you are worried about it."

Christian hesitated, then nodded his head, sighing again.

"I am going to beat you if I end up being the one coshed and robbed," he grumbled as Matthew turned to go in the direction Drake had departed, and Christian joined at his side.

"You can always go home."

"No, because if you do end up dead in the streets tomorrow morning, I'll be furious at myself for not having been at your side on the night your luck ran out, and everyone else will be furious at me."

Matthew chuckled. It was not like Christian to be alarmist; of all his fellow dukes, Christian tended to be the one with the most sense of adventure, which just went to show exactly how dangerously Matthew was behaving right now. But such was his confidence in his luck.

"I will do my best to keep us from becoming another set of tragic dukes," he said. Though, of all of them, Christian had the least responsibilities, other than to his tenants. Matthew had his grandmother to take care of. Both of his sisters, neither of whom he'd been close to, had been married off years ago by his father, the same years as their debuts.

Christian had no older relatives living with him nor had he had any siblings.

"If it comes down to it, let me take the fall," Christian murmured, as if agreeing with Matthew's thoughts. "I would rather die than have to explain myself why I let *you* die to your grandmother. No one will miss me if I am gone."

Shooting him a look, Matthew frowned as they reached close to the area where Drake had turned. He was not sure which of the narrow streets the other man had taken. The area was not well lit, and the fog on the ground was thickening, giving the Warrens an extra eerie feel.

"All of our friends would miss you just as much as they would miss me."

"Yes, I meant... well, you know what I meant."

Matthew was not sure that he did, but there was no use pressing Christian to talk about it, that he knew. The other man did not enjoy talking about serious matters. Which Matthew did not blame him for, it was hardly his favorite thing either.

Which street, the first or the second?

Should I take the first street?

He flipped the coin over onto his wrist.

No.

"Why are you flipping your coin over streets?" Christian asked.

"This way," Matthew said, nodding at the second street. "I want to know what Drake is up to."

"He's going to his carriage..." Christian's voice trailed off, and he frowned as he realized that the direction they were going in, the direction Drake had headed in, was taking them deeper into the Warrens. Matthew knew that's what Christian was thinking because he was thinking it, too. "What the bloody hell is he up to?"

They'd lost sight of him, but it did not matter.

There were times that Matthew did not need his coin, times that he could feel his path as if fate was guiding him down it.

This was one of those times.

He turned again.

And again.

Christian followed him silently, without complaint.

Suddenly, Matthew stopped, holding out his arm and barring Christian from moving forward as well.

Light suddenly illuminated through the fog, revealing a shadow standing in a doorway. No, two shadows.

One of a large man, a guard at the door.

The other was Drake.

"You have the Devil's own luck, I swear," Christian murmured.

Not only had they not been coshed and robbed, but they'd also caught up to Drake, even though they had not been able to see him until this moment.

Drake and the man exchanged words, then the guard stepped back, letting him in. That feeling of impetus, of forward motion, pushed at Matthew, and he stepped out as the door closed.

Christian's hand caught his arm.

"Wait... how are you going to get in there?" he hissed.

"I am going to use Drake's name."

"What if that doesn't work?"

Matthew shrugged. He would figure it out then.

"Are you coming, or not?"

Groaning, Christian released Matthew's arm.

"I want to know what he's doing, too."

Leading the way to the door, Matthew knocked on it with confidence, ignoring the way Christian was muttering under his breath behind him. The door opened, revealing the same man who had been there before. He was a big bruiser with a cauliflower ear and a nose that showed signs of having been broken more than once.

"We're here with Ormonde," Matthew said simply, before the other man could speak.

The bruiser gave both him and Christian a once-over, then nodded, stepping back.

"Seriously," Christian muttered once they'd walked past the bruiser and into the hallway. There was another door at the end of it, and Matthew sauntered confidently to it. "The Devil's own."

Glancing over his shoulder at Christian, Matthew grinned as he put his hand on the doorknob and opened it.

What they walked into on the other side was not at all what he would have expected.

Matthew had heard that Drake was frequenting houses of ill repute, but this was more than a bawdy house. There was an aura of darkness and desperation in the air. The waitresses were walking around the scattered tables with a hollow-eyed look, barely flinching when a man groped her or swatted her ass. Other women, the actual brothel tarts, were smiling, but they had the same look in their eyes as the waitresses.

As much as Matthew wanted to intervene, he could not take on the entire crowd. His jaw clenched as he moved through the men, looking for Drake. For all of Drake's rebellions, he could not imagine his friend *here*, in a place like this, indulging in pleasures of the flesh with these women.

This was the kind of place anyone with any sense of morals eschewed.

At the far end of the room, there was a stage, tattered and ratty, with a crowd drawn round it. Matthew thought he saw Drake near it, but then someone walked in front of him, cutting off his view.

Growling under his breath, he darted around the man and kept walking toward the stage, ignoring Christian's curse from behind him.

They needed to find Drake, ask him what the hell he was doing here, then go home. Why his coin had indicated he should follow, Matthew had no idea. This was certainly the most confounding path it had ever sent him down.

A man walked out onto the stage, a greasy smile on his face. His evening finery was well made but tattered and quite a few years out of style. Beside him was a woman in a low-cut dress that threatened to reveal a nipple from her fantastic bosom if she breathed wrong. Likely both at once.

"Good evening!" The man grinned, his eyes sweeping the small crowd in front of him. "Who is ready for our special auction this evening? A real, live virgin!"

The crowd cheered, more men coming down, crowding around Matthew, who had ground to a halt.

A virgin? In a place like this?

The very idea made his blood run cold.

Likely, it was some doxy they'd coached into the part. Bloody hell, but he hoped it was the case.

"She's a sweet one, alright. A real lovely *lady*, if you get my meaning." He winked at the crowd. "The likes that we have not seen since the Tramp claimed his lady."

Bloody hell.

There had been rumors that the Tramp's lady had once been a debutante who'd gotten lost in the Warrens or been kidnapped away to the Warrens. Matthew had never truly believed it. It was very likely that the auctioneer was capitalizing on the rumor.

That or a young lady had actually been kidnapped from the *ton*, though surely they would have heard... unless her family had fallen on terribly hard times. Or if they'd neglected to raise hue and cry over worries for her reputation. Perhaps Drake was here to rescue her?

But if that were the case, surely he would have told Matthew and Christian. He would not attempt something so astounding on his own. But if that were the case, where was he? Matthew scanned the crowd again, looking for some sign of Drake, but finding none. If he had been in this group, he'd disappeared entirely.

Yet Matthew could not make himself move to go find Drake.

Perhaps it was curiosity, perhaps it was intuition, but he could not leave until he'd seen this virgin lady being offered to the rowdy crowd of slavering men.

"Come on out, sweetheart, let them get a look at you," the man said, leering. The woman at his side moved away, back toward the side of the stage, reaching out her hand as if coaxing the woman onto the stage. The lady stepped out, her head down, hands clenched at her sides.

Pale blonde hair hung down, obscuring her face from the now roaring crowd.

A lady fallen on hard times.

That was Matthew's first thought, due to the condition of her grey dress. Similar to her surroundings, it had once been fine but now was tattered and in need of repair. Pity stirred in his breast. She was not being forced by the auctioneer, he realized.

She was not a victim of kidnapping but of circumstance.

Though she had to be coaxed onstage, she walked on of her own accord, her fear and reluctance in every line of her body. Both of which would whet the appetites of the sadists in the crowd, those who delighted in causing fear and pain, who considered the right to brutalize their lovers as their due because they'd paid for it.

The sound of the crowd seemed to have increased tenfold by the time she reached the center of the stage. Something about her graceful movements, her blonde hair, even her dress, was plucking at his memory.

But it was not until she looked up and he saw her face that he realized.

He was far too far away to see the color of those wide, terrified eyes, but he knew.

He knew.

They were a startling shade of violet-blue.

It was Lady Johanna. The young woman who had left Lady Astrid's party early.

He'd barely noticed her there because her stay had been so short and she'd been so quiet. The companion she'd been with, Miss Belle, had made far more of an impression.

Vaguely, he recalled something about a sick mother.

The family must be in dire straits. Even more dire than Nathanial's. At his worst, Nathanial had never had to worry about one of his sisters selling her virginity.

I have to rescue her.

Right. Of course, he should. That was the right thing to do.

"Let us begin the auction! A real live virgin should be worth at least a hundred pounds, eh?" The auctioneer winked and laughed as bids immediately started being shouted at the stage. Even in such horrid surroundings as this brothel, a virgin would fetch a stunning price, though she could have gotten far more at a more respectable place.

What had brought her here?

Matthew reached for his coin.

He'd meant to ask if he should buy her. Because even though he knew it was the right thing to do, it was such a major thing. There might be something else he was supposed to do.

But that was not the question that flitted through his head.

The question that flitted through his head, as he flicked the coin into the air, was the one that he asked every time he found a debutante that he was at least somewhat attracted to. A question he had *not* asked about Lady Johanna at Blackstone Manor but which came to him now, to his utter surprise.

Should I marry Lady Johanna?

The coin fell into his hand, and he slapped it down on his wrist. His heart had started pounding in time to the shouts around him as the bidding continued.

He lifted his hand and stared at his answer.

******

The Lord of Luck's story continues in The Duke's Indecent Purchase.

ABOUT THE AUTHOR

Golden Angel is a USA Today best-selling author of heart and bottom warming romance.

She is happily married, old enough to know better but still too young to care, and a big fan of happily-ever-afters, strong heroes and heroines, and sizzling chemistry.

When she's not writing, she can often be found on the couch reading, in front of her sewing machine making a new cosplay, hanging out with her friends, or wandering the Maryland Renaissance Fair.

www.goldenangelromance.com

BB bookbub.com/authors/golden-angel
g goodreads.com/goldeniangel
f facebook.com/GoldenAngelAuthor
instagram.com/goldeniangel

FOREWORD

After I came up with the idea for the series of the Indecent Dukes, I realized that even the deaths of their father's might not be enough to push them towards immediately searching for brides. They're young, cocky, it would be natural for them to assume they have all the time in the world.

Which is how I came up with the idea for an eighth duke, one whose death pushes them towards action. Because they can see for themselves that they might not have the time they think they do.

Isabella is the fiancé who is left behind. As often happens with me, sometimes I'll come up with a side character who won't stay quiet. Will she get a book? I don't know. But I had the idea of doing a diary for her.

She's an outlooker watching the goings-on of the series from her own perspective. Someone who might have been a part of it under other circumstances. And it's given me the unique opportunity to explore a major theme of grief, which I don't often get to do as a romance author.

These are the little tidbits, one chapter for each book, to watch her progress along with our dukes. And perhaps, one day she'll get her happily-ever-after too.

I hope you enjoy my side project,
Golden Angel

45

ENTRY 1

Sinclair is dead but not buried.

His funeral service was today.

To grieve without a body, without a last look upon his face, seems somehow worse than if he were there before me. William told me of his last glimpse of Sinclair, the waves pulling him away from the ship during the storm. I understand that they could not recover him from the middle of the Atlantic.

Sometimes I dream of him, myself standing in William's place, running to the rail of the ship and trying to throw myself overboard after him. Trying to save him.

But the waves pull him under before I can touch the water.

I wonder how he felt, as he watched the distance

between himself and the ship grow. If he felt dread. If he felt fear.

If he thought of me.

Selfish creature that I am, I hope he thought of me because I think of him daily.

I believe I will do so for the rest of my life.

It has been years since I kept a diary, but today I felt compelled to write. To remember. Because it feels as though otherwise he will be completely lost to me. I do not want to forget a thing about him, and yet already it is difficult to recall things.

The mind does not retain memories of him the way I wish they would.

I can remember the touch of his hand, the way his lips would brush over mine, gently at first and then more firmly, deepening the kiss.

Yet I cannot remember exactly where each of our kisses happened.

I remember the first one, two years ago on my birthday. I remember the dress I was wearing. I remember his crisp white of his shirt against the sharp black of his jacket, the way his dark hair waved back from his face. I remember the way my nose bumped against his, how I gasped when his tongue slid between my lips and into my mouth to touch mine. I remember the way my body tightened against his and how he held me as my head whirled and my knees weakened.

But what about the second kiss? The third? The fourth?

My mind strains but I do not know.

And I weep not only for the loss of him, but for the memories I have already forgotten. That I did not anticipate would be important holding onto. Because I thought we had forever ahead of us.

William has assured me that as Sinclair's heir, he will take care of everything. He has offered to allow me to go through Sinclair's things, if there is anything I want to keep to remember Sinclair by - that is not entailed to the estate or part of the family's heirlooms of course. He has reassured me that I need not return the engagement ring, as Sinclair bought it for me specifically.

Looking down at the opals and diamonds still adorning my finger, I almost wish that he had demanded its return, because how shall I ever bear to make the decision of when to remove it myself?

I cannot imagine ever doing so and yet I know that eventually I must. My parents expect me to marry. They will not push me while I'm in mourning, but unless I plan to become the spinster aunt, forever supported by my brother or his heir, I know I have no other choice.

My heart grows heavy with these thoughts, even knowing that it is a necessity that I think of my own future. Sinclair would want me to. He would want me to take care of myself and secure my future - in truth, he would be quite angry with me if I did not.

But for now, at least I have six months of full mourning before I have to entertain any such notions. Six months to gather myself and think about what I shall do next. What I want from a life without Sinclair.

Today, though, I am going to sit and dream of the life we would have had together.

The life we should have had together.

As ever,

Isabella

46

ENTRY 2

The Season is in full swing, the world moving on with me. Moving on without Sinclair.

The letters I receive from London are full of gossip and news. Most of it means nothing to me. I feel as though it should, and yet I cannot bring myself to care. My parents are trying to be patient, but I can tell they are worried at my continued despondence. I cannot find the words to explain to them that nothing feels like it matters without Sinclair by my side.

There have been two pieces of news that have somewhat lifted my spirits - two of Sinclair's friends have married. Rather unexpectedly in both cases. I feel that he would be highly amused by the circumstances.

Astrid has kept me apprised of Sinclair's friends, as though she knows I long for the semblance of normalcy even though I loathe the reminder that Sinclair is no longer among the cadre.

Gregory has married. Sebastian's sister, of all things, whom I have never met. This was her first Season and although it has been touted as a love match, the truth is that he found himself alone in a library with her, and rather than escorting her out, he decided to kiss her. According to Astrid, her mother was rather horrid and did her the disservice of dressing her in unfashion- able, unflattering clothing. Now that she is a Duchess in her own right and no longer under her mother's thumb, it sounds as though she has blossomed.

I look forward to meeting her. Eventually. Sinclair would want me to.

Nathanial has married as well.

His marriage sounds even more scandalous.

Caught in a lady's bedroom by her maid!

It is certainly the most excitement that one of Lady Astrid's house parties has ever seen, which is truly saying something. Not just the scandal, but the wedding which occurred quickly thereafter.

Her letters bring me much more joy than William's visits, though he is very solicitous. It is difficult to hear of his endeavors on Sinclair's estate. I know it is William's estate now, but in my heart and mind, it is Sinclair that I picture there. Riding atop his horse, over- looking the land, the way he was wont to do.

But he will never do so again.

I feel as though I must write those words over

and over again to remind myself. Too often it feels as though he is merely traveling somewhere. That he might appear at my door any moment to tell me it was all a horrid dream. That he is here and he loves me and we shall have the future we always planned.

The times I forget are the hardest, because when I remember, the grief hits me afresh. Like I am being informed of his loss all over again. So as difficult as it is to acknowledge his death, it is better than forgetting only to remember and be mired in a fresh wave of desperate tragedy.

I wish someone would talk with me about him. Remember him with me. Even after the funeral, I feel as though I have not been able to properly let him go. I do not know if talking would help, but not talking is certainly not helping.

My parents avoid the subject assiduously. William is always happy to discuss the estate or Sinclair's people, but not Sinclair himself. He seems so uncomfortable. Perhaps because he is not only grieving his cousin, but because he had to step into his shoes.

I miss Sinclair so much.

As ever,

Isabella

OTHER TITLES BY GOLDEN ANGEL

Historical Spanking Romance

Domestic Discipline Quartet

Birching His Bride

Dealing With Discipline

Punishing His Ward

Claiming His Wife

The Domestic Discipline Quartet Box Set

Bridal Discipline Series

Philip's Rules

Gabrielle's Discipline

Lydia's Penance

Benedict's Commands

Arabella's Taming

Pride and Punishment Box Set

Commands and Consequences Box Set

Deception and Discipline

A Season for Treason

A Season for Scandal

A Season for Smugglers

A Season for Spies

Desire and Discipline

A Season for Bliss

A Season for Desire

A Season for Christmas

Indecent Dukes

The Duke's Indecent Scandal

The Duke's Indecent Match

The Duke's Indecent Purchase

The Duke's Indecent Desire

The Duke's Indecent Proposal

The Duke's Indecent Secret

The Duke's Indecent Courtship

Standalone

Marriage Training

The Duke's Pursuit

Rogue Booty

Contemporary BDSM Romance

Venus Rising Series (MFM Romance)

The Venus School

Venus Aspiring

Venus Desiring

Venus Transcendent

Venus Wedding

Venus Rising Box Set

Stronghold Doms Series

The Sassy Submissive

Taming the Tease

Mastering Lexie

Pieces of Stronghold

Breaking the Chain

Bound to the Past

Stripping the Sub

Tempting the Domme

Hardcore Vanilla

Steamy Stocking Stuffers

A Sassy Christmas

Entering Stronghold Box Set

Nights at Stronghold Box Set

Stronghold: Closing Time Box Set

Masters of Marquis Series

Bondage Buddies

Master Chef

Law & Disorder

Switch Play

Legally Bound

Shallow Submission

Hidden Away

Secret Submission

Third Wheel

Black Fox Security Doms

Danger and Dominance

Cuffs and Cupcakes

Security and Submission

Whips and Weddings

Rescue and Ropes

Bondage and Bad Guys

Dungeons & Doms Series

Dungeon Master

Dungeon Daddy

Dungeon Showdown

Dungeons & Doms Boxset

Daddies Everywhere

Chef Daddy

Foosball Daddies

Taco Daddy

Cheese Daddy

Garden Daddy

Daddies Everywhere Boxset

Cherry Popping Daddies

Emily by Golden Angel

Lottie by Stella Moore

Titania by Raisa Greenwood

Standalone Daddy Dom

Little Villain

Sci-fi Romance

Tsenturion Masters Series with Lee Savino

Alien Captive

Alien Tribute

Alien Abduction